THE
ROGER SCARLETT
MYSTERIES

THE ROGER SCARLETT MYSTERIES

VOL. 1

THE BEACON HILL MURDERS

THE BACK BAY MURDERS

COACHWHIP PUBLICATIONS
Greenville, Ohio

The Beacon Hill Murders, by Roger Scarlett
The Back Bay Murders, by Roger Scarlett
© 2017 Coachwhip Publications
Introduction © 2017 Curtis Evans

The Beacon Hill Murders published 1930
The Back Bay Murders published 1930
No claims made on public domain material.
Cover image: Harrison Gray Otis house, Boston.

CoachwhipBooks.com

ISBN 1-61646-421-6
ISBN-13 978-1-61646-421-9

BEHIND EVERY GREAT MAN IS A WOMAN (OR TWO)
Dorothy Blair (1903-1976), Evelyn Page (1902-1977) and "Roger Scarlett" (1930-1933)

CURTIS EVANS

Part One
Clues to Mr. Scarlett

Between 1930 and 1933 Roger Scarlett produced finely finished models of classic crime fiction in five mystery novels, all of them set in New England: *The Beacon Hill Murders* (1930), *The Back Bay Murders* (1930), *Cat's Paw* (1931), *Murder among the Angells* (1932), and *In the First Degree* (1933). These accomplished and entertaining tales—initially modeled most obviously along the lines of the detective fiction of Arthur Conan Doyle, renowned creator of Sherlock Holmes and Dr. Watson, and S. S. Van Dine (Willard Huntington Wright), a bestselling mystery writer in between-the-wars America, both of whom published tales where investigations into complex crimes are conducted by a brilliant male detective and his far less astute yet intensely admiring male friend—were in fact composed by two women, Dorothy Blair and Evelyn Page, who during the time of the composition of their novels lived contentedly in a companionate relationship in Boston and rural Connecticut. Like the influential English detective novelist Dorothy L. Sayers, who graduated from Somerville College, Oxford, Dorothy Blair and Evelyn Page were educated at elite all-female institutions, the former woman at Vassar and the latter at Bryn Mawr, both of which schools were part of the loose association of northeastern American women's colleges known as the "Seven Sisters" (comprised of, in addition to Vassar and Bryn Mawr, Barnard, Mount Holyoke, Radcliffe, Smith and Wellesley). Whether the detective story truly is the "normal recreation of noble minds," as the English barrister and author Philip Guedalla is reputed by Sayers to have pithily put it, it emphatically was, during the period known as the Golden Age of detective fiction, the addictive plaything of the highly educated, as the lives and the admirable tales of Dorothy Blair and Evelyn Page evince.

The ancestral lines of both Dorothy Blair and Evelyn Page go back to the northeastern United States, the traditional intellectual citadel of the country. Dorothy Blair's parents were Dr. James Franklin Blair, who was born in Mercersburg, Pennsylvania, and Elizabeth Pickering Healey, who though born in New Orleans, Louisiana, had roots that ran deep into New England's past. After graduating from the University of Vermont, James F. Blair, a dashing, mustachioed gentleman of initiative and vibrancy, practiced medicine at the State Farm Institution at Bridgewater, Massachusetts (today the Bridgewater State Hospital for the criminally insane). After completing further studies at Harvard Medical School and the School of Medicine at Trinity College in Dublin, Ireland, Blair wed Elizabeth P. Healey in 1902 and departed with her from Bridgewater to Bozeman, Montana, then a town of some 3500 people and home to the Agricultural College of the State of Montana (today Montana State University). There Dorothy was born the next year, on the tenth of March.[1]

In contrast with Massachusetts, whose inception as a white settlement went back to the establishment of the Plymouth Colony in 1620, Montana at the time of the Blairs' arrival in 1902 had been a state for barely more than a dozen years; yet Frank Blair was quick to make a home and a name for his family in the developing western town, which had claimed a population of merely 168 in 1870. Before settling permanently in Bozeman, Blair had purchased, from the widow of its founder, the Bozeman Sanitarium, an ornately turreted and gabled thirty-two room private hospital erected in 1894 at the cost of over $30,000, which he promptly renamed, in an unabashed show of self-assertion, the Blair Sanitarium. Dr. Blair achieved considerable prosperity in Bozeman, evidence of which can be seen in his construction as his family's domestic residence of a stylish brick colonial revival structure complete with a glassed-in sunporch and a second-story ballroom and in his sending Dorothy back east for her education to Vassar, located in Poughkeepsie, New York, from where she graduated in 1924. At his death in Bozeman nine years later, Dr. Blair left his widow and daughter an estate worth, in modern value, over three-quarters of a million dollars.

Though comfortably circumstanced on account of her parents' wealth, Dorothy obtained a position as a junior editor at Houghton, Mifflin, where she met the similarly employed Evelyn Page, a Bryn Mawr graduate four months Dorothy's senior (Evelyn was born on November 9, 1902) who came from a socially prominent Philadelphia family descended from James II, King of Scotland, and Scotland's influential Hamilton clan. Evelyn was quite active in student affairs at Bryn Mawr, serving as class vice president and treasurer during her senior year, as well as an editor on both *The Lantern*, the college literary magazine, and *The Sportswoman*, a nascent periodical that was of the first to be devoted exclusively to women's athletics. (The latter publication had been founded by Constance Applebee, a native Englishwoman who directed athletics at Bryn Mawr for nearly a quarter of a century and today is best known for having introduced field hockey to the United States.) Graduating magna cum laude and earning a BA from Bryn Mawr in 1923, Evelyn obtained an MA at the same institution three years later.

With a couple of years spent reading manuscripts at Houghton, Mifflin behind them, Dorothy and Evelyn in 1929 left regular salaried employment to launch joint careers as the mystery author "Roger Scarlett," a pseudonym the two women presumably derived from *The Scarlet Letter*, a landmark American novel by Nathaniel Hawthorne. (One of the major characters in the novel, which is set in the seventeenth century in the Puritan Massachusetts Bay Colony, is Roger Chillingworth, Hester Prynne's coldhearted and vengeful husband.) Just as the two women wrote novels together, they resided together as well, first at Boston and then in Abington, a village located in northeastern Connecticut, on a farm which they kept for the rest of their lives. The farmhouse was an "early nineteenth-century stone house . . . [s]urrounded in the spring by daffodils and violets, set in an isolated valley from which one saw no other houses." In this remote spot Dorothy and Evelyn dedicated their mornings to writing and the rest of their daylight hours to coping "unaided with forty acres and two ponds, and the painting, plastering, preserving, cooking, washing, wood chopping and gardening pertaining thereto."[2]

The couple made forays into the outside world as well, however. Evelyn introduced Dorothy to Philadelphia society when Dorothy was Evelyn's guest on the occasion of the pair's visit to the City of Brotherly Love over the Christmas season of 1931-32. Mrs. Bertram Lippincott, who, along with her prominent publisher husband was a leading light of Philadelphia's most elite social set, honored Dorothy on this occasion with a luncheon at the Lippincott mansion.

Dorothy and Evelyn produced no more books of any sort together after the publication of the last Roger Scarlett mystery in 1933, yet they kept busy intellectually. Both women, but particularly Dorothy as we shall see, were friends of the distinguished longtime Smith College professors (and lifelong companions) Mary Ellen Chase, a bestselling regional novelist, and Eleanor Duckett, a medieval historian. Dorothy and Mary Ellen Chase had originally met in 1916, when Chase, a native of Maine, was teaching primary school in Bozeman, where doctors had sent her to cure her tuberculosis, and Dorothy had been one of Chase's young students. (Dorothy was 13 and Chase 29.)

Over three decades later, in 1949, Dorothy, now 45, reintroduced herself to the 61-year-old Chase at Smith College, causing the delighted Chase, who recalled Dorothy as "a little girl in a red coat in the snow of Montana, a radiant memory," to write, "I like her hugely, and we had an exciting three hours. She is most attractive, tall, healthy, and looks 35 though she must be 45. I do not know when I had so thrilling a day." Chase, who was then writing a commissioned biography of John D. Rockefeller, Jr.'s late wife, Abigail, engaged Dorothy as her research assistant on the project, with Rockefeller's full approval; and she wrote much of the book at Dorothy and Evelyn's farmhouse, effusively declaring that Abington was her "shelter in this whirlwind, the one material means by which the book has been accomplished."[3]

"During their collaboration on the book," notes Chase biographer Elienne Squire, Dorothy and Chase "became lovers" (with the knowledge of their own respective companions), traveling together to Europe for a seven-week holiday that Chase termed the "New Experiment." Those weeks, an enraptured Chase wrote in the personal journal she kept, "will always be borne within us. They have meant everything to me and I know they have meant the same to her." Dorothy later would stay at Windswept, Chase's home in Maine, for several weeks in the summer of 1951, when Duckett was conveniently away in England researching a book; and the pair would spend two months together in France in 1953.[4] Over the rest of her life Dorothy, whose "astute mind and sunny disposition" utterly "captivated" Chase (in the words of Elienne Squire), served as a reader not only for the books written by Chase and Duckett, but for those written by her companion Eleanor, who led by far a more visible public life than Dorothy.

For two years (1938-1939) Evelyn contributed an interesting book review column to the *Washington Post*, taking notice mostly of mainstream fiction, though she allowed the occasional mystery to make an appearance. Mainly on account of its appealing central character, an elderly English gentlewoman and incidental amateur sleuth, she favorably reviewed the short detective fiction collection *Mrs. Warrender's Profession* (1939), by the prominent English intellectual couple Douglas and Margaret Cole; though she took time to peg as the "best baffler" in the collection "The Toys of Death," which nearly a half-century later was anthologized by Martin Greenberg and Bill Pronzini in the book *Women Sleuths* (1985) and in 2015 was highlighted by me in my study *The Spectrum of English Murder* (Coachwhip).

During the Second World War Evelyn served consecutively as an aircraft inspector for the Navy Bureau of Aeronautics (1942-1945) and a sergeant in the Women's Army Corps, or WAC (1945-1946). After the war years she boldly stormed the groves of academe, obtaining a PhD at the University of Pennsylvania in 1952 and positions consecutively at Smith College (1949-1956) and Connecticut College, where she was an assistant professor of English and history (1956-1964). Additionally she served for four years (1956-1960) as principal of the Williams Memorial Institute (today the Williams School), a girls' prep school affiliated with Connecticut College that was founded by the nineteenth-century New England feminist philanthropist Harriet Peck Williams.

Three times during the 1960s Evelyn secured appointments as a Fulbright lecturer at overseas educational institutions, initially at Mashad, Iran, and later at Seoul, South Korea and Saigon, South Vietnam. Having clearly developed a taste for sojourns in what was then known as the "Third World," the globetrotting Evelyn was visiting Morocco in 1977 when she died suddenly on the 13th of December, little more than a year after her partner Dorothy, who had passed away on September 5, 1976. (Mary Ellen Chase preceded her two younger friends in death by just a few years, passing away in 1973, while Eleanor Duckett expired in 1976, at the venerable age of 96.) During her later years Evelyn published two more books: *The Chestnut Tree* (1964), a gently satirical novel concerning life in genteel Philadelphia society during the early twentieth century, and a historical literary study, *American Genesis: Pre-colonial Writing in the North* (1973), which is still cited in scholarship today.

In the acknowledgments to *American Genesis*, Evelyn circumspectly thanked "Miss Dorothy Blair, former reader at Smith College," for the "time and attention" she had "generously spent . . . in reading and criticizing my manuscript." Although they had published only five Roger Scarlett detective novels over a short span of four years during the midst of the Great Depression, the two clever women behind Roger Scarlett remained, to the end of their lives some four decades later, the closest of compatriots and collaborators. Mystery fans now able to read the Scarlett mysteries, left unaccountably out-of-print (in English) for over eight decades, should be grateful for Dorothy and Evelyn's intensely fertile creative collaboration, which produced some of the brightest murder puzzles from the Golden Age of detective fiction.[5]

PART TWO

MAYHEM IN THE MANSION: ROGER SCARLETT'S DETECTIVE FICTION

I. *THE BEACON HILL MURDERS* (1930)

The Beacon Hill Murders, the first Roger Scarlett detective novel, was published in the United States in February 1930 by Doubleday, Doran's Crime Club, then one of the most important mystery publishing imprints in the world, and later that year in the United Kingdom by William Heinemann, whose impressive and eclectic list of genre literature around this time included the excellent Ludovic Travers series mysteries of Christopher Bush; the popular romantic mystery thrillers of American writer Mignon Eberhart; the high-toned crime novels of Marie Belloc Lowndes, celebrated author of *The Lodger*; Graham Greene's superior "entertainment" *Stamboul Train*; J. B. Priestley's superb frightener *Benighted*; C. P. Snow's classic foray into detective fiction, *Death under Sail*; Ivy Low Litvinov's unusual *His Masters Voice*, set in the Soviet Union (the author was the wife of Soviet foreign minister Maxim Litvinov); Helen Simpson's marvelous macabre short story collection *The Baseless Fabric*; and F. Tennyson Jesse's notable gathering of tales about a female psychic detective, *The Solange Stories*. Roger Scarlett's accomplished first novel, which laid out the template for the four additional Scarlett tales to follow, merits a place in this distinguished criminal company. In "The Book Survey," his syndicated review column, the young American journalist Bruce Catton (1899-1978), a future winner of the Pulitzer Prize in history (for *A Stillness at Appomatox*, 1953), highly praised *The Beacon Hill Murders*, declaring it "well worth your trouble if you're a mystery story addict" and that "it will puzzle you considerably before you finish it."

The Beacon Hill Murders introduces Roger Scarlett's brilliant series sleuth, Inspector Norton Kane, along with his avidly admiring chronicler, a staid attorney named Underwood, who provides narration in the first three novels in the series and appears as well in the fourth. Also debuting in *The Beacon Hill Murders* are the dutiful but not overly perspicacious Sergeant Moran and his dim minion in blue, McBeath. (This pair also takes part in the next two novels in the series.) In each of the Scarlett mysteries Kane must solve a murder or murders that take place among upper- or decayed upper-class denizens of an old Boston mansion or brownstone townhouse. In *The Beacon Hill Murders*, Boston's Beacon Hill—an exclusive neighborhood of old homes and old money—has recently been invaded by a family of parvenus, the Suttons. As Underwood—Frederick Sutton's genteel attorney and a grudging dinner guest in Sutton's house—condescendingly explains:

. . . . I was walking up Quincy Street toward the Sutton house, which stood by itself, cut off from its neighbors, in the middle of a small plot of ground. As I approached it, I could not help being impressed with its air of dignity and age. It was typical of the best houses on Beacon Hill, and, like many of them, had fallen into evil days. Its original owner, endowed with the traditions of good taste and gentle living, could not have imagined that it would fall into the hands of Frederick Sutton, the stock exchange gambler, who had risen from nothing to a huge fortune.

. . . . I was reluctant and annoyed at the thought of the evening before me. As Sutton's lawyer, I had not been able to refuse his first invitation to dinner. He was obviously preparing to break his way into society, and I shrewdly suspected that he wanted to use me as a rung in the social ladder. I looked forward to an uncomfortable few hours spent in the company of the newly rich.

To the prim and proper Underwood's horror, murder, surely the most egregious of social errors, invades the Sutton mansion when Frederick Sutton is slain in his private sitting room by a single gunshot. It appears that only one other person was in the room with Sutton at the time he was killed, but it is difficult to believe that this particular individual would have committed such a crime. Shortly afterward, a second violent murder takes place in the spare bedroom of the Sutton mansion, this time right under the noses of the police. Both killings are essentially clever locked room problems that should severely test the acuity of the reader. (Three floor and room plans are provided to help her/him along.) Additionally, a surprisingly dark thread of Freudian psychology is woven into the dénouement of the novel, the authors arguably having in this respect drawn somewhat on their own personal backgrounds.

Like his most immediate model, S. S. Van Dine's Philo Vance (not to mention Ellery Queen's own Ellery Queen, who had debuted on the mystery stage one year earlier in *The Roman Hat Mystery*),

Norton Kane remains throughout the series an essentially sexless sleuth with no personal life to speak of, in contrast with the police detectives of modern crime fiction, whose lives commonly are steeped in storm and stress. (In the Scarlett mysteries readers are provided with those qualities by the troubled individuals implicated in Kane's murder cases.) To be sure, we learn from Underwood that despite Kane's "hard directness" he has "the look of a visionary, with his thick black hair and his fine forehead," while his "abrupt, ugly features" bring out by contrast "the sensitiveness of his eyes." Underwood, himself a rather squeamish soul for an attorney, wonders how such a man as he imagines his friend Kane to be can stand to "spend his days in the pursuit of the sordid and the horrible," but we never see foul play induce in the policeman any of the symptoms of existential crisis that afflict today's angst-ridden fictional detectives. Kane is an implacable problem-solving machine, and a most efficient one at that.

II. *THE BACK BAY MURDERS* (1930)

Inspector Kane ventures from Boston's stately Beacon Bill to another fine local neighborhood, Back Bay, in *The Back Bay Murders* (published in October 1930), when he is called upon to solve the mysterious slaying of a neurotic young man named Arthur Prendergast, one of the "paying guests" at Mrs. Quincy's refined boarding house. "There was certainly very little to distinguish the house from its neighbors," pronounces the discriminating Underwood when he and Kane first arrive at the boarding house, before murder has struck. "Like them it stood a little back from the street. A flight of steps led up to the front door, which with its heavy, handsome respectability, seemed to characterize the yet unknown inhabitants." However, as in Kane's immediately previous murder case (referenced in the current novel), these to all appearances highly respectable inhabitants prove a rum lot indeed, much to Underwood's mortification. As Kane lectures Underwood: ". . . . you ought to be better prepared to meet the unforeseen. You ought to know that under the surface of normal existence there are hidden currents which sometimes burst through. You shrink from them with horror, but I'm trained to expect their manifestations."

Before Kane is able to damn the hidden currents bursting over this particular Back Bay brownstone, however, there is another murder,

THE
BACK BAY
MURDERS

Roger
Scarlett

G&D
GROSSET
& DUNLAP

THE BACK BAY
MURDERS
By Roger Scarlett

Who left the
white feather?
on the corpse?

MYSTERY and MURDER in an aristocratic boarding-house

this time an ingenious poisoning. Once again Freudian psychology is invoked at the novel's dénouement and floor and room plans are thoughtfully provided for the scrutiny of readers determined to solve the puzzle for themselves. Although there is no locked room problem per se, the second murder presents aspects of one and the mystery plot overall is highly ingenious and rather bizarre, with such teasing clues as bloodstains that are not actually blood and a pet Persian cat toying with a feather. A worthy successor to its accomplished predecessor, *The Back Bay Murders* is, as William C. Weber avowed in the *Saturday Review*, an "American story that meets all the requirements."

A dastardly Englishman named Don Basil evidently agreed with the American reviewer, for in May 1931 he published, with the short-lived London press Philip Earle, a novel, *Cat and Feather*, which is nearly a word-for-word plagiarization of *The Back Bay Murders*. In his "The Uneasy Chair" column in the January 1978 issue of the landmark fanzine *The Armchair Detective*, edited by Allen J. Hubin, detective fiction collector Ned Guymon, who had corresponded about the matter a few years earlier with both Dorothy Blair and Evelyn Page, called Don Basil's *Cat and Feather* "probably the most glaring piece of plagiarism ever to exist." He amplified thusly:

> It is not similarity of character or plot or situation, it is a word for word copy. The English characters have different names, English locale has been substituted for American and there are a very few English words used to clarify American terms. Otherwise this book is a flagrant and larcenous case of plagiarism. You should see it to believe it.

I have seen a copy of Don Basil's book (which is extremely rare), and, having seen it, I certainly do believe it. Here are two pairs of matched quotations from the novels that illustrate the breadth and brazenness of Basil's plagiarism:

> I had known Kane for many years, but not until some months ago had I been associated with him in one of

his cases. On that occasion I had been present, as the family lawyer, at a dinner party which had a fatal ending, and had called Kane, my only friend among the police inspectors of Boston, to my assistance and to that of the Sutton family. His spectacular solution of that case, widely known as the Beacon Hill murders, had put him in the limelight as far as the public was concerned. (*The Back Bay Murders*)

I had known Richard Kirk Storm for many years, but not until some months ago had I been associated with him in one of his cases. On that occasion I had been present, as the family solicitor, at a dinner which had a fatal ending, and had called Storm, my only friend among officials of Scotland Yard, to my assistance and that of the Stafford family.

His spectacular solution of the case widely known as The Bexhill Murder Mystery had put him in the limelight as far as the public was concerned. (*Cat and Feather*)

Twenty minutes later Kane was propelling me through the doors of Thompson's Spa. "Don't let a murderer get the best of your appetite, Underwood," he cautioned me, grinning down at my gloomy face, "whatever else he does to you. Here's an empty counter and an idle handmaiden. Sit down." He slapped a stool. Without a word I climbed up on it and he sat down beside me. "It's past eating-time and I know it. We'll have oyster stew, with flocks of oysters, and, let's see—for a climax—" He debated gravely, and then brought out with gusto, "Pumpkin pie."

I forced a smile. The mention of food gave me no pleasure. "That's just where you're wrong," Kane announced when I explained this to him. "You know," he looked at me quizzically, "I'd lay a bet that nine out of ten really good murderers lose their appetites right after shooting. And a heavy-eating gumshoe gets them on the hip every time. So forget your troubles."

He ordered for us both. When we were served I fished about in my stew with as good grace as I could muster. (*The Back Bay Murders*)

Twenty minutes later Storm was leading me through the doors of a restaurant. "Don't let a murderer get the best of your appetite, West," he cautioned me, grinning down at my gloomy face, "whatever else he does to you. Here's an empty table and an idle handmaiden. Sit down."

Without a word we sat down at the marble table. . . .

"It's past lunch-time, and I know it. We'll have steak and kidney pie, with stacks of chips, and, let's see—for a climax—" He debated gravely, and then brought out with gusto, "College pudding."

I forced a grim smile. The mention of food brought me no pleasure.

"That's just where you're wrong," Storm announced, when I explained to him. "You know," he looked at me quizzically, "I'd lay a bet that nine out of ten really good murderers lose their appetites after the murder. So forget your troubles."

He ordered for us both. When we were served I toyed with my food with as good grace as I could muster. (*Cat and Feather*)

Aside from changes in paragraph structure and in character names (Kane becomes *Storm*, Underwood *West*, the Sutton family *the Stafford family*, the Beacon Hill murders the *The Bexhill Murder Mystery*), as well as some alterations of Americanisms (police inspectors of Boston becomes *officials of Scotland Yard*, lawyer *solicitor*, Thompson's Spa *a restaurant*, oyster stew *steak and kidney pie*, flocks of oysters *stacks of chips*, pumpkin pie *college pudding* and fished about in my stew *toyed with my food*), the text of *Cat and Feather* is identical to that of *The Back Bay Murders* all through the book. Irony is added, as Ned Guymon noted, by the fact that "Don Basil" (if that truly was the author's name) dedicated "his" novel as follows, "To Basil Holland, who once said, 'Uncle, please write a detective story for me'." To this Ned Guymon witheringly commented: "Basil Holland got his detective story all right but his uncle didn't write it, he copied it."[6]

III. *CAT'S PAW* (1931)

After the publication of *Cat and Feather* in England, where Basil's blatant plagiarism of *The Back Bay Murders* went undetected (Roger Scarlett's *The Beacon Hill Murders* had been published in the UK by Heinemann, as mentioned above, but I do not know whether the later Scarlett novels were so as well), the egregious rip-off was picked up for fall publication in the United States by Henry Holt and Company, one of the oldest of American publishers, but the plagiarism revelation resulted in the book's immediate withdrawal from the market. "Don Basil" deservedly disappeared, as far as we know, from the annals of mystery writing, but Roger Scarlett produced another fine detective novel in the fall of 1931, one whose title may well have been inspired by the recent Don Basil brouhaha: *Cat's Paw*.

In this third Scarlett mystery, Kane, along with his loyal chronicler Underwood and his assistants Moran and McBeath, is tasked yet again with solving a diabolically clever murder in a mansion filled to the rafters with genteel suspects. The novel has the most unusual structure of the series, being divided into four parts, the first part, "The Question," being a short prologue; the second, "The Evidence," a depiction of the days of family discord leading up to the murder; the third part, "The Case," Moran and McBeath's ultimately stymied preliminary investigation; and the fourth part, "The Solution," Kane's dramatic exposure of the culprit. (Only the prologue and the final section are narrated by Underwood, although the middle parts, told in the third person, ostensibly are written by him for Kane's perusal.) In the section of his "Book Survey" column devoted to mysteries, Bruce Catton, evidently having come down with Scarlett fever, deemed *Cat's Paw* "another good one," based upon a classic situation: "The eccentric old uncle gives a house-party to his nephews and nieces, and gets done in just after announcing that he's going to change his will. The suspects are singularly hateful, and you keep hoping that all of them are guilty. The result may surprise you, though."

With *Cat's Paw* Roger Scarlett continued his generous habit of lavishing floor and room plans upon readers of the Norton Kane series, in this case providing an endpaper map of the second story of the Martin Greenough mansion, an anachronistic survival along Boston's Fenway, a thoroughfare laid out by the great Victorian landscape architect Frederick Law Olmsted along the southern and eastern edges of the Back Bay Fens in the Fenmore-Kenway neighborhood of Boston (home, from 1912 onward, of Fenway Park). The forbidding mansion in this novel is a "huge Gothic house" surrounded by a "high stone wall," which in turn is surmounted with "threatening spikes of broken glass." Understanding the intricate physical mechanics behind the mansion murder is essential, yet again, to any reader attempting to descry a solution to the puzzle; yet so is comprehending the novel's fairly complex (for the genre at this time) character psychology.

Cat's Paw is the most implicitly subversive as well as the wittiest of the Roger Scarlett novels. Elderly cat fancier "Cousin Mart," as he is known to his relations, resides in improbable sin with a middle-aged woman, the respectably widowed Mrs. Warden, to whom he is not married, scandalizing, much to the reader's amusement, the flummoxed Sergeant Moran when he arrives upon the scene. Cousin Mart himself, in the classic manner of the murderee, enjoys deriding his outwardly decorous but inwardly seething dependents, even mocking the masculinity of his nephew Francis:

> Francis had turned to Mrs. Warden. "That's a most becoming dress," he said. "I like that electric blue."
>
> "Electric blue!" Cousin Mart snorted, and examined his companion's gown with a belligerent eye. "Blue, I call it. What makes your generation talk like men milliners? In my day, the man who knew the difference between sun-tan and flesh pink would keep still about it."

If discriminating nephew Francis stands accused of being something of a Deco era metrosexual, there is an androgynist appeal to outspoken niece Anne, who, in contrast with the rest of her family, had the gumption to tell Cousin Mart precisely where he could get off:

> By the table, facing them, stood a lithe, graceful girl, wearing a loose camel's-hair topcoat and no hat. She had a well-shaped face, nicely cut around the chin, and small, boyish features. Her blonde, wavy hair was cut short like a boy's and fitted her head like a cap except where the end of some rebellious curl escaped insolently upward. One hand was shoved deep in her pocket, while the other held onto the edge of the table, as if for balance. She smiled at Amelia a little defiantly.
> "Hullo," she said abruptly. "Hullo, everybody."

IV. *MURDER AMONG THE ANGELLS* (1932)

The setting of the fourth Roger Scarlett novel, *Murder among the Angells* (1932), is the strangest Boston mansion yet in the series, in its baroque artificiality resembling something out of an outré Ellery Queen novel, like *There Was an Old Woman* (1943) and *The Player on the Other Side* (1963), not to mention S. S. Van Dine's *The Greene Murder Case* (1928) and *The Bishop Murder Case* (1929). (There are no less than six floor and room plans provided.) Both of the Van Dine novels, just a few years old when *Angells* was published, were then regarded by a bevy of awestruck American mystery fiction reviewers as the apotheosis of detective fiction. Particularly marked is the resemblance of *Angells*—like Ellery Queen's better-known *The Tragedy of Y* (1932), which appeared in print the same year—to *The Greene Murder Case*, whose distinctive qualities are aptly summarized by the translator and blogger Ho-Ling Wong: "A family forced to live together though a horrible will of a deceased family patriarch, the absolute hate that exists among the family members, who will work together and betray each other whenever it suits them, the changing shares of the inheritance when one dies. . . . " These are all features as well of *Murder among the Angells*.[7] One might also be reminded of the fact that the New England horror writer H. P. Lovecraft, a contemporary of Dorothy Blair and Evelyn Page, grew up in nearby Providence, Rhode Island, in a large Victorian house on Angell Street.

The Angell house, located on Boston's Beacon Street, is a great L-shaped mansion curiously divided into two identical halves, respectively occupied by two aged brothers and their families and connected only by an elevator. It is in this elevator that the second of the novel's two murders takes place, in a classic locked room variant (an elevator slaying) which seven years later was employed to good effect in *Fatal Descent* (1939), a detective novel co-authored by the man who remains the greatest practitioner in this exacting subgenre, John Dickson Carr, and one of his closest friends, prolific British mystery writer John Street. The two Angell brothers, Carolus and Darius, have for decades been locked in a grim contest of survival in their divided mansion, on account of their eccentric health faddist father's queer will, which devises his entire estate to whichever brother outlives the other, as a way of encouraging the pair to live healthfully. Before the novel is over, however, both of the brothers will have died violently, presenting Inspector Kane with arguably his strangest and most puzzling problem in homicide yet.

Although *Murder among the Angells* seems to have been well-received by reviewers in the United States, the detective novel made by far its greatest impression in Japan, where it was one of the Western Golden Age mysteries that captured the imaginations of writers Yokomizo Seishi (1902-1981) and Edogawa Ranpo (1894-1965), leaders in Japan's embrace of "authentic" (i.e., fair play) detective fiction after the Second World War. When Yokomizo made a friendly wartime call upon Ranpo in Tokyo, notes Sari Kawana in *Murder Most Modern: Detective Fiction and Japanese Culture* (2008), Ranpo advised the younger author to read *Enjeruke no satsujin* [literally *The Murder of the Angell Clan*, aka *Murder among the Angells*]. The now hooked Yokomizo went on from there to reading translated editions of John Dickson Carr, which, he later declared, "forever changed his life as an author." In the first of Yokomizo's postwar, Western-influenced detective stories, *Honjin satsujin jiken* (*The Murder in the Honjin*, 1946), a locked room tale about a bride and bridegroom found brutally slain in a snow-shrouded annex that was praised by Edogawa Ranpo as "the first novel of reasoning in the Anglo-American style in the world of Japanese detective fiction, except for a few exceptional prewar works," the novel's narrator includes *Murder among the*

Angells in his list of foreign locked room mysteries that might possibly have inspired the murderer, along with Gaston Leroux's *The Mystery of the Yellow Room* (1907), Maurice Leblanc's *The Teeth of the Tiger* (1921), S. S. Van Dine's *The Canary Murder Case* (1927) and *The Kennel Murder Case* (1931), and John Dickson Carr's *The Plague Court Murders* (1934).

For his part Edogawa Ranpo wrote that for *Murder among the Angells* he had "nothing but admiration": "[T]he way the plot develops, the way the mystery is solved, the level of suspense, this novel has these elements in a strange way no other novel has. . . . [T]his is the style of writing I like best, that's what I think as I read every line." Ranpo included *Angells* in a top ten list and in 1951 even adapted the tale for a Japanese audience as the novel *Sankakukan no kyofu* (*The Terror of Triangle Mansion*).

Translator and Blogger Ho-Ling Wong has cited *Murder among the Angells* as an archetypal example of a *yakata-mono*, or mansion story:

> With many maps throughout the story, rooms that have doors at the weirdest places and the way people have to move about to get from one wing to another, this novel practically screams *yakata-mono*. The strange architecture practically functions as a silent extra character, not unlike the House of Usher, and succeeds in providing a very entertaining location for the murders. The movements of the suspects inside the mansion also play a big role within the story, with both murders being strongly connected with the way the mansion is built and the way the mansion has been divided into two wings. The Angell mansion is a very impressive force within the novel."[8]

V. *IN THE FIRST DEGREE* (1933)

In the fifth and final Roger Scarlett novel, *In the First Degree* (1933), Underwood, who took part in but did not narrate *Murder among the Angells*, is absent, as are Moran and McBeath, who had not appeared among the Angells either; yet the quintessential Scarlett murder mansion maintains as strong a presence as ever. This time the mansion that sets the stage for death is the historic Loring house, a rare survival of Federal period architecture on Cambridge Street in Bowdoin Square. (The authors liken the building to an actual survival, still maintained today as a museum: the Harrison Gray Otis house.) On leave while recovering from influenza (a situation somewhat resembling that of PD James' policeman sleuth, Adam Dalgliesh, in another architecture-obsessed mystery from four decades later, *The Black Tower*), Kane is importuned by a caller, John Faraday, to look into a sinister affair at the Loring mansion: a suspected plot to murder owner Aaron Loring himself. "You wonder, no doubt, why I came," Faraday rather melodramatically explains, "Death, Mr. Kane . . . death—it is a horrible thing to contemplate!" Lacking real evidence that would justify an official police investigation, but nevertheless intrigued as ever by the bright lure of murder, Norton in the guise of a lodger inveigles himself into the house (floor plans are again included). Most provokingly, however, a killing is committed at the Loring mansion, in spite of the freelancing inspector's presence. With this last novel Roger Scarlett departed from the stage in a blaze of glory, the *Saturday Review* declaring, "You'll never guess who did it and you must finish the book" and the *New York Times* avowing, "there is a surprise in store for the reader who thinks it is easy. . . . [T]he plot is as ingenious as it is unusual."

VI. Conclusion

In his review of *Murder among the Angells*, Ho-Ling Wong expresses his bemusement over the fact that the detective fiction of Roger Scarlett has been so utterly forgotten outside of Japan, where his work was championed, as mentioned above, by Yokomizo Seishi and Edogawa Ranpo:

> I'm actually quite surprised why nobody seems to know Scarlett outside of Japan. This encounter was pretty pleasant and [Blair and Page] did write five books in total, so why did the Scarlett name disappear *practically completely*? If I hadn't seen the name mentioned by Edogawa and Yokomizo, I doubt I'd ever

have found out about this book, actually. Which is a
shame because *Murder among the Angells* is an entertaining mansion-story which I think doesn't deserve to
be forgotten . . . *this extremely.*

Crime writer Shimada Soji has noted, in his introduction to the
2015 English translation of Ayatsuji Yukito's *The Decagon House
Murders* (1987), that in Japan, in contrast with the United Kingdom
and the United States, respect has been maintained for the *honkaku,*
or orthodox, mystery, "a form of the detective story that is not only
literature but also, to a greater or lesser extent, a game":

> Golden Age detective fiction is still alive and thriving
> in Japan today, whereas in the United Kingdom and
> the United States it seems to have shut up shop. This is
> because in Japan we have the concept of *honkaku.* The
> word refers not only to the novels themselves, which
> emphasize logical reasoning, but it is also a badge of
> pride to the authors who write *honkaku,* indicating
> they are writers from whose novels readers can expect
> a certain level of intelligence. *Honkaku* is a word that
> has given all Japanese writers, prominent or other-
> wise, the power to keep on writing.
>   It is my belief that if we can introduce this concept
> to the field of American and British detective fiction,
> the Golden Age pendulum [there] will swing back. . . .

Five years ago I urged a similar point in my book *Masters of the
"Humdrum" Mystery* (2012), arguing, after the fashion of the distinguished late public intellectual (and profound classic mystery fan)
Jacques Barzun, that the ratiocinative mystery apotheosized during
the Golden Age of detective fiction is a form of literature deserving of
critical respect, despite the opprobrium that had been heaped upon
it by critics and crime writers since the Second World War. Happily the last five years have seen a dramatic revival in the fortunes of
classic mystery, as publishers in the UK and US have finally re-
embraced it. Coachwhip's reprinting of the audaciously clever series

of austerely classical mansion murders designed by Dorothy Blair and Evelyn Page, the two highly educated women who for a brief but bountiful time masqueraded as Roger Scarlett, is not, then, an anomaly but, much to the contrary, a most promising sign of the times.

ENDNOTES:

[1] John E. Blair, a younger brother of Dr. Blair, also moved out west, serving on the faculty at Stanford Law School and finally settling in Spokane, Washington, where he became, as a partner in the firm of Burcham & Blair, one of the city's most prominent attorneys. The younger Blair brother lived through the Second World War, during which time he provided employment and safe harbor for a Japanese family of seven, who had fled from Seattle to Spokane in order to evade the harsh reach of the infamous federal government evacuation order directed against Japanese Americans. (Spokane lay just outside the government's evacuation zone.) See Jim Kershner, "Spokane's Japanese Community," 8 January 2007, *HistoryLink.org*, at http://www.historylink.org/File/8048.

[2] Description of Blair and Page's farmhouse and life there are drawn from Evelyn Hyman Chase, *Feminist Convert: A Portrait of Mary Ellen Chase* (Santa Barbara, CA: John Daniel, 1988), chapter 11 and a contemporary newspaper article.

[3] Chase, *Feminist Convert*, chapter 11.

[4] Elienne Squire, *A Lantern in the Wind: The Life of Mary Ellen Chase* (Santa Barbara, CA: Fithian, 1995), chapters 15 and 16. Squire notes that during a train trip from Edinburgh to Cambridge, Dorothy and Chase "bolted the door of their private compartment because they were terrified of being discovered" in intimate proximity (p. 150).

[5] The closest contemporaneous male mystery writing counterparts to Dorothy Blair and Evelyn Page may be the expatriate British couple Richard Wilson Webb (1901-1966) and Hugh Callingham

Wheeler (1912-1987), who under three different pseudonyms—Patrick Quentin, Q. Patrick and Jonathan Stagge—published a lengthy and important group of American crime novels between 1936 and 1952, a period during which they also resided together, much of the time, coincidentally, at a farm in western Connecticut. See my essay "Two Young Men Who Write as One: Richard Wilson Webb, Hugh Callingham Wheeler, Male Couples and *The Grindle Nightmare*," in Curtis Evans, ed., *Murder in the Closet: Essays on Queer Clues in Crime Fiction Before Stonewall* (McFarland, 2017), 139-155.

[6] I wonder, however, whether Don Basil, who clearly had a penchant for deception, might actually have been "Basil Holland," i.e., perhaps he dedicated to himself the book he had stolen from another author. No information about Don Basil has ever been discovered, to my knowledge, except for the fact that apparently he shamelessly renewed the copyright of *Cat and Feather* in 1958. Evidently even Don Basil did not quite know what to do with the picturesque passage "I'd lay a bet that nine out of ten really good murderers lose their appetites right after shooting. And a heavy-eating gumshoe gets them on the hip every time. So forget your troubles." The stumped plagiarist crudely sheared the passage to "I'd lay a bet that nine out of ten really good murderers lose their appetites after the murder. So forget your troubles." Basil's plagiarized version of *The Back Bay Murders* also omits the novel's floor and room plans.

[7] See Ho-Ling Wong, "Turnabout Beginnings," 15 December 2011, at http://ho-lingnojikenbo.blogspot.com/2011/12/turnabout-beginnings.html.

[8] Sari Kawana, *Murder Most Modern: Detective Fiction and Japanese Culture* (Minneapolis and London: University of Minnesota Press, 2008), 26, 193-93; Satomi Saito, *Culture and Authenticity: The Discursive Space of Japanese Detective Fiction and the Formation of the National Imaginary* (PhD thesis, University of Iowa, 2007), 172-74; Ho-Ling Wong, review of Murder among the Angells, 20 August 2011, at http://ho-lingnojikenbo.blogspot.com/2011/08/

blog-post_10.html. Ho-Ling Wong notes that while the term "mansion story" might suggest some kinship "to a term like 'country house murders,' a *yakata-mono* is distinctly darker than the more neutral 'country house murder' moniker. The mansion in question should almost act like a character itself in the story; this might be at an actual physical level . . . or at a more spiritual level, for example by acting as a place with a distinctly evil vibe." Confirming Ho-Ling Wong's view of the novel is the crystalline precision of Scarlett's descriptions of the dark and majestically menacing Angell mansion:

The house was very large, and was built, apparently, in the shape of a reversed L, the base of which stretched along Beacon Street, while the stem followed the blind street that ended at the Esplanade. The doorway was on the corner.

Architecturally, the house wore the frowning, repellent aspect of an Italian palace-prison. The high, narrow, leaded windows were set deeply into the walls, as their purpose was less to admit light than to provide the captive inmates with a contrast to their own sad darkness. Between the windows, at regular intervals, hung wrought-iron lamps, for ornament rather than illumination. The porticoed doorway was wide, the door of glistening mahogany surrounding a great oblong of plate glass. Over the glass a wrought-iron grating had been set. Not even the brilliant silver of the fixtures could lighten the impression of magnificence and gloom.

THE BEACON HILL MURDERS

To My Parents
Who are Innocent of Crime

CHAPTER 1

"Underwood!" Kane's voice was metallic. "You're letting this get the best of you. If I'm to find out what's happened, you've got to pull yourself together!"

His words broke into my incoherent story and brought me sharply to my senses.

"You telephoned me at this hour of the night to come immediately to the Sutton house. I'm here," Kane continued, "and you've wasted five minutes and told me nothing. All I gather is that you came here for dinner, and that something terrible has happened."

He turned to me more gently. "You're a lawyer, Underwood," he said, "and not accustomed, as I am, to violence and crime. But you ought to be better prepared to meet the unforeseen. You ought to know that under the surface of normal existence there are hidden currents which sometimes burst through. You shrink from them with horror, but I'm trained to expect their manifestations."

I knew that he was talking to give me time to recover myself, to lift the burden of horror which had oppressed me for the last hour.

Kane sat down facing me. In spite of his hard directness, he had the look of a visionary, with his thick, black hair and his fine forehead. His abrupt, ugly features emphasized the sensitiveness of his eyes.

How could such a man spend his days in the pursuit of the sordid and the horrible? How could he make murder the stuff of his life, his end and aim, as a police inspector, to bring criminals to justice?

"Now," Kane caught me up sharply, "put your personal reactions aside."

His presence was beginning to calm me. "I'm sorry," I said with an effort. "I haven't got over it yet. It happened only an hour ago."

"Never mind that. Sutton invited you here to a dinner party, you say. And that dinner party ended in murder."

He pulled out his watch. "It's twelve o'clock," he said. "I give you half an hour to tell me the story from the beginning."

At seven o'clock on the evening of September twenty-fourth I was walking up Quincy Street toward the Sutton house, which stood by itself, cut off from its neighbors, in the middle of a small plot of ground. As I approached it, I could not help being impressed with its air of dignity and age. It was typical of the best houses on Beacon Hill, and, like many of them, had fallen into evil days. Its original owner, endowed with the traditions of good taste and gentle living, could not have imagined that it would fall into the hands of Frederick Sutton, the stock exchange gambler, who had risen from nothing to a huge fortune.

I was reluctant and annoyed at the thought of the evening before me. As Sutton's lawyer, I had not been able to refuse his first invitation to dinner. He was obviously preparing to break his way into society, and I shrewdly suspected that he wanted to use me as a rung in the social ladder. I looked forward to an uncomfortable few hours spent in the company of the newly rich.

Sutton came to the door to greet me. His face was flushed, and his manner betrayed an excitement which struck me as both pitiable and ridiculous. As I shook hands with him I noticed that his palm was hot and moist with perspiration.

He took me to the room where his family had gathered and introduced me to his wife, who was standing before the fire. Her manner was ill-assured, and I thought that her stiffness was a result of timidity. Sutton hardly gave me time to speak to her, however, before he hurried me on to his daughter. After the introductions had been made, the four of us stood making awkward attempts at a conversation. Of the group, the daughter seemed the most self-possessed. About twenty-two or three, she had an air that set her apart from the usual young woman of my acquaintance. I should never have called her good-looking, and yet she expressed a kind of pride in her bearing. There was no doubt that she was intelligent, although she made no effort to be entertaining.

Faced with Miss Sutton's indifference, her mother's lack of confidence, and Sutton's nervous cordiality, I found talking to them uphill work and was relieved when Sutton, casting a look of angry impatience at the two women, drew me aside.

He clumsily maneuvered me into another part of the room, where we stood, uncomfortably, as far as I was concerned, engaged in a conversation that soon turned into a monologue. He was obsessed with the idea of his own success. For years it had been denied him—he spoke as though by the malice of the world—but he had conquered circumstance. Everything was at his command now, and he was ready to enjoy what he had won. He was like a man who had been starving for an audience, and I became the victim.

At the same time, behind his arrogance, it was easy to see his lack of assurance. He seemed to be trying to convince himself that what he said was true, and in the effort he became extravagant. His powerful, heavy face was flushed, and his eyes were bloodshot.

In an effort to distract him, I suggested that he show me a painting which he had just bought. He had paid a fabulous sum for it although there was some doubt as to its authenticity.

We walked over to the corner of the room where it was hung and I examined it with an interest more feigned than real, hoping that he would go off on the usual ignorant collector's jargon. Unfortunately, it served only as a starting point for the old subject, and in a minute he was talking in the same strain. In the midst of a sentence he was interrupted by a low chuckle.

"We're rich now, ain't we?" The question came in a thin piping voice which seemed childlike and absurd. It made me jump, for I had noticed no one in that part of the room besides ourselves. I looked around quickly and saw a slender little man emerging from the shadows. Apparently it was his voice that had cut short Sutton's tirade.

"My brother-in-law, Mr. Walton." Sutton introduced him abruptly and turned away from both of us, as if he were already ashamed of his outburst.

Walton came quite close to me, his small, beady, birdlike eyes fixed on my face. "He doesn't like me very much," he said, "and I don't like him. He said I couldn't come to-night, but my sister said I could." His manner was confidential, secretive. He began to strut up and down before me, more than ever like a bantam cock. "He needn't be so high and mighty," he continued, "other people can do things, too." He nodded mysteriously and retired again to his corner.

The half hour I had spent in the Sutton house seemed to me a most extraordinary prelude to a dinner party. Whatever I had contemplated in the way of boredom was nothing compared to the difficult position in which I found myself. My host had disappeared. Mrs. Sutton was sitting by the fire enveloped in a silence that did not invite interruption. She kept glancing toward the door, and it occurred to me suddenly that she was waiting, mentally bracing herself for an encounter with what or whom I could not know. Her daughter was standing nearby, and as I looked at her I saw that she was waiting too.

A second later I was tempted to laugh at the tricks my imagination was playing on me. The intensity which possessed all of them was natural enough under the circumstances. A year ago, no one had heard of the Suttons; now a considerable section of the newspaper reading public knew of their sudden rise to fortune. A year ago Sutton had been one of the crowd of stock exchange gamblers, playing on the narrowest of margins, losing one day what he had made the day before. I knew a good deal about his affairs, enough to realize how enormously luck had gone his way. It was natural that he should have been thrown into an abnormal frame of mind, and that his family should likewise have been deeply affected by the change in their circumstances. I was, in a way, fortunate in having the opportunity to witness their entry into a new world. It was a situation to be watched closely and with interest.

A ring at the door-bell disturbed my meditations, and the two at the fireplace stirred at the sound. Mrs. Sutton half turned toward the door, and then settled back into her chair again. Miss Sutton resumed her mask of indifference. Sutton himself reappeared in the room. He had recovered his exuberance, and glanced eagerly about him, as if to see that everything was prepared for the latest arrival. There was a pause, broken by the butler's announcement: "Mrs. Anceney."

Decidedly, I thought, this was to be an evening of surprises. I had met Mrs. Anceney, and at one time or another had heard of her a good deal as a woman of great charm. She went everywhere and knew everybody. No name appeared more frequently than hers in the social columns of the newspapers. She was a guest at Palm Beach or Newport. She had been seen at this wedding, and that hunt breakfast. The magazines printed pictures of her at Dinard and Deauville. Why should she, of all people, be a guest of the Suttons?

As she stood framed in the doorway, I looked at her with unconscious admiration. She was tall, and so dark that the lock of pure white in her hair added to her look of distinction. She did not possess beauty in the true sense of the word, nor youth, for she must have been forty or forty-five, but I could imagine no situation in which she would not have stood out as a personality. Her charm was elusive, indefinable, based on a combination of intelligence and good breeding. I noticed that she wore a spray of gardenias. Tradition had it that she never appeared without them.

At a signal from Sutton, Mrs. Sutton rose to speak to her. She did it clumsily, with more than a trace of reluctance in her manner. But at Mrs. Anceney's arrival everything seemed suddenly to become easier. Instead of being separate entities more or less antagonistic to each other, we became at least outwardly a pleasant gathering. If there were undercurrents I ceased to notice them so much.

When I found that Mrs. Anceney remembered me, I was pleased, although I doubt if Sutton was. He seemed to regard her as his special property, and demanded her whole attention, which she had the good sense not to give him. Instead she talked for the most part to Mrs. Sutton and Katharine, the daughter, and almost without effort drew them out of their isolation.

By this time I was beginning to wonder if the dinner to which I had been invited was ever going to take place. My anxiety on that point was allayed by the appearance of the butler with the cocktails. At his heels came a young man, whom I found to be James, Sutton's son, and an older man named Gilroy.

As I was sipping my cocktail I wondered again how Mrs. Anceney happened to be my fellow guest. Of all the people of my acquaintance she was the one least likely to know the Suttons at all, and yet she seemed to be on terms of familiarity with them.

When we went to the table I found myself seated between Mrs. Sutton and Katharine. Mrs. Anceney was on Sutton's right, with James on her other hand, and Gilroy at Mrs. Sutton's left. Walton took his place between Katharine and my host.

Thanks to Mrs. Anceney, dinner progressed smoothly. The conversation was general, and gave me an opportunity to observe more closely the strange group about the table. I decided that Mrs. Sutton was not as commonplace as I had at first thought her. She looked a good deal older than her husband, although she had apparently tried in every possible way to regain an appearance of youth. Her rather thin hair was carefully dressed, and although I was no expert in such matters, I thought that it had been touched up and restored to a color that might once have been natural but was so no more. She had used a little too much rouge, and her lips were too red. She was pretty much what I had suspected Sutton's wife would be, but I was surprised to see what startling eyes she had—eyes that were astonishingly clear and keen, that betrayed, behind the mask with which her hairdresser and her masseuse had provided her, the existence of a character.

We were having our coffee when Sutton became talkative again. A little flushed with wine and the success of his party, he started to take the conversation into his own hands.

"You're used to this sort of thing," he began, looking at me, "but I'm not—not yet. I'll get the hang of it soon, and maybe I'll have more to get the hang of. But it's funny to sit down to a dinner like this, in a room like this, and know that you own the whole house and everything in it. I used to feel rich when I had ten dollars to spare. I'll tell you this now—I wouldn't have told it to God himself once—I used to roll up cigar coupons, and put a couple of bills on the outside of the roll, so that it would look as if I had money in my pocket. Katharine knows all about it. I used to talk to her even when she was a kid. She believed I'd get what I wanted. She was like me, and still is, aren't you, Kitty? People like us never rest easy till we get what we want."

Katharine gave her father a quick glance, and murmured something inaudible.

Sutton turned to me again. "You wouldn't believe me if I told you the way I used to talk to her. She was the only one who would listen to me, and she'd do it for hours on end."

There was something likeable about him as he sat there. Behind his awkwardness and his ineffective speech there were sincerity and power. He looked again at his daughter.

"I've done everything for you I can. It's up to you to make something of it. You've got a lot to learn before you can knock the eye out of the world. Mrs. Anceney'll help you along." He looked at Mrs. Anceney inquiringly.

"Miss Sutton is much too clever to need my help," she replied.

Sutton laughed tolerantly. "You've helped her already, and you needn't think I don't know what you've done for all of us. Why, if it hadn't been for you, I'd never have had the sense to get this house, for one thing. You even got the servants and started us off right. I'm grateful to you, for one. And anyone who does anything for me, I'll see to it they don't exactly suffer for it."

He drew himself up, and looked around the table. His wife returned his glance steadily, and I thought there was something like a warning in her silence. James stared speculatively at his father, and Gilroy had a mocking smile on his face that did nothing to counteract the dislike I had already taken to him.

During the pause, Sutton was fumbling in his pocket. Finally he brought out an oblong jeweler's box, which he opened with an air of satisfaction. "This is what I meant," he continued ponderously. "I want you to know that I appreciate your help. Words are all very well, but they're cheap, and that's not my way. I want you to have something to show for it."

He handed the box over to Mrs. Anceney, and I think for the moment even her composure deserted her. The situation was absurd. Sutton seemed to have left behind him the elements of commonsense. If he had known no better, surely caution might have warned him that one did not give a woman of Mrs. Anceney's position jewelry as one might give a servant a tip.

"It is lovely," she murmured. I saw that the box contained a beautiful and intricately carved jade pendant.

She looked at the jewel appreciatively, and then continued, "Of course it is ridiculous of you to think of giving it to me." She seemed to be choosing her words carefully. "I'm delighted if my advice has been of any use to you, but you must be even more generous and let me have another sort of gift in exchange for it."

Sutton was perturbed. "Of course, if you don't like it, get what you want, and send the bill to me."

"I didn't mean exactly that," she replied. "You must let me continue to be a friend of yours and your family's. I should value that very highly."

For a moment Sutton's face was a study. Finally he flushed. "I see," he said, and his voice was soft. "You make me feel that I owe you more than ever."

I doubt if anyone around the table had preserved his self-possession. An embarrassed silence seized upon us. Sutton must have noticed our uneasiness, to say nothing of his own state of mind. With an effort, rare in him, to slide over our awkwardness, he said, "The fellow who sold it to me told me it had belonged to the Dowager Empress of China, whoever she was."

His ignorance of the Dowager Empress did little to conceal his pride in possessing a jewel once owned by royalty.

Mrs. Anceney still held the pendant in her hand, and her fingers caressed it gently.

"Yes," she said, "I saw in the newspapers that you had bought it. The article said that it had belonged to her. I don't think I've ever seen a more perfect piece of jade. Have you, Mr. Underwood?"

She showed it to me, and although I knew very little about it, I could see that she was right. It was a deep, translucent green, and although it was no larger than a man's watch, the carving was exquisitely finished. When I held it to the light, I noticed that both sides were identical except for three small marks.

"Isn't it rather unusual," I remarked, "that the same piece of carving has been done on it twice?"

"I'd have thought so," she agreed, as I handed it back to her, "if a friend of mine hadn't described it to me several days ago. He's been interested in Chinese jewelry and had heard of this. He told me that the carving represented the Empress's seal, and had been done by her orders."

She looked down at it. "You can see the two dragons," she went on. "The design at the bottom represents the waves. The figure at the top is a jewel the dragons are fighting for. The characters in the middle mean, as I remember, 'Heaven and Earth share the recurring spring.' It's a sort of pledge of happiness. The three little marks are her hall mark."

"How did he know so much about it?" Sutton asked abruptly.

Mrs. Anceney laughed. "You forget," she said, "you've bought something quite famous. A good many people know about it. As a matter of fact, he heard about it when he was in China, a little while after the Boxer uprising."

Again Sutton showed a childish pleasure. "I didn't know it was as famous as that," he said, "even though I did have to pay a thumping price for it."

"Didn't the jeweler tell you the legend about it?"

"Why, no." Sutton looked puzzled.

"Shall I tell you? It may make you uneasy, though I'm not superstitious." She hesitated as if she were doubtful whether to tell the story or not.

"Go ahead, go ahead. I don't take any stock in legends." Sutton made an impatient gesture.

She looked around the table, half apologetically. "This one is fascinating, I think."

"I'd like to hear it," I ventured, and the others seconded me.

"Well," she began, "I'll tell it as 'twas told to me, and remember I vouch for none of it. You probably all know that the Dowager Empress was a hot tempered and violent lady, but besides that she was devoted to the arts, and particularly loved jade. They say she would sit for hours fingering it. She loved the feeling of it. It's strange, isn't it, to think how often she must have had this in her hands."

She touched the pendant appreciatively. "According to the story, she was particularly fond of this, and people recognized it as a sign manual of hers, at first with no special feeling about it, but later with a good deal of fear. She gave it away once to one of her eunuchs, and in a little while he died. Somehow or other it got back to her, and again she gave it away, and again the possessor died. They say that one of the people she gave it to was the Empress A-lu-te, a rival of hers, whom she forced to commit suicide, At any rate, wherever it went, it was a sign of misfortune. The Chinese are very superstitious, you know. They would never put a symbol of bad luck in a piece of jewelry, and they are desperately afraid of such a thing as this.

"The story goes on to say that, during the Boxer uprising, the Empress's jade was lost or stolen. And they say, too, that whoever has owned it since then has had bad luck."

She looked at Sutton. "I suppose that's why the jeweler didn't tell you the story. He may have feared to lose the sale."

"I'm not afraid of any such cock-and-bull story as that," Sutton said emphatically. "He might just as well have told me about it. I'm not a fool," his voice became gentler, "though I didn't mean to pass bad luck along to you."

She laughed. "I should probably have liked it all the more for the legend. Other people's bad luck symbols seem to have a fatal attraction for me. I'll go out of my way to walk under a ladder, and as for mirrors, I break them as a matter of policy."

"Anyhow, I'm glad you know I didn't know the story," Sutton repeated with awkward sincerity.

She smiled at him, put the pendant back in its case, and handed it to him.

"You mustn't tempt me too long with something as lovely as that," she said. "It's never wise, is it, Mr. Gilroy?"

Gilroy, too smooth, too polite, replied, "That is a lesson that an attractive woman is often taught but rarely learns." He leaned back in his chair and stroked his small, carefully tended black moustache. There was something very annoying in his assumption of ease, something false in his mannered behavior.

Walton, who had sat quietly, like a well-trained child, throughout dinner, leaned forward and stared greedily at the box which lay by Sutton's hand. "I'd like to have a look at that," he said suddenly. "I'll give it right back."

Sutton looked at him impatiently, and hesitated.

"Let him see it, Fred," said Mrs. Sutton gently, as if she were used to humoring her younger brother. "It's pretty, Bert, isn't it?"

Bert nodded and handed the box back. Sutton slipped it into his pocket.

CHAPTER 2

I had my first opportunity to talk to Mrs. Anceney after dinner was over. I was curious enough to try to find out how she had met the Suttons, and why she had gone on with their acquaintance, but I discovered very little. Apparently their meeting was a happenstance, and occurred at a tea to which some business friends of Sutton's had invited him and his wife. Sutton at least had lost no time in singling her out. Still, I could not understand why she had let him show her such open admiration. He, of course, was the type to which concealment is impossible, but she was a woman of subtlety and fine distinctions. I could not believe that the realization that Sutton was in love with her would sweep her off her feet. She must have had several chances to marry again—she was a widow—but she had chosen not to do so.

During the short time that I was talking to her, I could feel Sutton's eyes fixed upon us. He had seemed hurt, at first, when she refused to take the pendant, but he had soon recovered. He must have realized that she was paying him a high compliment in saying that she valued nothing as much as his friendship. By now he had taken on an attitude of humble adoration, although like most worshipers he made a good many demands on his goddess. Again she managed him cleverly, and refused to let him monopolize her.

I thought that the difficult part of the evening had been got over, when Mrs. Anceney suggested that we play a rubber of bridge. With an embarrassed glance at her right arm, Mrs. Sutton said that she did not want to play. I had noticed during dinner that she made no use of it. From the way she managed it, it must have been stiff from the shoulder down. Her brother did not promise to be a very likely hand at the game, and Sutton and I decided to watch, so that Katharine, Mrs. Anceney, Gilroy, and James made up the table. Walton looked pitifully disappointed at being left out, but Mrs. Sutton whispered something to him, and he scuttled happily away. In a moment he returned with a parchesi board, and was soon absorbed in a game against his sister.

It was arranged that Mrs. Anceney and James should play together against Katharine and Gilroy. While they were cutting for deal, at Gilroy's suggestion they decided to play for a stake. The game began. Sutton pulled up a chair and took his place by Katharine's side, and I looked over Gilroy's shoulder.

The vague dislike which I had felt for him when we first met had become sharper during the course of the evening. The man looked like a wax dummy in a shop window. His manners were too good, and he was always conscious of them. I thought of him as an imitation gentleman and resented the cheap boldness of his glance.

My mind had wandered from the game, when I happened to notice that Gilroy was making a revoke, and, to judge by the malicious expression on his face, doing it on purpose. James was playing the hand. He had seemed certain to make game and rubber for himself and Mrs. Anceney. The revoke, however, turned the scales against him. Mrs. Anceney saw it, but being dummy could not say anything. James was oblivious of what was going on, and to his annoyed surprise went down.

After that, luck changed sides, and Gilroy and Katharine pulled steadily ahead. Sutton was becoming more and more interested. He leaned over Katharine's shoulder, advising her eagerly, and she accepted his suggestions with the ease of long habit. There was evidently a very close understanding between them.

Once or twice after Sutton had pointed out to her a good play, James seemed about to object to his father's interference. The boy's temper was not improving under adversity. He was a good deal like his father, I thought, although he was too much the young man about town to possess Sutton's brutal vigor. Neither one, however, could stand losing, even in bridge.

The cards continued to go against James, and his rather florid face reddened with annoyance. Finally, while Sutton was giving Katharine a direction, James leaned forward with an ugly frown.

"Let her play her own hand," he said.

Sutton glared at him angrily, but made no reply, and after a moment the boy's eyes wavered and fell. Without a word he went on playing, and Sutton continued his instructions to his daughter.

Meantime a rather flirtatious rivalry had arisen between Sutton and Mrs. Anceney. He took a childish pleasure in circumventing her plans, and in the interchange between them I could detect the overtones of a more serious situation.

As the game came to a close, Gilroy and Katharine (I might almost say Sutton) were several hundred points ahead. The former pocketed his winnings from James with ill-concealed satisfaction. As Mrs. Anceney was settling her accounts with Katharine, she remarked pleasantly, "You play a splendid game, Miss Sutton."

"She plays well enough when she remembers what I've told her," Sutton replied for his daughter.

The bridge party having broken up, Katharine and I drifted over to the fireplace. Sutton remained by the table, looking down at Mrs. Anceney and talking to her in a low voice. I am not sure, but I thought I overheard him apologizing for his stupidity at dinner and intimating that he realized she could not accept his gift.

He seemed to be urging her to do something. She hesitated, and he continued, becoming more and more importunate. At last she evidently yielded, and together they walked slowly toward the door.

Bert looked up from his game sharply. "Where are you going?" he asked, an expression of infantile curiosity on his face. Too late, Mrs. Sutton tried to stop him.

"Upstairs to my sitting room," Sutton replied impatiently.

"Mr. Sutton was kind enough to say that he would show me a bronze he has just bought," Mrs. Anceney explained.

"You will enjoy seeing it, I think." Mrs. Sutton looked up from her game with a curious expression.

They went out of the room, followed after three minutes or so by James and Gilroy, who seemed to find each other congenial. I took up a laborious conversation with Katharine and Mrs. Sutton. It was not long, however, before Katharine excused herself, and Bert, yawning prodigiously, followed her upstairs.

I did my best to talk to Mrs. Sutton, since I felt a good deal of sympathy for her. She seemed rather a pathetic figure. Sutton obviously believed that he had gone beyond her, and, indeed, she seemed helpless in her new life. But as our conversation limped along, realized that she was the kind of woman who needs neither pity nor sympathy. She was too self-contained, too unapproachable.

As we sat there, I heard Sutton, upstairs, laughing, and there was an exultant note in his laughter. I glanced at Mrs. Sutton, but she must not have heard him, for she gave no sign. Shortly afterward I heard a door close, and there were no more sounds from upstairs.

It was getting late, and I was anxious to return to my own comfortable apartment. I had made no headway at all with Mrs. Sutton, and the events of the evening had tired me. I wanted to leave, but in the absence of my host I felt a little awkward about doing so.

I murmured something to Mrs. Sutton about having to go, and was amused to see a shade of relief in her face. As far as discourtesy was concerned, Sutton was guiltier than I, and I could see no reason for staying any longer. I made my bow to Mrs. Sutton, therefore, and went out to the hall where the footman presented me with my hat and coat.

As I left the house and walked slowly down the street, it occurred to me afresh what an amazing evening I had spent, and how dearly some gossips of my acquaintance would love to have been in my shoes. The situation between Mrs. Anceney and Sutton would give plenty of opportunities for spicy comment, the more because, in their different spheres, they were both so well known. The Sutton family alone was peculiar enough to satisfy the most sophisticated dealer in personalities.

I had hardly gone half a block before I remembered that I had left my stick behind. It was one which I liked, and so I decided to go back and get it. I retraced my steps, crossed the little alleyway which bounded one side of the house, and rang the front door-bell.

The footman answered my ring, and when I explained what I wanted he went to fetch it. The hall was deserted, and there was no sound from upstairs. In the silence I heard the clock strike eleven.

There was a pause, and then a sharp explosion. Perhaps I should have thought the noise was made by a car if it had not been followed by a scream of terror. Now that the moment is over, I can explain to no one the effect that agonized cry had upon me. The world and life itself stopped for a moment. I was dazed, as though somebody had struck me in the face and blinded my eyes. I could not move during that instant when all my faculties were paralyzed. Another second brought me to my senses. I realized that a woman had screamed, that something horrible had happened, and that I was afraid.

I suppose that I stood motionless for no more than thirty seconds. I noticed that the footman had come back with my cane, and that his face reflected my fear, although he mechanically offered me my stick. As mechanically I took it, and the feel of it in my hands restored my courage. I pushed him aside and ran down the hall, the blood pounding in my temples. It seemed to take immeasurable hours to reach the stairs, and I was gasping for breath when I got there.

Still half unconscious of what was going on around me, I noticed Gilroy standing two or three steps up, as if he had been coming down the stairs when the unearthly sounds had arrested him. His face was pallid and beaded with perspiration.

"Something seems to be the matter," he stammered, his dummy-like smile fatuously fixed.

I wanted to shout at him, but dashed on. In the upper hall I saw Katharine, who was in a state of highly nervous excitement, coming out of her room. She must have been awakened by the cries, for she wore a dressing gown and slippers.

"Why did you cry out? What is it?" I said, trying to control my voice.

"It wasn't I," she answered breathlessly. "It came from in there." She pointed to a closed door.

Meantime James and Bert had joined us. The boy's studied coolness jarred on me disagreeably, no less than did Walton's gaping curiosity. Mrs. Sutton appeared in her doorway. On the far side of the hall, a group of servants stood, huddled together like sheep.

Still caught in an illusion of unreality, I walked to the door Katharine had indicated, and threw it open. Within, the room was dimly lighted, and at first I could see little or nothing. Then I made out the figure of Mrs. Anceney. She was standing, rigid, by a chair. Her hand was pressed to her mouth, as if she were trying to keep herself from screaming again. She saw me, and made an effort to compose herself.

"What is it?" I said. "For God's sake, what's the matter?"

She made a slight motion of her hand, and I looked in the direction of her gesture. Sutton was sitting nearby. I half expected him to get up furiously and order me out, but his head remained bent, and he said nothing.

"Look!" Mrs. Anceney cried. "Can't you see—"

I went nearer to him, conscious that the others were pressing close upon my heels. Still he did not move. Suddenly I saw a red spot on his shirt front. It grew larger as I looked at it. Only then did I begin to realize what had happened. I took his hand. It was limp, and I knew that he was dead.

I started back, and my eyes fell on a gun lying on the table in the middle of the room. Dazed, I glanced from it to Mrs. Anceney.

I remember making confused and unavailing attempts to keep the women from that ghastly figure. I suppose that the expression on my face was revealing enough to tell them, without words, what had happened. Katharine threw herself on her knees beside Sutton and burst into a wild fit of crying. Mrs. Sutton stood quietly by his chair, and taking the hand I had let fall, stroked it gently.

I turned to Mrs. Anceney. "What happened? Why did you do it?" I cried.

The sound of my voice seemed to break the spell of her horror. She became conscious of the present, realized that there were people in the room, and recognized the meaning of my words. She glanced at me as coldly as though I had asked an impertinent question.

"I have nothing to say now, do you understand? Send for my lawyer at once, please. I must talk to him." Her manner cut short any further protest I might have made.

"There is a small room on this corridor which is unoccupied," she continued. "I will wait there until he comes. You need not worry about my running away." She walked out the door without looking at any of us.

I had sufficient self-possession to dismiss the servants without further ado. The butler seemed to be a responsible man, and I put them all in his charge, telling him as forcibly as I could that no one must leave the house, or disturb anything in it.

I then turned back to the principal actors in the tragedy. A touch on the arm aroused James from his apparently stolid attitude.

"Get your mother and sister away," I said. He moved to obey me. Mrs. Sutton left the room without argument, but Katharine ignored his attempts to arouse her from her grief. She pushed away his hand and clung desperately to her place by her father. Finally he succeeded in getting her away, and taking her by the arm, led her to the door, where he paused and looked at me questioningly.

"You had better go to your rooms and stay there until the police arrive," I said in reply. "I will notify them immediately. Mrs. Anceney is taken care of."

I turned back to the others. Gilroy was standing absolutely motionless. His lips were twitching, and he glanced warily about as though expecting an attack. I told him to wait downstairs, and he obeyed without speaking.

After they had gone, I gave a hasty glance about the room to make sure that there was only the one entrance to it. As I did so I saw that Bert was still there, crouched in a corner. He looked wild with terror, and his eyes darted first in one direction and then in another, like those of a trapped animal seeking some way of escape. I shook him roughly and ordered him out. With a sobbing gasp, he ran to the door.

Moving carefully so as to disturb nothing, I assured myself that everyone had gone, that the windows were closed and fastened, and that the only way of getting into the room was by the door I had used. Fortunately there was a key in the lock. I turned off the lights, closed the door behind me, and locked it. The key I put in my pocket.

Downstairs I found that the butler had already notified the district police station. An officer stood at the front door. It was only two or three minutes before Moran, the police sergeant, arrived. I told him briefly what had happened.

"Then," I ended my tale to Kane, "I thought of you, and as you know, telephoned you at once. Nothing further occurred during the fifteen minutes before you came." I searched again in my mind for any additional details I might give him. As far as I could see, there was nothing. "That's all."

CHAPTER 3

As I concluded my story, I looked at Kane with some eagerness to learn what his reaction would be, but if I had expected to find him with knitted brow, I should indeed have been disappointed. He sat lazily fingering a Florentine leather match box, and his expression was as pleasantly interested as if he had been listening to an old wives' tale rather than the events of a cold-blooded murder. I found it necessary to remind myself that Kane's face was never an index to what went on behind it, and that no one could tell what his reactions would be to a given situation.

He seemed a curiously incongruous figure as he sat there. Feature by feature he was so ugly that it was rather a pleasure to look at him, in contrast to the neat conventional man of the advertisements. His thick black hair rebelled against discipline. Beneath it his forehead was heavily lined, and his thick eyebrows seemed startling in the pallor of his face. His eyes were deep-set, and their kindness belied the severity of his nose and chin.

He must have measured well over six feet, but his slight stoop took away from his height. Although I had seen him move as quickly and surely as a cat, as a general thing he managed himself awkwardly, and his long arms and legs gave him a look of rawboned, country breeding.

The workings of his mind were completely opposed to his physical appearance. I had first met him as a young man in college, where he was known as a brilliant student, obsessed with a strange curiosity about crime. For some years after that he had studied abroad, and worked with the experts in criminology and abnormal psychology. It had been something of a shock to me to learn that he had returned to become a police detective. However, in the few years during which he had applied himself to practice instead of theory, he had built up for himself a growing reputation. Although the murder of Sutton must have been by far the most spectacular case which had come into his hands, I could see, as I looked at him, no signs of excitement.

He was silent for a few minutes, then laid the match box down on the table, and knotted his long fingers together.

"Very excellent, Underwood," he said, with a smile. "Of course I'm referring to your narrative powers. Straightforward, to the point, and not an important detail missing, as far as I can judge. If all witnesses were lawyers, a detective could find time to lead a private life. I can see your characters perfectly. By the way, you've painted a glowing picture of Mrs. Anceney. Is it possible that that lady has touched your sensibilities also?"

"Not at all," I made haste to say, and then stopped short with some irritation, realizing that I was being taken for a ride, as the saying goes. Kane was looking at me with unconcealed amusement.

"Well, I'll pass judgment later on, after we've called on her." He sat up and stroked his chin thoughtfully. I realized that with the gesture he had abruptly sloughed off his inconsequential manner. The disinterested listener had become the keen investigator.

"She is being well taken care of, isn't she?" he asked.

I told him that she was waiting in one of the upstairs rooms and that McBeath, one of Sergeant Moran's men, had been posted outside. At her request, I had telephoned for her lawyer.

"When Moran and I posted McBeath there, she called me in," I went on, "and asked, as a particular favor, that nothing should be given out to the newspapers until she had seen her lawyer and prepared her statement. After all, it meant putting off the reporters for only an hour or so, so I was able . . ."

"So you were able to wangle that particular favor for her," Kane finished grimly. "Well, so much for the birth of chivalry. Now, Underwood," he said, thrusting his hand into his pocket, his manner serious enough to stifle my only natural indignation at his last comment, "I understand from what you say that you were distinctly surprised to find that Mrs. Anceney was a guest of Sutton's. You made quite a point of that, I remember. Didn't anything happen later that would explain her being there?"

I tried to think of something that would answer Kane's question, for he obviously thought that it was important.

"Nothing that explains it to me," I said finally.

"You're sure that she couldn't have been attracted to Sutton, just as he was to her?"

"Positive."

"You don't happen to know, do you, whether or not she stood to benefit financially by his death?"

Since I had drawn up Sutton's will for him, I could assure Kane that she did not.

"She was more likely then to want to have him alive?"

"I don't think she was trying to get money out of him, if that's what you mean," I replied. "She's fairly well off herself. And she's not in the least what they call a gold-digger."

Kane looked very thoughtful. "You see, if she didn't cultivate him for any of the obvious reasons, we'll have to find out what her motives were. As far as I can judge, she certainly had them. You admit, don't you, that she was wise enough to know the danger she was courting?"

"She certainly has had plenty of experience," I said. "And no one could call her stupid."

"You've never heard any gossip about her?"

"Nothing serious. Of course, there's gossip about everybody."

I had answered Kane's question quickly without thinking very much about it. But almost as soon as I had stopped speaking, I had a vague recollection of something I might have told him. He must have noticed a change in my expression, for he said quietly, "What was it about?"

"I can't quite remember," I answered, searching my mind. "It was so long ago, and it wasn't about her exactly. Some relative of hers got into a scrape, I think, and people talked."

Kane looked at me intently. "Not enough to damage her, I suppose."

"No."

He shifted abruptly. "How long have you known her, or known of her?" he continued.

"For twenty years, I should say. I went to school with her husband."

"I take it then that she isn't a native Bostonian?"

I was puzzled by Kane's insistence on questions that seemed to me so remote from the main issue. "I think not," I replied. "I can't be sure."

"You've never heard her refer to her younger days?"

"No."

"She seems to have made quite a place for herself here," he reflected.

I looked at him in astonishment. "It isn't only here that she's well known. You could say the same thing about New York or London or Paris. She has friends everywhere."

"I'll take your word for it," he said. His interest in the conversation had dropped. "It's time I got to work," he went on. "I've an idea I'd like to gumshoe a bit around the room in which Sutton departed this life. We may not find footprints in the snow, but there are always the forgotten calling card and the initialed handkerchief to be hoped for. Secondly, I've a growing curiosity to see this lady who has caused my hardheaded lawyer friend to lay his cloak upon the ground. Possibly that may end our adventures, but I've an odd hunch, Underwood, that it may only begin them. At any rate, let's do what we can now."

As he pushed himself up from his chair, I reminded him that Sergeant Moran was waiting upstairs to join us in any investigations we might make. Kane replied that he was glad Headquarters had sent Moran rather than someone else, since the murder was unexpected enough without having to cope with imagination in a police sergeant.

I had followed him as far as the door when I observed that he had paused with his hand on the knob. He turned around slowly.

"There's just one more thing, Underwood, that you can tell me. You say that when you entered Sutton's sitting room, Mrs. Anceney was standing by her chair. She had her hand pressed over her mouth. Isn't that right?"

I said that it was.

"Now what I want to know is this—what was the expression on her face *after* that moment?"

"Why, the natural one, I suppose, under the circumstances."

"Under what circumstances?"

"Under the circumstances of killing a man in cold blood and of being discovered with the body," I replied, a little puzzled at his persistence.

"All right," he said. "Now I should suppose that any woman who shot a man as Mrs. Anceney would seem to have shot Sutton acted on impulse and not on plan. Why? Because she was perfectly certain to be caught. In that case, it occurs to me that the woman would be momentarily horrified at what she had done, and, a second later, terribly frightened of the consequences. Do you agree?"

I said I did.

"Then you would answer my first question by describing Mrs. Anceney's expression as one of terrible fear?"

"She was horrified," I answered at once. "She had screamed. I was afraid she was going to scream again."

"But that was just as you came into the room, wasn't it, about a minute after the shot was fired? It's natural for anyone, innocent or guilty, to be horrified at murder. I'm speaking about the following moment, after the crisis, so to speak, was over. How did she act then?"

I tried to think. "She must have been terribly frightened," I said at last. "She was staring at Sutton's body. There were so many people about . . . I can't remember exactly," I concluded lamely.

"But you supposed that she was terribly frightened," said Kane quickly. "Well, it's natural to suppose so. She may easily have been. The difficulty is that after a time what one actually has seen and what one has expected to see merge into one impression and can't be separated. Now you have already told me that she was not so utterly upset as to lose all control of herself. She sounds to me rather self-possessed, in fact. Therefore, are you perfectly sure that you did not involuntarily read fear into her face, when actually it may not have been there?"

Kane was looking at me so sternly that I hesitated a long time before I spoke. "I'm not perfectly sure, no. I can't be, if you put it in that fashion. But," I added, "neither can I bring myself wholly to doubt the truth of my impressions."

Kane relaxed in that unexpected way of his. "Underwood," he said lightly, "if I was impressed by my skill as an inquisitor, you've taken the last breath of wind out of my sails. Nothing more or less than the truth can pass muster when faced with your New England conscience."

I paid no heed to his words, and as he turned around to open the door, I said, "You must remember, too, that Mrs. Anceney may have a more than ordinary control of her emotions." I had started to follow him out and almost trod upon his heels as he paused just inside the door. "I do remember that," he said slowly, as if to himself. We went out into the hall and up the stairs.

At the top of the stairs and just outside the door to the room in which, as I pointed out to Kane, Mrs. Anceney was being held, we found Sergeant Moran carrying on an apparently spiritless conversation with his minion McBeath. Moran came forward with alacrity as he saw us and gave Kane a hearty handshake.

"Glad to see you, Kane. I guess we won't have to spend much time on this business. Not much like the last case we doped out. That *was* a puzzler." He shook his round grizzled head ruefully, as if meditating on departed glories.

Kane gave him a brief smile. "Well, don't be too downhearted, Moran. We may be able to squeeze a little juice out of even this one." He looked over Moran's shoulder and laughed suddenly.

"Hello, McBeath. Comfortable?" he asked.

The patient McBeath, his heavy body wedged cautiously between the fragile arms of a small gilt chair, nodded dourly.

"I have sat here for an hour," he reminded us reproachfully.

"Then why the hell don't you stand a while?" snapped Moran.

"Because you said there'd be the devil to pay if you caught me out of this here chair before her lawyer comes. I will be so glad—" he was about to continue in the same slow, toneless voice, when Moran gave him a good-natured thump on the shoulder and turned to Kane. "I suppose you want to look over the ground, don't you?" he asked, and as Kane nodded he motioned us to follow him down the hall. We stopped before a door which Moran unlocked with a key from his pocket.

"Mr. Underwood had the sense to lock this door immediately after the murder took place," he explained to Kane. "He turned the key over to me when I came, but I haven't been in yet. So nothing's been touched."

He pushed the door open. Within there was utter darkness, and I remembered that I had turned the lights out before I locked the door. We all walked forward a few steps, and then Moran asked a little testily, "Where are the lights, anyhow? Do you know, Mr. Underwood?"

"Somewhere to the left," I replied, and fumbled uncertainly along the wall until finally my hand touched the button. Instinctively, as I pressed it, I tried to turn away from the sight of that figure which I knew I must face for the second time. But the only light in the room which responded to the switch was the standing lamp near the heavy wing chair, and the cone of brightness which its dark shade threw downward drew my eyes like a magnet.

The grotesque body of the murdered man, lurching over the arm of the chair, almost sprang into being, as if suddenly picked out of darkness by the glare of a malevolent searchlight. The red stain which marked his wound stood out on the gleaming whiteness of his shirt front. One limp arm hung over the side of the chair, with its fingers trailing on the polished floor, and on one of the fingers, half sunk into the flesh, a little diamond twinkled its contempt for all mortality. The sight of Frederick Sutton, alive, had never been pleasing to me, but I had not imagined that his dead body would fill me with the loathing and the dread I now felt.

Apparently my two companions were not concerned with such thoughts. Moran, with a brisk businesslike air, moved around the room turning on all the available lights. Kane remained standing just inside the door by which we had entered, and after a slow glance about, took a torn packet of cigarettes from his pocket. He pulled one out, tapped it deliberately on his thumbnail, and licked its tip.

"Match?" he queried sharply, and as I mechanically handed him my box, he took one look at my face, but lit his cigarette and put the matches in his pocket before speaking again.

"Thoughts on mortality, Underwood," he said quietly, "are always superfluous, and they are more than ordinarily ineffectual right now." He flung back at me as he walked away, "After all, our business here is with the living, and not with the dead."

Again Kane had brought me back from my thoughts into the present. His remark, coupled with the fact that I was keenly interested in his maneuvers, quashed my morbidity. He had gone over to the wing chair and stood looking down at the body. As I followed him, I began to notice the room itself, which was a fairly large one. It seemed to occupy a corner of the house, since there were windows on two sides. The fireplace in the long wall opposite the door was set in the center of the space between two tall, small-paned windows. The other two windows were in the left-hand wall, and evidently were front windows facing on the street. There were not more than eight or nine important pieces of furniture in the entire room, but as most of these were made of heavy mahogany they filled it adequately. I noticed a low couch between the two front windows and a desk against the right-hand wall. In the center of the room was a long table, and between this table and the fireplace were the standing lamp I have mentioned before and two large overstuffed chairs. It was the chair on the left of the fireplace which held the object of interest for Kane and Moran.

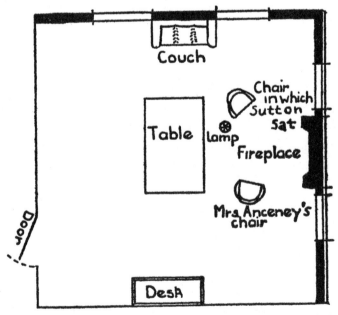

PLAN OF THE ROOM IN WHICH SUTTON WAS KILLED

I heard Moran say, "One shot did for him, all right, and there's the gun that did the work." He pointed to the automatic lying on the table. Kane took a pencil from his pocket, and sticking it in the barrel of the gun, held it up so that he could examine it on all sides. After a moment, he laid it on the table without comment.

"Moreover," Moran continued enthusiastically, "it looks to me as if the person that fired the shot must have stood just about here." He took up a stand at the far end of the fireplace, near the chair by which I had seen Mrs. Anceney standing. "What would you say, Kane?"

Kane drew a last puff from his cigarette and threw it into the grate before he replied. "I'd agree with you," he said, "up to a certain point. Undoubtedly the gun was fired from that direction. The position of the body and of the wound shows that. Sutton was obviously sitting so that he was directly facing that end of the fireplace when he was killed. The wings of the chair would have protected him from a shot fired from either side. After he was hit his body slumped over the arm of the chair as we see it now. Unless I'm very much mistaken, the medical examiner will confirm my opinion on that point. However," he paused, "I'm not quite as sure as you are that the person who shot Sutton stood near the end of the fireplace."

"Well, I'd like to know how you reason that out?" Moran inquired defensively.

"Quite simply, in fact by what is known as a personal application of the problem. I feel reasonably sure that if I were about to be shot by someone standing not more than ten feet away from me no sentiment of *laissez faire* could induce me to remain comfortably seated. Sutton was not afflicted by an aggravated case of myopia, as far as I know, therefore that part of the fireplace which you indicate must have been plainly visible to him. Still, he made no attempt, as far as we can judge from outward signs, to escape death."

Moran was not to be moved. "No, but look here. Let's make another personal application. Suppose the woman you'd been having an agreeable conversation with for the last hour or so suddenly pulled out a gun and told you not to stir a finger or she'd drill you through. What then?"

"I'd stay put," Kane immediately agreed. "Yes, I certainly would. Rotten of her, though, to shoot me down regardless." But he seemed unduly meditative.

Moran proceeded a little triumphantly. "And here's another point that fits in with my theory. If you agree with me, and you do, that he was shot from this angle," he swept his arm in the direction he meant, "then if your murderer didn't stand near the end of the fireplace, he must have been perched somewhere in a tree outside the house. Because you can't extend your line much more than two or three feet beyond the end of the fireplace before you run into the wall." He illustrated this remark by taking a step or two toward the window. "Do you see what I mean?"

"Certainly I do. Although," he said, "I confess I *hadn't* thought of that tree." He walked over to the window, looked out for a moment, then turned back to us. "No tree," he announced, and grinned.

Moran felt, perhaps, that he could afford a moment's indulgence. "Wouldn't cut much ice if there were one," he said kindly. "The shot didn't come through the glass. And Mr. Underwood here swears that all of the windows were not only closed but locked when he came into the room about a minute after he heard the shot."

I nodded. "That's right," I said. "I looked around at all the windows soon after I came in, and they were all closed. Moreover, I'm perfectly sure I would have noticed anyone's shutting one of them while I was in the room."

Kane had turned back to the window. "You score again, Underwood," he said. "And incidentally, I'm relieved to observe that careless housemaids aren't limited to bachelors' diggings. The next time one comes to me for employment, give her an examination in elementary dusting, and if she cleans the sill and neglects the crosspiece, she's completely and absolutely out." Moran and I stepped over curiously. Kane pointed to the frame and to the catch, both of which were filmed with dust. "Two days' accumulation, as I'm a housewife," he stated, with a great show of disgust.

Moran gave a grunt of satisfaction. "All of which means that this window has remained locked for two days," he said.

"Precisely," Kane answered. "You'll undoubtedly find the same evidence for the other three windows. Personally, I'm not interested."

But he was interested, very much interested, in something, I decided, in spite of the casual way he whistled between his teeth as he sauntered over to the table. There he sat down and kicked carelessly at the figures in the rug with a large black shoe. At intervals the whistling would stop suddenly and the dangling leg become motionless, and I could see him frown impatiently, then sigh, and soon after the whistling would begin again.

Meanwhile Moran had been checking up on the other three windows. He reported that they were all in the same condition as the first one we examined. "Which leaves us with pretty much the same watertight case we started with in the first place," he said. "There's no way to get around it. I don't pretend to know why she shot him, but the facts are, she did. I suppose he said something that made her mad. Oh, there are lots of motives, if that's what's worrying anybody. He might have been carrying on an affair with her, and he was a married man, which—"

"—is not unusual," Kane finished mockingly. "Let this be a lesson to you, Moran. You're a married man, yourself."

I thought this was a little mean, and didn't blame Moran for looking annoyed. But he continued his story.

"There's not a shred of evidence to indicate there was anyone else in this room from the time that Sutton brought Mrs. Anceney up here after dinner to the moment that Mr. Underwood and the rest rushed in to find that Sutton was murdered. There's one door to this room. Sutton's bedroom is next to this but there's no connecting door between them. These four windows in here are locked tight. All that means that a third person would have had to make his getaway through the door into the hall after he'd fired the shot. And in that case, he'd have been caught in the act." He turned to me. "How about it?" he asked. "Wouldn't he have been seen?"

"Yes," I replied without hesitation. "I don't see how he could have avoided it. In the first place, as you come up the stairs, you are facing this door. So I would have seen him coming out. And Gilroy, too, was on the stairs, so he," involuntarily I paused, then continued, "would have seen anyone."

"Well, there you have it," Moran concluded with a take-it-or-leave-it air. "No one could have escaped from this room. And that's pretty damned conclusive. For my part, I'm satisfied we've done all we can."

"I think we've turned up as much as we can at present," Kane agreed seriously. "At any rate, we'll wait to hear what Mrs. Anceney

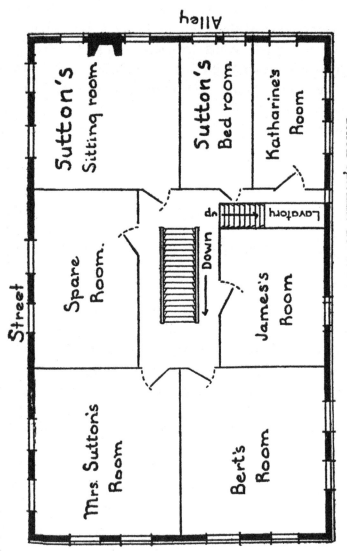

PLAN OF THE SECOND FLOOR OF SUTTON'S HOUSE

has to say in her own defense, after she has talked with her lawyer. Something tells me that that may be surprisingly interesting. I think I'll look in on her for a moment now."

We left Moran to attend to locking up the room. As we walked down the hall together, I asked Kane whether he thought the evidence so far was enough to convict Mrs. Anceney in case she refused to confess to the murder.

"Overwhelmingly enough," he said emphatically.

"Is there no loophole?" I asked. "What about my meeting Gilroy on the stairs?"

"That fact alone won't carry us very far."

Kane continued. "You asked me about loopholes, Underwood. There are none that I can see at present. However," he paused so significantly that I looked at him quickly and saw that his face was peculiarly intent, "there is one curious fact which impressed me, a fact which Moran was too busy with his own train of thought to notice. If Mrs. Anceney shot Sutton on the impulse of the moment, *why* did she wear a glove or hold the gun in her handkerchief?"

I stared at him in bewilderment.

"There is not one fingerprint on the handle of the revolver," he said.

CHAPTER 4

It was not without misgivings that I tapped on the door of the room in which Mrs. Anceney was confined. I felt a little hesitation about intruding upon her at this time, but mixed with that feeling was a desire to see how Kane would meet and deal with a woman of her type. Receiving an immediate answer to my knock, I entered and Kane followed me. The room in which we found ourselves was, I imagined, one of the guest chambers. It was now only partially illumined by a table lamp but I could see that it was furnished with some taste, and designed to please the feminine eye. After the heavy severity of the room we had just left, associated as it was with the gloomy character of our errand there, these surroundings were a relief. It was a small room, longer than it was wide. Its two windows evidently looked out on the street, although I could not be sure of this since the heavy curtains, hanging to the floor, were pulled almost across them. A canopied bed occupied most of the space.

Mrs. Anceney was sitting on the right-hand side of the room, the lamp on a table by her side. The high back of her chair was toward the door but she leaned over the arm as we came in and greeted us in what seemed to me a curiously bright manner, under the circumstances. I introduced Kane, who was not so surprised at her assurance as to hesitate in taking the apparently friendly hand she offered him.

"You know," she said, smiling at me, "I think I should have been quite frantic if I hadn't felt sure that you would break in upon my isolation sometime during the evening. Now do sit down, both of you, and talk to me about something that's cheerful. And, please," she turned half pleadingly, half reproachfully to Kane, "not about this evening, because, you see, I'm holding that subject in reserve for a later time, and I've an awful feeling that it will be utterly threadbare before morning." She sighed in a mock-desperate fashion, but one glance at her pale face and the tense lines around her mouth told me, in spite of her words, that she was laboring under a great nervous strain. And I felt that Kane would not be deceived.

He seemed to have some appreciation of the effort she was making, for after pulling up a chair onto which he eased his length of limb, he proceeded to enter into the spirit of her conversation with much more grace than I could have mustered. "On the contrary, Mrs. Anceney," he said, smiling at her, "the only thing that induced us to intrude was the desire we have for an unprofessional half hour." He pulled out his package of cigarettes. "Will you smoke these, or do you prefer Underwood's tainted Egyptians?" I reached hastily into my pocket, but she had already accepted one of Kane's.

After he had lighted it for her she leaned back in her chair, and laid aside on the table the magazine which had been lying in her lap. As she did so, she raised her dark eyebrows quizzically.

"Reading *Vogue* is a fairly nonchalant gesture, don't you think?" she asked Kane, and as he laughed she added, "Furthermore, it's quite distracting, I assure you, even in the shadow of the guillotine, to learn that the style of one's new gown is completely passé, according to Patou."

Kane met this comment with some light retort, and so the conversation continued. I was completely disregarded, but I confess to no talent for trafficking in repartee at such moments. I was conscious, however, of an undercurrent of purpose beneath the surface of their banter, and could not help admiring the woman for the gallant manner in which she rose to the situation.

After somewhat more than a quarter of an hour, the conversation began to flag. Even Mrs. Anceney could not resist the atmosphere of suppressed intensity, or keep out of her mind the event which had brought about our meeting there. Her face had become very pale. As she moved her hands, I saw that her fingers were shaking. She could control them so little that the cigarette which she was holding dropped on the floor.

As I hastily picked it up, and at a nod from her stubbed it out, I was suddenly overcome by a flood of pity for her, not because she was a woman—and therefore, perhaps, to the masculine mind weak—but because she was both strong and helpless. No courage of hers could deliver her from the toils of circumstance, no fineness of mind overcome the brutality of the trial she must go through.

I should have been glad, phlegmatic as I ordinarily am, to pay her some tribute of admiration, but I could think of nothing to say or do. Then, too, whatever her reasons for her actions, she guarded them tacitly in a privacy upon which it would have been an impertinence to intrude.

Kane had fallen silent with her, but in a moment or so he aroused himself.

"I have a request to make, Mrs. Anceney," he said. "I promise you that I'll ask you nothing about this evening. That can wait until your lawyer comes. But I'd be very grateful indeed if you would help me on one paint. I promise you, too, that whatever you say I'll listen to as a private individual and not in my official capacity."

His speech, worded as it was with a good deal of delicacy, seemed partly to restore her composure.

"I don't want to refuse you," she replied, smiling a little, "but under the circumstances would it be too much if I ask you what your question is before I agree to answer it?"

"No one trusts a policeman," Kane laughed ruefully. "Nor do I. But to come to the point"—his face became grave again—"I've found in the course of my experience that to deal successfully with such cases as this, I must know the people involved. With Underwood's help, and my own eyes and ears, I can find out what I want to know about most of the people here to-night. But there is one person I can never know, and he is the central figure of the story."

As Kane spoke he kept his eyes fixed on Mrs. Anceney's face. She returned his gaze questioningly.

"I don't want to ask too much," he went on, with some slight hesitation, "but you have seen and known a great many people. If I'm not mistaken, you are a wise and just judge of them. Will you tell me what your impressions of Sutton were, and what sort of man he was?"

I was distinctly surprised at Kane's request. After all, it seemed extraordinary to ask her to discuss the character of the man she was accused of murdering.

There was a rather painful pause. "I can't see why I shouldn't," she answered at last. "But he wasn't a simple person, you know, and that makes a fair judgment of him difficult."

"So I gathered from what Underwood said of him," Kane replied. "Also that he was the sort you might either like or dislike strongly."

"No one could have been indifferent to him," Mrs. Anceney agreed. She spoke calmly enough, but her eyes had wandered from Kane's face.

"Probably more disliked than liked, wasn't he?"

"Probably."

"And yet he was inclined to be generous?"

"Yes." She hesitated a little. "He liked to be lavish, but if anyone asked him a favor, I think his first impulse was to refuse."

"Wasn't he rather unscrupulous in his own way?"

Mrs. Anceney took the cigarette Kane offered her and tapped it thoughtfully on the arm of her chair; then, without answering, lighted it from the match he held.

"I don't know that 'unscrupulous' is the word," she replied slowly. "I doubt if he ever considered that another person might not see eye to eye with him. He never let anyone stand in his way."

"I suppose he was decent enough to people who didn't bother him."

"Oh, more than that," she said, emphasizing her words. "He went out of his way to be pleasant to them. For one thing he liked to make them extravagant presents."

She seemed to be making a needless effort to speak of Sutton's virtues, and I wondered if she were afraid of giving Kane too black a picture of him.

"Money didn't control his calculations, then," Kane remarked.

"Not when he had it," she replied, "but he always wanted something in return. He couldn't help that. It was in him to be shrewd."

"Shrewd, but not very intelligent."

"He never had time to be intelligent. Neither time nor patience." She paused as though she had been on the verge of saying more but had decided not to.

"Did he ever talk to you about the time before he made his success?"

"A little. Very much as he did at dinner to-night." She looked at me for understanding. "He had a very hard time, and I don't think he ever forgot it."

Kane nodded slowly. "I suppose that accounts for his feeling of inferiority."

"It must have had a good deal to do with it. It must have made him even more determined to get everything he wanted."

As though the words had some special connotation for her, she bent her head a little, and put the fingers of her right hand to her temple. It was a gesture I had seen her use before.

"He should have taken Wolsey's advice."

She looked over at Kane with quick understanding. "'Cromwell, I charge thee, fling away ambition: by that sin fell the angels.'" She repeated the words softly. I realized again what a beautiful voice she had.

Kane and she smiled at each other as though there were some secret kinship between them.

"Have I told you what you want to know?" she asked.

"Yes." Kane jerked himself out of his momentary abstraction. "Sutton must have been a very powerful figure."

"Very," she said quietly. "And power is a dangerous thing to have, and a dangerous thing to be near."

After the calm, impersonal discussion they had been having, her words brought me sharply back to the concrete present. I think all three of us felt the change. They had talked of Sutton as though he were a mutual friend who had died peacefully in his bed. But Sutton had been murdered, and the woman who was talking to us was charged with his death.

Kane rose awkwardly. "I haven't thanked you for helping me," he said abruptly. "It was very good of you."

"It was very good of you to come and talk to me," she answered lightly. "The debt is on my side. I feel much better. In fact I'm thoroughly prepared to meet you in your official capacity as my antagonist."

"I'm sorry that has to be," Kane rejoined.

"Oh, don't think of that," she hastened to reassure him. "When it's all over and done with, I'll look forward to seeing you again, and I promise to bear no hard feelings." She paused, and the strained look came back into her eyes. "I hate to have you go."

Kane seemed to share her reluctance. "I'm afraid we must get on to less pleasant occupations," he said. I was perhaps maliciously amused to see that he was not wholly impervious to Mrs. Anceney's charms.

Mrs. Anceney looked so loath to have us go that I asked whether there wasn't something we could do to make her more comfortable.

"How about some wine?" I asked.

She seemed grateful for the suggestion. "Thoughtful man," she exclaimed, somewhat to my embarrassment. "I *should* like a small glass. Sherry, I think. Not to raise my spirits, you understand, but to keep them at their present high level."

"I'll have it sent up right away," I said.

As we went out again into the hall, McBeath gave us such a glance of distrust that Kane was moved to ask him whether he suspected that we had Mrs. Anceney concealed beneath our skirts. But McBeath, impatient of such folly, made no answer.

"A good man," Kane said, when we had passed out of earshot, "but, shall we say, unimpressionable."

I was eager to know what he had made of Mrs. Anceney, but to my query he would only make one of his characteristically evasive replies.

"Quite delightful," he said, "and capable of dangerous cleverness in an hour of need. You may be a thoughtful man, Underwood, but it requires a wise one to cope with such a woman."

As we reached the head of the stairs, I stopped.

"But she's more than you say she is," I protested. "Surely you see that. She's not the type that would commit murder. I admit I thought she must have at first, but I can't believe it now."

"It's dangerous to generalize about the type that commits murder," Kane retorted. "You can't tell by appearances, you know."

"I suppose that's true." I felt rather nonplussed. "But even you have to agree that she's unique."

"Yes, I do. But," he spoke very sternly, "I can't let my personal feelings influence me. Every obvious element of the case is against her. It's easy enough to construct a motive out of the situation she got herself into. Sutton was in love with her. You told me that yourself, and it didn't take you long to find that out. At least five people can swear that she was in the room with him at the time he was killed. And they can swear, too, that they found no third person there. The windows were closed and locked and had been for two days. You say that you would have seen anyone who left Sutton's sitting room by the door into the hall. There is no other door, or any other way by which the murderer could have got out of that room. According to what you said, Gilroy would have seen him, if you did not."

"But Gilroy himself—"

"We have no time to discuss him now," Kane interrupted me. "That can come later. There's one other thing to add to the case against Mrs. Anceney: the fact that there was a weapon found on the scene of the crime."

"It wasn't in her possession," I said. "I can swear to that. It was on the table."

"But it was in the room, and she could easily have used it," Kane replied quietly. "You know," he said, with a change of tone, "I told you once that it puzzled me to find there were no fingerprints on the gun. It still does, if this is a murder on impulse. Under the circumstances, why should she have wiped them off?"

Kane's expression was very grave, and he stared intently at the floor. He left his question unanswered, and I did not attempt to answer it for him.

"I have certain suspicions," he went on, "but I'm not ready to talk about them yet. There's no sense in discussing theories unless you have the facts. The night isn't over yet, and I think we'll know more than we do now before morning."

"Enough to acquit her?"

Kane looked impatient. "I can't say that," he said. "I can't say any more than I have. I don't think there is a jury in the world that wouldn't believe her guilty, if the evidence we've already got was presented to them. And whatever we find out in the next few hours, she stands in very grave danger."

As he finished speaking, I heard a slight noise. I looked up quickly and saw James standing across the hall. He could not have helped overhearing Kane's last speech.

"I beg your pardon," he said with a smile. "I thought I heard voices."

"You did," Kane said abruptly. The boy turned and went back to his room. We started downstairs in silence. Kane looked worried until, as we reached the first floor, he made an involuntary gesture which seemed to banish his thoughts. He turned to me again.

"This being my evening with the ladies," he said, "I'd like to talk to Mrs. Sutton and her daughter, separately or collectively—though perhaps separately would be better. We'll find Moran first—he'll want to sit in, I suppose."

We found Moran in the living room downstairs, chewing glumly on the end of a dead cigar and considering an old Sunday supplement with a complete lack of interest. He was not the only occupant of the room. On the other side sat a slender, dark girl whom I recognized with surprise.

"There's Miss Sutton now," I said to Kane.

But there was absolutely nothing about this motionless figure to remind me of the startled girl who had thrown her arms so passionately around the body of her dead father. Her wild grief had faded into a patient acceptance of her loss. Since I had last seen her she had changed into a dark woolen dress which further enhanced the pallor of a face in which only the eyes now seemed alive.

Kane turned and she met his questioning regard without change of expression, but as he walked over toward her, her long fingers began to twist themselves in her lap and she looked up at him with silent appeal.

"Miss Sutton?" he asked. She nodded, and he went on to explain who he was. I hadn't known that he could speak so gently. His voice apparently reassured her, and she finally found her tongue.

"I couldn't stay in my room." She hesitated. "It's so—quiet." Kane seemed to understand. "I'll go now," she said.

"You can come back here in just a few minutes," Kane said to her kindly. "But now we want to see your mother and ask her some questions. Then you can come down and stay as long as you like. If you feel able, we'd like to talk to you too, for you can, perhaps, help us more than you realize. But if you'd rather not—" She burst in upon him before he could complete the sentence.

"Oh, but I will!" All her apathy was gone in a flash. "If it's about my father. I knew everything about him." There was a curious mixture of pride and sorrow in her tone and in the quick way she lifted her head to look at Kane. Without waiting for another word from him, she rose to her feet and started out of the room. But Kane called after her.

"Miss Sutton, on your way will you please stop and ask your mother to come down." She nodded and went out.

Moran aimed his cigar butt at the fireplace and put his paper down impatiently. "Now what hunch are you running down?" he asked, not too courteously. "I don't see any earthly sense in monkeying around with a lot of witnesses when Mrs. Anceney is only waiting until her lawyer comes to spill the whole truth. Where is that old snail, anyhow? He should have been here an hour ago." He turned on me irritably.

"I'm sure I don't know," I answered smartly, for I was provoked with his stupidity. "I telephoned to him myself, and he said he would come right away. However, he lives on the other side of the city."

Moran muttered something, still annoyed, but Kane stepped in to placate him. He explained that since we had some time on our hands it was just as well to get from Mrs. Sutton certain information which we might need, even if Mrs. Anceney did make a full confession. Moran finally saw the wisdom of this program.

Meanwhile Mrs. Sutton had not appeared, and as we waited for her I suddenly remembered the wine I had promised to send up to Mrs. Anceney. I hurried out and found one of the servants to whom I entrusted the matter. When I returned to the room, Mrs. Sutton was there.

She sat obediently facing Moran, her face tired but composed, her eyes heavy with weariness. Moran, who had evidently elected himself to conduct investigations, was putting questions to her in a tone carefully calculated to match Kane's most tactful manner, and she answered each one without taking her eyes from his face. She acted as if this interview were an ordeal she had made up her mind to endure.

"I went upstairs to my own room right after Mr. Underwood left," she was saying. "I'm not sure what time it was. Before eleven, I think. I started to undress—"

"You didn't stop anywhere before you went to your room, did you, Mrs. Sutton?" Moran asked.

"No, I didn't." She cleared her throat.

"And when you heard the shot you immediately ran to your husband's room?"

"Yes."

"Then how does it happen, Mrs. Sutton," Moran continued slowly, "that you were one of the last to enter that room? Your room is as near, isn't it, as any of the others, and yet they were all there before you. Mr. Underwood tells me that you were just opening your door as he started to enter your husband's room."

The woman gave me a sidewise glance which made me feel vaguely uncomfortable.

"I—I don't know," she said hurriedly. "I think I was afraid. I may not have gone right away. I wasn't sure it was a shot. I stood there and then I heard people running in the hall." She stopped, and as Moran made no response to her words, she turned to Kane. He had been standing restlessly at the window, but now he came forward and made a sign to Moran which the latter seemed to understand.

"It's very natural to be almost physically paralyzed at a moment like that," he said, looking away from Mrs. Sutton rather than at her. "You heard the shot and were startled. When you realized what it was, you were so frightened you couldn't move. That's what you mean, isn't it?"

"Yes, it is," she said quietly, and waited.

Kane continued. "You understand, don't you, Mrs. Sutton, that we are not asking these questions for the purpose of frightening you. A woman's conviction for first degree murder may depend on the evidence we are able to collect. We are trying to give her every chance we can." Kane's voice was now as stern as his words. Mrs. Sutton looked at him without a change of expression.

Moran resumed his examination. "There are just one or two other things, Mrs. Sutton," he said. "Now, Mrs. Anceney was a guest at your dinner party. Yet after Mr. Underwood's departure you prepared to go to bed. Isn't it singular for the hostess to retire before all her guests have left?" He paused, but the woman made no move to reply. "Didn't you, perhaps, think of joining them when you went upstairs?"

Mrs. Sutton answered this with no uncertainty.

"No," she said.

"But why didn't you?"

"Because," she answered, "my husband would have objected." There was no apparent resentment in her manner.

"I take it then that your husband preferred to entertain Mrs. Anceney alone?" Moran queried in a tone which did not conceal the import of his question.

"Oh, yes." The answer was completely matter-of-fact and emotionless. Even Moran looked uncomfortable. It seemed to me that certain facts of the case had been sufficiently well established and I hoped he would call an end to the present examination. Evidently the same thing occurred to him, for after a brief and fidgety silence for at least three of us, he told Mrs. Sutton that she might go.

Not more than a minute after her mother had left us, Katharine came in. Without hesitation she sat down and looked expectantly from Moran to Kane. Finally, she said quietly, "I'm ready now—if there is anything you want to ask me." Her voice was neither agitated nor listless, and I marveled at her new composure. Kane's appeal to her had evidently borne fruit. There was now a faint color in her cheeks, and she seemed possessed by a steady determination which had been utterly lacking a half hour before.

At Moran's request, she explained her movements during the time preceding the murder, saying she had gone upstairs somewhat before half-past ten and, being tired, had gone to bed almost immediately. She supposed she had fallen asleep. She was suddenly awakened by a loud report followed by an unearthly scream. She had got up and had hurried out into the hall.

"Where you saw Mr. Underwood and Mr. Gilroy?" Moran asked.

"Yes."

"Miss Sutton"—it was Kane who spoke—"until this evening have you ever had any reason to suspect Mrs. Anceney of holding a grievance against your father?"

The girl rubbed her hand across her eyes in a bewildered fashion, and then looked impulsively at Kane.

"Never," she said quickly. "That's the horrible part of it. I can't believe—" She bit her lip nervously and stopped.

A second later, she continued. "You probably know that Father had very few friends. But he liked Mrs. Anceney. They had a great deal in common."

Moran looked at her curiously, and cleared his throat. "Miss Sutton," he said gravely, "I'm sorry I can't mince matters, but didn't you suspect that your father was more than ordinarily interested in Mrs. Anceney?"

The girl caught her breath sharply, and her eyes narrowed with anger. For a moment I feared that she was about to spring at the defenseless Moran, but soon she controlled herself, and when she spoke her voice was painfully steady.

"So you've heard that too. Well, that's not true," she said slowly and distinctly, clipping short each word. "He liked Mrs. Anceney—that's all—because she amused him. Why can't people believe the truth? I suppose because it doesn't make enough gossip. *I'll* tell you some gossip that may interest you. If you knew the pleasant family feeling in this house you wouldn't believe what they say for a minute. They'd do anything to hurt him, even now. They hated him—even his own son did." She laughed bitterly and then was silent.

At that moment I heard the front door-bell—ring sharply. The lawyer, at last!

Almost simultaneously, there were steps in the hall, and I looked in that direction, expecting to see the footman on his way to the door. But it was Mrs. Sutton, presumably going upstairs from another part of the house.

Kane saw her almost as soon as I did. "Mrs. Sutton," he called, "may we see you once more, please? Your daughter has just been telling us something that we'd like to ask you about."

With a sharp glance at Katharine, the woman came in the room.

As she sat down, the bell rang again, more insistently. Moran got up impatiently and walked over to the door.

"McBeath," he roared, with little ceremony, in the general direction of the second floor. "Answer that bell, will you, and take the man up to Mrs. Anceney. Damn servants . . . all asleep," he muttered irritably, without regard for Mrs. Sutton's presence, as he came back and sat down. We heard McBeath's heavy feet descending the stairs none too rapidly.

Kane made some remark of a general nature to Mrs. Sutton but I did not understand what it was, for I was momentarily distracted by the sound of a loud conversation in the hall between McBeath and a gentleman who seemed to be explaining at length why he had been so delayed in arriving. Presently I heard them going upstairs.

Kane was drumming his fingertips on the table, with his chin sunk thoughtfully in his other hand. Finally he raised his head and addressed Mrs. Sutton.

"We understand from what your daughter says—" he was beginning, when suddenly we heard from above a loud, sharp exclamation, and in a moment there were heavy, rapid footsteps on the stairs.

McBeath burst into the room, his round eyes almost starting from his head.

"Mrs. Anceney—" he began, and stopped for breath.

We were on our feet in a second. Moran seized McBeath by his coat, as if to shake him into speech.

"She's got away?" he cried.

McBeath shook his head dumbly.

"No," he said, and his red face was as uncomprehending as a child's, "she's dead."

CHAPTER 5

For a full minute, or so it seemed to me, the six of us stood as if turned to stone, Moran still clutching McBeath's coat. Then Kane leaped forward as if shot into motion. His face was as sharp and keen as a hound's. "Mrs. Sutton," he said swiftly, "you and your daughter please go to your rooms. Come on, Moran." And in a moment his long legs were taking the stairs three at a time, and we followed close behind him. A little man, clinging to the banister and retreating fearfully downward, quavered, "How did it happen? I really had no idea . . ." Kane knocked him aside and we rushed past him, up the stairs, and into the room.

But nothing was confused there. Nothing overturned, or broken. No sound to shake our incredulity. Everything was exactly as I remembered it before, the table lamp burning steadily, Mrs. Anceney's arm resting quietly on the chair. I could even see the top of her head leaning comfortably against the back as she read. Only we four were out of place, breathing hard, staring stupidly. McBeath . . . the fool. . . . Kane strode over and stood in front of the chair. He did not speak. I remember walking over to him. I saw a magazine in Mrs. Anceney's lap. And then I realized she had stopped reading.

I knew people died. I knew death was not always beautiful. But it was calm, and one could wait by the bedside, prepared, and then, after a while, go sadly away, a little upset, perhaps, to tell friends it was all over. So this wasn't death, though it was very still. It was something else, a thing that for the second time that night had been thrust without warning into my commonplace existence. Life suddenly extinct.

There was blood, not on her face, but everywhere else, on the front of her dress, on the seat of the chair. And what had been her body sat there, heedless of its ruin, careless of our horror.

Her throat had been cut. There was a long ivory-handled razor with its blade covered with blood lying near one of the hands.

I turned away with an effort from the awful fascination of that figure. I saw that Kane was still looking down with narrowed eyes which moved swiftly over the body of the woman. They were missing no detail of its appearance and attitude. There was a cold, almost unnatural concentration in his glance, and his set face reflected the grimness of the sight before him.

I was surprised to see that Moran, who stood beside me, was more affected than Kane. He shifted awkwardly from one foot to the other, and moistened his lips with his tongue. At last he cleared his throat hurriedly and moved away. He began to bark staccato questions at

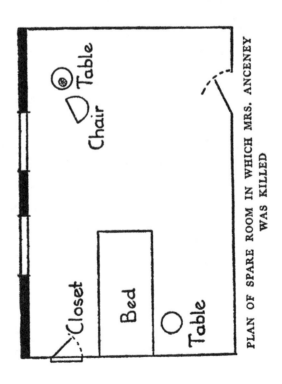

PLAN OF SPARE ROOM IN WHICH MRS. ANCENEY WAS KILLED

McBeath, whose face was suffused with a guilty terror. I could see the fellow's fingers waggling nervously below his coatsleeves.

"You told me to answer the bell," he kept repeating. "You yelled at me, 'McBeath, answer that bell.' I was sitting here all the time like you told me, and when you said that I got up and went down and let him in." He jerked his thumb at the little man who had entered unnoticed by me. "And when he told me he was the guy Mrs. Anceney'd phoned for, I said to him, 'Come along upstairs,' and we went right up, now, didn't we?"

He turned fiercely on the man, as if to divert Moran's attention from himself.

But at this point, Kane, roused from his examination of the body by McBeath's loud words, turned his head to say, quietly but emphatically, "That'll do, McBeath. Moran, let's get all that later. If everyone but you and Underwood will clear out, we can take a look at this room. McBeath, you, and you, sir," he indicated the man who stood hesitatingly near the door, "please wait for us downstairs. We'll want to talk to you in a few minutes." At these words the two he had addressed left the room with more relief than reluctance.

When they were gone, both Kane's attitude and Moran's seemed to change. They had the manner of being no longer concerned with the fact that Mrs. Anceney was dead, but with the possible cause of that death. I marveled at their being able to cast off the grip of dread which had fastened itself on my imagination. Perhaps, I reasoned, had they seen Mrs. Anceney as I had, only that evening—a beautiful, charming woman of gracious manners and quick wit—they would be as horror-stricken as I by this travesty of her former self.

To escape from my thoughts and my terrors, to forget the body in the chair, I forced myself to watch them as they began a businesslike examination of the room. I noted how different were their methods of procedure. Moran would look at an object long and closely; Kane stood farther away from it, and seemed more interested in its relation to surrounding objects. Moran examined everything with equal care, while Kane seemed satisfied with a casual glance in most cases.

Such a glance he gave to the two windows in the room—merely looking carelessly out of each and then walking away. But Moran examined the locks, and tried to push up the sashes. Did he think that someone had entered by one of them, armed with that keen, deadly weapon, impelled by a sinister motive to take the life of the woman who sat so securely, she thought, within a guarded room? Had she seen him before he reached her side and guessed his purpose too late to cry for help? Would her dead face betray her fear? Involuntarily my eyes moved toward the body, but before they had seen more than the bloodstained dress my throat grew tight with dread. I shuddered and turned away.

Moran was saying curtly, "Nobody got in by the windows at any rate. They're locked tight."

"I thought not," Kane said, moving over to a small table on the opposite side of the room from the chair in which the body lay.

Then how? The door was guarded. No one could have got in. Did that mean, I found myself wondering almost calmly, that she took her own life? Perhaps that was the truth of it. It was more reasonable, certainly, to suppose so.

"Moran, come here a minute," Kane directed, and as if I too had been addressed, I went over to where he stood. On the table before him was a small tray, holding a decanter and a wineglass. With a rush of memory I recalled that *I* had ordered that wine brought to this room. I remembered, too, as if they had been uttered long ago, her cheerful words when I had asked her if she would like it. "I should like a small glass. . . . Not to raise my spirits, you understand, but to keep them at their present high level." "Their present high level"—the irony of the last few words we had heard her say cut me like a knife. I almost heard again her pleasant laughter as Kane and I had left the room. Or had she laughed? I could not remember.

Kane had picked up the wineglass and was holding it toward the light. "Nothing was drunk from that glass, or even poured into it," I heard him say. He handed it to Moran who made a careful inspection.

"No," Moran agreed, setting it back on the tray, and making a survey of the other articles on the table. When he had finished, he walked over and threw open the door of a clothes closet near the bed. I heard him rummaging in this for a minute or two.

Meanwhile Kane was again standing by the window which was near the fatal chair. He seemed to be giving it a rather aimless inspection. I hardly dared keep my eyes upon him for fear they would fall undirected on the awful thing so near him. But suddenly I saw him reach up and take something apparently from within the heavy folds of the window draperies. As his back was toward me, I could not see what it was. He appeared to hesitate a moment, and looked irresolutely toward the open door of the room.

I expected to hear him call Moran. But he did not. Instead he pulled out a large handkerchief in which he quickly wrapped the object, whatever it was, and stuffed the bundle into his coat pocket. When he rejoined me, as he did immediately, his expression was curiously unconcerned. I did not know what to make of his behavior and, catching his eye, I directed a significant glance at his pocket, which bulged noticeably. He frowned and turned away. I felt uncomfortably rebuked, and held my tongue.

Moran, with a last glance around, came up to us. "Well, I'm satisfied, if you are," he said shortly, looking up at Kane. When Kane nodded, I was intensely relieved. I wanted to leave that room forever, to forget, if I could, that I had ever been there. Somehow I felt the presence of a living evil within those four walls.

"There isn't anything out of the ordinary here," Moran continued gloomily. "The obvious solution is all I can make out of it. It's plain suicide. The woman shot Sutton, then realized all of a sudden what she was in for. So, she avoided the consequences. You can't blame her for doing that." Even as the import of Moran's words sank into my consciousness I resented vaguely his calling Mrs. Anceney "the woman." She had been more than that once, surely, though now—but I shrank from my thoughts.

"You're probably right," Kane was saying. "We'll have to hear what McBeath has to say. At any rate there's nothing more for us to do here."

I had started for the door, when I heard him add, "I think I'll take this razor with me. I'd like to find out something about it. Lend me your handkerchief, Moran." I saw him take the handkerchief, and pick up the razor in its folds. Holding it carefully, he walked out of the door and into the hall, where I had preceded him. Moran, who was the last to leave, stopped outside and locked the door.

"Give me the key, will you, Moran?" Kane directed, and as Moran obeyed, he continued: "You and Underwood go downstairs. I'll be with you in a minute."

Silently Moran and I descended the stairs. Although the spell of the death chamber was still upon me, I felt that every step I took away from it was loosening the tension of my nerves. I drew a deep breath and was glad that I could. I even wondered what McBeath would have to tell us. How much had he seen?

CHAPTER 6

McBeath and the man I judged to be Mrs. Anceney's lawyer were waiting for us in the living room. As we reached the first floor we heard McBeath's dull voice raised, apparently in reply to a question of his companion's.

"I don't know a thing about it, I tell ya. You'll just have to wait."

But further waiting seemed to be impossible for the nervous gentleman he was addressing. He got up quickly upon seeing us at the door and took short anxious steps toward Moran.

"Could you tell me," he began, peering apprehensively at us through his rimless spectacles, "when I may be allowed to go home? I—I feel a little shaken."

And, indeed, he looked so.

But Moran was not affected. "You can go when we're through with you, and not before. Sit down. We'll wait for Kane." Startled, the man did as he was told.

I found myself a chair and was surprised to find how tired my knees were. They felt as though I had been standing for hours. I began to go through those mechanical actions a man will perform when he finds he can relax after a period of great strain. My eyes hurt—I rubbed my hands across them. I pulled my collar down a little, leaned back, and stretched out my legs. One didn't go through an experience like mine very often, thank God. That last half hour put a lot behind me. I wondered what was ahead.

With that thought, I came sharply back to the present. There was a great deal ahead. We would all know soon.

Kane came into the room a moment later. With hardly a glance at the rest of us, he said briefly to Moran, "The razor is Sutton's. There's a box for it in his bathroom." As if that ended the subject, he sat down and turned his attention immediately to McBeath.

"McBeath, I understood you to say that you were right outside the door to Mrs. Anceney's room when you heard Moran call to you. Is that so?" he asked in a quiet voice which failed to mask the sharpness of his question.

His tone plucked the slow-moving McBeath into uneasy attention. "Yeah," he said, his face red with unaccustomed worry, "I was sittin' there."

"And you came downstairs, answered the bell, and returned immediately?" Kane put a significant stress on the last word.

McBeath rose to the challenge almost physically, as if the opportunity to do so was one he had long awaited.

"I did, right away. Immediately," he added in the manner of an afterthought, and was about to continue with further emphatic statements when Moran, who had been observing the conduct of his minion with some impatience, cut in with "All right, all right. Now, did you go straight in the room?"

As affairs were thus snatched from his hands, Kane gave Moran a quick look of disapproval, but a second later he evidently decided to let things run their course, for, with a slight shrug, he settled quietly back into his chair.

McBeath had turned to his new inquisitor. "No, I didn't," he said in reply to the latter's question. With a vague motion to his left, he went on, "*He* did. I was just a-settin' down in my chair again when out he come, screechin' something terrible."

It was difficult to imagine the little man to whom Moran now shifted his questions emitting such boisterous sounds as McBeath had described. As attention was turned on him, he made a visible effort to control his perturbation.

"You're the lawyer for whom Mr. Underwood telephoned this evening?" Moran asked him.

"Why—I really don't know the identity of the person who telephoned me," he answered, and then, as Moran made an impatient gesture, he continued hurriedly, "That is to say, I understood that my client, Mrs. Anceney, wished to consult me. I was surprised to be called at so late an hour, but made such haste as I could under the circumstances. It has been raining, you know, and it took me all of an hour to secure a taxicab. When I arrived here, this gentleman," he indicated McBeath, "met me at the door and conducted me upstairs. Imagine my astonishment, sir, when—"

"We can," Moran broke in drily. "But look here, Mr.—Mr.—"

"Titterton, Leroy Titterton."

"Tell me, Mr. Titterton, in as few words as possible, what you noticed as you entered the room."

"I knocked on the door, and thinking I heard someone say 'Come in,' I opened it. I saw someone sitting by the table, but as the back of the chair was toward me, I could not distinguish whether or not it was Mrs. Anceney. So I said 'Mrs. Anceney?' but she did not answer. I assure you I experienced a strange feeling. However, I walked over until I could see her face—"

"You can stop there," ordered Moran. "We know what you did next." He tapped the arm of his chair thoughtfully. "One more thing," he said. "When you came up the stairs, did you see anyone in the hall, or near the door of the room?"

Titterton said that he had not, and McBeath, at Moran's request, corroborated his statement.

"And Mr. Titterton, there was no one else in the room when you entered it?"

Titterton gave a faint shudder, whether at the thought, or under Moran's boring scrutiny, I could not tell.

"I saw no one," he answered.

Moran scratched his head. "Well," he said, "I guess that's all for you. We can let him go, can't we?" he asked Kane. The latter nodded, and Titterton, with ill-concealed relief, got up from his chair. At Kane's suggestion, he left a card with his address and telephone number on it. As we heard the front door close behind him, a silence fell upon all of us, which Moran was the first to break.

"Well," he sighed, and then stated in a matter-of-fact tone, "I guess she preferred the devil to the deep blue sea. It was the easiest way out for her, maybe. It looks to me as if she'd been waiting all evening for something to take McBeath away from her door."

Kane's smile betrayed a hint of malice. "Do you mean by that, Moran," he asked, "that Mrs. Anceney could have come out of her room, found Sutton's bathroom, taken the razor, got back to her own room, and killed herself during the three minutes McBeath was on his way to and from the front door?"

"Certainly not," Moran countered truculently. "She had the razor already, of course. All she wanted was the chance to kill herself without running the risk that McBeath would hear her and prevent her from doing it."

"Oh."

"And, by God, McBeath, if you hadn't been so damn slow on your feet, she might be here yet."

McBeath shot his jaw forward stubbornly. "All right, mebbe so," he said with heavy defiance. "I don't pretend to be no fairy. An' it would have took one of those to git up and down them stairs quicker'n what I done. I wasn't gone more'n three or four minutes."

Kane interrupted. "Look here, Moran, I realize that all the evidence points to suicide. But even so, you're traveling pretty fast."

Moran shrugged his shoulders. "What else can you make of it? Seems to me it's the obvious solution. She shoots Sutton and finds herself in hotter water than she'd expected. So, presto—and she's out of it. Are you trying to argue, Kane, that someone killed her during the three or four minutes that McBeath was downstairs?"

"No, I'm merely considering the possibility," Kane answered carelessly.

"Well, remember then," Moran suggested, "that if anyone did murder Mrs. Anceney, he couldn't have got in the room by the windows."

"Right," Kane agreed serenely. "If there was a murderer, we've got to accept the fact that he entered the room in quite the normal fashion."

"And broke all speed records getting out again," Moran added with derision.

Kane smiled. "Not necessarily. There were—let's see—about five minutes to work in."

But McBeath contradicted loudly. "I said three."

"I remember you did," Kane said agreeably. "But look here. When you found Mrs. Anceney was dead, you ran downstairs. Isn't that so?"

"Yeah."

"And did Mr. Titterton remain in the room?"

"I'll say he didn't."

"In fact, I remember passing him at the bottom of the stairs as we came up. Don't you?"

"Guess so."

"Then here's the possibility. You and Titterton could have given a murderer an additional two minutes to escape. Understand, Moran, I'm not stating there *was* someone else in the room when Titterton came in. But I do say that there *could* have been someone, and that he could have made his escape into another part of the house while McBeath and Titterton were running down the stairs. Their backs would have been toward the door, you know." Kane stopped and looked at Moran. "Of course, I admit that that point may be absolutely unimportant. But it makes your objection to a murder theory on the basis of time less binding, doesn't it?"

Moran considered. "Well, yes, it does," he admitted. "But where does that get you? It seems to me you're putting the cart before the horse. What's the evidence to prove it was murder?"

"That's the difficulty." Kane spoke cheerfully. "We've nothing very tangible to work on. However, if a mere suspicion of mine would interest you, I might state that I *think* you'll find no fingerprints on the handle of that razor when you turn it over for investigation. But that's something that can't be proved without closer examination. However, it would be curious, if true, wouldn't it?" He smiled at Moran's puzzled frown. "In the meantime, let me ask McBeath a few more questions."

At these words, McBeath fixed on Kane a look of stolid attention, but the latter failed to continue at once and seemed to be absorbed in thought. Finally he said, "Am I right in assuming that you sat outside the door of that room from the time you saw Mr. Underwood and me go downstairs until Moran called you to answer the bell?"

"Yeah."

"You didn't as much as get out of your chair during all that time?"

The man was about to say "No" when a sudden thought seemed to strike him. He looked away from Kane and shifted his feet. Kane noticed his uncertainty, and said quickly, "You did get up, then?"

McBeath hesitated and looked down anxiously at the floor, as if searching there for relief from this quandary. His answer was unwilling.

"All right, then, I did. Once. But that was before I took the wine in. I had to, I tell ya," he ended defiantly.

"Where did you go?"

"Oh, I went down the hall." He motioned vaguely with his head.

Moran leapt upon him before he could continue.

"Well, for God's sake!" he exploded. "Who told you to wander around the halls?"

But his scorn failed to wither McBeath. "Nobody did," he replied with some dignity. "But I'd set in that there chair for about two hours. I'm human, ain't I? Don't ya understand, I had to *go* somewhere," he stated truculently, and with a rising inflection.

Kane hastily concealed a smile. "That's all right, McBeath," he said soothingly. "It was nobody's business but your own. But how long do you think you were gone?"

"Not more'n a minute. I hurried," McBeath added earnestly.

"Have you any idea what time it was?"

"Oh, it must 'a' bin about half-past one." McBeath seemed reassured by Kane's manner. "Yeah, that's about right. I know because I couldn't 'a' bin back more'n five minutes when one of them butlers or something come upstairs with the wine. I was gettin' pretty tired, and I asked him what time was it, anyway, an' he looked at a little watch on his wrist and said twenty-five to two."

"Did he take the wine in to Mrs. Anceney?"

"No siree, he didn't. I did."

Kane continued. "McBeath, when you went in the room, did you notice anything strange in Mrs. Anceney's manner?" McBeath looked puzzled. "I mean, did she seem—excited?"

McBeath turned the word cautiously over on his tongue. "Excited?" he repeated to himself, and then as if finally recognizing the word as a familiar one, he ventured a statement. "Oh, no. She wasn't excited, I don't think," he said slowly, emphasizing each negative with a shake of the head. "She was sittin', readin', when I come in. I said here was the wine she ast for, and she told me 'Thank you' and to put it on the table by the bed. And I did, an' then I went out. No," he concluded, with an air of having given his best judgment to an important question, "I couldn't hardly say she was excited at all."

"If I may say so," Moran began with slow decision, "it seems to me that you're making your own difficulties, Kane. Understand, I believe in being thorough, and in considering the thing from every angle. But you've been airing your theory now for some time, and I don't see that you've found so much as one piece of tangible evidence to support it."

"I haven't," Kane agreed. "That's just why I insist on wasting even more time to find it. Right now I want to ask McBeath if he saw anyone in the hall tonight after Underwood and I went downstairs to join you."

In reply to this question, McBeath said that the only persons he had seen were Mrs. Sutton and her daughter, going downstairs or returning to their own rooms, and "that funny little guy with the squeaky voice."

"He means Bert Walton," I explained to Kane.

"Yeah, that's the one," said McBeath. "Well, he come around, but that must 'a' bin earlier. I guess it was about twelve. Say, ain't he funny actin' though! He walked right clost up to me, quiet, like a mouse, and stood there lookin', and not saying a thing. Pretty soon, he set hisself down on the floor, all hunched over, and begun to rock back and forth. It give me the creeps, it did, and I said quick, 'What's the matter with you, anyway?' Then he looked at me sudden-like, an' he had the funniest face I ever *did* see. 'I'm afraid,' he says. His mouth was all puckered up an' his eyes was popping like marbles. Then he said nobody would talk to him. I said, 'The idea of you whinin' around when don't you know something important's happened to-night.' That made me real mad and I told him so. An' he went away then, but he kep' lookin' back at me an' grinning. Honest, Mr. Kane, don't you think that guy's a loony?"

"I haven't ever seen him, McBeath," Kane replied, smiling, "but I'd like to. Well," he continued after a moment of thought, his expression more serious, "I guess that's all."

"You mean you're ready to give up?" Moran asked quickly

"You might call it that," Kane answered. "At any rate," he said, almost apologetically, "upon thinking the matter over, I've come to the conclusion that your theory has been right all along."

Moran was momentarily startled, and I no less than he, by this un-expected surrender. "You mean," he asked hesitantly, "that you now believe that Mrs. Anceney committed suicide?"

"Exactly. She undoubtedly killed herself in a fit of depression."

I stared at him incredulously.

I could see that Moran was inclined to be mildly triumphant, but Kane cut short his expressions of gratification. He pulled out his watch.

"It's almost three," he said, "and I've a suggestion to make to you and Underwood. It seems to me just as sensible for us to stay here for the rest of the night as to go home at this hour." As Moran looked puzzled, Kane explained. "I've telephoned the Medical Examiner to be here at eight o'clock in the morning. I don't want to bother with him to-night. Someone must be on hand when he comes. McBeath may as well go, but I think it's simpler for the three of us to remain. The Examiner will have to talk to us anyhow."

Moran seemed about to expostulate, but the determined tone in which Kane was speaking evidently made him think better of it.

"Someone must tell the family what has happened," Kane went on. "Will you do that, Moran? I'm particularly insistent that every one of them should be told. They've guessed by this time that Mrs. Anceney is dead, and it will relieve their minds to know we've definitely estab-lished it as suicide. Tell them that the Medical Examiner will come in the morning to make a final investigation, and that after that the affair is practically over, so far as we are concerned.

"And while you're doing that," he said seriously, "please ask Mrs. Sutton about putting us up for the rest of the night. I think Sutton had a bedroom adjoining his sitting room. I'll camp there, if she has no objection. In fact, Underwood and I will go up there now, and you join us as soon as you can. Tell Mrs. Sutton that Gilroy will have to stay here, too. She may not realize that." As he finished speaking, Kane got up. The three of us followed him out of the room.

At the foot of the stairs McBeath left us. Moran went up to talk to Mrs. Sutton, and Kane and I took possession of Sutton's bedroom. During the few minutes we waited, Kane addressed no word whatever to me, and as he seemed to be concentrating on some problem I knew nothing of, I did not venture to disturb his thoughts.

Finally Moran returned, saying that he had informed everyone of Mrs. Anceney's suicide, and that Mrs. Sutton had kindly arranged to put one of us downstairs for the night and the other in a bedroom on the third floor. "I'll go downstairs," he said. "I can sleep there as well as anywhere else."

At this point Kane roused himself to say coolly, "On the contrary, Moran, this is one night when you won't sleep at all."

Moran turned to him in quick bewilderment, but Kane silenced him. "I've something I want to show you," he said earnestly, "but I warn you beforehand to say nothing that may be overheard. Is the door closed tightly?" I tried it and told him that it was.

"First of all," began Kane in a low voice which commanded our instant attention, "I deceived you deliberately when I said I agreed with you that Mrs. Anceney had committed suicide—but I did it for a purpose which I will explain later. She was murdered, and by some-one who planned and executed the murder with the utmost skill and coolness. Her murderer—do you realize—is in this house, now. That is why I warn you that we must not be overheard."

As Kane spoke these words, I wondered whether the strange sensa-tions I felt creeping along my spine were what is popularly described as a cold chill. My tongue stuck to the roof of my mouth like a thick piece of dry leather.

Moran was leaning forward, asking incredulously, "But the proof? You said you had none."

Kane did not answer immediately. Instead, he picked a newspaper out of the waste-paper basket and spread it on the table near him, then took out the handkerchief which I had seen him stow away in his pocket. There were several blood spots on it. He unfolded it, and took out what appeared to be a piece of cloth about twelve inches square. It was covered with blood that was still wet. Kane laid it carefully on the newspaper.

"That's my proof," he said.

CHAPTER 7

Moran half rose to look at it.

"Where'd you get that?" he asked sharply, with an almost hostile tone in his voice. But Kane was not disposed to be hurried. I suspected him of enjoying Moran's confusion.

"Well, not where it should be found in a well-conducted suicide, at any rate," he evaded. "It was rather curiously placed. I picked it out of one of the inner folds of the window draperies just above the point where they are drawn back toward the sash. I went so far as to assume that someone had put it there for purposes of concealment. Since it's Mrs. Anceney's blood on the cloth—you'll allow me that, won't you— it's hardly likely that *she* hid it there. Even steady determination, you know, won't keep you on your feet after your jugular vein has been severed."

Moran had jumped up in a fever of excitement.

"Who killed her then? Where did you find it? Why did you say it was suicide?"

"Because I had a sudden inspiration," Kane answered the last question. He got up from his chair.

"And I'll tell you about it in a few minutes. Neither of you will believe what I have to tell you unless I can offer concrete proof. I'm going now to see whether I can find it." He opened the door. "Back in a minute," he said, and went out.

Moran settled himself again and glared at me as if I had been the cause of this delay. I was impatient, too, but I kept myself from visible fidgeting. Finally, he walked over and commenced to wrap up in the newspaper the bloodstained cloth which had been left lying on the table.

"What d'you suppose anybody'd use this for, anyhow?" he asked as he did so.

I had wondered about that myself, but since Moran's question had been addressed more to the air than to me, I said nothing. Moran put the package in his pocket and sat down again.

I was glad when Kane returned. His face showed no trace of excitement, but there was a matter-of-fact briskness about him which convinced me that his quest had not been in vain. Moran and I got to our feet eagerly.

Kane looked at his watch. "We haven't more than a half hour to work in," he said, "and we've got to travel fast. So come on."

We followed him out of the room. As we went down the hall I noticed with surprise that there was a light in the room where Mrs. Anceney's body lay. Moran noticed it too, and turned to Kane sharply.

"You left that door unlocked," he exclaimed.

"I did it on purpose," Kane replied curtly.

He had opened the door to Sutton's sitting room and was motioning us to come in. I saw as we entered that only one light was burning, the lamp near Sutton's chair. Moran promptly made a move to turn on the overhead lights, but Kane stopped him.

"This is all the light we'll need," he said, and crossed the room to the end of the fireplace. He took up a stand facing the body of the murdered man. "Moran, come here," he ordered, and when Moran stood beside him, he continued. "We're now going to settle, I hope, an argument we had earlier this evening. You said, as I remember your words, that Sutton was shot by someone who stood approximately where we're standing now. You intimated that Mrs. Anceney had suddenly taken out a revolver and shot him down as he sat there in his chair talking to her. I agreed with you entirely in this particular—that he was shot from a point along a line drawn from his chair and passing through this spot we stand on. But I was inclined to believe, contrary to your opinion, that Mrs. Anceney had *not* killed him, and that the murderer, whoever he was, had not stood here when firing the shot. Now wait a minute," he cautioned, for Moran's mouth was about to fly open with the force of his protest.

"I know you're itching to repeat exactly the argument you put forward two hours ago. So I'll do it for you. You want to say that no one could possibly have shot Sutton from the direction I indicate without standing approximately where we are. Because, as you've said, you can't follow out our line without going through the wall of the house. Do I interpret your objection?" he asked, raising his eyebrows slightly.

"Well," Kane went on, "on that last point you're right. But the cold fact is that the murderer was on the other side of the wall. Sutton was shot by someone who was outside the window." Kane paused, and with the two of us desperately clinging to his last words, and breathlessly awaiting his next, coolly lit a cigarette. It struck me at that moment, with some irritation, that Kane's sense of the theater was the one supremely childish thing about him.

He took one or two drags from the cigarette. Though Moran was either too bewildered or too stubborn by this time to voice the expected question, Kane took up his discourse again as if in answer to the unspoken query.

"I know that this window was shut and locked before the murder, and that it remained so during and after the murder. Nevertheless, the shot came through that window." He took a small flashlight from his pocket and threw away his cigarette. He turned to me.

"Underwood," he said, "you're not accustomed to second-story work, so watch your footing. There's a ledge outside these windows which runs the length of the house. I'm going to take you out on it so that you can see for yourselves how Sutton was shot." He crossed to the window on the other side of the fire-place, unlocked it, pushed it up, and clambered awkwardly over the sill. Moran and I, who had followed his movements eagerly, saw that he was standing on a stone ledge, about a foot and a half wide, somewhat below the window sill. Moran started to climb after him and I was not far behind.

"Hang on to the stones that stick out from the wall," Kane directed, and moved farther down the ledge.

I felt a slight giddiness as I crawled out on to the shelf and looked below me, but once I was standing erect, with my face to the wall of the house, and a firm clutch on the projecting stonework above my head, I saw that progress was not impossible. Kane and Moran were moving rapidly down the ledge. Finally I perceived with relief that they had stopped. After a few seconds of painful effort I reached them. Moran helped me to secure a less precarious handhold. We were standing outside a window and I realized immediately that it was the one through which Kane had said the shot had been fired. I looked inside and appreciated how well Kane had set the stage. Almost directly before the window, but removed from it by about three feet, was the chair in which, presumably, Mrs. Anceney had been sitting. To our right was the fireplace and in front of that the light shone directly down on Sutton's body. From this position his white shirt front would have been an unmistakable target. But at this point my thoughts ceased to function. Could a bullet pass through a window without breaking the glass?

"Given an opportunity like this, what man couldn't do efficient murder," Kane was saying. "However, let me remove the element of mystery." He turned his flashlight on that part of the window which was three or four feet above the ledge. It was a small-paned window, as I had noticed before, with heavy leading between the panes. As Kane focused the light more closely, I distinctly saw a black smudge on two adjacent panes.

"Powder marks, eh, Moran?" Kane suggested. Moran grunted something which I took to mean agreement.

Holding the flashlight in his left hand, Kane pulled gently, with the thumb and first finger of his other hand, at the thick piece of leading between the two panes. It came away easily, with almost no sound, leaving, between the panes, a rectangular space approximately six inches long by half an inch wide.

"Well, I'll be—damned," Moran muttered in solemn astonishment. "I never saw that before."

Kane smiled. "I think it's rather neat, myself. You see the opening is just wide enough to shoot through if you hold the revolver close to the panes."

"Let's go back now," he concluded. "I'll take this piece of leading with me." Without further remark we made our way back to Sutton's bedroom. As we went through the sitting room, Kane turned off the lights and locked the door.

Once seated, Moran began doubtfully, "Don't you think it's rather a coincidence that the window should have been fixed that way?"

"Not necessarily," Kane answered. "In the first place I don't think for a minute that Sutton's murderer used the ledge for the first time to-night. He'd undoubtedly been out on it, not once, but many times before—probably for the purpose of spying on Sutton. He may have discovered, on one of those times, that the piece of leading was loose. Or he may have loosened it himself." Kane flashed his light on the object he held in his hand, and examined it on all sides. "However, there are no marks on it, so I think it wasn't pried out forcibly. It was probably insecurely fastened from the beginning, and the murderer may have come upon that curious fact while engaged in the comparatively innocent occupation of eavesdropping. At any rate, that's the way I've worked it out for myself."

"How about the ledge?" Moran asked. "What windows does it connect with?"

"Now that," Kane answered, "is the most baffling, or I may say intriguing, part of the whole discovery. The ledge runs the entire length of three sides of the house. I was careful to find that out. It doesn't run across the front of the house. Mrs. Anceney was killed in a room which, you remember, is on the front. That means, as I see it, that the windows of every room on the second floor, except those that face only on the front, open on this ledge. However, that point is not too important. In any event, the murderer could have gained access to the ledge through the windows of this room, Sutton's bedroom, which was temporarily unoccupied."

Moran, whose eyes had been fixed on Kane in squinting concentration, pursed his lips at this statement and tapped a warning finger.

"Just a minute!" He turned to me.

"Mr. Underwood, seems to me you noticed pretty accurately what rooms the different people came out of. But I don't remember your saying anybody came out of this room."

"No one did," I replied, "at least not when I was standing outside the door of the sitting room before I went in. They came from their own rooms, as far as I was able to judge."

Moran looked wisely at Kane, as much as to say "There, you see."

But Kane was not disturbed. "I don't doubt you for a minute, Underwood," he said. "I'll take my oath on it that you saw no one coming out of this room—and that furthermore you saw every member of the household emerging from his or her room or coming from the far side of the hall. However, in spite of opposition," he smiled ruefully, "I *still* think the murderer could have made his exit through this door."

"Well, I don't see *why* you do," I countered, for I remembered the moment distinctly, and was sure my impressions were not mistaken.

"All right, I may be wrong," Kane agreed easily. He sighed and rose unwillingly to his feet. "Come along, anyhow. We'll test it out."

He threw open the door, and we followed him into the hall. Somewhat to my surprise, he led us down the stairs. Three or four steps from the bottom he stopped, and turning around, pointed upward.

"How much can you see?" he asked quietly.

I understood immediately. From where we stood all we could see of the second floor was the door to the sitting room, which was straight ahead. The bedroom door, to the right, was not visible.

Kane spoke in a low tone. "While you were on your way up, Underwood," he said, "someone could have slipped out of the bedroom, and keeping to the left of the stairs, or to the right as we're standing now, gained the other side of the hall without your seeing him."

I nodded, realizing that not until my head was almost level with the second floor could I have noticed anyone passing above.

"And Gilroy, whom you met coming down," Kane continued, "would have been at the same disadvantage. So, there were several moments after the shot was fired when neither of you was in a position to observe what was going on up there. Satisfied?" he queried of us both.

"Yes."

Without further words we went back to the bedroom.

"Well, I guess that means," Moran suggested, after the door had been closed, "that anyone who was in the house to-night could have got out through this room, with small chances of being caught in the act."

"Exactly," Kane agreed, "especially since these windows have apparently been open all evening. However there are probably others which have been open also."

Kane paused for a moment, as if he were collecting his thoughts, then went to the heart of the matter without delay.

"There is no doubt in my mind," he said slowly, "that whoever shot Sutton also killed Mrs. Anceney."

Moran nodded. "We can take that for granted."

Kane continued thoughtfully. "We have no means of knowing at present what the motive was that prompted Sutton's murder. But I doubt that Mrs. Anceney was killed for the same motive. If she had been, she and Sutton would have been shot down at the same time. No, I think her murder was an afterthought. You remember how near her chair was to the window through which the shot was fired. Why wouldn't she have turned instinctively and have caught a glimpse of the person who stood on the ledge? Perhaps she saw him clearly enough to identify him—perhaps she didn't, and the murderer only suspected that she had. But it makes no difference whether she did or didn't—the person guilty of Sutton's death killed her because he feared that she would expose him. He was forced into committing two murders in order to shield himself from the consequences of the first. Doesn't that seem logical to you?"

Moran admitted that it did. "But there's one thing I don't get," he said. "If she wasn't guilty, why on earth didn't she clear herself immediately? Why did she wait?"

"There again," Kane replied, "I can only guess at her reasons. If she had any more than the ones I've figured out for myself, they may turn up later. One thing I am certain of is that if she *had* cleared herself immediately, she would be alive now. However, she couldn't have known for a moment that she was in any danger whatever. From what Underwood has told me of Mrs. Anceney, I assume that her position in her social world was of the utmost importance to her. As a witness in the Sutton murder trial, she would be thrown into a spectacular light, and she would certainly want to avoid that as far as possible. You must remember too that her presence in Sutton's sitting room, and even in his house, for that matter, might have a double meaning for some. I think she realized that in a flash—and that she felt the need of legal advice. Titterton could tell her, after hearing the circumstances, just where she stood, and just what was likely to be required of her later on. In other words, she could find out how *little* she needed to say. She knew that every word she spoke, after the murder had been discovered, would be remembered. She was a discreet woman, and she feared publicity more than anything else. Underwood, you were helping her a great deal when you put off the newspaper men.

If affairs had turned out as she planned, the morning papers would have held little enough to affect her future standing in the eyes of the world. From her own point of view she was wise. She had nothing to lose and everything to gain by the delay. But she would have been wiser to consider the present as well as the future."

"Well," Moran said heavily, "of course it's hard for me to follow an argument like that. But I guess you're right. Anyhow, it doesn't do any good to hash it over now." He picked meditatively at his front teeth. Suddenly he frowned and looked at Kane. "See here, if Sutton was shot from the ledge, how do you explain away the fact that we found the revolver on the table in the room where he was killed? Don't you think that was the gun used?"

"Yes, I think it was. The only person who can identify it beyond the shadow of a doubt, of course, is an expert on firearms. I'll have it examined to-morrow just to confirm my own belief. By the way, I happened to notice that there were no fingerprints on the handle."

"You don't say," Moran exclaimed in surprise. "Guess I couldn't have looked at it very carefully. That means gloves, I suppose."

"Something of the sort," Kane replied. "And a clever criminal, to boot. So far he's been damned negligent about leaving us the usual helpful clues. His disposal of the gun was as daring and as neat a strategy as any I can imagine. And so much more artistic than trying to conceal it."

"What do you mean?"

"I mean that after having shot Sutton and re-entered the house by a window, he carefully wiped all fingerprints off the handle of the re-volver, walked in to the scene of the crime with the rest, and with truly devilish coolness laid the weapon on the table. No one saw him do it."

"Whew! That narrows down our possibilities, all right," exclaimed Moran.

"Does it now?" Kane spoke more to himself than to us. "At any rate they're not too narrow to be interesting. Remember that in Sutton's room, a moment after the crime had first been discovered, there were, besides Underwood and Mrs. Anceney, the servants—five of them, weren't there?—Mr. Gilroy, and the Sutton family. Any one of them had the opportunity to put that gun on the table. No one else could have done it.

"As I see it," Kane continued, "we know three fairly definite things that narrow down our prospects. First, the criminal must have been in the sitting room when Sutton's death was discovered. We know exactly who was there. Second, to commit Mrs. Anceney's murder, he must have been able to keep a close watch on McBeath's movements. As far as we know now, this bars none of the people to whom the first point applies. Third, the murderer is someone who is well acquainted with this house. That's obvious, of course, from the fact that he knew about the ledge. It seems to me that Mr. Gilroy is the only one whom this point could possibly exclude. If we find that he was merely a chance visitor to the house, then he's beyond suspicion.

"So you see the possibilities aren't so narrow. If you take the five servants into account, we have ten people on our list any one of whom may be the criminal. Personally, I'm in favor of excluding the servants altogether. I can't bring myself to suspect that a butler or a housemaid could have committed these particular crimes. That leaves us five possibilities, I think." He ticked them off slowly on his fingers. "Mrs. Sutton—Katharine Sutton—her brother James—Bert Walton—and Mr. Gilroy."

Moran and I were respectfully silent for a moment, and then Moran cleared his throat suddenly. "I think we can cut it down to four," he said. "Could Mrs. Sutton have used the ledge?" he asked Kane directly. "Her arm, you know—"

"Unfortunately, we have no time for any more discussion," Kane said, taking out his watch. "Look here, we've serious work ahead of us within five minutes. I want to explain to you why I acted as I did to-night. When I found that bloodstained cloth, I was on the point of showing it to you all immediately when suddenly a better idea came to me. First of all it occurred to me that the cloth had been wrapped around the handle of the razor in order that no fingerprints might be left. Naturally it became drenched with blood. It was unfortunate. The murderer had to make his escape through the door by which he had entered. McBeath was presumably away from that spot at the time, but he might encounter him as he went down the hall. Or he might meet someone else. In any event he couldn't carry that bloody cloth in his hand. His clothes would be badly stained if he concealed it on his person. He had to be rid of it, so he stuck it in the fold of the draperies.

"I can't be sure," he went on, "that the murderer intended Mrs. Anceney's death to appear as suicide from the beginning. Possibly he did. At any rate, after he had escaped from the room, I should imagine that an announcement by the police that it was suicide would leave little to be desired, as far as he was concerned. The whole affair would be concluded. The police would leave, satisfied. Mrs. Anceney had shot Sutton, and then killed herself. It was all a perfect shield for the real murderer. That is, perfect except for one flaw.

"That was the bloodstained rag he'd been forced to leave behind him on the scene of his crime. If that were discovered, there would be no question of suicide. It gave me an idea.

"I agreed with your theory. I told you to tell every member of the household that Mrs. Anceney had committed suicide, and to make our remaining in the house overnight plausible on the ground that we were waiting for the Medical Examiner who would appear early in the morning to make his routine investigation.

"Now this is what I've been leading up to. I have reason to expect that before morning someone, not knowing that we have discovered the cloth, will attempt to remove the evidence of murder from the room in which the body is now lying. I propose to find out who that person is."

Moran could contain his excitement no longer. "You mean," he broke in, "we are to lay a trap for him? We are to hide ourselves in the room?"

"Yes."

"But what's to prevent his having searched the room while we've been sitting here?"

"No fear of that. Anyone who is awake now knows that we are too. Besides, I turned on the light in the room to prevent his going in there until we were ready for him. And the hall lights are still on. No, he' wouldn't have tried it yet. It's too much of a risk. He'll wait until he thinks we're all asleep. You see I wanted him to be sure, too, that the door would not be locked."

Kane stood up, and we instantly followed his example.

"This is the plan. Moran, you take Underwood to his room on the third floor. Mrs. Sutton told you where he was to sleep. I'll stay here meanwhile, and turn off my light, as if I were going to bed. When you come down again, turn out all the lights on this floor, including the one in the room where you're supposed to be. Do all this obviously, you understand. After about six minutes—you both have watches, haven't you—both of you are to leave your rooms as quietly as you can. Join me right outside the door of that room. As little noise as possible, remember. Get the lay of the land before the lights are turned off. Understand?" We nodded. "All right, then." He opened the door of his room, and we went out.

"Good-night," Kane said, in a conversational tone of voice.

"Good-night," we answered. He closed the door.

Moran and I went down the hall, our heels clicking sharply on the floor. There was no evidence of anyone's being awake at that hour. We went up to the third floor and Moran showed me into the room intended for me. Then he left and I heard him descending the stairs.

I took off my shoes, and after two minutes turned off the light and sat myself on the bed to wait. I tried to count off two hundred and forty seconds in my head, and then looked anxiously at my watch. There was one minute to go.

At the end of that time I got up, opened the door quietly and stepped out of the room. I expected an unearthly noise at every step I took, but none resulted. As I cautiously descended the stairs, my hand was so moist with nervous perspiration that it refused to slip easily along the polished banister. I could hear no sound from the darkness below me, nor could I tell when I had reached the bottom of the stairs. There was one less step than I had expected and my outstretched foot suddenly hit the hall floor with an impact which I fancied reechoed from every wall. I stood still with fright and actually expected to feel hairy hands closing upon my throat, but I took courage and proceeded to feel my way down the hall to the spot which Kane had designated. At this point I was careful to convince myself that if anything *did* touch me, it was bound to be either Kane or Moran. In spite of this desperate communion with myself, I could not keep from starting when I felt a hand touch my arm.

It was Kane. I had reached the meeting place. Moran was there too. We followed Kane into the room.

"Go over there and stand behind the curtain of that window," he told me in a whisper that might have seemed low at any other moment.

"Moran and I will stand inside the closet by the bed. Don't move unless I give you a signal."

Without another word, he and Moran moved quietly away. I could dimly see the outlines of the window he had pointed to, and it came to me with a burst of relief that it was not the window by which stood the fatal chair. In another moment I had managed to pick my way across the room and had stepped behind the heavy curtains.

CHAPTER 8

The room was completely dark. Even though knew that the door in the wall opposite was open I could not distinguish its outlines. Through the windows a street light shone faintly, throwing on the floor two dull yellow patches which only emphasized the blackness before me.

I stood rigidly, afraid to move lest I be heard by the visitor for whom we were waiting. All the small sensations which at another moment I should have disregarded took on a heightened keenness—the musty smell of the curtain which hung before my face, the roughness of it where it touched the back of my clenched fist. The point of my collar was digging into my neck, and the slight irritation which it at first caused me soon became an unbearable pain. I stood it as long as I could, and then put a cautious finger to my throat and loosened it a little. I was amazed to discover that my face was damp with sweat.

A curious trick of memory sent me back to an episode of my youth, when I had gone walking at night with some friends of mine. I could never remember how I lost them but I did. Then as now darkness had closed in upon me like an impenetrable wall. I felt again the horror of night, the desolating loneliness that I had first known in my childhood. The silence was hostile, implacable, unbroken.

What were we waiting for? Would the person who had that night committed two murders betray himself to us? Would we know in a few moments beyond the shadow of a doubt which of the people whom I had accepted as casual acquaintances was guilty of the worst of crimes?

I strained my eyes trying to pierce the blackness, and it was blackness no longer, but a thick cloud of heavy purple, which eddied and shifted like a veil of smoke, but never cleared away. My eyeballs had begun to throb, and still I saw nothing.

A sudden creak, as though someone had stepped on a loose floor board, broke the silence like a pistol shot. Every muscle in my body became tense. I thought of my fellow watchers and wondered if they had heard it as I had, if they were suffocating as I was with a choking suspense that was beyond excitement. I held my breath and waited for another warning.

The creak was not repeated, but the silence was gone forever. I became aware of a hundred sounds I had not heard before. The room seemed suddenly to have come alive—to be filled with hushed whispering. All the familiar noises of a house at night centered there, but they had become strange and threatening.

I thought of the dead woman who shared our watch, and a new horror seized upon me. What if the merciless hand that had killed her were to be turned against us, were to come out of the darkness, strike, and vanish, never having really appeared!

I tried to tell myself that I had become hysterical, that I was losing control of myself, that I must try not to think, that I must simply wait, but I doubt if any self-command of mine could have brought me to my senses. I had a sudden, over-mastering desire to look at my watch, to see how long I had stood there. I turned my wrist slowly so that I could see the luminous hands. I had lived through eternity in four minutes.

The sudden shock of reality restored my reason. I considered rather grimly the fact that four minutes had brought me as near insanity as I ever wanted to come. I made up my mind that I would wait until doomsday, if necessary, and to the best of my ability see things through.

How long I actually did wait, I never knew. At any rate I settled down, in something approaching calm, knowing that I could never again, no matter what happened, be so completely unnerved.

My thoughts drifted away, and I had almost forgotten what I was doing, when something indefinable told me that Kane had been right. There was no new sound, I could see nothing more, but I knew with a freezing certainty that someone had entered the room.

What was Kane going to do? He had laid his trap and it was sprung. Someone had fallen into it. He had only to snap his flashlight, and we would know the answer to the puzzle. I held myself in readiness, expecting from second to second that he would show himself, light up the darkness, and reveal the criminal he was seeking.

The fact that someone besides the three of us had come in was unmistakable now. I heard a soft footfall on the carpet, the sound of someone brushing against a chair. I thought I could detect the slight noise of breathing, and the impact of a fumbling hand against wood.

I could barely keep myself from taking action. What was Kane thinking of? In another minute it would be too late. The murderer would have come and gone, and we would be left in ignorance of his identity. Had Kane gone to sleep? Had he forgotten what he had to do? I felt a bitter impatience at the thought of the torture I had gone through for nothing. Then I remembered Kane's words, the sternness with which he had commanded me not to move. He was letting his plan be ruined, but it was his and not mine to decide what the result should be.

Whoever the intruder was, he moved with a deadly quietness and caution. The sounds that betrayed his presence were so slight that I could hardly believe my ears. But my intuition served me better than my hearing; I knew beyond the possibility of a doubt that he was there.

Suddenly the darkness was broken by a circle of light, directed full on the body of Mrs. Anceney. My eyes were so blinded by it that for a second I could not see who held the torch. Then he leaned forward a little and I could distinguish the features of—Gilroy.

Even in the intensity of that moment I was repelled by the expression on his face. Completely callous to the horrifying figure before him, he stared at the murdered woman as though his keen eyes were searching the depths of her cold ones to find out if she could still betray him.

He moved a little, as though his scrutiny had satisfied him, and I waited breathlessly to see him approach the window. In a flash I realized that that was the decisive action for which Kane was waiting.

As he turned away from the body, there was another sound from the doorway. Startled, he swung his flashlight in a wide circle. The tense silence was broken by a woman's voice.

"Who are you? What are you doing here?"

There was a click, and the room was flooded with light. At the door, her hand still on the switch, stood Katharine. Her face was very pale, framed in her dark hair.

Gilroy, all his swift assurance vanished, shrank back. For once I saw him as he really was. All his suavity, all his coolness were gone, and in their place he wore a look of vicious cunning. His eyes were narrowed cruelly, and his lips were drawn back from his teeth. I think if he had dared he would have sprung on the girl who had revealed him, who confronted him like an accuser.

"What do you want?" he said roughly.

"I want to know what you are doing here. I followed you to find out," she replied. Her voice was low and controlled.

Gilroy straightened himself as though he were trying to throw off the burden of fear she had put upon him.

"Go back to your room," he retorted. "This is no business of yours."

If he thought he could frighten her into obeying him, he was mistaken. "I won't do that," she said quietly. "Why are you here? Shall I call Mr. Kane and let you explain to him?" She took a step backward into the hall.

Her words stirred him to action. "Come back here," he said with a threatening gesture. He seemed to be trying to collect himself, to think of something that would prevent his ruin.

Katharine obeyed him and came slowly back into the room. Her compliance restored his boldness.

"Don't be a fool," he said in cold triumph. "Let me give you a warning. I make a bad enemy. Tell Kane you found me here and I'll make you suffer for it. It's up to you."

The girl seemed utterly defenseless before him. "I don't mean to do anything against you," she said wearily, and continued almost to herself, "It can't make any difference. You were my father's friend. I won't say anything unless they ask me; if they do, I'll have to tell them. It's all much too horrible already. If you'll go away now I won't say anything."

Gilroy seemed to think that a bargain had been struck between them. There was a disagreeable familiarity in the way he looked toward her. "I'm going, all right," he said. "I advise you to do the same.

Remember I can always find a way to get back at people who make trouble for me."

With catlike steps he crossed the room and went out. As he passed Katharine the girl shrank away from him. She turned as if to follow him, but with her hand on the door-knob she hesitated. Then her eyes turned involuntarily toward the corner of the room where the body lay. She seemed to become aware for the first time that Gilroy had left her alone with Mrs. Anceney.

As though she were spellbound under an awful fascination she moved slowly toward the chair. With uncertain steps she drew near to it, and, helpless under the power which controlled her, let her eyes fall for an instant on that mutilated figure. Then with an intake of her breath, she covered her face with her hands.

I could not bear to think what she must have suffered at that dreadful revelation. In sudden pity for her I looked away, and when I raised my eyes again she was at the door, her fingers seeking for the switch. She pressed it, and we were plunged in darkness.

My mind was tired and I could make nothing of the tangle, except that we had failed through Katharine's interference. If Gilroy had been left to himself only a few seconds longer we would have accomplished our purpose.

As I stood there, weary and numb, I heard Kane whispering to me. "Come on, Underwood." When he touched me on the arm I jumped like a shying horse, but I managed to follow him and Moran quietly out of the room. Kane turned to lock the door behind us, and as he did so, the last strange episode of that terrible evening occurred.

Each one of us heard, and stood straining his ears. Someone had been waiting outside the door and frightened by our approach was making cautious efforts to get away. A sharp creaking betrayed every step he took. He must have realized that, and abandoning any attempt at concealment, he began to run swiftly down the hall to our right.

Quick as a shot, Moran pulled out his flashlight and threw its beam from one dark corner to another. He found no one.

"It's no use, Moran," Kane whispered. "He's gone. Put it out." There was one more failure to add to our discouragement.

Kane led the way back to Sutton's bedroom, and once there dropped into a chair and stretched his long legs wearily. For the first time he gave evidence of the strain he had been under, he more than Moran and I, for the responsibility had been his. Moran looked utterly discouraged.

"I thought that was a pretty cute plan," he said at last. "But here we are. We wait for the murderer to come and Gilroy comes, but he doesn't do a damn thing we can use against him. I wish to God Katharine had stayed in bed. Then we go out in the hall and hear some other bird making his getaway. Now what's the answer?"

"You don't think Gilroy was the man in the hall?" Kane asked him.

"No, I don't. Why should he hang around out there?"

Kane nodded. "I don't think he was either. For one thing, his room is in the third story. And whoever we heard didn't go upstairs. He went into one of the rooms off the hall. We can cancel Gilroy as far as that one thing's concerned."

Moran seemed to find one grain of comfort in his bewilderment. "Anyhow," he said, "we know what's what with Gilroy, and we can find a way to wring the rest out of him."

"That's just what we can't afford to do," Kane replied with decision. "We've got to go slowly, Moran. That whole business to-night is good for one thing. It shows that there's a lot more to this affair than there seems to be. We have nothing against Gilroy or anyone else that we can act on. If we move too soon, God only knows what may happen. I tell you if we had the strongest case in the world against anyone I'd hesitate before I used it. There isn't going to be any strong case until we know who did the murders and know beyond the shadow of a doubt."

His evident anxiety impressed Moran. "You mean that we'd better lie low and see what Gilroy does?"

"Yes," Kane replied. "Do you agree, Underwood?"

"I suppose so," I said. "We have got to have more than this to go on."

Kane passed his hand through his hair as though the gesture helped him in his perplexity. "We'll be better men in the morning," he said in a flat, tired voice. "If we don't go to bed now I'll be forced to give you a lecture on the wickedness of human nature. I can feel it coming over me." His smile was a feeble salute to the spirit of mockery.

He went with us to the door of his room. As we left he looked at us quizzically. "I feel like the well-known Roman lady," he said. "You are my jewels."

CHAPTER 9

After a sleepless night, I left the Sutton house early, changed from my dinner clothes at my apartment, and had breakfast on the way to my office. Even after the strange and terrible events of which I had been a witness, the habits of years were strong. I read and answered my letters and tended to my routine business as though I had passed the preceding evening at the club, where nothing exciting has ever occurred, and where the chief topic of conversation is the goodness or badness of the food.

Nevertheless I could not shake off a feeling of unreality. Had my mind played a trick on me, and invented the dinner party, with its tragic conclusion? It seemed impossible that of that group of eight people two had met violent deaths and one was a murderer. And here was I, thrown out of the maelstrom, calmly sitting at my desk dictating letters.

About half past ten I sent my office boy out to get the papers. Definitely as I had expected it, the announcement of the crimes gave me a distinct shock. The headlines seemed to make the murders more concrete, and as I read through the sensational accounts, it was my daily life which became unreal, while the melodrama in which I had played an involuntary part was reenacted before my eyes.

Almost the whole story had been given to the reporters—Sutton's murder and the grave suspicion against Mrs. Anceney, her supposed suicide, the proof that Kane had brought out to show that both she and Sutton had been killed by the same person, and the statements of the various witnesses, mine among them. Following the account of the crimes were others giving the history of the Sutton family, the career of Mrs. Anceney, and my own modest achievements. The wording of the last gave me an uneasy idea that the press would be delighted to flaunt in the later evening editions some such headline as "Boston Lawyer Slays Two."

Just as I had finished my fascinated examination of the newspapers I had a telephone call from Kane. His voice was cool and his manner amused.

"Seen the papers?" he inquired. I said I had.

"They did us up very brown, didn't they? By the way, you may not know it but a considerable portion of the force has been busy keeping the reporters away from you. I know it's not necessary to say this, for people in your trade never tell anything, but don't inadvertently nod your head in answer to any of their questions. I'll see that our misdeeds get sufficient publicity."

"I wish that you would see that mine get a little less," I replied somewhat tartly. "It seems likely to me from what I read that I may take a trip to jail at any moment. This, for instance: 'Mr. Underwood has as yet made no statement to the public as to why he was in the Sutton house at the time of the crimes. A policeman stationed at the door of his apartment refused to allow our representative to interview him.'"

Kane laughed uproariously. "I will use all my influence," he answered, "to see that you get a life sentence instead of the chair."

His voice became serious again. "You're by no means through with this business, you know. I wish you'd drop whatever you're doing and come around to the Sutton house right away. I want to clear the stage a little and I need your help."

To be honest with myself I had to acknowledge that I was glad enough to go. My one dose of adventure had given me an appetite for more and made my customary occupations dull beyond description.

At the outer door of my office I found a lounging group of half a dozen newspaper men whom my appearance excited to hectic activity. To my relief, the imperturbable McBeath was there also, and under his solemn and powerful guidance I made my way to a taxicab. He took his place beside me, saying nothing, and to save my life I could not tell whether he thought he was watching the criminal or protecting another prospective victim. His vigilance was, however, unceasing.

We arrived at our destination in short order, and found Kane and Moran waiting for us. Having turned me over to them, McBeath left me, as his manner plainly said, to my fate.

"Been behind the bars, Underwood?" Kane greeted me with deep amusement, his dark eyes brilliant for a moment.

I grunted something in answer, and acknowledged Moran's curt nod. We had met in Sutton's sitting room, and I for one was glad that it was broad daylight, and that the ghastly figure was no longer slumped in the chair. I found out that both bodies had been taken to an undertaker's.

Kane seated himself at the desk and spoke briskly to me. "I'm sorry to have to disturb you this morning, but as you know we are all likely to be disturbed until we bring this matter to a conclusion. In the first place Moran and I realize that so far you have been invaluable to us. You know the situation we have to deal with better than we can hope to, except through the information we get from you. We agree that it would help a lot if you would go on working with us. We recognize the fact that our legal right to your aid is doubtful, but we are confident that your duty as a good citizen is clear to you, and that you will assist to the best of your ability in the execution of justice."

I recognized in the pompous manner of his conclusion an imitation of my own way of speaking. "I'll be glad enough to do what I can," I answered feebly.

Kane acknowledged my reply with a smile, but Moran was impatient of our delays. "All right, Moran," Kane said in answer to his glance. "We'll get to work. Suppose we take the servants first."

There were five of them, the butler, the footman, the cook and two maids. Moran discovered that the three women had been together during the evening, and observing that the two maids were too frightened to give clear reports of themselves, he singled out the cook, a middle-aged Norwegian, for examination, and sent the rest from the room.

The woman sat down at Moran's bidding, and calmly hung the heels of her square shoes on the rungs of her chair. From this position she regarded us distrustfully, but with a certain bright-eyed interest.

"I understand, Mrs. Christiansen," Moran began, "that you were in the house at the time that Mr. Sutton was killed."

The woman took this as a statement of fact, and made no answer.

"You were, weren't you?" Moran persisted.

"Yah."

"In what part of the house?"

"Oh, where we sit in efening."

"That's a room near the kitchen, is it?"

"Yah."

It was with difficulty that Moran succeeded in drawing from the woman replies of more than one syllable. When she finally became more voluble we learned that Nellie and Marie, the two maids, had been entertaining their "yong men" in the servants' sitting room—and that the "yong men" had been drinking what they told her was "hot stuff." She, the cook, had not been invited to remain at the party but had declined to leave because she suspected the nature of the "hot stuff" and was afraid they would break the Victrola record she had "yust that day bought." No, they had not heard the shot because the Victrola was playing, but the footman, with a "vite face, pore fella," had burst in to tell them about it, whereupon the young men had left precipitately, and the rest of them had gone upstairs.

At the time of the second murder, which she had not learned of until that morning, she and the two maids, unable to sleep, had been sitting in her bedroom, talking and wondering "Vy that woman killed Mr. Sutton."

At this point Kane interrupted her story to ask whether she had ever seen Mrs. Anceney before the murder.

The cook replied "No," but that she had heard of her. Asked what she had heard, she answered that Tom, the chauffeur, had talked. One day, it developed, when Sutton had given the chauffeur the afternoon off and had driven the car out himself, Tom had winked at her and had said that Sutton was going on "private business." He had further remarked "Bet she don't go ridin' with him. She never has yet," and when, a half hour later, Sutton had returned, red-faced and impatient, she and the chauffeur had watched him from the window, and had "laughed and laughed." Whereupon, it seemed, Tom had passed certain insinuations which she had not completely misunderstood, foreigner though she was.

I could see that Kane was not only amused, but somewhat interested in this latter part of her testimony. Nothing more was to be learned from this source, however, and he dismissed her abruptly, asking that she send in the butler.

When the man came, I recognized him immediately as the servant to whom I had spoken about taking the wine to Mrs. Anceney. He testified that at the time of Sutton's murder he had been downstairs in his pantry. He had followed out my orders about the sherry a few minutes after I had talked with him and had taken the tray upstairs.

"Where you delivered it to Mrs. Anceney?" Moran questioned.

"No sir, I didn't," the man replied. "The policeman outside her door wouldn't let me take it in, so I gave the tray to him."

"Do you know what time it was then?"

"Yes, sir. I happened to look at my watch because he asked me for the time. It was twenty-five minutes of two."

At this point Kane made a curt gesture to Moran who told the butler that he might go.

After he had left, Kane remarked cheerily, "At least, we've found two people who tell the same story."

We concluded our examination of the servants with the footman, who could add nothing to what I had already said for him.

"No leads there," Moran said disgustedly, when he had finished his testimony.

"Oh, well," Kane replied, "it's encouraging to know that Underwood and McBeath are honest and remain untainted by the wickedness of the world. Let's go looking for another honest man."

"Who?" the sergeant inquired.

"Bert first, don't you think?"

"Don't expect to find anything honest about him." Moran's face was glum. "He's a damn queer specimen."

We found Bert in his room across the hall, diligently pasting clippings in his scrapbook. As I glanced at it casually I saw to my horror that he was occupied with the various accounts of the murders.

He seemed frightened when Kane asked if we might come in and talk to him. His small eyes narrowed, and his pale, pointed face was anything but prepossessing.

Kane disregarded Bert's uneasiness, and sat down as though he had come to pay a social call. On a table near his elbow was a heap of books similar to the one with which Bert had been busy when he entered.

"May I see your scrapbooks?' he asked. "I used to keep them myself when I had time."

Bert was obviously placated by the request, and to some extent lost the antagonism he had at first shown toward us. He set himself at once to explain to Kane that he put in the books everything that he wanted to keep. They were all in order. He had started five years ago, and he had already filled ten. He sorted them carefully, and gave Kane the earliest to look at first. When Kane praised their neatness, he became still more pleased and excited, drew himself to his full height (five feet two, perhaps), and balanced himself on his toes, swaying slowly up and down, the embodiment of swelling pride.

Kane turned the pages over quickly as he talked, taking the trouble to skim through more than one of them. Meantime he conducted his casual interview with Bert.

"You've lived with your sister and brother-in-law ever since they were married, haven't you?"

"Oh, yes," Bert replied in surprise. "Ellen couldn't get along without me."

"Nice room you've got."

Bert looked around, a shade of discontent on his face. "It's all right," he said, "but it's not the one I wanted. I wanted one on the street. I like looking out of the window. I ought to have had the one Fred took for his sitting room."

"It's a nice house altogether," Kane continued, ignoring Bert's remarks. "Your sister is lucky to have married a man who was so successful."

Bert blazed up. "*She* wasn't lucky at all. I often told her she was silly to let Fred put upon her so. I would have taken better care of her than he did, and been nicer to her, too. He wouldn't say a decent word to either of us for weeks. He was downright nasty—always talking about what *he* would do and what *he* wanted. Nobody ever stood up for her but me, and she wouldn't let me say anything against him."

"Didn't Katharine side with her mother?" Kane asked.

"She didn't at all," Bert replied indignantly. "She always sided with Fred. She acted as if he were God Almighty, always hanging at his heels even when she was little, and taking everything he said for Gospel truth."

"How about James?" Kane continued to flip the pages of Bert's scrapbook, as though he didn't care whether his question were answered or not. Moran looked at him with growing impatience. He was leaning heavily on the back of Kane's chair as though he were utterly weary of this beating around the bush.

Bert considered Kane's question judicially, as though he didn't wish to be swept away by the memory of old wrongs. With a distinct effort at fairness he replied, "You have to remember that he is young. That's what Ellen said. I said he was selfish and out for what he wanted just the way his father was."

Moran had evidently held in as long as he could.

"You don't like any one, do you?" he burst out.

"Yes, I do," Bert protested, "I like Ellen."

"But you didn't like your brother-in-law?"

Bert checked the words on the tip of his tongue, and looked suspiciously at Moran. "Oh, I liked him all right," he said finally.

Moran was evidently determined to take the interview out of Kane's hands. "Where were you last night at eleven o'clock?" he continued.

At the abrupt question Bert shrank like a pricked balloon. His frightened eyes darted from the one to the other of us.

"I was here in my room," he replied.

"You heard the shot fired and ran out to see what was the matter? Had you any reason to suppose that anything was the matter?"

"No, I hadn't." His voice had become shrill. "What do you think when somebody fires a gun?"

"How did you know it was a gun?"

"It was, wasn't it? I know lots of things."

"What did you do after Mr. Underwood turned you out of the sitting room?"

"I went to my sister, and she told me to come back here and wait."

"You were here when Mrs. Anceney was killed?"

"I suppose so."

"You stayed here all the time?"

"Yes, I did."

"How does it happen then that McBeath saw you skulking in the hall about twelve o'clock?"

Moran's questions and his manner had so thoroughly frightened Bert that for an instant he could do nothing but babble disconnected words. "I—I forgot," he cried finally. "I was there but I didn't do anything." He cowered away from Moran.

"That's enough for to-day," Kane interrupted briskly, and we left the room with no more ado.

Moran was annoyed. "Why didn't you let me go on? I had him nicely scared," he said as we went down the hall.

Kane looked at him in half irritation. "You won't get anything that way, Moran. Personally I'm satisfied with what we found out. Let's fish another creek. By the way, I understand that Gilroy went to his office this morning. Why don't you send for him, and save time? We can talk to James while he's on his way here."

Moran barked an order at McBeath, while Kane knocked on James's door. James, clad in a brilliant lounging robe, let us in rather grudgingly.

"I thought you'd probably be after me," he said in a sulky voice.

"We'd be glad if you'd tell us what you know," Kane replied, and tacitly handed the interview over to Moran, who took it up without delay.

James's statements were not particularly illuminating. He and Gilroy, after leaving the rest of us downstairs, had settled down to gin and ginger-ale in his, James's, room. Gilroy hadn't been with him when he heard the shot, having left a little while before—two or three minutes, James supposed—to go home. He repeated my story of the finding of Sutton's body, told of taking Katharine and Mrs. Sutton to their rooms. He had then gone downstairs, and finding the police in charge had obeyed Moran's suggestion that he take himself out of the way. He was in his room at the time of Mrs. Anceney's death, which he had understood was suicide. He had gathered from the morning papers that the police no longer believed that, but thought that both Mrs. Anceney and Sutton had been killed by the same person.

He told a straight story without hesitation. His manner was cool and indifferent, and he seemed to take almost no personal interest in the proceedings. From his attitude it would have been difficult to deduce that his father had been murdered the night before.

One point of more than minor interest came out in the examination. The only member of the Sutton family who owned a gun, to James's knowledge, was his father. Sutton was accustomed to keeping a Colt .32 in a drawer of his desk.

After he had listened to the matter-of-fact story James told in answer to Moran, Kane put a few questions to the young man.

He began with some hesitation. "I don't like to seem unduly curious, Mr. Sutton, and if I could avoid it I wouldn't ask you the things I am going to. You must understand that there is no one else who can give me the information I need. I want to know whether in your opinion there was anything more than a friendly relationship between your father and Mrs. Anceney?"

"I can't give you a straight 'Yes' or 'No' to a question like that because I really don't know," James answered with a disagreeable smile. "But I suppose the answer might as well be 'Yes.' My father was the kind to make a fool of himself over women."

"Did your mother ever seem to resent his attentions to Mrs. Anceney?"

"I can't say if she did or not. She never told me about her feelings."

Kane changed the subject abruptly. "Tell me something about Mr. Gilroy," he said.

"What do you want to know?"

"Had he known your father very long?"

"Perhaps a year," James answered briefly.

"Was he a friend of your father's?"

"Not particularly. He was his secretary."

"Did he come to the house very often?"

"He was here a good deal of the time, but he spent most of it with me."

"Then he was a friend of yours?"

"We used to see the town together." There was something ugly in the ease with which James adopted Gilroy as a cicerone.

"Did your father and Gilroy get along, as far as you know?"

"Oh, yes. Though he didn't care much for the way we made the money fly."

"I see."

There was obviously nothing more to be learned from James. As far as I was concerned I was glad to be rid of him. I had never seen anyone of his age so thoroughly lacking in human feeling. He certainly cared neither for his father nor his mother. I agreed with Bert. Youth could not excuse or explain his cold detachment.

Back in the sitting room, we had only a few minutes to wait before Gilroy made his appearance. At Kane's suggestion we had schooled ourselves to be as matter-of-fact toward him as if we knew no more than he thought we did.

He was as dapper and smiling as ever. His clothes were immaculate, and carefully planned to give an effect of a style too extreme for my taste. In fact, everything about him displeased me, from the top of his sleek head to the toe of his polished shoe.

He had the effrontery to greet me as an old acquaintance.

"Good-morning, Mr. Underwood. I'm glad to see you again, though I'm afraid last night's affair was rather extraordinary for an introduction." He smiled knowingly. I was relieved that I did not have to shake hands with him.

"Won't you sit down, Mr. Gilroy?" Kane asked politely, adopting Gilroy's urbanity. "I'm sorry to take you away from your private affairs, but you know—"

Gilroy interrupted quickly. "Certainly, Mr. Kane. The ordinary procedure, of course. No apology necessary. As a matter of fact I was just on the point of coming around to offer my services when your man called. Though I'm afraid I can't tell you much," he concluded ruefully.

"A new point of view on things we already know may help us," Kane put in smoothly, and I could have laughed at the placid manner in which Gilroy received so true a statement of the case.

"Then I suppose that the first thing the law requires," Gilroy suggested with intended facetiousness, "is a detailed report of my whereabouts during the evening. That so?" He raised his eyebrows at Kane.

"Exactly, Mr. Gilroy."

"Let's see." He stroked one side of his moustache softly. "First off, I was a dinner guest here last night, as Mr. Underwood may have told you. So far, so good, eh? Well, after dinner, I stuck around a while, and then James and I went up to his room."

"How did you happen to do that, Mr. Gilroy? Are you a particular friend of James's?"

"Oh yes, we get together now and then. As a matter of fact, the boy thought the old man's cocktails a bit weak, and suggested we go to his room and have a few snifters."

"I see. Go on."

"We had a drink or two—sat around—talked. Suddenly we heard a shot—I ran out—"

Kane lifted what seemed to be a mildly puzzled face.

"Now that's funny, Mr. Gilroy." He spoke wonderingly, as if he were confused. "James just said—"

But Gilroy sprang immediately to the business of righting his craft.

"Oh, that's right, that's right. I'm all balled up." He laughed deprecatingly. "Awfully sorry. Must be nervous, I guess." He looked around for appreciation of his joke, and Kane returned a good imitation of an understanding smile. "Of course, I'd left the room, that's it, I'd *left*. I wasn't with James at all." His manner implied a great discovery. "Funny how I got mixed up."

"Don't let us confuse you," Kane commented dryly. "But tell me— did you happen to notice what time it was when you left James?"

Gilroy's assurance had returned. "As luck would have it, Mr. Kane, I did. I looked at my watch, and I said to James, 'Good God, man! It's two minutes of eleven, and I've got work to do before I can get to bed to-night!'"

Kane took this calmly. "Rather a happy chance, wasn't it, Mr. Gilroy," he said carelessly, "that you chose that moment to look at your watch? Do you"—his eye traveled rapidly over Gilroy—"always carry a watch?"

"Oh, yes." Involuntarily the man looked down and realized that his open coat could hide no lack of a watch chain. "That is, always in the evening," he corrected himself, smiling.

Kane accepted his statement with no surprise. "Now, let's see, where were we?" he began absentmindedly. "Oh, yes, you were saying you had left James's room when you heard the shot. Were you in the hall, then?"

"On the stairs. Just going down. Fact is, Mr. Underwood saw me just where I was when the shot was fired." He smiled at me with a great assumption of ease. "I guess we're in the same boat, Underwood, far's this case is concerned. They'll have to tar us with the same brush, eh?"

I forced a feeble smile at this audacity, but Kane laughed out loud as if he were enjoying himself. Soon he became serious.

"Did you happen to see anyone in the hall as you went downstairs?" he asked.

Gilroy considered. "No," he said.

At Kane's direction, Gilroy went on with his story, and explained that at the time of the second murder, he had been downstairs in the library. He had spent the night in the house, in accordance with the police orders. Mrs. Sutton had given him a room on the third floor, he said. Being profoundly shocked by the events of the evening, and particularly by the murder of so charming a woman as Mrs. Anceney, he had retired as soon as he was able to.

"Did you sleep well?" Kane was idly twisting the end of a silver pencil.

Gilroy darted a sidelong glance at his questioner. His well-manicured hand fingered his lip, but in a moment dropped again carelessly, and he replied.

"Why—yes. Very well, thanks. Why the question?"

"I just wondered," Kane returned aimlessly. "So many of them seem to have spent sleepless nights. But naturally you wouldn't have been so deeply affected, being outside the family. By the way, do I understand that you had met Mrs. Anceney before last night?"

Gilroy swung one leg over the other, and carefully pinched the crease of his gray trousers. He looked away from Kane and smiled.

"I don't believe I've ever been asked the question," he replied.

"Had you?"

"No. Attractive woman, wasn't she?" The heel of his right shoe beat a faint tattoo.

Kane ignored the query. "But you knew Sutton fairly well, didn't you?" he pursued.

"I ought to."

"You were a kind of confidential secretary?"

"More or less. A Jack-of-all-trades fills the bill."

"How long were you with him?"

"Oh . . ." Gilroy was in no hurry to remember . . . "about a year, I guess."

"Then, Mr. Gilroy, perhaps you can tell us this—did Sutton have any enemies?"

"Undoubtedly." There was real enthusiasm in the reply. "Dozens of 'em."

"Do you think so?" Kane's interest seemed real. "You're the very man to help us. If you'll give us the names—"

But Gilroy showed a slight alarm.

"Well, now, Mr. Kane," he hesitated in becoming fashion, "one hates to brand a man in a situation like this. You know how it is. I—I should dislike to be the cause . . . Perhaps I should have phrased my reply in other language. I merely implied that Sutton was not what you might call 'popular.' And that's natural, isn't it? Such a man is likely to be misunderstood."

"Oh, yes." Kane was in perfect accord, it seemed. "And now, Mr. Gilroy, I've detained you longer than I intended to—"

"Not at all."

But Gilroy did not seem averse to leaving our company. He got up immediately, shook hands all around, with a word for each of us.

"And if," he had paused with his hand on the doorknob, "I can help you in any way, you'll keep me in mind, won't you?"

"We'll keep you in mind," Kane assured him.

CHAPTER 10

"Now that we're here," Kane said when Gilroy had left us, "we may as well look up Sutton's gun." At his suggestion Moran rummaged through the drawers of the desk without finding it.

"I think we can take it for granted," Kane remarked finally, "that Sutton was hoist by his own petard. The gun we found on the table was a .32, if I'm not mistaken. We'll have the rifling of the gun and the bullet compared, but for the moment we can let the point go."

Moran grunted his assent but continued his aimless search through the drawers. "Might be something here," he said, pulling out a bundle of letters and old dusty photographs. He began shuffling through the latter. In a moment he had paused curiously and was picking out of the bunch a small snapshot, printed in blue and yellowed around the edges. Suddenly he let out a guffaw. Kane looked up quickly and Moran held out the picture.

"Take a look at that, will you," he laughed. "If that didn't come straight from the funny papers, I never saw one!"

Kane took it and in a moment he, too, was laughing.

"Capitalist and Family, As They Were," he chuckled.

"God, I bet Sutton would have sweated blood if the papers had ever got hold of that," Moran suggested gleefully. "Oh boy, what a Past!"

Kane flipped the picture over to me and the moment I saw it I understood their laughter. It was an old-time exposure taken when James and Katharine were about five and eight years of age. The family were posed rather than seated on a stiff wooden bench. From left to right there were Bert, or rather a third of him, James, Katharine, Mrs. Sutton and Sutton. But the curious effect of the whole arose from

127

the fact that Sutton, although very much in the picture, had taken it himself by means of a bulb attachment plainly visible in his left hand. This phenomenon had wreaked havoc with the facial expressions of the group. Mrs. Sutton was the only one looking into the camera, and that not without difficulty, for Sutton, in his excitement over being not only subject but *deus ex machina*, had thrust his large head well toward the center. The children were gazing with bated breath at the bulb, while Bert, at the extreme left, had evidently been talking during some part of the exposure, for his mouth and nose were inextricably mingled. It was Sutton, however, who looked most ludicrous, for he wore the eager yet glazed expression of one who tries to do two things at once and hopes for the very best.

I put the picture back on the desk. Moran had meanwhile been turning over other photographs which illustrated in a curious fashion the history of the Suttons. One family group had been taken on the porch of a cheap suburban house. Sutton himself in a checked suit dominated it, his large square figure casting into the background his wife's less imposing presence. It was easy to see from the photograph just what they had been. Sutton must have been under thirty when the picture was taken, but his face already showed signs of self-will and restlessness. His heavy jaw was firm and defiant, and he stood poised as though he were ready and eager to move forward. His wife sat, typically enough, in his shadow, but I could see that she too was already set in the mold of what she would become. Her plainness, her lack of obvious self-assertion, emphasized her strength. Everything in the picture, the people, their attitudes, their clothes, showed their self-consciousness.

Another group illustrated their rise in the world. It was taken before a larger house and made an effect less suggestive of a poor photographer. Sutton had become even more forceful, but he no longer wore the checked suit. Already he and his family belonged to the upper middle class.

Besides the larger pictures there were snapshots of James, a younger physical edition of his father, and Katharine, easily recognizable as a child, with her thin, rather sallow face, and straight dark hair.

The letters and papers were such as any man might keep, old receipted bills for small amounts, notices of new issues of stocks, statements, and so forth. Scattered among these were letters from various members of his family, from Mrs. Sutton who had been away on a visit, from James at school, and from Katharine. Many of them had been written by her, and it offended me vaguely to see Moran opening one after another of them, and to hear him reading the childish phrases which disclosed the intimate and tender relationship which had existed between the girl and her father.

Moran ran through them rapidly, then pushed them back into the drawer and shut it.

"That's all," he said dourly. "Let's go."

"There are just a few things I want to show Underwood," Kane interposed, "before we eat."

He spread out on the desk a number of objects which I had seen before and some which were new to me. The gun, the razor, the blood-stained rag, a slip of paper and some jewelry.

"That's all we've got to go on," he said, "so far." He went on to explain that the watch and the keys which I saw had been taken from Sutton's pockets, while the two rings and a pin were Mrs. Anceney's. Obviously as evidence they were worthless. He had been confirmed in his opinion that there were no fingerprints on either weapon. I examined the slip of paper with some interest. It was nothing more than a scrap torn from a desk pad. A meaningless series of figures had been written on it.

"You remember," Kane reminded me, "that Mrs. Anceney was reading a magazine when we went to talk to her. She evidently used that to mark her place, for I found it this morning between a couple of the pages."

He seemed to show more interest in his find than I could see any reason for, but I was somewhat shaken from my indifference when Moran snatched the paper from me, leaned over the desk and fitted it neatly to the jagged half sheet on Sutton's calendar.

"Good work," said Kane approvingly, "that's where it came from all right. I wonder who tore it off and why."

I glanced at it again. The numbers looked as if they had been scribbled at random. They read 153225475.

Kane gathered up his scanty collection. "I'm hungry," he said. "While we're having lunch we can consider the past and the future."

As we were leaving the room, McBeath entered and handed Moran a couple of reports. They came from the Medical Examiner's office, and said in technical language what we already knew—that Mrs. Anceney had been killed by the severance of the jugular vein, and Sutton by a single bullet that penetrated the heart. Death in both cases was instantaneous. One detail added the finishing touch to Kane's theory of Sutton's death. The path of the bullet was slightly downward, as it would have been had he been shot by someone standing on the ledge.

With parting instructions to McBeath to keep all journalists out of the house, we made our escape by the back door. Kane and Moran insisted on eating at a quick lunch place, to my disgust. Both devoured their food with gusto, and refused to talk until they had eaten the last scrap of huge slices of pie.

"Nothing gives me as good an appetite as a murder," Kane remarked with the air of a ghoul. "Now I'll have another cup of coffee, and we can converse peacefully. I propose that Underwood, being a lawyer, should review the case for us, Moran. It's a good idea to get the bare facts straight before we go any further."

Moran agreed to the proposal, and I did my best to give them a clear and brief statement of the case as I saw it.

Sutton was murdered at eleven o'clock by one of the people who had been in the house during the evening. The murderer could have got onto the ledge by the windows of any room except those which opened on the front. He may have gone through Sutton's bedroom which was unoccupied. At any rate he made his way by the ledge to the window of Sutton's sitting room. There he removed the loose leading and fired at his victim, killing him at once. He would have had time to make a show of having been in his own room, if he were a member of the household, or, in Gilroy's case, to have made his way down half a flight of stairs, before being discovered.

At that time, according to the evidence given, James was in his room, as were Bert, Katharine and Mrs. Sutton in theirs. Gilroy, as I had said, was on the main staircase. There were, then, no alibis available for any of the people who might logically be suspected, but neither had we succeeded in proving that any one of them had given a false account of his or her movements.

As far as the second murder was concerned, it had taken place between five minutes of two and two o'clock, during the time when

McBeath had left his post to let Titterton in. The murderer had been watching McBeath's movements, and had probably been able to accomplish his purpose before Mrs. Anceney became aware of his presence. He had made his escape either before Titterton entered, or afterward when McBeath and the lawyer had run downstairs to tell Kane what had happened.

Of the five people in the house under our consideration, any one of whom might conceivably have been guilty, James, Bert, and Gilroy could offer no proof as to their whereabouts. The two women, Mrs. Sutton and Katharine, were at that time with Kane, Moran, and myself.

"That'll do for a basis," Kane said, when I had finished. "Now I want to cover ground that is a little less secure. I think you'll both agree with me, though, that both murders were planned. No one would have taken a gun, and, knowing about the opening in the window, gone out on the ledge without definite premeditation. The same thing is true of Mrs. Anceney's death, too, although that plan must have been made in a shorter time. The murderer had to keep track of McBeath in order to get at her."

"Sure. That's all right," Moran said impatiently. "Anyone could see that, but where does it get you?"

"Just this far," Kane replied slowly. "It means we have to deal with a high grade of cunning. Both of those affairs were pretty well managed, you know. Another thing—both were carried through in cold blood. The person we're looking for wasn't swept away by impulse."

He paused and looked sharply at Moran and me. "Before I go on," he said, "I want to be sure that you agree with me that we are looking for one person. I base my opinion on the fact that the two crimes are logically connected; in the first, the murderer intended to have the blame fall on Mrs. Anceney. Having failed in that, and believing that he would be exposed as soon as she made her statement, he killed her, simulating suicide. You see, in both crimes he arranged not only to avoid detection, but also to provide an obvious solution for us."

Seeing that we followed him, he went on, "If you agree with me there, the next question is, what was his motive, not for killing Mrs. Anceney—we've made a good guess at that—but for killing Sutton? You understand, I'm not speaking of the motive that any one person may have had, but of the motives inherent in the situation. As far as I can see there are three. In the first place, Sutton was a very rich man. Someone who stood to benefit by his death may very possibly have killed him. In the second place, he was married, and was nevertheless carrying on an affair with another woman. It seems inevitable that jealousy should enter into it, perhaps in an obvious, perhaps in a more subtle way."

"Wait a minute now," Moran interposed. "I'd think that too if we didn't know that Mrs. Sutton couldn't have—"

"You don't understand, Moran," Kane interrupted him, "I'm taking this as an abstract situation, without regard to the peculiarities of this particular case. I think from that point of view I'm justified in saying what I have. Take those two things, then, money and jealousy. There's something else we must take into consideration—the fact that Sutton was a brutal man, who wouldn't have hesitated to override anyone in his way. He may have used his power unwisely, that is, until the worm turned."

Kane's head was bent over the table, and he spoke as though he were talking to himself rather than to us.

"At any rate," he went on, "you see we have to look to Sutton's murder for the motive, whatever it is. On the other hand, if the murderer has left clues behind him, we must look for them in the case of Mrs. Anceney. There was a larger element of chance in that."

"I see what you mean," Moran agreed. "But I think we have one definite lead. I want to follow that, and find out about motives later."

"I'd like to do that too, if it were possible," Kane replied, "but we've tried to walk straight forward once, and tripped. Now I want to find some other way. And I believe we'll find that way by studying the whole situation."

"Between Sutton and Mrs. Anceney?"

"That of course, but more than that. I wonder what Katharine meant by saying that they all hated Sutton. You see there's Mrs. Sutton, the injured party, so to speak. I can't quite make her out, except that she sticks by Bert, and he by her; then Katharine who always sided with her father, and has no particular feeling for the rest of the family; and James who cares for no one but himself; and Gilroy who must fit in somewhere. Over the whole thing there's the shadow of Sutton. I've got to know more about him, and more about Mrs. Anceney. She was a clever woman, who had her reasons for doing as she did. Why did she ever take up with Sutton? Why did she lead him on as she must have? Why did she carry with her this slip of paper?"

With an abrupt shift from the abstract to the concrete, he flipped across the table the torn sheet on which the numbers were written.

"That brings me down to earth," he said briskly. "Well, Moran, what have you to suggest?"

"Let's get back to where Mr. Underwood left off," the sergeant replied. "There's something nobody's paid much attention to. We said in the beginning there were five people we could suspect, Katharine, Mrs. Sutton, James, Bert, and Gilroy. We know Katharine and Mrs. Sutton were with us when Mrs. Anceney was killed, and that brings it down to three. Now let's go on from there. You found that rag, and we all agreed the murderer would come and get it. Gilroy came, and we'd have had him then and there if it hadn't been for Katharine. What are we going to do about him now? We can't let him slip through our fingers."

"He won't do that, Moran," Kane said. "He's an ugly customer and tricky. Luck was on his side for once, but it won't be always. He's a friend of James's as I remember, and we may be able to get at him through James. Meantime I want to repeat what I said last night. This isn't a simple business at all. We aren't going to get to the bottom of it right away. Until we find out all about it, we won't get to the bottom of it at all. We've got to move very slowly. The person who was cruel enough and clever enough to commit these murders isn't going to stop at anything to keep us from finding out who's guilty."

He got up from the table, and Moran and I followed his example. As we were going out the door, he said curtly, "Let things go their own way, and keep your eyes open. I'll take charge of Gilroy."

CHAPTER 11

Immediately after lunch I read Sutton's will to his family. There was nothing in this commonplace document to indicate that one member of his family would benefit more immediately by his death than another. The bequests were exactly what one might have expected. He left his whole fortune, which was somewhat smaller than it was supposed to be, in trust. I was named an executor, together with the Boston City Trust Company. A half of his money went to Mrs. Sutton. On her death the greater part of her portion descended to Katharine, the rest to James. Each of the children was to receive the income from a quarter of the total at once. Neither could touch the principal.

Outside his immediate family, I was the only person mentioned. There was a bequest to me of ten thousand dollars, made, I presume, because I had consented to become an executor.

The contents of the will were of course known to me before they were made public. Kane did not lose the opportunity of declaring to Moran, after I had explained this to him, that I belonged among the suspects for I certainly had a motive and an opportunity to commit the first crime, if not the second.

Kane had nothing for me to do, and so I returned to my office, but my state of mind was such that although I busied myself there I could do little justice to my own affairs. By the middle of the afternoon I had almost resigned myself to my stupid lot when my office boy announced that Moran was waiting to see me. I shoved my papers whole-heartedly into a drawer and sat up with new interest.

Moran nodded to me complacently, and flicked a half inch of cigar ash into my pen tray before he spoke.

"Well," he said, dropping heavily into the chair I pointed out to him, "I came around to see if you can give me any dope on a new development.

"You remember that jade whatcha-may-call-it Sutton gave to Mrs. Anceney at the dinner party?" he continued.

"Yes, it was a carved pendant," I said. "But she didn't take it, you know."

Moran dismissed my objection impatiently. "Well, however that may be, it's aside from the point. I understand, anyhow, that it was worth lots of coin. That right?"

"Undoubtedly. It would probably take five figures to cover what Sutton must have paid for it."

"H'mm." He rotated his cigar between his teeth. "Very interesting. Fact is, it's vamoosed."

"What?"

"It's gone—disappeared," he explained. "Kane found that out just now. He asked the family—nobody knew a thing. Hadn't even thought about it, I guess. So we searched the likeliest places. Of course, we knew it hadn't been on either of the two bodies, or it would have turned up before. We went through Sutton's room first, and then through the room Mrs. Anceney was killed in. Mrs. Sutton looked in the safe they have. No soap."

I was silent, trying to puzzle out the import of what Moran was telling me.

"I had an idea," Moran continued, "that you might remember seeing that piece of jade later on in the evening."

I shook my head. "No, the one and only time I saw it was when Sutton took it out at the dinner table. After that he put it back in his pocket."

"You didn't see it lying around somewhere in Sutton's sitting room?"

"I don't remember seeing it," I said. "I don't say it wasn't there, but I didn't notice it."

Moran looked disappointed. "Well, I didn't expect you would, but I thought I'd ask anyhow."

"Sorry to be of no help," I said. "It looks to me as if the disappearance of this jade puts a new complexion on the whole affair."

"Seems so," Moran agreed. "At any rate, we've now got a definite motive for Sutton's murder."

"Theft, you mean?"

"Sure. If anything worth as much as that is missing after a murder, you can be pretty sure it explains the whole business. Our hunch is to look for a fellow who needed money."

"What does Kane say?" I asked.

"Damn little," Moran replied shortly. "But he's pulling a long face."

"I should think it would interfere with some of the ideas he's been holding up to this time," I suggested.

"That's the trouble. It does," answered Moran rather pleasantly. "He doesn't half like it."

"Where is he now?"

"At Sutton's. You'd better come over there." Moran got up abruptly and clapped his hat on his head. "Something's bound to turn up, no telling when. If Kane'd let me have my own way I'd find that jade soon enough, but he says I've got to look for it so's nobody'll know I'm looking. How can I help it when the whole damn family sticks around?"

I had work to do at the Sutton house at any rate, and I was glad enough of an excuse to be there. I accepted Moran's suggestion, and we walked over to Quincy Street together. I found Kane alone in the upstairs sitting room, pacing slowly up and down, and leaving a trail of cigarette ashes to mark his progress. He greeted Moran and me with a nod.

Moran looked at him half defiantly. "I was thinking of looking for that jade," he said.

Kane turned on him sharply. "Don't be a fool, Moran. Do you want to raise a hornet's nest? We've got to work quietly. You can't do it now. Every single one of them is here."

Moran accepted the rebuke in sulky silence and took himself off.

"Nothing's happened, then?" I ventured.

"Nothing you don't know," Kane answered.

I explained to him that I had to examine some papers of Sutton's, but he looked at me so absentmindedly that I could not tell whether he had heard or not.

"This complicates the whole affair, you know," he said after a long pause.

"The pendant?"

"Yes." He took a long, slow drag on his cigarette. "When a thing like that disappears at the time of a murder there are certain conclusions to be drawn, and certain dangers to be avoided. That's why I warned Moran to go slow. This business is too important to be bungled. I'd forgotten the story about the jade till now," he continued slowly. "It did bring Sutton bad luck, didn't it?"

He took up his restless march again, and since his silence did not invite interruption, I settled down to work at the desk.

I had been there perhaps an hour, and had become thoroughly absorbed in my task, when I was startled, on looking up, to see that Bert had entered the room. For all I knew, he might have been watching us for quite a while. At any rate, there he was, perched on the arm of a chair, a keen observer of what we were doing. When he realized that I had at last become aware of his presence, he chuckled as though he had just got off a successful joke.

"You didn't hear me when I came in," he said, "did you?" My denial increased his pleasure.

Kane looked at him with tolerant amusement. "You certainly can move quietly," he said.

Bert's self-satisfaction increased visibly. He seemed to have lost his fear of us. I suppose that he had become so accustomed to seeing us around the house that he accepted us as part of the scheme of things. At any rate, curiosity had overcome his apprehensions as his next remark showed. "I want to know," he said, in an important manner, "if you have any idea who killed Fred?"

Kane humored him. "We'd like to say we had," he replied. "And of course any report we had we'd make to you, since you are really the head of the family now. I'm sorry to say we don't know yet. You must excuse us, for this is a very mystifying case."

Bert was content with the answer. He and Kane continued to chat together amicably, while I went on with my work, but I was doomed to further disturbance, and this time James was the offender. His manner was self-assured as usual, and nettled me a good deal. With a glance at Kane and Bert, he said to me, "I should like to speak to you alone."

I was in no mood to grant his request. "I doubt if your uncle and Mr. Kane will bother to listen to what you have to say," I replied sharply. "I'm afraid you'll have to talk to me here or not at all. I am very busy."

My refusal to comply with his request made him slightly uneasy. For the first time I noticed on his face signs of experience prematurely gained. He belonged to that detestable type, the old young man.

He shot a sharp look at Kane and Bert, and seemed satisfied that they were paying no attention to us; then he turned back to me.

"I want to draw on my share of the estate for a sum of money," he said curtly, as though his desires overruled all other considerations.

"For how much?" I asked without comment.

"Forty thousand dollars," he replied.

I looked at him in utter amazement. "My dear young man," I said, "you were present at the reading of your father's will. As you know, the money he left to you is in trust. You cannot touch one cent of the principal, and the amount you mention is something more than your income for a year. Neither I nor anyone else has the power to give you any such lump sum. The idea is absurd."

There was no mistaking his anger and surprise. "Do you mean to say that I cannot have money that is my own, now that my father is dead?" he cried.

"You will get your income at stated times, and nothing more."

"In other words you, instead of my father, will give me an allowance?" he exclaimed in amazement.

"If you choose to put it that way."

At that, his indignation completely upset him. "Let me tell you one thing, Mr. Underwood," he said, leaning toward me with a look of ugly determination. "I will not be treated like a child, and I intend to have that money. I've got to have it. If you won't give it to me willingly, I'll take steps to make you."

"Do whatever you like," I replied with equal force. "But let me give you a little advice. You will get nothing but trouble from trying to break your father's will."

He got up abruptly and without another word walked out of the room. If I had ever thought him emotionless, that idea was destroyed forever.

I was aroused from my own angry meditations by Bert's piping voice. "He didn't get it out of you, did he?" He laughed maliciously. "I thought he wouldn't. He didn't get it out of his father either."

CHAPTER 12

At Bert's announcement, Kane made a sudden movement, but the face he turned to Bert showed only disinterest. "So James asked his father for money, did he?" His tone was as remote as if he had been talking about the weather.

"Oh, yes." Bert's voice held more than a note of exultation. He looked like a robin who had just pulled out of the ground a particularly pleasing worm. "They had quite a time about it; they certainly did. I don't know that I've ever seen Fred so mad. He got so mad he couldn't talk. He looked like he was going to have a fit." Bert considered the question thoughtfully. "No, I can't ever remember seeing Fred as mad as that, even at James."

Kane took up a little box that had been lying on the desk, and squinted at it. "When did all this happen?" he asked carelessly.

"It was last night. Just before dinner."

He looked quickly at Kane.

"How did you happen to know about that?"

"Oh, I heard. I was in my room," Bert answered, offhand.

"Where were they?"

"Down in Fred's sitting room."

Kane continued to toy with the box he had picked up. "And you could hear what they were saying?"

"Uh-huh."

"You must have pretty good ears. Your room is quite far down the hall. Weren't you nearer than that?"

"I don't know." Bert shifted uneasily, and his eyes avoided Kane's.

Kane hastened to reassure him. "It doesn't matter. I just wondered if you happened to walk down the hall."

"Well, I guess I did once," Bert admitted. "But I didn't let Fred know I was there. He'd be mad at me."

"What were they talking about?"

"Oh, they were fighting, I told you," he added petulantly. "Fred was telling James he'd never give him the money, and James said just what he did to you." Bert looked over at me sympathetically.

"And what was that?" Kane asked.

"That he'd get it somehow. He had to have it."

"I wonder what James wanted money for. He didn't happen to say, did he?"

"Yes, he did. He said he owed it to Gilroy."

Kane tossed his little box in the air and caught it again. "What did Sutton do when James said he had to have money?"

"He got up out of his chair and stood over James and he said, 'Do you mean to defy me?' Fred was very mad," Bert nodded his head slowly as if to confirm his recollections. "I didn't like it at all. I didn't think I'd better stay there any longer; so I went back to my room."

"I suppose nothing happened after that," Kane was tugging at the lobe of his ear. I knew enough of his habits by this time to realize that he was not as disinterested as he seemed.

Bert was annoyed by Kane's assumption that the story was ended. "A lot happened after that," he said indignantly. "You didn't give me a chance to tell you. I went back to my room, but Fred'd closed his door, and I couldn't hear a thing. So I went back again."

"Was he still quarreling with James?"

"I should say he was. He was furious. He wouldn't let James get a word in edgewise, just kept yelling at him." Bert became still more confidential. "But he wasn't still talking about money." The little man hugged himself in his excitement. "He was talking about Mrs. Ance-ney, and saying that James had better be more polite to her than he had been, or he'd know the reason why. Fred said he wouldn't have him or anyone else treat her the way James did. He said anyone who insulted her insulted him, and he wouldn't stand for it. Fred was in an awful state. Why, he came bursting out of that room and slammed the door behind him. But he was so mad he didn't see me at all. His face was all red, and his eyes looked like they were going to pop."

"Was James as mad as his father?"

"I guess he was. But I don't know. I didn't see him."

Bert's dramatic sense had almost carried him away. He waved his arms around as he told his story, and glanced eagerly now at the one, now at the other of us to see if his tale were having its proper effect.

"Don't you want to hear about it?" he asked, like a child who has been trying in vain to amuse his elders.

"Why, of course we do," Kane assured him. "You are a very good story teller. What happened then?"

"Nothing much," Bert replied in an anticlimactic fashion. "I waited around, but I couldn't hear anything unless I put my ear right close to the door. Then I heard James moving around. I wanted to see him come out, but he didn't. I'd have waited longer, but I had to get dressed for dinner."

"There's only one thing I don't understand," said Kane. "You say he was moving around. What do you suppose he was doing? Why didn't he go back to his own room after his father left him?"

"I don't know," Bert said, his interest in the subject having apparently waned. "He was keeping pretty quiet, I know that. I could hardly hear a thing. He crossed the room once or twice, and pulled out a drawer and closed it. I guess that's all. I thought it was funny myself that he stayed in there so long."

"James and his father didn't get on very well, did they?"

"Oh, my, no! They couldn't stand each other."

Bert's volatile gaze shifted about the room. Obviously he had come to the end of his conversation, and he was restless to be on to some other place. He began picking nervously at the arm of the chair on which he was seated; then suddenly he bounced to his feet.

"Good-bye," he said, and to Kane, "You'll be sure to tell me anything you find out, won't you? I'll be glad to help you any time I can, and you can depend on me."

He strutted away, playing the role of the head of the house. I looked after him in utter stupefaction. Didn't he know what he had been saying? He had given evidence against his own nephew.

After Bert had left the room, Kane walked over to the window and stared out of it as if he expected to find some answer to the questions which beset him floating in the empty air. As for me, every new development so far had increased my bewilderment. I tried vainly to puzzle out the significance of Bert's casual disclosures, and to determine their importance.

Kane interrupted my thoughts by turning to the telephone. He asked for Moran, and when he had got through to the sergeant told him to come at once to the Sutton house.

"Yes," he said, apparently in answer to a query of Moran's. "New lead, I think. I'll tell you about it when you get here."

Ten minutes later Moran joined us. "What's up?" he asked eagerly.

"Not so fast," Kane cautioned him. "Wait a minute and I'll explain things."

He settled himself in an easy chair, and in his quick, accurate fashion described Bert's joining us, James's request for money and my refusal, and Bert's comments on his nephew. Then he launched into the story Bert had told of James's interview with Sutton. When he had finished, Moran looked at him thoughtfully.

"Let me be sure I've got this straight," he said "Bert hears James quarreling with Sutton yesterday evening. James wants money, and his father won't give it to him. They're both pretty mad, and James says he'll get it anyhow. Bert's scared for fear they'll catch him listening in, so he gets out, but he's too curious to stay away, and comes back to listen again. Sutton's giving it to James hot and heavy. After he's finished he bursts out of the room, leaving James behind. Is that right?"

Kane nodded.

"Bert didn't have anything more to say after that?"

Kane gave him a significant glance. "Just one more thing," he replied quietly. "Bert said that James stayed in the sitting room alone. Bert couldn't see him or tell what he was doing, except that he opened and shut a drawer."

Moran was puzzled for a moment, and then gave a loud whistle of astonishment.

Kane did not seem to think it was necessary to make further explanations. "Don't I remember," he asked, "that James told us where his father kept an automatic?"

I remembered that in our first talk with James he had betrayed his knowledge of its whereabouts.

Moran corroborated my opinion. "Sure," he said. "That's right. And what about this money business? Does that seem to you to connect up with anything?"

"You mean the jade?" Kane returned. "If that's true we'll soon know about it. Now I propose we go and talk to him. I'd like to know what he has to say for himself."

Kane rose, and led the way down the hall. As we entered James's room, its owner cast a surly look at me. Obviously he thought that I had set Kane on his trail, and that this interview was a consequence of his conversation with me—it was, of course, although not as directly as he suspected. He did not seem to feel the necessity of speaking to us, or of attempting any semblance of cordiality.

"Sorry to bother you," Kane said by way of introduction, "but we need some information you can probably give us."

"Well?" James's attitude was certainly not promising.

"I suppose you know from your mother," Kane continued slowly, "that so far we haven't been able to find the jade pendant your father wanted to give to Mrs. Anceney. Now from all we can discover he had it at the time of his death. Did you notice it anywhere in his sitting room when you entered after the firing of the shot?"

"I wasn't looking for jewelry at the time." James's retort was so nearly insulting that I marveled at Kane's forbearance. He, however, refused to be disturbed.

"I understand then," he went on, "that you didn't see it. Have you any idea what could have become of it since then?"

"No. Is there any reason why I should have?"

Kane looked disappointed. "I suppose you can't help us." He paused. "By the way, Mr. Sutton, when did you last see your father alone?"

James did not answer at once. His face grew a shade paler, although his assurance did not fail him. "Just before dinner last evening," he replied finally.

"He didn't say anything to you that would indicate that he was unusually disturbed?"

"Nothing."

Instead of pressing the point, Kane took up another topic.

"You know," he said, as though he were trying to satisfy himself, "I don't believe we know all that you can tell us about your father's devotion to Mrs. Anceney. Are you quite sure that it didn't have a greater effect on your mother than you suggested before?"

"I can't tell you any more than I have," he replied with an unpleasant, worldly wise smile. "I should say the chances were she wasn't pleased by it. Why don't you consult my uncle? He is the only one of us she confides in."

Kane considered the suggestion. "It might be a good idea to talk to him, but he's a little difficult to deal with."

James laughed. "My father thought so," he said. "He tried to put the old fool in a sanatorium where he belongs, but my mother wouldn't have it."

"I see." Kane straightened himself in his chair, and there was a distinct change in his manner as he did so. "I asked you a few minutes ago, as you may remember, whether your father seemed disturbed during your last conversation with him, and you replied that he did not. There's just one other thing I want to ask you. What did you and your father talk about when you last saw him?"

"Oh, nothing much," James answered quickly.

"You didn't talk to him then about the money you owe Mr. Gilroy?"

There was a long pause. James stared at Kane as though he were trying to find out how much the detective knew.

"I said something about it," he admitted finally.

"I think you told us before," Kane went on, "that your father objected to Gilroy on the grounds that he made you spend too much money. And yet you say he wasn't disturbed when you told him about your debts?"

James made no reply.

"I think I've been beating around the bush long enough," Kane said sternly. "Suppose I tell you we already know that you and your father quarreled on that occasion. It is really only as a matter of form that I ask you whether or not it is true. Is it?"

James's face was white, but this time he was wise enough to answer. "Yes," he said truculently.

"You talked about nothing but money?"

"No."

"What did you do after your father left the sitting room?"

James's glance wavered. "What do you mean?" he asked warily. "He didn't leave the room. I left when I couldn't stand him any longer."

"I see," Kane murmured. "In the course of that conversation you both used rather strong language, didn't you?"

"No!" James looked desperate, in spite of his denial.

"You didn't tell your father that if he didn't give you the money, you'd get it somehow?"

James held himself rigid as if he were afraid to move. Once he moistened his lips as if he were about to speak but he made no answer.

Kane continued to press his advantage. "You see, Mr. Sutton, we knew before we came here that you and your father did not get along together. We also knew that you had quarreled with him on the evening of his death, and that you more or less explicitly threatened him. I want you to remember that you may do yourself a great injury by denying the truth. When I asked you what you did after your father left the room, you replied that you left before he did. We have reason to believe that that is not so. We have been told, too, that your father was angry with you not only on account of your demand for money but also because of your insulting rudeness to Mrs. Anceney. Have you anything further to say on either subject?

James made an effort to pull himself together. He seemed to be considering his words carefully, and spoke with a calculated emphasis. "As I told you, I went back to my own room, leaving my father in his. As far as I can remember, Mrs. Anceney's name was not mentioned."

"Can you offer any proof of your statements?"

James thought for a moment, but finally shook his head.

"Didn't you tell us, the first time we questioned you, where your father kept his gun?" Kane's voice was very soft.

James's face was entirely expressionless. "Why, yes," he said. "In the drawer of his desk."

"Are you quite sure," Kane went on, "that you didn't stay in his room alone, and open and shut a drawer?"

James leaped from the chair in which he had been sitting. "So that's what you've been trying to make me say?" He was choking with either anger or fear. "Well, you can't get me that way. Do you think

I'm such a fool! I didn't, I tell you. Get out! Try and see if you can get anything against me! Get out!"

"Sit down, Mr. Sutton," Kane said sternly. "I'm giving you your last chance. Did you or didn't you stay in your father's room alone?"

Again the younger man made an effort to collect himself. "No, I did not," he said defiantly.

CHAPTER 13

The following morning Kane called me. "Underwood?" His voice came sharp and impatient over the telephone. "Get over here right away, will you? Moran's got something up his sleeve."

He did not even wait for my assent, and I had no opportunity to ask him what it was all about. As quickly as I could I made my way across the Common and along the streets, now more than familiar to me, that led to Sutton's house.

I found Kane upstairs as usual, and Moran, bursting with excitement, joined us immediately. Obviously he had news, but this was his moment, and apparently Kane was not the only one who disliked being hurried. Moran sat down and looked sharply at us both.

"You've found it, haven't you?" There was an anxious look on Kane's face.

"Yes," Moran said complacently. "I've found the jade. I'd have found it long ago if you'd let me have my own way. I did some looking last night after we talked to James, and this morning I found it."

"Where?"

"It was rather unexpected to find it where I did. I warn you, it's going to shock you both."

Kane made no comment but waited for him to continue.

"I noticed that there was a secret drawer in a certain desk. They're simple to open, you know, once you've spotted them. Well, I did open it, and there was the jade right on top."

"But whose desk?"

Moran paused a moment, and then said laconically, with an air of believe-it-or-not, "The daughter's!"

"Not Katharine Sutton's!" I exclaimed.

Moran's composure was not to be disturbed. "Certainly. The desk in her bedroom. If you want proof, I'll show it to you. I left it there and shut the drawer."

I looked quickly at Kane and was relieved to note that for once I was not alone in my astonishment. For one moment the surprise on his face was not to be disguised. Although he came to himself almost instantly and turned away from us to another part of the room, Moran too had seen his expression.

"Well, Kane," said that person, in a conciliatory tone, "knowing what the possession of that jade implies, I was damned well astounded myself. I really was," he added slowly, with what seemed a sincere effort to be just. "And then I said to myself—why not? Why shouldn't she be considered?" He turned on me almost hostilely, "Don't say anything until I've finished." I was obscurely irritated at this injunction, inasmuch as I had no intention of opening my mouth. Nor had Kane, it seemed. He was standing quietly at the window, his hands in his pockets, with such a look of deep reflection on his face as to make me doubt that he heard Moran at all. I saw him frown once, in the manner of a man being forced into accepting the incredible.

"After all," Moran was continuing, "Katharine had as good an opportunity to kill her father as anyone else had. From what we know, Sutton went upstairs with the piece of jade in his pocket a little after ten. A few minutes later Katharine makes some excuse and follows him up. She had time enough to plan and execute the crime. She knew about the ledge, of course. The windows of her room open on it, unless I'm much mistaken. Isn't that right, Kane?" he asked pointedly.

"Quite," Kane answered without hesitation from his post by the window. But Moran was not satisfied.

"And you'll admit, won't you," he pursued, "that she had a perfectly good chance to kill Sutton?"

"None better," came the serene reply. "The actual physical opportunity was as great for her as for anyone else."

This lack of opposition acted as a spur to Moran's eloquence. "And you can't say," he went on, "that theft is too ignoble a motive to inspire the murder of one's own father. Take that last Springfield case—where the girl stabbed her mother. There's an instance."

"And there are others," Kane murmured.

"In this case," Moran continued, unheeding, "the object of the theft was worth a small fortune. There's more than one person in this world who would do murder without compunction for that. So," he concluded firmly, "in view of the points I've just brought up, I'm not so unwilling now to accept Katharine's guilt as I was when I first discovered the jade in her possession. There are the plain facts right before you. You've got to consider them pretty damned seriously, haven't you? Wouldn't you say so, Kane?" he insisted.

Kane turned slowly away from the window. The puzzled expression had left his face. He walked over until he stood directly in front of Moran's chair.

"Yes," he said, with apparent gravity, "the facts *should* be considered seriously, and," he added lightly, as he swung on his heel and turned a deliberate back on us, "with becoming caution."

I thought he was about to supplement this latter statement when he suddenly faced us again, and smilingly addressed himself to Moran. Had it not been for that smile I might have been able to believe his words were as earnest as they sounded.

"Moran," he said, "possibly my wits are becoming dulled by this constant pursuit of the elusive. Sometimes I boggle at points which, to a quicker man, might not even seem difficult. Your assumption, excellent as it may be, that Katharine, led on by an insatiable desire for the jade pendant, shot Sutton, leaves me with one question in my mind which I fail utterly to answer. So I'll propose it to you, in the hope that you can clear up the mystery. How could Katharine have killed Mrs. Anceney? You remember where she was when McBeath was answering the door-bell."

Moran was, for a moment, frankly disconcerted. Then he gave an impatient sniff. "I'd just like to remind you, Kane," he said somewhat pettishly, "that it was your idea, and not mine, that the same person committed both murders. Under the circumstances, I don't think it's at all necessary to hold to that theory."

"Well," Kane replied gravely, "there our paths divide. I'm too set in my ways to give up the idea that one person is responsible for both crimes."

"I think that theory is shutting your mind to possibilities," Moran said firmly.

"Perhaps."

"Another point," Moran began, "I think we've relied entirely too much on hearsay regarding the relation between Katharine and her father. How do we know she was so crazy about him? She's acted the part, I admit, but she's clever enough to put all that on if she wanted to, isn't she?"

"Undoubtedly," Kane agreed.

"Then why let it influence us? This undying affection for her father's memory is all very pretty, but after all it's our business to be hard-boiled. Personally, I'm not deceived by appearances, and that's all we've got to go on. I'm ready to believe that Katharine's whole attitude has been a pretense."

"Just a minute, Moran." Kane spoke very quietly, but there was command in his voice. "You're going pretty fast, you know. I'm sorry to say this, but I think you're too ready to believe a lot of things for which you have no foundation. I admit there's a big danger in believing everything you see, but to my mind there's just as great a one in believing nothing. When I confess that I *do* believe in Katharine's love for Sutton, you'll say that I'm taking too much for granted. However, we have evidence and concrete facts to prove the reality of her affection. for him. As far as I'm concerned, I think that Katharine cared far more for her father than most daughters ever could."

Moran set his mouth stubbornly. "What you say is all right, but I'm talking about facts too. I mean that Katharine Sutton has, in her possession at this moment, the piece of jade that disappeared on the night of the murders. If you can get around that, I'll be willing and ready to withdraw every statement I've made."

Kane looked at him quietly for a moment, and seemed to be considering the problem. Then he asked, "Where was Katharine when you were searching her room?"

"Downstairs. You told me to work on the quiet."

"She doesn't know, then, that you've been in her room?"

"No."

"Now describe to me as carefully as you can the exact place where the jade is."

"Why don't you let me show it to you?"

"Because I'd rather let Katharine show it to me," Kane replied calmly.

Moran made a gesture of bewilderment and started to ask something, but Kane cut him short and repeated his question. Thereupon Moran described the position of the secret drawer in Katharine's desk, and explained that he had opened it with a penknife. The jade was lying right on top, he added.

"Now let's find Katharine and we'll go over the room," Kane said when Moran had finished speaking. "This is another instance," he went on, "in which I prefer to have you believe the evidence of your own eyes rather than what I can tell you. And, by the way, I wish you'd both leave the conduct of this affair entirely in my hands. You'll understand my reasons later on."

He walked toward the door and I went with him, a little hesitantly. Moran, a somewhat doubting Thomas, to judge by his expression, dogged our heels as we went down the hall. I knew we were both wondering what on earth Kane was trying to prove. Wouldn't the jade be there after all when we came to search the desk? That seemed a bit fantastic. Moran's eyesight at least was beyond reproach. But that was the only explanation I could summon at the moment.

We were descending the stairs as these thoughts went through my mind, and when we had reached the lower floor, Kane went at once to the library where we found Katharine reading a book which she put aside as we came in. I looked at her keenly but I could detect in the faint smile with which she acknowledged our presence no sign of the surprise or alarm which I had half expected. Her eyes were swollen and there were deep circles under them, but she was obviously making every effort to control herself. Yet, with a kind of horror, I realized that Moran might be right. Both he and Kane had been looking for the person, man or woman, who had the jade pendant, and Moran was still unshaken in his statement that she had it.

Kane sat down on the edge of a couch and faced the girl.

"Miss Sutton," he began, "as you know, a valuable jade pendant disappeared on the night of your father's death. Now, it's been necessary for us to take certain steps in an effort to recover it, not only because of its intrinsic value but because it is thought to have some connection with the crimes that were committed that night."

Katharine nodded gravely, and kept her eyes fixed on Kane as he spoke. Perhaps she failed to realize how sharply the three of us were searching her face for telltale evidences of guilt. At any rate, whatever her state of mind, it could not be denied that she had herself well in hand, for she seemed unconscious of our scrutiny. She pushed her book a little farther away from her, however, and began to finger the pages, as though Kane's seriousness had made her a little nervous.

"You realize, don't you, that it is very important for us to find it? that we must make every effort to do so?"

"Yes, of course." She spoke rather breathlessly. "But—" Whatever she was going to say, her words trailed off into silence.

"As a matter of routine," Kane went on, "we've gone carefully over every room in the house. We have just been through your bedroom." Kane made what seemed to be a conscious pause at this point. The girl did not shift her eyes, but her face had grown a little paler. Whether she were guilty or innocent, she must have realized how closely everything that had to do with the Sutton family was being observed. Still she showed no fear.

"Yes?" she questioned, as if encouraging him to continue.

"Your desk has a secret drawer in it, we find. I'm afraid we'll have to ask you to open it for us."

The words I had been waiting for seemed to have little effect on her. She still fumbled at her book. I waited anxiously for her to speak, but instead she frowned and looked toward the window. It was the first time she had taken her eyes from Kane's face.

Slight as the indications were, they were enough to give Moran an air of triumph and to make Kane's expression still more anxious. I held my breath for a long moment, until she finally said, as if in explanation of her hesitation, "I was just wondering where the key is. I haven't used it for so long I'm not sure I can find it right away."

Moran uttered an inarticulate noise. I was forced to agree with him that the girl was putting us off.

"You see I don't keep anything of value in it," she went on. "Father had a safe put in for the silver and our jewelry." She paused again, as though she were thinking of something more to say.

"I may have to keep you waiting while I look for the key," she glanced at Kane and from him to Moran. She must have had a sudden feeling that the police sergeant was her enemy, for her face contracted a little, and she looked away from him.

Kane's attitude remained completely casual. "We understand that, of course. As a matter of fact," he continued carelessly, "it's quite all right if you don't want to look for it now. We can do it to-morrow."

I heard Moran make an impatient movement and understood what he was thinking. Didn't Kane realize he was giving her an opportunity to escape? She could get rid of the jade a thousand times over by tomorrow. Of course, now that she knew how important the police considered it, she could accept the delay, wait till we had gone, take the jade out of the drawer, and dispose of it forever. Whatever Kane thought he was doing, he was playing the fool with his chances of success. And if I was not mistaken he would get the fool's reward.

"It's just that I don't want to keep you waiting," she repeated. Her voice was apologetic.

"We have lots of time. You needn't think of that," Kane replied cheerfully. "But we don't want to bother you any more than we have to. We'll put it off until to-morrow. In the meantime, you can be thinking where the key is."

At this my amazement was redoubled. Kane was not only giving her a chance to escape. He was forcing it upon her. My calculations were cut short by Katharine's unexpected reply.

"It's silly of me not to remember. Of course I can think of three or four places where the key might be. I might just as well look for it now. I'd really rather. Will you come with me?"

She got up and led the way to the door. As Kane also rose, he smiled at Moran and me. In a somewhat dazed condition we followed them upstairs and into Katharine's room. I was beginning to understand faintly Kane's object, but one glance at Moran's face told me that if not completely mystified, he was still stubborn.

When we reached her room, she turned to Kane. "That's the desk you mean, isn't it?" She pointed to one standing in a corner.

"That's it." Kane's eyes wandered over it.

She sat down in the chair before it, and fumbled in the pigeon holes, pulling out letters and papers, and piling them in front of her. Finally an idea seemed to occur to her, and she pulled at two pieces of carving, which came free in her hands. They slipped out, and showed two narrow drawers behind them.

"These aren't the drawers you mean, are they?" I thought there was a shade of propitiation in the way she looked at us.

"No, they're not." Moran's voice was surly. "It's the one in the center."

Katharine nodded uncertainly. "That's the one that has a key."

She crossed the room to her dressing table. Moran's gimlet eyes followed her every movement. He was uneasy and distrustful:

On the table there was a leather box, the contents of which she dumped out. She tossed them over without success, and then turned her attention to the drawer. She looked closely through its contents. As she turned them about, I heard a faint metallic ring.

"There it is," she said.

Without a word, Kane held out his hand, and she gave him a small metal rod.

I turned to Moran. He was no longer sneering, nor did he look very stubborn. But he was puzzled, perhaps as I was, as to what would happen next. Then I looked at the girl. She was white, and she leaned back against the wall as though she needed its support. Still she showed no signs of regretting her action, and made no effort to stop Kane in his search.

I stood by Kane's side as he fitted the rod into a hole cleverly concealed by a wooden panel in the upper central part of the desk. There it seemed to stick. He turned to the girl, who stood on his other side.

"Miss Sutton, will you get me a nail file, please?"

As she crossed to the other side of the room, and was in the very act of picking up a file from the dressing table, Kane suddenly pushed the rod, pulled out the drawer, and, so swiftly that I could see little more than a flash of green, took something out and concealed it in the palm of his hand.

When Katharine returned, he said quietly, "Sorry to have bothered you. It came open finally."

While the girl watched him, he made a pretense of rummaging through the papers in the drawer with his free hand. When she turned away, he slipped the jade back into the drawer, closed and locked it, and, smiling, handed her the rod.

"That's all," he said, "and thank you."

It had been a neat performance. Without frightening her, Kane had succeeded in demonstrating the truth of the situation to us both.

When we were back in what we called our own room again, Moran said with heavy frankness, "Well, you're right again, Kane. I guess I got your point this time. The girl didn't even know the jade was there."

"She couldn't have had an idea it was," Kane agreed, a little wearily, I thought. "It gave me a bad start when you told me you'd found it in her desk. The only explanation I could possibly find was that someone else had put it there. As you must have noticed I gave her a perfectly good chance to avoid opening the desk to-day. When she rejected that, I was absolutely certain she knew nothing about the matter. No, the jade was planted in her room, for a motive which I think I can explain."

"But—who?" I exclaimed.

"Do you know who put it there?" Moran flung an excited question at Kane.

Kane examined the burning end of his cigarette with half-closed eyes. "Yes," he said. "I'll tell you what I know."

CHAPTER 14

"This is going to be a somewhat extended explanation," Kane continued, "so make yourselves comfortable. I appreciate the fact that you want to hear nothing more or less than the name of the person who deliberately planted the jade pendant in Katharine Sutton's desk. Well, I can tell you that, but not, however, until I've gone into certain other matters which may seem to you to be digressions from the main point. But they're not very far removed, as you'll soon see; so have patience."

Moran and I settled ourselves into attitudes which suggested more repose than we felt, and Kane continued.

"You remember the slip of paper with the figures on it which we found in the magazine Mrs. Anceney was reading before her death?"

We nodded.

"Well, it occurred to me that those numerals might be the combination for opening a safe. Yesterday afternoon, when we were looking for the pendant, Mrs. Sutton opened a safe, which, she said, was the only one they have in the house. I made very certain that the combination on the paper didn't fit that. So, I thought to myself, there must be another one somewhere. I took a look around, particularly in this room." Here Kane raised his hand and pointed to a large picture hanging on the wall opposite. "Behind that picture I found a small wall safe. Presumably, Mrs. Sutton didn't know of its existence. At any rate, my combination opened it. I think I half expected to find the jade, but it wasn't there. There was nothing in the safe but these interesting documents."

Kane drew a leather wallet from his pocket. He unfolded it and took out a sheet of paper to which were clipped two canceled checks. He gave this to Moran, who examined it with painstaking interest before handing it over to me. I looked first at the two checks which carried dates of about four months back, and were signed with the name of Frederick Sutton. They were made out to the order of cash for five thousand dollars each. Then I glanced at the sheet of paper, on which was written one sentence. "I hereby confess that the two checks attached to this paper were forged by me with Frederick Sutton's name." The signature was that of Frank Gilroy.

I returned the papers to Kane without a word, and he slipped them back into his wallet.

"You see," he said significantly, "Sutton had Gilroy just where he wanted him. The noose was around his neck. It must have given him some pleasure to tighten it now and again. How Gilroy must have wanted to get those papers back! I suppose, though, that Sutton might never have exposed him, as long as he continued on his good behavior. What was ten thousand dollars to him compared with the fun of playing cat to Gilroy's mouse!

"I imagine you're wondering at this point," Kane went on, "why Mrs. Anceney, of all people, should have had the combination of the safe. I wondered at that, too. Remember there was absolutely nothing in it except those papers which concern Gilroy alone. Why should she have had any earthly interest in them?

"The long and short of my speculations was that I decided I knew far too little about her. And she was worth knowing. So I went to Titterton, principally because I knew he had handled Mrs. Anceney's affairs for a number of years. He was a gold mine, once he had shed his verbosity, and he told me, not without a good deal of hesitation, something he had known for a long time. Underwood, have you ever happened to look up Mrs. Anceney in the Social Register?"

I said I had not.

"If you had you might have noticed her maiden name. It was Gilroy. Frank Gilroy is her brother.

"According to Titterton, Gilroy decamped from this part of the country after some minor scrape about fifteen years ago. A few years afterward he became embroiled in a scheme for floating fraudulent bank stock, and although Mrs. Anceney did what she could for him, he got a short prison term. Since then he's been in one second-rate confidence game after another, but he never was clever enough to make a go of any of them. So he called on his sister to pay the piper more than once, and she was glad to do it if it meant she could hush the affair up. But it was the last straw when she found out, about a year ago, that he was here in the city. Titterton says she was very much upset about it. He'd got himself attached in some capacity to Frederick Sutton with whom Mrs. Anceney was not acquainted at the time.

"That was all Titterton could tell me, but the rest is easy to follow. From the dates on the checks I should say that Sutton met Mrs. Anceney remarkably soon after the day when he forced Gilroy to confess his forgeries. I should make a shrewd guess that their meeting was not the happenstance it seemed to Sutton.

"Gilroy made a bad break when he used Sutton's name in vain. And it was a bad break for Mrs. Anceney, too. Money meant nothing to Sutton. She couldn't buy him off. I imagine she felt her small world crashing about her ears. So it was perfectly understandable that she should have used the only other weapon she had against a man like Sutton to stave off the catastrophe. She arranged to meet him and set her feminine charms against his egotism. He fell in love with her, and that too is not beyond comprehension. She should have won her point.

"What happened was something like this. On the night of the dinner party she'd arranged with Gilroy to make an attempt to get the papers. First she would appeal to Sutton frankly. If that failed, she'd get the combination of the safe in which the papers were kept. Incidentally, Gilroy probably knew which safe it was. That combination she planned to give to Gilroy later on, and the rest was up to him.

"So she appealed to Sutton, told him Gilroy was her brother, and that it meant everything to her to get those papers. There is no reason in the world to believe that Sutton refused her the substance of her request. He was too far gone to fail her utterly. But there is sometimes a queer streak of stubbornness in men like him which makes them hesitate before unconditional surrender. Also he may have wanted a hold over her. Sutton probably said, 'All right, if you feel that way about it, I'll let him off.' And he would have. But, unreasonably, he refused to make the gesture of handing over the papers to her, saying perhaps not to worry about them, that he'd destroy them anyhow later on. And Mrs. Anceney, having staked so much, was afraid to take the risk. So she wrote down the combination of the safe. He had probably taken the papers out sometime during their conversation, and she had a chance to look over his shoulder at the dials. That slip of paper she carried with her out of Sutton's room into the room where she was confined after the murder, intending to give it to Gilroy at the first opportunity.

"Let's consider Gilroy's situation. We know that he is an entirely unscrupulous man. We know also that he was completely in the power of an equally unscrupulous man, whom he had good cause to hate. All that supplied him with a strong motive for murder.

"Now turn to another aspect. Through his sister, Gilroy had made satisfactory arrangements for getting back the checks. He must have been sure she would be successful, either by one means or another. In the final analysis, therefore, Gilroy had no earthly reason for killing Sutton. Whatever else I may be uncertain about, I know one thing— that Gilroy is not the man we're looking for.

"But at least we've found out why he fell into the trap we'd set for the murderer. From the beginning, I couldn't believe he was the guilty person—yet I couldn't account for his presence in the room. Of course, now I know he was looking for that slip of paper. Or for the note and the checks themselves. He didn't know which he'd find, because, re-member, he hadn't had a word with his sister since Sutton's murder was discovered. But he was sure one of the two was there since the police hadn't announced finding any evidence of the sort. It was im-portant, in fact, imperative, for him to remove the checks before we found them. So he went, but unfortunately Katharine blocked his game, and he failed to find what he was looking for. However, he suc-ceeded in one thing, for which he gets no thanks from me. He threw a monkey wrench into the machinery of our neatly planned trap—for naturally the murderer would not enter the room while he was there."

Kane paused for a moment, and I seized the opportunity to open a package of cigarettes. I held them out to Kane, and he took one, but absentmindedly refused a light when I offered it to him. Finally he laid the cigarette down on the table.

"Now that's one reason why Gilroy came into the room that night," he stated thoughtfully. "But I'm fairly sure of my ground when I say he had another motive for doing so. And here's where the jade pendant enters our scheme of things."

It was a shock to me to realize that it had been the discovery of the jade pendant in Katharine's possession which had given rise to these amazing revelations.

"When Sutton and Mrs. Anceney went upstairs after dinner," Kane began, "Sutton had the pendant in his pocket. Since he saw no one but Mrs. Anceney, she was the only person to whom he could have given it. Therefore, whoever stole it must have taken it from one of two places—from Sutton's room or from the room in which Mrs. Anceney was sitting when she was murdered. I say that because I can see no reason why Sutton should have taken the trouble to put it elsewhere. Now if we consider that it may have been taken from Mrs. Anceney's room, we immediately assume that she had accepted a gift previously and publicly refused. Otherwise the jade wouldn't have been in her possession. I can't see why we should entertain very seriously the possibility that she changed her mind so completely about the matter. Particularly since she was so afraid of being compromised. For all practical purposes, then, we can say that the jade was stolen from Sutton's room.

"That leaves us with the fact pretty evident that the thief took it from Sutton's room at that very important moment when the first murder was discovered. If it had been stolen *before* the murder, an alarm would certainly have been given."

"But what I don't quite get," Moran interposed heavily, "is why the murderer couldn't have taken it at the time he shot Sutton."

"You're forgetting, Moran," Kane answered, "that the murderer was outside on the ledge, not in a place where he could commit robbery.

"Therefore," Kane continued, "we have two very neat pieces of action going on at that time, both unnoticed by at least nine of the people who were in the room. That lack of observation explains to me why so many of the conjurors in the world are able to make a living. They focus the spectator's attention on their right hand while they quite openly do the trick with their left. Just as, in this case, the jade was stolen, and the gun used for the murder laid on the table, while the possible witnesses to both actions stared wide-eyed at the body of the murdered man.

"Now I tried to figure out for myself," he went on, "who would be most likely to steal the pendant at that moment. First of all, I discarded the members of the family, even James, though we knew he was in need of money. What reason would any one of them have for taking such a senseless risk, when he probably could get the pendant by other means than theft, later on? That's the reason I was so astounded when I heard that it was in Katharine's desk. It seemed almost incredible until the explanation came to me that it must have been planted there by the real thief.

"And the real thief was not one of the servants, I'm sure. That's the second possibility we have, if you can call it a possibility. No one of them would have taken the jade. In the first place they wouldn't have had the slightest idea of its value. And if they did know enough to realize its value, they would have realized at the same time that it would be absolutely impossible for them to sell it. That jade pendant was, as I understand it, what might be called a museum piece. Sutton paid a small fortune for it. I remember reading about it in the papers. It was, by its very nature, something that couldn't possibly be sold without comment.

"No, the only person who could have taken that pendant was the one who would have been able to realize on its money value. And that was Frank Gilroy."

"But how could he have sold it," Moran queried impatiently, "any more easily than the others? The sale would be noticed just the same and he could be traced."

"Certainly," Kane agreed. "But *he* could say that Mrs. Anceney had given it to him, having proved that he was her brother. And she would be bound, at that time, to confirm what he said, to protect him once more as she had always protected him. It would be easy for her to say that after the dinner party she had decided to accept Sutton's gift, and that she had subsequently given it to her brother to sell. Don't you see, at the moment when Gilroy took the pendant, Mrs. Anceney was *still alive*."

Suddenly I understood the trend of Kane's argument. "Then you mean," I said, "that after her death the jade was no longer of any use to him?"

"Yes, that's just what I mean," Kane replied. "Her death completely turned the tables, as far as he was concerned. Mrs. Anceney could no longer protect him in any way. He could still prove that he was her brother, but he could offer no evidence whatever to show that she had given him the pendant, prior to her death, or even that she had finally accepted it from Sutton. As a matter of fact, there were any number of reliable witnesses who could state that Mrs. Anceney had not so much as spoken to Gilroy since the dinner party. Moreover, Gilroy was bound to realize that the theft of the jade would be sooner or later associated with one, if not both, of the crimes. The possession of it had become an active menace to him.

"Naturally, he decided to put it back before its loss was discovered. So, that very night, when he thought everyone was asleep, he probably tried to enter Sutton's sitting room. But that door was locked, you know. Then he made up his mind that the next best place to put it was on his sister's body. And there you have the second reason for Gilroy's presence in that room. He wanted to leave the piece of jade at the same time that he looked for the paper with the safe combination on it. Unluckily for him and perhaps for our subsequent peace of mind, Katharine kept him from accomplishing either purpose.

"I can only surmise what happened after that, but it works out fairly logically. Gilroy certainly put the pendant in the drawer of Katharine's desk, and his motive for doing so is the only thing that requires explanation. I think he put it there intending to use it as a hold over her. You see, he was in mortal fear Katharine might tell us of trailing him into the room that night. Under the circumstances, it was a suspicious action, and Gilroy had enough to hide as it was. He intended that through his sly suggestion Katharine should find the jade in her desk. He would then let her understand that he knew about it and threaten to tell us if she gave him away first. Of course, his whole plan has been ruined, although he doesn't know it yet, by the fact that Moran discovered the pendant before he had a chance to suggest to Katharine that she look in her desk drawer. In order to keep him from frightening the girl to death, we'll have to indicate very tactfully to him that the lost has been found, and then watch his expression. But I'd advise going no farther for the moment, as far as he's concerned. We've bigger fish to fry."

Kane ceased speaking, crossed his long legs, and leaned back in his chair with a certain air of finality. He picked up his unsmoked cigarette and lit it. "That, gentlemen, ends the harangue, from my point of view at least," he said, cheerfully, between puffs. "And it ends, too, the pretty little story you were telling me about the jade, Underwood. It seems too bad we couldn't ring in something supernatural about a bad-luck stone. However, in strict honesty, we can't." He laughed. "Now, I'd like to know that you're satisfied with my diagnosis."

Moran stroked his chin slowly, a doubtful expression on his face. "Well," he said, "I'm satisfied that your diagnosis is O. K., but I can't say I'm exactly satisfied with the way things have turned out. Where does it get us, that's what I'd like to know."

"It gets us farther than you may think, Moran," Kane answered. "That it gets you no farther in your own mind is because, from the beginning, you've laid too much emphasis on the wrong theory. You're disappointed now, naturally enough, because you assumed that when you found the person who had stolen the jade you would have Sutton's and Mrs. Anceney's murderer. I've never expected so much, simply because I didn't believe that theft could have been the motive for the crimes. They carry none of the earmarks of robbery. No, I believe that the impulse guiding the murderer has resulted from a much darker and more esoteric derangement than you have tried to conceive of.

"While the solution of the pendant's disappearance has not led us to the criminal we seek," Kane went on slowly, "it has played a great part in clearing up certain elements of the situation. For one thing, we need bother no longer with Gilroy. We know now why he walked into our trap, and though guilty of theft and of forgery, he is certainly too pinwitted for greater crimes. For another thing—and this, with its possible complications, cannot be considered too significant—we understand Mrs. Anceney's connection with Frederick Sutton.

"Above all, the explanation of the jade episode has warned us to concentrate our attention henceforward, not on a thief or a forger, but on a murderer whose criminal instincts were fired by a passion far more compelling and extraordinary."

CHAPTER 15

As I was thinking over what Kane had just told us, it occurred to me that the checks forged by Gilroy, which Kane had found, were the property of Sutton's estate, and that Mrs. Sutton, the person most affected, could insist on a prosecution, or at least an attempt to recover the money they represented.

"I suppose she might," Kane said thoughtfully. "Ten thousand dollars is a lot of money. You'll have to talk to her, won't you, Underwood?"

"Yes."

"I wish you'd explain to her that any such issue brought up now will make things more disagreeable for her than they already are. It doesn't matter particularly, but we won't be able to keep any such business as that out of the papers. By the way," he went on, "I wish you'd come over to my office after you've seen her. I'm on my way there now."

It was with a good deal of reluctance that I approached my conversation with Mrs. Sutton. I found her downstairs in the sitting room, where I had first met her as my hostess on the night of the dinner party. It struck me that she was very little changed, except in one small thing. She no longer wore make-up—otherwise, her husband's death, which must under the circumstances have shocked her profoundly, had apparently left no mark upon her. It was as though her existence moved at the same even rate no matter what the exterior circumstances. The idea came to me that for such a woman life was something that went on only within herself and had no physical manifestations.

She asked me quietly whether the police had as yet identified the murderer, but hardly listened to my answer. I went on to tell her that our search had had one definite result, and explained as briefly as I could the matter of the checks. When I told her that she would probably have the deciding vote as to whether or not Gilroy should be prosecuted, she looked at me sharply.

"I've always believed that people should answer for what they do," she said as though that settled the question.

"We all believe that," I answered, "more or less. But that can't have too much influence in this case. You know of course that your name is a byword to a large number of people by this time. But I don't think you realize that anything that happens to you or your children is bound to receive undue attention. Even though you are clearly in the right, the consequences of any further publicity are bound to be disagreeable to you."

"You mean that you are advising me to let this matter drop?"

"Yes," I answered. "There is not only what I have just said, but also the fact that you probably couldn't collect ten thousand dollars from Gilroy. I should certainly do nothing about it."

She looked at me in silence for a moment. Several times she seemed on the point of speaking, but checked herself. Finally she said, "I have never liked Mr. Gilroy," and waited as though she expected me to reply to her. When I did not, she spoke again. "I have never trusted him."

There was nothing for me to say. Whether or not she felt I disagreed with her, her dislike of Gilroy became more apparent. "You advise me to let him go scot free?"

I nodded.

"I suppose," she continued, "that a man like that is likely to get off—to get out of anything." She looked away from me for a minute, as though collecting her thoughts. "You say that the police know about this? Aren't they going to do anything about it? I thought that when murder had been committed they at least considered—"

She stopped short. In a moment she went on, in her usual emotionless fashion, "Very well. I shall take your advice. Mr. Gilroy is in luck, I see."

Feeling very uncomfortable, I left her to go to Kane's office and make my report to him. He sent for Moran as soon as I arrived, and the two of them listened to me closely. Kane remarked as I had that

Mrs. Sutton was obviously a woman of strong feelings, however carefully she concealed them.

"Seems to suspect Gilroy, doesn't she?" Moran broke in.

"Her suspicions might have excited me once," Kane replied. "I can't say they do now. There is only one thing we know, and that is that Gilroy himself is out of it. If he were to sign and seal a confession I wouldn't believe that he had committed the murders."

"I wonder why she was so set against Gilroy," Moran went on.

"Probably because she can't fail to realize that if Gilroy didn't kill Sutton one of her family did," Kane was quick to reply. "She may be afraid."

He paused to light a cigarette. "By the way," he continued, "I called on our friend Gilroy before I came here, and told him that we knew a little more than he thought. When he got a bit excited, I explained that we weren't accusing him of murder. After that, he took it more calmly, and didn't seem to mind confessing to forgery. I also said we had seen him go into the room where Mrs. Anceney's body was, and asked him why he did it. He simply answered that he had persuaded her to get the combination of the safe for him. She was to have done it that night. He admitted that she had cultivated Sutton for his sake.

"As I left, I mentioned in an offhand fashion that we had found a piece of jade we were looking for. His eyelids flickered a little, but he didn't say anything and neither did I. We won't hear anything more from him."

Kane sat back easily in his chair. "That being that," he said, "I think the time has come to talk over some of the things that have happened recently. Now that we can see more clearly, I've prepared a careful schedule of time that may help us. Of course the times have to be approximate but they are relatively correct. It starts at the moment when things got important."

He showed us a typed sheet, which both Moran and I examined closely. It read:

10:15	Sutton and Mrs. Anceney went upstairs, leaving the rest of the party together in the downstairs sitting room.
10:20	James and Gilroy went to James's room.

10:25	Katharine excused herself and went to her room.
10:30	Bert, leaving Underwood and Mrs. Sutton, went upstairs.
10:55	Underwood said good-night to Mrs. Sutton and left the house. Mrs. Sutton went to her room.
10:58	Gilroy left James.
11:00 the	Underwood, standing in the hall, heard shot which killed Sutton.
11:05–11:20	No certain knowledge where the various people were, except for Mrs. Anceney, who was waiting in the spare room, guarded by McBeath. According to the testimony given, all the members of the family were in their respective rooms.
1:20–2:00	No definite information as to the whereabouts of James and Bert. Both, according to their evidence, were in their rooms. Gilroy was alone downstairs during this time.
1:20–1:40	Mrs. Sutton downstairs being interviewed by Kane, Moran, and Underwood.
1:35	McBeath took wine in to Mrs. Anceney.
1:40–2:00	Interview with Katharine at which Mrs. Sutton was present during last six minutes.
1:54	Door-bell rang and Moran told McBeath to answer it.
1:58	McBeath away from Mrs. Anceney's door.
1:59	McBeath announced Mrs. Anceney's death.

Moran looked up from his scrutiny with a satisfied air. "That's useful," he said, "and taken with other things it seems almost conclusive. It's a pity that James didn't get away with the jade instead of Gilroy."

"If he'd had an equally good alibi, he probably would have," Kane replied. "But of course there's another thing. James thought he would have all the money he wanted after his father's death."

"Bert must hate James," Moran put in, "to have told that story on him."

Kane blew a smoke ring and watched it vanish into thin air before he replied. "I suppose James was like his father. Neither one of them ever showed any consideration for Bert. And he was wily enough to seize an opportunity to get back at James."

"Well, at any rate," Moran continued cheerfully, "we have something to work on, though I wish there were a little more to it. We know James had no alibis, we know he fought with Sutton, we know when he got the gun. He hated Sutton, and he needed money. Do you think that makes a case?"

"There's one great difficulty with it," Kane answered, frowning, "which you probably see. The whole thing depends on Bert's evidence. And somehow I can't see him standing cross-examination. That's why I talked to James. If he had admitted staying in Sutton's sitting room, it would have been plain sailing. If he had explained why he did it, we could have weighed his statements, and decided whether or not they were true. But a flat denial is more difficult to deal with."

"I don't see why you need to bother about that," Moran protested. "Of course, he denied it."

"It's not so much the fact of his denial that bothers me," Kane answered. "It's that I can't see Bert facing that denial and keeping to his story on a witness stand."

"You mean we can't depend on him? Then I guess we're stumped."

"Not stumped for all time," came the quiet reply. "I don't think we can do anything yet."

Moran was discouraged. "What gets me," he said, "is that the very night of the murders we thought we were going to catch the person who did them. A lot of good that trap did us!"

"I did make a mistake," Kane admitted, "in thinking that we could catch the murderer so easily. The trap failed, but its results still interest me."

"You mean the man we heard in the hall?" Moran's voice was alive with a new interest.

"I should like very much to know who he was," Kane answered. "You see, Moran, I've got an idea about this case, and everything that's happened so far confirms it, but we haven't got the conclusive evidence. That's what I'm waiting for."

The three of us continued to sit silently around the table. A stenographer brought Kane his mail, and he turned to examine it with a look of relief, as though he said to himself, "Here at last is something I can handle, something that exists outside my own mind."

Disappointment was in the air. It occurred to me forcibly how many chances were on the side of the criminal. He at least could plan intelligently, act quickly, and retire into the obscurity from which he had never really emerged. He was troubled by no sense of justice, had merely to carry out his own desires, and since no one could be pointed out as the type of the murderer, he would find a disguise ready for him in the character with which people of his everyday acquaintance had endowed him. We were, after all, at the mercy of chance, and every small advantage the fickle lady gave us we must use at three or four times its face value.

I was aroused from my meditations by an exclamation from Kane. I looked up, and found him staring at a letter he held in his hand. "The gods are good," he said. "Perhaps they've given us what I wanted. Read this."

He handed Moran the letter. The sergeant read it, and his face betrayed his surprise and exultation.

"Well, thank God!" he exclaimed, "that begins to sound like business. I was beginning to think we were stuck for good."

I took the letter from him. It read:

MY DEAR MR. KANE:
I think that you, as one of those interested in unraveling the mystery which surrounds the deaths of Mr. Sutton and Mrs. Anceney, may wish to examine a letter which I have just received. It was apparently written by Mr. Sutton only a few hours before his death. I should of course have received it yesterday, but I was out of town.

If you will make an appointment through my secretary, I shall be glad to show you the letter, which may have some bearing on the case.

Sincerely yours,
CARTER SIMONDS.

"What does he mean?" I asked. "Who is Carter Simonds?"

"One of the foremost psychiatrists of this country," Kane replied, and without further explanation he picked up the telephone. He carried on a brief conversation, at the end of which he turned to us.

"Well," he said, clapping Moran on the shoulder, "he's got something for us, I think."

He pulled out his watch. "It's almost three o'clock now. Dr. Simonds said he would meet us at the Sutton house as soon as he could make it. I think we may as well go out there now. You have your car, haven't you, Underwood?"

I nodded, and Kane pushed his chair back abruptly and got up. Soon we were on our way. Kane sat in front with me, smoking silently, and paying little or no heed to Moran, who, leaning forward from the back seat, shouted excited opinions on one thing and another into our ears.

CHAPTER 16

When we arrived at the house, McBeath met us and ushered us into the hall, reporting weightily that nothing had occurred during Kane's absence. We were about to go upstairs when Kane, glancing into the living room, turned and walked in that direction. As we entered, we heard Bert's voice.

"There, you see, Ellen, I've got twenty-four red ones, and thirty white ones, counting the shells, and nineteen green ones. Now, *do* look, Ellen," he insisted.

"Yes, I see. That's very pretty," his sister answered. Her back and Bert's were toward the door and she had not seen us. Katharine, who was facing both of them, looked up.

"Mother, here's Mr. Kane," she said quickly. Mrs. Sutton's sewing dropped abruptly from her hands as she turned to speak to us. She started to get up, but evidently thought better of it.

"What—" she began in surprise, and then stopped and looked away, as if realizing that she had nothing to say after all. Kane made her hesitation even more awkward by refusing to step into the breach with his usual kindly word.

Meanwhile, Katharine's announcement of our presence had sent Bert into feverish activity. Without as much as a glance in our direction he swept into a heap the objects which were lined up on the card table before which he was sitting. They dropped into a box in his lap with a loud staccato rattling. Katharine turned on him nervously at the sound, and I could imagine the defiant look he gave her in return.

Then Bert swung around to us and grinned. "How do you do," he said pleasantly. "We didn't expect to see you again."

175

Kane's somber expression lifted. "No?" he said carelessly. "Then it must be a surprise to you." He walked over to Bert's chair and picked something up from the floor. "This is something you forgot," he said, holding it out. I moved over casually until I could see that it was nothing more than an irregular red stone, rather prettily colored.

Bert took it shyly. "Thanks," he said, and sliding back the lid of a wooden starch box not more than an inch, dropped it in.

Mrs. Sutton smiled deprecatingly. "Bert collects stones and shells," she explained.

"Is that so," Kane murmured absent-mindedly. "You must show me your collection sometime." He put his hand on my shoulder. "Let's get on," he said. "By the way, Mrs. Sutton," he added, swinging around to her, "I've asked a man to come here to see me this afternoon. I tell you so that you'll know I'm expecting him. McBeath will bring him up."

We went out into the hall. I heard Bert get up and follow us, a little behind. With his foot on the first step of the stairs, Kane stopped and raised his head, as if listening. Then he turned around and smiled down at Bert.

"New shoes?" he asked.

Involuntarily Bert looked down at his rather small black oxfords. "No," he said, eyeing them uncertainly. Moran and I were turning stupidly from Kane's face to Bert's feet and back again.

"But you haven't had them long, have you?" Kane was continuing calmly. "I'll tell you what I'd do if I were you. I'd give them a good soaking in hot water overnight. It'll take out that squeak."

He started up the stairs, leaving Bert staring blankly at us. After another perplexed examination of the offending footwear, I followed Kane, pondering on his disturbing fondness for pleasantries. At the top of the stairs, he told us to go into the sitting room. He would join us there in a few moments.

We had not been in the room more than a minute or so when he walked in, his hands comfortably thrust into his pockets, and something like a smile on his face.

"Well, I've a nice fat worm for you," he announced in a curious tone. "Tear it apart." He sank into a chair, leaned his head back, and closed his eyes before he said softly, "Our piece of jade has disappeared again."

Before we could recover from our surprise, Kane raised his hand as if in protest at our exclamations. "Yes, it's gone from the drawer of the desk. I don't know where—I can only suspect," he continued, without opening his eyes. "But I'd enjoy some silent thought on the subject, if you don't mind."

Moran resentfully composed himself in his chair once more and chewed at his thumb nail. This effort at reflection threw him into a state very much resembling bad temper, and the expression on his face led me to believe he considered the second disappearance of the jade in the light of a personal hostility. I could understand why he scowled each time his glance fell on Kane's recumbent form, for the apparently complete repose of the latter gave little evidence of mental activity, and suggested that he had washed his hands of the whole affair. Only once did I see him draw his brows together; then he sighed heavily and sat up.

A few minutes after this there was a heavy knock at the door, and at Kane's sharp "Come in," McBeath entered, followed by a tall, dignified man, with an intelligent, pleasant face.

Kane got to his feet at once. Without waiting for McBeath to speak, he held out his hand to the newcomer. "I'm Norton Kane, Dr. Simonds, and these are my colleagues. We appreciate your coming here to-day." As we shook hands, McBeath went out and closed the door. Dr. Simonds sat down in the chair Kane pulled up for him.

"Well, Mr. Kane," Dr. Simonds began slowly, "if I had been able, I would have communicated with you before this. As I wrote, I was away yesterday, and when I returned I discovered this letter from the late Mr. Sutton."

Kane nodded, and Dr. Simonds reached into his breast pocket and pulled out an envelope.

"I may as well tell you now," he continued before handing it to Kane, "that I have no idea to whom the letter refers. Mr. Sutton has never consulted me before on this or any other matter. I had never met him or his family, and knew of them only by hearsay. However, when I found out that you were in charge of the case, it seemed to me that I should pass the letter over to you. Perhaps you can make something of it." He held out the letter to Kane, who took it and pulled it out of the envelope.

As Kane unfolded the letter and began to read, the three of us sat watching his face. I followed the movement of his eyes across and down the page, but his expression did not alter. When he had finished, however, he did not immediately hand the letter over to Moran, but let it fall into his lap while he stared off into space without saying a word. Finally he said quietly, "Thank you, Dr. Simonds. I think this letter will be very useful to us. Yes," he added, drawing a long breath, "it's one of the trump cards in my game."

Moran meanwhile had snatched the letter from Kane, and was reading it with ejaculations which further confounded me and added to my impatience. I took it eagerly when he had at last finished. The letter began:

> My Dear Dr. Simonds:
> For the past year or so I have been somewhat worried about the mental condition of a member of my family. Perhaps I have fooled myself into believing that the situation was harmless, and that there was no need to do anything about it. I was very much troubled, therefore, when I happened to read in a recent article of yours that a condition such as this is not only harmful but malignant. The truth of that was proved to me today when an actual threat against my life was made by the person in question. Under the circumstances, the threat itself is absurd, but as an indication of the psychological disturbance behind it, I can't take it lightly. I feel that I have been tolerant long enough, and must take stronger measures.
>
> I would like an appointment with you as soon as you can arrange it, to talk over the matter, for I am deeply worried and annoyed under the existing conditions.

The letter was signed "Frederick Sutton," and was dated September 24th. It was the day of the murders. I saw that the envelope was postmarked 6: 30 P.M.

I noticed all these things mechanically as anyone who is bewildered will clutch stupidly at small details for support. My mind was in such a confusion of half-conscious theories suddenly uprooted that I found myself almost incapable of putting any two ideas together for a fresh start. In despair I saw that even Moran was not lost in such a sea of doubt and perplexity as I, for although more excited than I had ever seen him, he gave evidence of having grasped some vestige of truth from the chaos.

And Kane was strangely calm. "You've thought so all the time, then?" I heard Moran ask him wonderingly.

"I wouldn't go so far as to say exactly that," Kane answered quietly. "I've had certain confused ideas about the situation, but I don't know myself when I first began to suspect the truth. This letter has removed any doubts I might have had."

"Then it has helped you." It was Dr. Simonds who spoke. I had almost forgotten his presence.

"More than I can tell you. It's given me the courage to stick to my convictions. You see, this case has been particularly baffling for a number of reasons. The clues we've followed out recently have been disheartening because, on the surface, they've seemed like blind alleys. I've believed all along that each one of them would prove of value—that they would complete the picture sooner or later. Meanwhile I've been holding on to my original theory with only half confirmations to help me to believe in it. But no matter now—the letter has given me the strength of ten. There's just one more thing I must find out," Kane's voice was far away, "and when I can explain that to myself, and to a jury if necessary," as he spoke, he opened his long hand, and then closed it with a significant gesture, "we'll have it all clinched."

"Look here, Kane," Moran said earnestly, "if there's any small thing we need besides that"—he pointed to the letter with a stubby forefinger—"you can be darned sure we're going to get it, and soon. I've got a hunch I know just where to look for it too. Now let me have Mrs. Sutton in. She'll shed some light on the whole business or I'll know the reason why."

"Oh, no!" Kane said quickly, as if in dismay, and then explained almost apologetically, "I don't think she could help us very much, Moran."

"Well, I'd like to try," Moran insisted. "Why not? It can't do any harm."

"I suppose not," Kane agreed. He shrugged his shoulders. "All right, then, do as you wish. But remember, I have nothing to say to her." He turned to Dr. Simonds, who was patiently waiting. "I suppose you'd like to go now, and I don't want to keep you any longer. You've helped us a great deal. I'll have McBeath take you down to the door."

He called. McBeath, who had been outside in the hall, came in, and listened stolidly while Kane directed him to conduct Dr. Simonds downstairs. He was turning to obey when Moran said, "And McBeath, tell Mrs. Sutton I want to see her."

When the door had closed behind McBeath and Dr. Simonds, Moran got up and walked over to Kane's chair. Somewhat ostentatiously he put his hand on the latter's shoulder.

"Well, Kane," he said, "I guess I've got the sense to admit I've been tearing off on a lot of false trails. Perfectly frankly, I've got to hand it to you."

From beneath his thick eyebrows Kane looked up at him. "Thanks, Moran," he said quietly.

Moran was occupied with his own thoughts. "I hate to think how ready I was to pin it on James," he said at last.

Kane shook his head. "It wasn't James."

"Oh, I know that now. There's only one person that letter could point to."

"Just one."

"Have we got enough to make an arrest?"

Kane turned a troubled face toward the window. "There's only one thing we can't explain. But I'm not downed yet. We'll get it."

Moran looked at him questioningly. "Well, let's hear what it is," he suggested. Suddenly he frowned, as if a disturbing thought had struck him. He pulled his watch out of his pocket and exclaimed in vexation, "Damn it! It's four-thirty, and I'm due at Headquarters right now. Why didn't somebody remind me? I damn near forgot all about it. Hold everything, Kane. I'll be back as soon as I can make it, and we'll dope out anything that puzzles you. I've got to beat it," he added as he started for the door in haste.

I called after him to take my car, and he thanked me and said he would.

I had half expected that Kane would unburden himself to me on the subject of the letter when we found ourselves alone, and I was disappointed to observe that he seemed in no mood for conversation. He sank more deeply into his chair, and when he was not running his fingers nervously through his hair he stared in a preoccupied fashion through and beyond me.

"Just one obstacle, Underwood," he said, with something like despair in his tone, "just one. But it's between me and the goal. Well," he slapped the arms of his chair, and got up. "I've got to figure that out, in spite of everything else we know." He began to walk absent-mindedly in little circles around me.

At that moment the door opened and Mrs. Sutton came in, followed by McBeath. Without a word she walked over and sat down in the place Kane had just vacated. He turned questioningly to her and waited for her to speak. At his silence, she began to pick nervously at the handkerchief in her lap. Finally Kane, observing her embarrassment, asked, "Do you want to see me, Mrs. Sutton?"

She looked at him quickly, with a queer expression on her face. "Why, no—that is," she stammered, "I was told you wanted to see me." She motioned vaguely toward McBeath.

Kane appeared to be suddenly enlightened. He smiled. "Oh, I'm sorry, Mrs. Sutton. It was Sergeant Moran, not I, who asked to see you. He had to leave unexpectedly."

But Mrs. Sutton was not satisfied. She looked suspiciously at Kane and then at McBeath. The latter came slowly to his own defense.

"Didn't you ask me, Mr. Kane, to bring Mrs. Sutton up here?" he asked, his face growing redder with perplexity.

"No, McBeath, you misunderstood. It was Moran."

"Oh." But McBeath seemed still doubtful as he left the room.

Mrs. Sutton, meanwhile, had got up from her chair in some confusion. With a half apology, and a glance at both of us in which there was not a little distrust, she went out.

Kane laughed shortly and took up his pacing again. I ventured no comment for I knew he did not want to be disturbed. A minute or so passed, with no noise in the room except Kane's regular, heavy tread. Finally I noticed that his steps had become slower, and then stopped altogether. I heard an exclamation and turned quickly to look at him. He did not appear to see me.

"By God," I heard him say softly, "so that's it."

He had a look of exultation. "And how utterly stupid of me not to have suspected it before. I'd completely closed my mind to that possibility."

Quickly he walked over to a table at the side of the room and picked up the telephone.

"Haymarket 6400," I heard him say, and then, "Let me speak to Moran." His words were clipped short with excitement. After a short wait, he continued, "Moran? Drop everything else and get out here as quickly as you can. We'll make an arrest to-night."

CHAPTER 17

It was growing late, and in the dying light of the afternoon the three of us were once more assembled in the sitting room. Moran had arrived a short time after receiving Kane's message, his excitement subdued a little by the quiet tone of the latter's greeting. The last act of the drama was about to unfold.

Up to the last few hours I had believed that we were doomed to follow will-o'-the-wisps, and to end in an ever thicker tangle of lies and speculations. But now the unknown person with whom we had matched our wits had emerged from his obscurity.

As Kane sat facing us, the deep lines of his face showed sharp and dark in the fading light. He looked tired; the strain of the last forty-eight hours had left its mark on him. His mouth was stern and set as though he had taken on the attributes of the impersonal justice whose instrument he was.

He was saying slowly, "I couldn't quite get things straight till now, though I've suspected the truth for some time. You remember I foresaw how difficult this was going to be. The crimes were so simple and nothing is as hard to deal with as simplicity. They were the product of a brilliant mind, if you can admit that brilliance may be directed to an evil end."

"While I was away, then," Moran interjected, "you figured out the thing that was bothering you? In other words, we've got a plain case."

Kane roused himself from his abstraction. "Yes," he said, "it's quite plain. We know now what Mrs. Anceney may have known before her death."

"Well, I'll take your word for it," Moran said. "How you got on the right track from the start I don't quite get—and I don't understand either why there was anything to worry you after you'd read the letter. But we can pass over those things. I'll believe you."

Kane frowned. "And that, Moran, is exactly what I *don't* want you to do. I want your personal reaction to the concrete evidence we've found—not your belief that what I say is right. What do you think? Have we conclusive proof?"

Moran lost no time in meditation. "Conclusive! Certainly. There's nothing we need do but snap on the handcuffs. And I'm not taking your word for it either. It's all straight now. Of course," his tone was so honest that I felt a sudden liking for him, "I'll say frankly that I was about as far off the track as anyone could be till this afternoon. First off, I was dead sure it was Gilroy."

"That was reasonable enough," Kane assured him, "until we found out that Gilroy was guilty of theft. After all, we couldn't consider theft a motive in this case. And we could explain every suspicious action of his entirely satisfactorily on other grounds. That put him out of the question."

"And James had me stumped, too," Moran admitted ruefully, "a long time after that."

"I spent some time wondering about him myself," Kane answered. "So many things were against him. He's a disagreeable young man, and if anyone would take parricide coolly, he would. He felt no affection whatever for his father—in fact, they were more or less hostile toward each other. And he'd quarreled with his father on the very night of the latter's death. To cap the whole thing, his evidence on this point contradicted Bert's evidence. Yes, James was in a bad position. But I kept wondering whether he could ever feel violently about any person except himself."

"All the same, I'd have clapped him in jail if I'd had my way," Moran persisted. "Thank God that letter of Sutton's turned up when it did. You couldn't make any mistake about what person *that* meant. And it didn't take me very long to drop James."

Kane nodded thoughtfully. "Yes, the letter cleared the decks of all but one person," he said.

There was a short silence after this remark, and then Moran looked wonderingly at Kane.

"You know," he said slowly, "I didn't realize there was any homicidal tendency there. Did you, before you saw the letter?"

"Yes, I did, Moran. It's an abnormal mental twist. I suspected it to be a very dangerous one, too, and as a matter of fact, that suspicion served as the foundation for my whole theory of the crimes."

"I would have said it was perfectly harmless."

Kane looked at him quickly. "That's what Sutton thought, too. Remember what he said in his letter. It was Simonds's article that finally brought him to his senses. By the way, I looked up that article. We can use it as evidence."

But Moran was engrossed in reflections of his own. A question was on his lips before Kane had finished speaking.

"Tell me one thing, Kane. It was Bert then, was it, who ran away from us down the hall, the night we laid our trap?"

"Yes."

"How did you ever find that out?"

Kane gave a short laugh. "Just think a minute about the situation that night. We'd made our plans for the trap, and they'd failed. As we left the room, we heard someone running down the hall. Now, do you remember anything peculiar about the sound that person made?"

I tried to put myself back to the moment of which Kane was speaking. We were standing in the doorway, Kane, Moran, and I, when we first heard the cautious footsteps, and knew that someone was trying to get away from us. For all his care he could not muffle the sound of his movements. That was all I could recall. I looked inquiringly at Kane.

Seeing that Moran and I were at a loss, Kane answered his own question. "It may seem ridiculous to you, but the humor is rather sardonic. The person who ran had a squeaking shoe. Did you happen to notice the sound Bert made to-day when he followed us out into the hall? I have a good auditory memory. It was exactly the same."

The point had not occurred to Moran any more than it had to me, but I could see that he recognized it, as I did, as another link in the long chain of evidence.

"Well, I'll be damned," he muttered. "That's a fine way to be caught." His astonishment soon passed. "I had my suspicions all along," he continued, "about the story he told of James's quarrel with his father. It sounded fishy to me."

"Some of it was true," Kane interrupted. "James did quarrel with Sutton that evening, and Bert overheard him. But they weren't quarreling about Mrs. Anceney, and Sutton didn't go off leaving James in the room. He also indicated that he'd heard James getting the gun out of the drawer. That wasn't true, either. The thing that made me doubt Bert's story was the fact that with no hesitation at all James had informed us that he knew where his father kept his gun. If he'd been guilty, I think he would have shown a little more sensitiveness on the subject. Other things made me think that James was telling the truth. He didn't stay in the room alone. He left it when he said he did, while his father was still there. And that was the time when the real criminal entered."

"In other words," Moran stated grimly, "Bert gave us the story just wrong enough to throw us off the track."

"Exactly," Kane replied.

Moran snorted contemptuously. "And I thought he was feeble-minded! That's a joke on me, all right. The whole thing was right before me and I couldn't see it. Why, I remember now—the first thing I ever heard about him was the way he jeered at Sutton. And he admitted himself that he hated him."

Kane rose abruptly from his chair. His expression was more than weary. He went over and stood by the window. Although it was almost dark in the room, the faint light outlined his tall figure and showed me that his head was bent.

Moran paid little heed to Kane's movements. "I wish I'd had the sense to connect up a few things," he mused disgustedly. "I knew Bert didn't have an alibi for either murder, and besides, McBeath said he was in the hall before Mrs. Anceney was killed. And how about those scrapbooks of his—pasted up with every account of the murders he could lay his hands on." He fell into a brief silence, only to break out with, "By God, Kane, here's something else. I'll bet Bert's got that jade pendant right now. It'd make a good addition to that bunch of colored rocks he's got."

With an effort he curbed his excitement. "Well, I guess that's aside from the point. The main thing is to get a warrant."

He lifted himself out of his chair. "It certainly is funny the way these things end," he remarked as he started for the door.

Kane swung around and faced him.

"Where are you going?"

"Why, to swear out a warrant against Bert," Moran answered.

"Then you'd better wait a minute. I've already sworn out a warrant," Kane said, and then, as Moran turned back from the door, he added quietly, "but it's not against Bert Walton."

Moran did not move, or try to speak.

"Bert is not guilty," I heard Kane say, as if from a great distance, and in the tense silence that followed, his words seemed to reecho through the room.

His mouth half open, Moran stared at Kane as at one gone suddenly mad. When he spoke, it was with great effort, in a strained voice.

"What do you mean?"

"I mean that Bert is an eavesdropper, a sneak, and a talebearer, but he is not a murderer."

Moran recovered himself. "What in damnation are you driving at?" he shouted. "We've got a case against him, haven't we? Are we going off on another wild-goose chase?"

"Not a wild-goose chase this time," Kane said quietly. "Listen to me. We have a case against Bert. The weak point in it is that he isn't guilty."

"But Kane," Moran cried, in real desperation, "what've you been talking about all this time? You just said yourself that Bert was the person in the hall that night!"

"He was," Kane replied, "but I didn't say he was the murderer." His manner changed, and he put his hand on the other's shoulder. "See here, Moran. Sit down, will you? I've got a lot of things to explain to you and Underwood, but you must let me do it in my own way."

Slowly Moran obeyed, and Kane began his story.

"You've worked up in your own mind a case against Bert, and for our mutual satisfaction I'm going to check off the points against him.

"First, his motive. We know that he had a possible motive; hatred of Sutton, love for his sister, and jealousy for her against Mrs. Anceney.

Set against those facts others: he was, and is, small-minded. Spite is the equivalent of hatred in his mind; he has taken no pains to hide his sentiments, but rather seized every opportunity to give them an outlet. He's told tales against James; he's taken a malicious satisfaction in collecting newspaper stories of his brother-in-law's murder. Such a man is not the remorseless egotist we're looking for.

"Next, we have a number of what I may call suspicious circumstances which weigh against him, most of which have their roots in his character. His habit of eavesdropping, his abnormal curiosity, have brought him time and time again into compromising positions. That's why he was in the hall that night. He wondered what was going on and came to find out. His oddities show that he is an example of retarded development, not that he is a homicidal maniac. In fact, the very things that point against him are proof enough that he could not have committed the crimes, which were the products of a subtle intellect set in activity by distorted emotions."

Moran objected stubbornly. "But Kane, you can't get around the fact that Bert lied about James. You said so yourself. And how about that letter? Do you mean to say that was a fake?"

"One thing at a time, Moran," Kane replied. "I didn't say that Bert *lied*," he continued. "I said that only part of his story was true. The other part was wrong, but that wasn't Bert's fault. He simply got the facts twisted."

"I don't see what you mean." Moran was completely upset.

"I'll explain. Bert heard and saw James the first time he went to spy on him and his father. When he returned the second time to listen at the door he neither saw nor heard him. He simply took it for granted that Sutton was quarreling with the same person, that is, James. Bert didn't know that during his absence James had left the room, and another person had come in."

"You can't prove that."

"I can prove it by proving a lot of other things. But for example, the subject of the quarrel had changed. Sutton was no longer berating someone about money, but for rudeness and more or less open hostility to Mrs. Anceney. James felt no particular antagonism toward her. He didn't care enough about her or about his father. Whether or not you accept that distinction, I can show you later on that it was not James who seized the opportunity Bert described to get Sutton's gun."

"What are you going to say about Sutton's letter to Simonds?" Moran put in doggedly.

"As to that," Kane took up the challenge, "I've two points to make. Do you remember the wording of that document? Sutton expressed himself as being *deeply worried*, or something like that, over the state of mind of a member of his family. Sutton didn't give a damn what happened to Bert, either in mind or in body, and he wasn't the man to disguise his indifference."

He glanced at Moran. "You don't read the more or less learned journals, do you?"

The red-faced sergeant looked at him in bewilderment, and did not answer.

"Well, you remember," Kane went on, "Sutton's reference to a recent article of Dr. Simonds's which had induced him to write to the psychologist. Now, some time ago I noticed a copy of the *Psychological Review* hanging around here, and I wondered who was interested in such subjects. Apparently, Sutton had need to be. I still wonder how he came to be so scientific about his troubles, but I suppose psychology is in the air just now. At any rate I consulted the magazine—August issue, I think—and found the article. It proved to be very illuminating. I won't quote it to you now because you wouldn't accept it as evidence if I did. But in its proper place it's almost conclusive."

Kane took a long drag on his cigarette, and sat down with his back to the window. Against the light I could see nothing of him but a black silhouette. As he turned his head so that I saw him in profile his ugly rugged features stood out with startling distinctness. When he faced us and took up his argument again, he became nothing but a voice proceeding with a curious clarity from what seemed to be the dummy figure of a ventriloquist.

"It's time to build up a true case. We've been misled enough, although everything that threw us off the track fits in to the true solution. Now I'll give you definite evidence against the real criminal."

We strained our eyes toward Kane's dark shadow. He straightened himself in the chair.

"First of all, the motive for the crimes. We have already decided on the motive for the second crime. It was fear. The murderer thought Mrs. Anceney could identify him. Whether she could or not is beside the point. The possibility brought about her death. The motive for killing Sutton was a very different thing. There wasn't a shadow of impulse in it. It was something that had been built up gradually over a long series of years. And the most powerful element in it was love. You remember, 'Unnatural vices are fathered by our heroism.' When I say 'love,' I don't mean the ordinary, commonplace affection to which we are all subject. I mean an emotion as much hotter as the sun is hotter than the moon—an emotion which overpowers all scruple and all reason. Hate enters into it, of course, a hate born of resentment at being rejected for another person. Jealousy, too, the child of love and hatred."

We heard him sigh and then begin again.

"As I told you, it was McBeath's mistake a little while ago that really concluded my case. He's a good fellow, faithful and conscientious, but God might just as well not have given him his eyes and ears. He's another one who could have told us the whole story.

"But there's this much to be said for McBeath," he continued. "Mrs. Anceney was sitting in a wing chair. Do you remember the room, and the way the chair was placed? As nearly as I can judge, the room measures about twelve feet in depth, that is from the door to the windows. From side wall to side wall it must measure about eighteen feet. Mrs. Anceney's chair was to the right of the door, about seven feet in from it; on the other side it was about two feet from the window. There was a small table beside her chair. In the part of the room to the left of the door as you enter, there is a bed and another small table.

"You remember McBeath's enforced absence, lasting, he assures us, not more than a minute. On his return, he took Mrs. Anceney's wine from the butler and carried it into the room. The back of her chair was toward him. According to his account she was reading quietly. He told her he had her wine, and she thanked him and told him to put it on the table by the bed. He did so, and left the room. Now I want you to pay particular attention to two things. McBeath was told to put the wine on the *far* table, for one; the second thing is that the wine was not poured into the glass at all. It was left untouched. Do those facts mean anything to you?"

"No," Moran replied curtly.

"Well, they mean a lot to me." Kane looked at the two of us intently, leaning forward in his chair. His voice was deadly serious, and emphasized the gravity of his words.

"They mean that Mrs. Anceney was dead when McBeath brought the wine in."

Moran gave a strangled gasp. "For God's sake," he cried, "do you think McBeath has hallucinations? He heard her speak."

"McBeath heard someone answer him, Moran," Kane replied grimly, "but it wasn't Mrs. Anceney. She was dead."

The room was almost dark. For a moment the only sound I heard was Moran's excited breathing. I was too dumbfounded to speak.

Kane continued. "The first time McBeath left his post the murderer entered the room. The murder then took place earlier than we thought. And that difference in time is the basic fact of the true case."

His words were heavy with significance.

"At the time," he said, "when we once thought the murder occurred, we were talking to Katharine and Mrs. Sutton."

"You mean," Moran burst out, "that to change the time of the murder is to destroy their alibis?"

Kane nodded.

"I have one more point to bring up," he said, "a small point about voices. McBeath thought Mrs. Anceney spoke to him. I doubt if even McBeath would mistake a man's voice for a woman's."

He stopped.

"So much for the first part of my case," he said, after a moment. "It was a woman who killed both Sutton and Mrs. Anceney."

CHAPTER 18

As he finished speaking, Kane got up and pushed his chair roughly to one side. He began to take slow steps up and down the room. The familiar sounds broke the stupefied silence his last words had cast about us and lifted a little the cloud of horror that threatened to shut us in.

The thing he had said was execrable. "Kane, I can't believe this," I began. My voice was hoarse and I stopped to clear my throat. "These women aren't the sort . . ."

Kane's voice was metallic in its coldness. "One of them is," he said, and his face was as rigid as a mask. "Don't be a fool, Underwood. Throat-cutting isn't a typically feminine act, you think! You seem to forget that most of the really horrible crimes we know of were either committed or instigated by women. When it comes to downright cold brutality, a man is more likely to shudder at its execution than a woman. Lady Macbeth is true to her sex."

His words stiffened us both. Moran's eyelids narrowed. I knew what he would ask.

"Which one was it?"

"You'll know within ten minutes, Moran. For I'm going to give you the facts in the least pleasant manner possible." His laughter was disagreeable, and when he spoke again he bit off his words as if he loathed each one.

"We have one more scene before us, in which both of our characters will appear. It will be short. I need you as witnesses."

"What's the idea?" Moran asked quickly.

"I'm going to show you which one is the murderer. Now I have certain preparations to make. I want you and Underwood to stay here until I've set the stage." In another second he had left us.

Moran and I had waited no longer than five minutes when he returned.

"All right. Come with me," he directed. We left the room and followed Kane down the hall. He stopped before a familiar door. It was the one that opened into the room in which Mrs. Anceney had been killed. McBeath was guarding it, much as he had on that memorable night.

Kane turned to us. "Remember," he said sharply, "you're my witnesses, and I'm depending on you. But keep out of sight."

He opened the door, and we went in. The room was empty. Everything in it was placed as it had been on the night of the murder—the wing chair, the lamp, the tables. But the chair had no occupant, although my memory leaped to supply one.

Kane had thrown open the door of the closet. I understood what he meant and stepped inside. Moran followed me, and Kane pushed the door to until there was just enough of an opening to permit us an unobstructed view of the room. Then, without a word, he left us and went out. We waited in the semi-darkness of the closet.

Presently there were voices in the hall. Katharine Sutton came into the room, Kane with her. I looked for Mrs. Sutton to follow them, but she did not.

"It isn't a matter of persistence, Miss Sutton," Kane was saying. "We've done all we could. We've followed up every lead. That's why I want to see if there isn't some help you can give us."

The girl looked up at Kane. "I don't know," she said slowly. "If I can . . ." She left the sentence unfinished.

"Sit down, won't you?" Kane requested. He was standing in front of her in such a manner that the seat nearest her was the wing chair by the small table. She sank into it and raised her eyes questioningly to his.

An expression of annoyance crossed his face. "Excuse me for a minute, will you?" he asked. "I've forgotten something. I'll be right back."

He left the room. As she heard the door close behind him, the girl looked momentarily puzzled. She glanced suddenly at the chair in which she was sitting, and instinctively lifted her hands from its arms. For one moment I could have sworn she was afraid. Then her face cleared. She glanced down at one of the satin slippers she was wearing and bent over to straighten its buckle. As she leaned back again there was the sound of the door re-opening.

But it was not Kane who entered. It was McBeath, and he carried a tray on which were a decanter and a single wine glass.

When he was well within the room, before the girl had turned to see him, he spoke slowly, stupidly. "Here's the wine you asked for."

Katharine swung around to face him with startled eyes.

"Thank you. Please put it on the table by the bed." The answer came in a strange, low voice.

Suddenly I knew it was not Katharine who had answered, although the words had come from her direction. The girl's lips had not moved. Now she had stiffened in her chair, and was staring toward the window.

McBeath was stolidly obeying the command of the voice. His back was turned to the girl and he was approaching the table when suddenly the draperies of the window nearest Katharine were thrown to one side. Another instant, and the figure of Mrs. Sutton came from behind them and moved quickly and silently across the room and out the open door.

At the same instant, a startling change took place in the girl. She sprang to her feet with the speed of desperation, and stood looking from side to side of the empty room as though she were surrounded by foes. The whites of her eyes gleamed, and she took short breaths like a panting animal. For one minute she was motionless, crouching a little, her arms held rigidly in front of her as if to ward off an expected blow. Then a veil of cunning fell over her face. With long, noiseless steps she moved toward the door.

"Get back there!" The command rang out like a shot. It was Kane, but he spoke in a voice I had never heard before, the harsh, relentless voice one uses to a treacherous beast.

The girl recoiled, but sprang forward again almost at once. Kane stood squarely in the doorway, his mouth a thin, hard line, his eyes unwavering and cold. He spoke almost in a monotone, and his words were short and menacing.

"There's no need for any more tricks, Miss Sutton. You see, we know now how you did it."

The girl rushed at him with a demoniacal ferocity. Moran and I emerged quickly from our hiding place, but Kane motioned us to stand back.

"Let me by," she shrieked, "or I'll kill you."

"Just as you killed them both," Kane flung back at her. "Just as you shot your father down, without a word of warning." He had seized her clawing hands, and held her while she writhed impotently. But at his last words she caught a gasping breath and looked at him wildly.

"You fools!" she cried. "It wasn't my father I killed, don't you know that!" She laughed hysterically. "It was someone else, someone *she'd* changed him into. She'd ruined my life—taken everything I wanted. I hated her. I'd do it again, no matter what happened."

She jerked herself free from Kane's grasp, and glared at him in unholy triumph.

"I got the best of her! He came back to me again after I'd killed him. And then I killed her, so she couldn't tell. I'm glad, I tell you, I'm glad!"

Her body rocked with sobbing laughter, and she swayed as if she were about to fall.

Kane motioned to McBeath. "Take her away," he said dully. "She's all right now. And let her sleep." He dropped into a chair and covered his face with his hands.

CHAPTER 19

Half an hour after the scene I have just described, Kane, Moran, and I were seated in Kane's office, whose businesslike air seemed to give the lie to the drama in which we had taken part.

Kane broke the long silence. "I know there are things you want me to explain," he said, addressing us both, "and I'm ready to answer anything you wish to ask."

Moran had been waiting for this opening. "Well, then, I'm curious about this, Kane," he stated. "Didn't you ever suspect Mrs. Sutton?"

"I couldn't," Kane replied. "In the first place, to murder Sutton, she would have had to use the ledge. Her crippled arm would have prevented her from doing that. In the second place, she never showed any emotion toward Sutton but indifference, or possibly a mild affection. She is a harsh but a just woman, whose actions are regulated by her convictions. She showed that in her attitude to Gilroy. Then, too, she made no bones about Sutton's devotion to Mrs. Anceney, while Katharine denied it. There's an interesting difference there. In admitting it, Mrs. Sutton showed her almost complete lack of feeling toward the situation. Katharine, on the other hand, would not acknowledge the truth. She acted on what she knew, and immediately afterward denied its existence. It was necessary for her to recreate in her own mind her father as she wanted him to be. To cap the climax as far as Mrs. Sutton was concerned, there was one great reason why she couldn't have been guilty. At the time Mrs. Anceney's death really occurred, Mrs. Sutton was downstairs giving us her evidence.

"Therefore, when I realized that Mrs. Anceney might have been killed a half hour earlier than we thought, and that consequently her murderer was one of the two women, I knew that only Katharine could be guilty. But to put my conclusion beyond the possibility of a doubt, it was necessary to force Katharine into admitting it. And I used the only means at my disposal.

"Moran, at one time you came close to the truth," he continued, "but it was for the wrong reasons. When you found the jade in Katharine's desk, you tried to build up a case, using the jade as the only evidence against her. It was too early then for me to lay my cards on the table. I hadn't enough of them. Besides that, I couldn't believe that Katharine had stolen the pendant. As we found out later, she hadn't.

"By the way, I haven't ever told you what eventually happened to that piece of jade. That's quite interesting, if you haven't already figured it out for yourselves. Gilroy planted it on her, as we know. He wanted to have a hold over her so that if she told her story he could tell his. As luck would have it, he picked the person for whom it would have the most significance. You remember that when I opened the drawer of the desk I was careful not to let her see the jade. But I left it where it was. She was bound to find it sooner or later, and think that it had not been there at the time of my search. I reasoned that if she were innocent, if my whole theory were wrong, she would bring it to me. Well, she did not, but the jade disappeared from the drawer, as you know. She thought we were ignorant of its whereabouts, and got it out of her possession. That made me sure I was on the right track."

"Look here, Kane," Moran interposed, that stubbornness I knew so well creeping into his tone, "you've got to admit you haven't always been on the right track. I can tell you one time you were wrong."

Kane smiled good-naturedly. "All right, Moran. Let's hear it."

"The time you said our trap had failed," Moran stated triumphantly. "It didn't fail. Katharine came."

"But it failed for all practical purposes, Moran. What evidence did we have against her? If she'd had the time and the opportunity, she would have given herself away. But circumstance prevented. And the circumstance I refer to was the unexpected arrival of Gilroy on the scene."

"What do you mean—the unexpected arrival of Gilroy?" Moran queried sharply. "Gilroy was there before she came."

"No, he wasn't, Moran." Kane laughed. "I see there's more to explain than I'd thought. Well, this is the truth of the matter. All of Katharine's actions in that room were a play to the grandstand, and the grandstand was not Gilroy, but you and Underwood and I. You see, she knew we were there. She realized she must play innocent, and she did it supremely well. Let me tell you how I've figured it out. It was she who entered the room first. She moves very quietly, you know. She became aware, somehow, of our presence. Perhaps she saw Underwood's outline against the window, and knew someone was lying in wait for her. Meantime, she heard the sound of another person, Gilroy, coming into the room. She let him pass her, and edged her way to the door, so that when she spoke to Gilroy, and switched on the light, she gave the impression of just having come from the hall. That's what I meant when I said, do you remember, that the murderer would not have entered the room while Gilroy was there. Katharine had entered the room *before* Gilroy came.

"And that solves that mystery, I hope, Moran. Now just to put all perplexities out of your mind, I want to finish an explanation I gave you in partial form this afternoon. The person whom Bert overheard quarreling with Sutton over Mrs. Anceney was not James, as he thought, but Katharine. She had joined her father while Bert was away from the door, and after James had left. It was she who got the gun out of the drawer."

Kane fished a cigarette from a rumpled package and lighted it. "I wonder if you are as struck as I am by the diabolical cleverness Katharine showed, not only in planning the crimes, but in acting on the spur of the moment when no plan was possible. The existence of the ledge, and the loose piece of leading in the window served, as she knew they would, to cloak her connection with the first crime, and to throw the guilt on Mrs. Anceney. She was shrewd enough to leave no fingerprints on the gun or on the razor, and to leave both weapons on the scenes of the crimes. Dropping the gun on the table of Sutton's sitting room, in the presence of nine or ten other people, was a feat in itself.

"She had a rare ability to carry through a deadly purpose without a tremor. Fearing that Mrs. Anceney could betray her, she seized a hairbreadth chance to silence her forever.

"Just imagine," Kane said softly, "what her state of mind must have been when she heard McBeath's conversation with the butler, and realized that he was going to catch her literally red-handed. She hid and kept her nerve enough to answer him in Mrs. Anceney's stead. When his back was turned, she slipped out of the room, as you saw Mrs. Sutton do. What had been her greatest danger turned out to be her greatest safeguard. McBeath was ready to swear that Mrs. Anceney was alive when he brought her the wine.

"Think, too, of the fact that at the time of her greatest peril, she kept her wits about her enough to slip the bloodstained cloth into the window draperies. In that and every other situation up to the end she showed a cunning beyond description."

Kane ceased speaking for a moment, as if to collect his thoughts. Finally he said, "Let me remind you again of what I told you this afternoon—that the deepest and strongest part of the motive for the crimes was love. Do you remember the letters you found, Moran? Letters from Katharine to her father? They meant something to me, even at the time. One fact you must accept, otherwise the truth seems absurd. Katharine's love for her father was real. It was the center of her life. She had a strange heredity, both from her father and from her mother. And there was another quirk in her mind which prevented her from finding normal outlets for her feelings. I think they call people of that type introverts. We can, at any rate, since we're not speaking scientifically."

He turned to Moran. "You thought Sutton's letter referred to Bert. But let me read you a part of the article he mentioned, and you'll see your mistake. It's a paragraph Simonds quotes from Freud."

He picked up a magazine that lay by his elbow, and flipped through the pages. "Here it is," he said, and began to read:

> "The son, even as a small child, begins to develop an
> especial tenderness for his mother, whom he considers
> as his own special property, and feels his father to be
> a rival who puts into question his individual posses-
> sion; and in the same manner the little daughter sees
> in her mother a person who is a disturbing element in
> her tender relation with her father, and who occupies

a position that she could very well fill herself. . . . Furthermore the Œdipus-complex is more or less well developed; it may even experience a reversal. . . . In addition, children frequently react to the Œdipus-idea through stimulation by their parents, who in the placing of their affection are often led by sex-differences, so that the father prefers the daughter, the mother the son."

Kane put the magazine down on his desk. "You see," he said, "that's the sort of situation we were dealing with—or rather with a reversal of it. In her father Katharine found the only object of her affections, and he fostered that tendency in her by treating her as an equal and a confidante. Up to a few months ago, she was satisfied. Then Mrs. Anceney came along to tread on delicate ground. She involuntarily turned Sutton away from Katharine and aroused the girl's fierce jealousy. You see, Katharine was in the position of a woman who has been betrayed by her lover. Add to that the fact that she knew no scruples, had no moral convictions, and an unbridled temperament, and you have the makings of the tragedy.

"Whatever you do, don't yield to pity for her," he continued. "I doubt if anyone ever deserved it less than she does. She wasn't insane, you know, except as we are all slightly insane. She was supposedly a responsible person who saw fit to commit an unnatural crime. She is dangerous, merciless, violent, and unbalanced."

I had to agree with him.

For all of us, the case was ended. There was nothing more to do, and so I rose to make my departure. Seeing that I was about to go, Kane got up.

"I have rotten manners," he said apologetically. "I haven't thanked you at all. You just take that for granted, will you? You know you're much too good a sleuth to be wasted. The Sutton case is done with, but there are a lot of things waiting for me. One of them may be promising. I'll let you know."

He grinned at Moran and me in a friendly fashion.

"Good-bye for the present. Remember, 'in thunder, lightning, or in rain.'"

THE BACK BAY
MURDERS

Affectionately Dedicated
To
E. S. M. and S. M.

CHAPTER 1

"You can't always tell," Kane was saying, "just where you're going to end up when you start out chasing your hat. You may land in jail, or you may be run over, or you may go peaceably home with your hat under your arm." He stared out of his office window at the busy street below.

"You think there may be something in this, then?" I asked.

"Don't make me into a prophet, Underwood." He turned, half-smiling, half-impatient. "I can only say this—and I've never known it to fail: when a queer thing happens there's usually something queer-er behind it. And the gentleman who called me up just now wasn't feeling calm by any means. I'll make a guess, too, that he's a fairly peculiar person."

There was a familiar light in Kane's eye, a light that I had seen before. It gave him a curiously aloof and intent look, as though he were already working on a problem that as far as I was concerned did not yet exist. It always fascinated me to see him so eager to get something out of nothing. He had that kind of imagination, the kind that seizes upon a few seemingly disconnected facts and fits them into a clear and logical sequence.

I had known Kane for many years, but not until some months ago had I been associated with him in one of his cases. On that occasion I had been present, as the family lawyer, at a dinner party which had a fatal ending, and had called Kane, my only friend among the police inspectors of Boston, to my assistance and to that of the Sutton family. His spectacular solution of that case, widely known as the Beacon Hill murders, had put him in the limelight as far as the public was concerned. Between the two of us it had strengthened the friendship of years, and although I still played an active part in the law firm of which I was a member, I spent a great deal of time following Kane in his more thrilling profession.

"Do you want to go with me to see Prendergast, on the chance that something comes of it?" he went on.

"I don't know yet what 'it' is," I said, "but of course I want to go with you." Kane seemed to expect that after hearing one end of a telephone conversation I would understand the other.

"Well, 'it' is an unusual report of a housebreaking," he answered. "The man who called me up is named Prendergast. He lives in the house of a Mrs. Quincy, over on Beacon Street. Someone has broken into his room. He sounded almost crazy. He kept saying that he couldn't stand it, and begging someone to come over. He said something about blood that I couldn't quite get. The man was pretty much on edge, and not on account of a possible burglar either."

Kane was busy at his desk, picking up papers and loading his pockets, which always bulged with an assortment of objects. Finally he got himself to his feet, put on his hat and started for the door.

He was in no mood for conversation, and we walked in silence downstairs and into the street. Kane's long legs covered the ground rapidly. It seemed strange to be trying to keep up with his stride again. Of course, I had seen him often since the conclusion of the Sutton affair, but it was a very different thing, after meeting him casually, to see him at work. I felt the old excitement coming over me once more. After all, the things that Kane, as a police inspector, accepted as part of his day's routine, were like Arabian tales to me. He could safely say that his business was like chasing a hat, but the hats he dealt in were likely to lead him into devious and dangerous ways. Still it was hard for me to fancy that this expedition of Kane's, that took us along familiar streets colored by the brilliant sunshine of early November, might come to a strange conclusion.

We had been walking about fifteen minutes, when Kane stopped abruptly before a brownstone house.

"That's the number," he said. "It doesn't seem as though anything very extraordinary were likely to happen here."

There was certainly very little to distinguish the house from its neighbors. Like them it stood a little back from the street. A flight of steps led up to the front door, which, with its heavy, handsome respectability, seemed to characterize the yet unknown inhabitants. A brass plate underneath the bell bore the name of Quincy.

We mounted the steps and Kane rang. As we stood there waiting I could not help wondering what that noncommittal door would reveal.

In a few moments Kane's ring was answered by a manservant, who seemed to expect him.

"Mr. Kane?" he said in a surly, Irish voice, and motioned to us to come in. "Mrs. Quincy'd like to speak to you."

He knocked on a door to the left of the hall, and, opening it, stood aside to let us enter. Then he closed it silently and disappeared. The room in which he left us was comfortably arranged with dark, massive furniture. It was handsome in a way, and yet old-fashioned enough to be significant of a past rather than a present splendor. The windows looked onto the street. There was a door at the farther end. As I glanced toward it, it opened and a woman entered.

Kane walked towards her. "I'm Inspector Kane, Mrs. Quincy," he said. "I understand that your house has been broken into."

Mrs. Quincy returned his gaze with a look of surprise. "You come from the police?" she asked. Evidently Kane's tall, awkward figure did not fit in with her idea of his profession.

Kane nodded in answer to her question, then turned back to me. "Mr. Underwood," he said, in introduction. "You want to speak to us?"

"Yes." She came forward to the lighter part of the room. She was a woman of middle height and middle age, who expressed in her bearing, curiously enough, both self-assurance and insecurity. As she sat down she passed her hand nervously over her forehead, pushing back her iron-gray hair, which she wore in a loose pompadour. Her forehead was heavily lined, and her shrewd brown eyes looked on the world with suspicion. But whatever lay behind her fears, she was obviously prepared to deal efficiently with any attack that might be made on her.

She motioned to us to sit down, and once again turned her gaze on Kane. She seemed to be measuring him and at the same time steeling herself against any contingency that might arise. She sat quietly, her hands folded in her lap, and waited, not for Kane to speak, but until she herself was ready to do so.

She began slowly. "As you know, Mr. Kane, it was not I who called you up. It was Mr. Prendergast, who lives in this house. Some of my rooms are taken by people of my acquaintance, who prefer that way of living to an apartment house or a hotel."

"He lives here alone?"

"No. With his mother." She brushed Kane's question aside. "I was very much disturbed to learn that he had called the police. You understand that I have to think of the other people who are living here. Naturally they wouldn't like anything of the sort."

"I see." Kane looked at her reflectively. She could not hide the fact that she was worried, and now that I knew something about her I could understand her defensive attitude. She belonged among the impoverished well-born, whose first effort is to gloss over indigence with carefully nourished pride. She was fighting tooth and nail, probably, to keep her place even there, by the hard career of the hostess of paying guests. "I'm afraid there's nothing I can do but go ahead," Kane continued, "now that Mr. Prendergast has called me."

"I suppose not," she answered a little wearily. "But there's one thing I want to explain to you. Mr. Prendergast is rather difficult to deal with. When you see him, you must remember that he isn't quite like other people. I don't mean to say"—she corrected herself hastily, as though she were afraid of being overheard—"that he is insane at all, but he has queer ideas. Of course, something has happened, but it may not be quite what he says, or thinks."

She checked herself again, trying to avoid saying too much, and afraid of saying too little. "I don't mean that he doesn't tell the truth," she amended herself. "He seems to suffer from hallucinations, almost."

She looked at Kane as though she distrusted his understanding. His air of intelligence encouraged her. "You know what happened, don't you?" she continued.

Before she could go on, Kane interrupted her. "If you don't mind, Mrs. Quincy," he said, "I think I'd like to see for myself. Where is Mr. Prendergast?"

"Upstairs."

She seemed to realize that the affair had got beyond her control, but she followed us to the door as if she were reluctant to let us go.

"You won't forget what I said, will you?" she reminded him. "Mr. Prendergast is very excitable, and—unbalanced."

Kane made a reassuring gesture and led the way to the hall, Mrs. Quincy had evidently made a sudden decision to come with us. She pushed her way past Kane and began to mount the flight of stairs. Her left hand gripped the balustrade firmly and she stepped with quick determination.

I could hear voices coming from above, and as we reached the second floor we found a group of people collected in the hall, centered about a young man. He sat huddled in a chair, his head bowed, and his hands pressed over his eyes. His long black hair was disheveled and hung lankly over his fingers. An older woman bent over him nervously.

"Now, Arthur. Now, Arthur." She repeated the words over and over again, her hands fluttering ineffectually. Finally she turned a bewildered, childish look on the others. "I can't seem to do anything with him," she said. "He won't even pay attention to his mother." She pouted helplessly. "Can't you do something, Doctor?"

A slim, dark man came to her side. "You must not be so distressed, dear lady," he said. "These gentlemen are ready to take charge now." She turned and saw us for the first time.

Kane stepped forward. "Mrs. Prendergast?" She gave him a faint smile. "I think your son telephoned me."

At the sound of Kane's voice the young man leaped from his chair. "Yes, I did," he said wildly. His angular features were distorted and his black eyes shone unnaturally. "I called you. You've got to do something, understand. I can't stand this any longer. People are doing horrible things to me, and I can't stop them. It's horrible."

An embarrassed silence fell on the whole group. They looked at one another uneasily. No one seemed to know what to say. Finally a white-haired man, wearing a skull cap, walked slowly across the hall toward Prendergast. He had a cane in his hand, which he held a little before him. He turned an expressionless face on the young man and spoke to him in a slow, gentle voice.

"Never mind, Arthur. Never mind. You mustn't think such things. It's all right, all right."

Prendergast swung away from him. "It's not all right, I tell you. No one believes me. Everything's against me. But I won't stand for it any longer. I know who—" Frightened, he checked himself, and with a sudden rush of courage, "I'll—I'll—oh, God, I can't!" His voice had taken on a hysterical shrillness, and he turned a despairing face on Kane. "Can't you do something?"

Kane took charge of the situation. "Suppose you show me what it's all about," he said briskly. "And then I'll know what's to be done."

Prendergast gave a jerk of his head and pushed his hair back from his forehead. "I'll show you," he said, "but I won't go in." He shuddered a little.

He shoved the elderly man to one side, and ignoring the other two men who stood in the hall led the way toward the front of the house. He turned suddenly and put his hand on the knob of a door to his right.

"This is my room," he said, his voice shaking. He threw the door open and stepped back quickly. "You can see for yourself. It's everywhere. Blood!"

CHAPTER 2

At first glance the room looked peaceful enough. The glowing sunlight of the late afternoon streamed through the window. It fell in a distorted oblong upon the floor, in the middle of which a white Persian cat was playing. The animal was intent on his game. He paid no attention to us, but continued to toss his plaything, a white feather, into the air, and leap after it with wicked grace. When it fell, he moved it gently with his paw until the breeze caught it and whirled it over his head.

There seemed to be nothing out of the ordinary in the place, nothing that would explain Prendergast's fears. I glanced about the room but my eyes were blinded for the moment by the sunlight, and I could see little but the outlines of a bed, a desk, a chair. What could have come over the man?

Then I looked down at my feet. Just inside the sill, the floor was stained a thick, reddish brown. Blood. There was a pool of it near me, and farther inside the room the floor was discolored and spotted as though blood had rained down from the ceiling.

Now I saw that everything was in disorder. The drawers of the bureau had been pulled out and ransacked. Papers were strewn over the desk and on the floor. There was a towel lying near me, on its white surface a telltale red stain.

The place gave me a weird feeling. It was as though some mysterious crime had been committed there, leaving behind it every sign of violence but one. Where had the blood come from?

There was something uncanny about it, something threatening, as if a ghastly joke had been played to arouse perverted laughter.

After a moment or two Kane stepped into the room motioning me to stay where I was. At his entrance the cat looked up, gave a terrified start, and darted through the doorway to my right. He left his feather on the floor behind him.

Kane moved quickly and carefully about the room, avoiding as far as he could the stains of blood. He paused by the desk and picked up a metal box, the lid of which had been wrenched off. He examined it closely and then spoke to Prendergast.

"What do you keep in this?"

There was no reply. I looked back into the hall. Prendergast was standing pressed against the opposite wall. His head was bent a little forward and he was staring into the room, his brilliant eyes unnaturally fixed.

When Kane repeated the question, he came somewhat to himself.

"Nothing," he said, with a quick, sobbing breath.

"You kept it locked, didn't you? You must have had something in it. You had better look and see if there is anything missing."

Kane held out the strong box, but Prendergast did not move toward him.

"I won't go in there," he said, shrilly. He began to tremble again.

Kane did not insist but went patiently to work, examining everything, asking Prendergast where he kept this and that, what valuables he had, whether or not he kept money in his room. His patience had one result. He found that Prendergast had been robbed of nothing.

Before Kane left the room he took out his penknife and carefully scraped up from the floor a clot of blood. He put the scrapings in a paper, folded it, and slipped it in his pocket. As he closed the door and came out into the hall he said to Mrs. Quincy, "You can have the servants clean the room now."

A look of relief came into her eyes, and she hurried away.

The people who had been in the hall when we first came upstairs were still there. The dark man who had gone to Mrs. Prendergast's side stepped forward to meet us. He assumed the air of a master of ceremonies.

"You will want to ask us some questions?" he queried, smiling. "We'll be very glad." His easy glance took in the other occupants of the hall. "My name is Spinelli. Dr. Spinelli. You know Mr. Prendergast. His mother, Mrs. Prendergast." He bowed toward the nervous lady. "This is Mr. Weed." With a graceful gesture he brought the white-haired man into the circle.

Weed stepped forward uncertainly. "How do you do?" he said, extending his hand in our direction. "Mr. Kane?" His voice was inquiring. "You'll have to excuse me. I can't see, you know." He was gently apologetic. I noticed that blindness had not disfigured his pale gray eyes, except by giving them a look of vacancy.

Kane shook hands with him, and then turned to the others, whom Spinelli had brought forward.

"This is Mr. Wainwright." A rather formal gentleman of fifty-five or so acknowledged the introduction. He was meticulously dressed, and his manners were of the old school. He had an air of intelligent, if somewhat cold, reserve.

"Mr. Vincent." A younger man came forward. He was tall and extraordinarily good-looking. His dark hair was brushed back from a high forehead, whose whiteness was emphasized by his black eyebrows. His eyes were deep-set, his features almost perfectly formed. He wore a small mustache. And yet, for all his charm of manner and appearance, no one could have thought him effeminate, for he was powerfully built, and he had an air of vigor and health that I liked. As he shook hands with Kane, I noticed two other significant things about him—his engaging, easy smile, and the shape of his hands. It gave me something like a shock to look at them, for while otherwise he was really a type of masculine beauty, they were ugly and ill-formed, the palms heavy, the fingers short and spatulate.

The doctor continued to take charge of the proceedings. "You will take us in turn?" he suggested. "May I ask that you speak to Mrs. Prendergast first? She is very much upset. She should rest."

Mrs. Prendergast, who had been sitting down, rose nervously. "What is it?" she asked, her hands fluttering. "What do they want to say to me? I don't know anything about this dreadful thing." Her voice rose in a childish wail of self-pity. She appealed to the doctor. "Can't you tell me what to say?"

He shook his head gently. "These gentlemen won't trouble you any more than they can help. It will be only a minute."

He herded the others to the end of the hall, and without bothering to go to another room Kane began his investigation. Mrs. Prendergast could tell him nothing. She had been out all afternoon, and had returned to find her son in a state of excitement and distress. After a few questions, Kane let her go and talked to the others, one by one. Like Mrs. Prendergast, they had nothing to offer. Wainwright, Vincent, and Spinelli had come home at five o'clock. About half-past five they had heard Prendergast storming down the hall. They had gone to see what was the matter, and had seen, but had not entered, his bedroom. Spinelli had taken the trouble to make sure that no one disturbed it before Kane's arrival.

Weed, on the other hand, had been in the house all afternoon. He had heard nothing until Prendergast's outburst. With the passive serenity of the blind he was untouched by the prevailing excitement. He was troubled only by the fact that his cat had got out. Someone had told him that the cat had been in Prendergast's room. When Kane said that he might go, he ambled uncertainly down the hall, calling, "Sheba! Ni-ice Sheba!" Mrs. Quincy evidently heard him, for she called to him that the cat had gone back to his room.

Prendergast had disappeared, and when Kane asked for him, Dr. Spinelli answered in his stead. "May I suggest," he said smoothly, "that he be allowed to rest for a few moments? That is, if you approve."

Kane seemed satisfied. "I want to talk to Mrs. Quincy," he said. "Send him to her sitting room when he's quieter."

We went downstairs again and found Mrs. Quincy. She looked at Kane anxiously, but he made no answer to her unspoken question.

When he had made himself comfortable in a big armchair, he said, "What's your explanation?"

"I haven't any. I can't imagine how it could have been done."

"Could any intruder have got in by the front door?"

"Certainly not. I am very careful about that. I had a new lock put on last week, and only my guests have keys."

"The back door?"

Mrs. Quincy was very decided. "I asked the servants just now. They have been in the kitchen all afternoon. No one came in or went out that way."

"And there is no possibility that the house could have been entered by the windows?"

She made a gesture of denial. "You can see for yourself. The lower ones are barred. The upper ones couldn't be reached."

Kane reflected a moment. "By the way," he went on, "have we seen everyone who is staying here?"

"I don't think so." She thought the question over. "My husband is out. You haven't seen Mr. Lovejoy, have you? Or Mrs. Balbirnie?"

"I don't think I have."

"Well, you'll hardly need to wait for them. Mr. Lovejoy is a nice young man. Perhaps a little weak." She gave a short laugh. "You've seen Mr. Prendergast. Even he calls Mr. Lovejoy a coward. The man can't even look at a cut finger without turning white. As for Mrs. Balbirnie"—for once she gave her shrewdness full rein—"she might have a great deal to say, but it would scarcely be to the point."

Kane said nothing. Mrs. Quincy became impatient. She glanced at her watch, almost as though she were giving a caller a polite hint to leave. "It's almost dinner-time," she murmured.

With a humorous twist of his lips, Kane put the suggestion aside. "Has anything ever happened before," he said slowly, "that might lead you to expect this—episode?"

Mrs. Quincy gave him a hostile look. "I don't think you understand, Mr. Kane"—she spoke with crisp decision—"that the people who live in my house are not the sort. . . Things don't happen to them."

"I wonder if they don't, occasionally," Kane replied in a quiet voice. "However . . ." he pushed speculation aside. "We're waiting to see Mr. Prendergast. Isn't this the best place for us to stay until he's ready to talk to us?"

She agreed silently and left us, saying something about the servants and dinner. When she had gone Kane turned to me.

"What do you make of it?" he asked.

"Somebody must have broken in and looked through Prendergast's things," I said. "Then, when he was opening that strong box, he must have cut himself on the edge of it. That would account for the blood."

"That's simple, all right," Kane agreed, "but nothing was stolen. Also, the lid of the strong box had a blunt edge, and the box itself had no blood on it."

I looked at him helplessly and said nothing.

Kane pulled his awkward length out of the chair, walked over to the mantelpiece, and leaned against it. "There's something intangible about the whole thing," he said, as if to himself. "I can't get the hang of it. After all, as far as the law's concerned, nothing much has been done. We can't do anything about it, yet."

He flipped the ash of his cigarette into the fireplace. "I suspect Prendergast holds the key to this riddle. Perhaps we'll get something out of him when he's calmer."

We had only a few minutes to wait before Prendergast appeared. He moved and spoke more quietly, but the signs of strain had not left his face. He did not sit down, but took a stand at the door, as if he wanted to be near a way of escape.

"I seem to have been a fool again," he said, with a sickly attempt at a smile. "Everybody says nothing can be the matter. I'm sorry I called you."

"Oh, that's all right," Kane tried to reassure him, but the kindly, intelligent look he gave the younger man brought no response. "We'd be glad to help you," he added.

Prendergast did not reply. "You see," Kane pursued his monologue, "if you could tell us a little more, we might be able to do something."

Prendergast's eyes were fixed on Kane's face, but still he did not say anything. There was a strange tensity about him.

"You're sure you have nothing to tell us?"

"Nothing. No, nothing." He spoke as if he were appealing to us. He bent his head so that we could not see his face.

"You couldn't say, for instance, who did this?"

Prendergast started as if he had been shot. He looked up. His eyes were tragic. "No," he whispered. "I can't. I can't say."

Kane got up. "That's all I wanted to know," he said, his words breaking a strained silence. "If anything turns up, I'll let you know. There's nothing more we can do here. Let's be on our way."

CHAPTER 3

The next evening I met Kane at his hotel for dinner. I waited until we were having our soup to refer to our last night's adventure. His spoon was halfway to his mouth, but at my comment he put it down untouched. Our waiter, observing that Kane was leaning back in his chair with the air of having finished, came up quietly and took away his plate. He seemed unconscious of its disappearance.

"Underwood," he began, frowning at the tablecloth while he outlined an intricate pattern on it with his forefinger, "I don't know what you think but I'm certain there's more in this affair than meets the eye."

I made no reply for a moment. Then I said, "All those people are so surely entrenched in respectability. It's a strange place to have anything like that happen."

"Yes, it is," Kane agreed. "I wonder how they all happen to be living in Mrs. Quincy's house. For the sake of companionship with their own kind, I suppose. Except for the Prendergasts, they seem to be solitary individuals without immediate family connections. Probably they could well afford to have their own homes, if they wanted to live alone. But Mrs. Quincy's establishment offers them comfort, as much luxury as they want to pay for, and human society. Moreover, Mrs. Quincy's shrewd eye is their assurance that no undesirables will be foisted upon them."

I nodded and waited for him to continue. Finally he looked up at me. "By the way, Underwood," he said, "those blood spots tested out just as I thought they would."

"What do you mean?"

"I mean that the stains so carefully deposited in Prendergast's room weren't bloodstains."

"Not blood!" I looked at him in astonishment. "Then what were they?"

"Oh," Kane made a careless gesture, "mercurochrome, tomato catsup, a red dye—any one of a hundred different things. All I care about is the fact that they weren't blood."

"But how do you explain their being there? Something spilled by accident?"

Kane shook his head. "Well, it wasn't an accident that anyone cared to own up to."

"Then," I suggested, "if, as you say, the stains weren't blood, isn't it possible that Prendergast staged the scene himself?"

"You mean from some crazy delusion?"

"Yes," I defended myself. "You know there are people who do things like that to gain notoriety."

"Of course," he answered, "but did Prendergast seem insane to you for all his fears?"

"No."

"He didn't to me either. And he'd have to be well off his head to fabricate such a situation."

He began to eat his fish. "How would it suit you," he asked, after a moment, "to walk around to Beacon Street with me? That is, if you're interested."

"I'd like to go."

"All right. You see, I'll have to go around there sometime within the next twenty-four hours. Got to explain to them, with some difficulty, I expect, that what looks gory isn't always blood. Calm their fears, and depart in peace. Waiter!" He signaled to the hovering black-coat behind my chair and told him that we were in a hurry for the rest of our dinner.

Twenty minutes later we passed through the revolving doors of the hotel and out into the street. I noticed that the clock over the desk said 9:01.

Kane lit a cigarette and looked speculatively at the sky. "Stopped raining. Guess we can make it between drops," he commented, and then added, glancing at the crooked handle over my arm, "though I see you've brought a stout umbrella to protect us both."

"And we would have needed it half an hour ago," I returned defensively. "Looked like a downpour to me. Be thankful I'm not wearing rubbers!"

Kane laughed and we set out in the direction of Beacon Street. It was about fifteen minutes' walk from the hotel, and soon I could pick out the brownstone front of the house to which we had been summoned, under such peculiar circumstances, the evening before. As we drew near we saw that the house was ablaze with lights.

"Not risking another mysterious visitation, I guess," Kane said.

We mounted the steps. Kane pressed the bell and turned toward the street, waiting. In the moment of silence, we heard a confused murmur of voices from an open window on the second floor of the house. There was no answer to our ring, and Kane pushed the button a second time, with the same result. Suddenly, from the murmur above us, there materialized a low sound of sobbing. I turned questioningly to Kane. Without a word he grasped the handle of the door and pushed it open, admitting us to a small vestibule. The glass door beyond did not yield to Kane's repeated attempts to force it.

Now the sounds were distinct, but through the door of the vestibule we could see no one on the first floor. The ceiling above us resounded to hurried footsteps, and there was a frenzied haste in the incoherent words that reached us. All at once we heard a voice nearer than the rest, shouting to someone.

"Tell her I can't get the inspector. He's not there. But they're sending someone else right away. What? My God, yes, of course they'll hurry!" The man's voice was shaking with either anger or fear.

The words we had heard startled Kane into action. Seizing my umbrella, he hammered on the glass with its wooden handle, at the same time rattling the door knob noisily. In a moment there were steps on the stairs. A man appeared in the hall and looked fearfully toward the door of the vestibule. He was thin and gray-haired. I did not remember having seen him before.

As he hesitated, Kane thrust his face closer to the glass.

"Open this door," he called menacingly.

"What do you want?" the man countered. Without replying, Kane flipped back his lapel and showed his badge.

The man gave it one look, and then, with a start of surprise, hurried to obey. As he threw open the door he quavered, "Thank the Lord you're here!"

Kane grasped the man by the shoulder.

"What's up? Who are you?"

"Quincy." He swallowed convulsively and with a nerveless hand pointed toward the upper floor.

Kane's grip tightened. He looked searchingly at him, then shot out one word:

"Prendergast?"

The man nodded and seemed to be on the point of recovering his tongue. But at his nod Kane released him and started for the stairs.

Quincy babbled disconnectedly as we mounted the steps to the second floor, but Kane ignored him. Questions were unnecessary—the hysterical crying we had heard from outside and the murmur of voices led us directly to the doorway from which they issued. The instant we reached it I knew it was the room Kane had been called to examine the night before—the room of the mysterious bloodstains.

For a second we stood outside the open door, unnoticed by those within. Every light in the room had been turned on. In their unshaded brightness were standing six or seven people whose frightened faces and strange attitudes I could not explain. Apart from them, a woman, her hands pressed to her eyes, was uttering regular, terrified moans.

Without thinking what I did, I looked down toward the place on the floor where, the evening before, I had seen the red stains. Only the polished surface of the boards met my glance, and I felt a sense of relief that the spots had been removed. But as I slowly raised my eyes, they fell suddenly upon a larger, much more horrifying stain on the light gray rug near the table in the center of the room. It was a glistening, dark red pool, which grew larger as I watched it—and even Kane could not doubt that this was blood, for near it lay the body of Arthur Prendergast. He had fallen on his right side. One arm was outstretched, the other drawn up so that his clenched fist pressed against his throat. His knees were bent. From a wound in the left side of his neck a red stream had oozed. He was dead, I knew; the glazed, staring eyes in the distorted face could not have belonged to a living man.

As we entered there was a heavy silence, which was broken by a sound I had not heard before—a steady, regular tapping which set my nerves on edge. Only one explanation entered my mind—that it was blood falling drop by drop upon the floor. I looked toward the corner, in the direction of the sound. I could see that the floor there was wet, and the ceiling above it discolored. Then I saw a drop of water splash on the bare boards. Rain! It had leaked in, as if some gruesome intelligence had willed it to give the final touch of horror to the room.

A sudden cry distracted me. Mrs. Quincy, catching sight of Kane, broke from the group, and came swiftly toward us. She moistened her lips spasmodically in an effort to control her agitation. With an instinctive gesture, she half held out a trembling, blue-veined hand.

"Mr. Kane," she began, with a sharp intake of breath after the words, "I didn't know you'd come. Mr. Prendergast . . . you see . . ." She stopped helplessly, and motioned vaguely behind her. Then she went on: "I found him right here. We don't know anything, any of us." She bit her lower lip nervously.

Kane gave her a cool glance, then he stepped past her into the center of the room. Two men, one of whom I recognized as Vincent, made way for him awkwardly.

"Dr. Spinelli!" Kane addressed the man who, leaning on the table, was surveying the face of the corpse with an almost dispassionate interest.

"Yes?" Spinelli looked up in surprise.

"Mr. Prendergast is—dead?"

"Yes." His voice was calm.

"You've made an examination?"

"Certainly."

"H'mm." Kane crouched on one knee and bent over the body. Soon he straightened himself.

"Did you discover him?" he asked Spinelli.

"No. I was called in afterwards."

"How long had he been dead then, can you say?"

Spinelli pulled at the cuff of his shirt. "A little less than a half hour, I think. I should say death occurred at about ten minutes of nine." He looked up and gave Kane a glance of appraisal.

At this moment Mrs. Prendergast, whose sobbing had long ago ceased to be an interruption, raised her head.

"Ten minutes of nine!" she cried unbelievingly, her face piteously tear-stained and discolored. "Almost as soon as I'd left! Oh, my God, my God, if I only hadn't gone!" She bowed her head once more and swayed to and fro, her fingers tearing frenziedly at her hair.

Kane had stood silent during this interruption, making no attempt to quiet the woman. Now he turned abruptly and faced us.

"I must ask you all to leave the room."

Vincent and a man whom I supposed to be Lovejoy started to obey, and Mrs. Quincy was turning reluctantly toward the door when Kane's voice snapped "Just a minute!" in so sharp a tone that almost in concert they swung around.

"There are one or two things I want to find out before you go," he said. "First off," he looked around him quickly, "who found the body?"

"I did." The answer came in a soft, almost effeminate voice. It was Lovejoy who spoke. "That is," he hesitated uncertainly, "Mrs. Quincy and I did. We—"

"All I want to find out, Mr. Lovejoy," Kane cut in, "is whether you touched anything, picked up any object, while you were in the room."

"We went right out again," Lovejoy was almost breathless. "No," something like a shudder crossed his face, "we didn't touch anything."

"And when you came into the room a second time?" Kane persisted.

"Not then, either. Dr. Spinelli told us—"

Spinelli, on the far side of the room, cleared his throat. "I warned them all on that subject."

Kane raised his left eyebrow. "I see," he said quietly. "Now," he continued, addressing Quincy, who had been standing in a kind of stupor at my side, "we overheard you telephoning Headquarters. They're sending someone else around?"

Quincy nodded.

"Good. Then that's all. No one may leave the house, for I shall want to see you in a few moments. Dr. Spinelli, will you see to Mrs. Prendergast, please?"

Spinelli touched Mrs. Prendergast's sleeve, and without a backward glance she allowed herself to be led unresisting from the room. The rest followed after them.

As they went, I turned around to watch them and saw Weed standing in the hall near the door. He must have been there for some time, although I had not seen him before. He did not seem to understand what was going on, but he went quietly away with the others.

CHAPTER 4

Scarcely had they left when Kane and I heard ascending footsteps on the stairs. A man spoke gruffly, and there was something familiar in the voice. Kane heard it too, and a ghost of a smile flickered on his lips. He beckoned to me.

"Come on," he said. "Something tells me an old friend of ours has been detailed to this case." We went out into the hall.

Two men were standing at the head of the stairs, one a thickset, middle-aged man with a square face; the other was shorter and carried a small black bag. I recognized the former as Sergeant Moran, who had worked with Kane on the Sutton case the year before.

Moran acknowledged my presence with a surprised grunt and shook hands with Kane.

"We musta made a name for ourselves, eh, Kane, to have 'em put us in the same team again?" he suggested.

Kane made some reply and introduced me to Dr. Sloan, the medical examiner.

"What's the case, Kane," Moran asked bluntly, "suicide or murder?"

"Come and judge for yourself," Kane answered. We returned to the room.

Moran sucked in his breath sharply as he looked down at the grotesque figure stretched out on the floor, and the pool of blood beside it.

"Doesn't look much like suicide to me," he said heavily, bending over to study the body more closely. "That's a nasty gash in the neck, and the man's hand isn't even bloody. Any weapon?" he asked.

"Haven't found any yet," Kane answered, "but we might take another look around. Are you through with the body, Moran? If so, Dr. Sloan can make his examination."

"Sure."

Dr. Sloan had taken off his hat and coat, and he now approached the body with a methodical calmness that astounded me, considering the hideousness of the object he was to deal with. I saw him bend over and lift the lifeless head—then I could look no more.

Meanwhile, Kane and Moran were making a careful survey of the room. I observed that Kane tried the windows and found them locked. All at once Moran, who had been peering at everything with strained attention, pointed to a spot on the floor near the window.

"Some more blood," he announced, in excitement at his discovery. "Didn't you see that before? There musta been some kind of struggle here, according to my way of thinking."

Kane suppressed a smile. "That's rain water," he said gravely. "I don't believe it means a struggle. It was leaking through the ceiling a minute ago. It's stopped now."

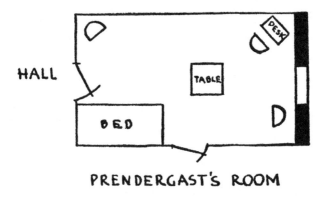

PRENDERGAST'S ROOM

Moran compressed his lower lip and said nothing. Presently he bent over and, with narrowed eyes, gave the polished table top a minute inspection.

"No good prints there," he said finally, drawing a heavy breath.

"No?" Kane queried casually. "Well, let's take a look at this," he remarked, picking up from the table an imitation tortoise-shell cigarette case and holding it at an angle to the light. "Yes," he continued immediately, "here are two distinct prints. Moran," he turned to the other, "have you an extra man with you?"

"Yeah. McBeath. Left him downstairs."

"Then let him take this case to be photographed right away. Tell him I want it back here to-night, within a couple of hours."

Moran wrapped the case in his handkerchief and went to carry out Kane's instructions. By the time he returned to the room Sloan had finished his examination.

He rose from his knees and began wiping his hands. He had moved the body slightly, and I felt an overwhelming relief that he had closed its eyes so that their ghastly stare was no longer fixed on us.

"What's your report, Sloan?" Kane asked him.

"Death from obvious causes," the doctor replied, pulling down his cuffs, and reaching for his coat. "The jugular vein is severed. Some sharp instrument used, probably a knife."

"Is it at all possible that he committed suicide?"

"Possible, but highly improbable. The wound is too large, and the position of it too far to the side. Have you found the weapon?"

"No, it's not in the room. Can you give us an idea of how long the blade was?"

"Five to six inches, I should say. Anything else?"

Kane pushed a long hand through his hair and frowned. "No, I guess not." Suddenly he looked at the doctor. "Wait! There's one other thing. When would you say he died?"

Dr. Sloan hesitated for a fraction of a second. "Well, I'd say," he answered slowly, "that he's been dead not less than half an hour, and not more than an hour."

"You can't approach it any more exactly than that?"

The doctor shook his head. "No, I can't be any more definite. It's impossible to put your finger on the exact time."

"Would you have been able to if you had examined the body twenty minutes sooner?"

"No."

Kane seemed satisfied. He took out his watch. "It's nine-thirty now. What you say means that Prendergast was killed sometime between eight-thirty and nine o'clock, doesn't it?"

"Yes." Dr. Sloan picked up his hat and his bag. "If that's all, I'll be going along."

"Just a minute." Kane stopped him. "Do you know a Dr. Spinelli?"

"That fellow who lives here?" Sloan asked in return. "No."

"Ever heard of him?"

Sloan snorted. "Yes, I have," he said. "He's a hand-holding lady-killer with a bedside manner. Tells every one of 'em she's a sensitive plant, and makes a lot of money by it."

"All right, and thanks," Kane replied absently.

As the door closed behind the doctor, Kane remained standing where he was, his long arms clasped behind his back and his head sunk upon his chest. He was staring moodily and almost unseeingly at the body of the dead man.

Presently his eyes became brighter, and his heavy brows drew together. His chin shot upward in that abrupt manner so characteristic of him; he took two long steps forward, and bent on one knee over the corpse. I saw him draw from beneath the twisted left shoulder, where it had remained concealed until Dr. Sloan had shifted the body, a small white object whose tip was soaked with blood.

Kane held it between thumb and forefinger. There was a strange expression on his face as he looked down at it.

"A feather . . . a white feather," I heard him say, as if to himself. "Now I wonder what that means."

CHAPTER 5

"Then I am to understand that Mr. Prendergast was—murdered?" Mrs. Quincy's small eyes fixed themselves intently on Kane as she asked the question, but she showed no sign of agitation. Apparently the half hour which had elapsed since the scene in Prendergast's room had enabled her to resume the composure which I had at first remarked in her. It was probable that Kane had counted on this capacity for self-control, for after coming downstairs he had not hesitated in summoning her to the living room.

Now the look he directed at her was as calm as her question. "Yes, Mrs. Quincy," he said steadily, "we think it was murder. But you,"—his voice rose a little—"you suspected that from what you saw, didn't you?"

"I suspected it." There was a pinched expression around the woman's mouth.

Kane nodded slowly and then his manner hardened. "Mr. Moran wants to ask you a number of questions, and I hope you'll be as direct as possible in answering." Having laid the burden of the interview on Moran's shoulders, he slumped down in his chair.

Moran cleared his throat. "Now, Mrs. Quincy, you found the body, didn't you?"

"Yes."

"All right. Tell us about it."

She hesitated. "I don't know just where you want me to begin," she countered, and then observing Moran's look of impatience she amended herself hastily, "but I suppose I'd better start at the time Mr. Lovejoy returned. He—"

229

"Who's Lovejoy?" Moran cut in.

Mrs. Quincy seemed startled at the interruption. "Mr. Lovejoy is one of the guests here, Mr. Moran," she replied coldly.

"All right," Moran dismissed the subject with a gesture. "Go ahead."

"Mr. Lovejoy knocked at my door at about five minutes past nine this evening, I think," she continued. "He had just returned from the political parade on Boylston Street, and wanted me to go upstairs with him. There was a leak in the ceiling of his room, he said, and he thought I ought to look at it. So we went up—"

"Just a minute," Moran stopped her again. "You say Lovejoy had just returned from the parade. Had he been up to his room before he knocked at your door?"

"No. He said he'd just come in, and he was carrying his hat." Mrs. Quincy glanced at Moran, but he gave no sign of having further questions to ask her, and she continued. "We went straight to his room on the third floor."

"Where you found a leak?"

"Yes. It was a bad one, and the ceiling was so discolored I was afraid the plaster would fall."

"And then?"

"I told him I would attend to it, and was about to go out, when he suggested that perhaps I'd better look in Mr. Prendergast's room too. You see, his room is below Mr. Lovejoy's and it was possible that the water might have gone through."

At this point, Mrs. Quincy's chair began to rock ever so slightly. She moistened her lips and went on.

"We knocked at Mr. Prendergast's door

"Mr. Lovejoy was with you, then?"

"Yes. It was he who knocked." She hesitated. "There was no reply; so I told Mr. Lovejoy we would go in anyhow, and he opened the door."

The woman's words, still cold and precise, had begun to fall a little hurriedly.

"I think Mr. Lovejoy took a step into the room. Then he stopped. I heard him scream. I couldn't imagine—I was behind him, you see." Mrs. Quincy put one hand to her forehead. "I suppose I pushed him to one side and looked into the room. At first I didn't see anything. But something frightened me, I don't know why." The expression of the woman's eyes belied the forced calmness of her words.

She continued quickly. "Then I saw Mr. Prendergast lying on the floor, in a—as you saw him. I knew he was dead." She stopped speaking.

Kane roused himself. "Did you go any farther into the room?" he asked.

"Well, yes, I did. I went over to him, to make sure. But I didn't touch him."

"What about Mr. Lovejoy?"

Mrs. Quincy's eyebrows went up and she gave a short laugh. "Mr. Lovejoy retreated to the hall. But Mr. Lovejoy, of course," she concluded, half-defensively, "is not what one might call a brave man."

"No," Kane agreed. "He doesn't seem to be."

At that moment we heard the sound of a door closing noisily.

"What's that?" Moran asked quickly, as he half-started from his chair. "Someone leaving the house?"

But his question was answered for him by the appearance of a man in the doorway, a man wearing a dark overcoat and hat, who looked curiously into the room, and seemed about to pass on down the hall. I recognized him as one of the people I had seen the night before.

Mrs. Quincy looked quickly at Kane. "Mr. Wainwright doesn't know what has happened," she said, in a low voice. "He has just come in."

Kane called Wainwright into the room. The latter came slowly, removing his hat in a mechanical fashion as he approached us. There was a questioning look on his face, as though he instinctively recognized the atmosphere of disaster but could not guess from what it emanated.

"Mr. Wainwright," Kane might have been announcing some topic of minor interest, so matter-of-fact was his tone, "Mr. Prendergast has been murdered."

Wainwright's starched collar moved visibly. His hand felt for his chin.

"Mr. Prendergast—" he repeated haltingly, as though mesmerized. "What?" A dull red crept into his cheeks. "I—I don't—understand," he stammered. Then his habitual formality reasserted itself, and he waited for someone to speak.

"No one is to leave the house to-night," Kane went on.

Wainwright's heavy face was almost expressionless. "I see," he said. He made an effort to change his position. I noticed that he did not bother Kane with useless questions.

The silence was broken by the ringing of the door bell. Kane turned to Mrs. Quincy.

"Is anyone else out?" he asked.

"Mrs. Balbirnie, possibly," she replied. "Mr. Wainwright, will you see who is there?"

Wainwright obeyed, and presently we heard him opening the door of the vestibule.

"Oh, Mr. Wainwright, thanks so much. Of course, I forgot my key again." The voice was deep and rather hoarse, but it was undoubtedly a woman who spoke. We heard her continue, more loudly, as if she were addressing someone in the street.

"Good-bye, girls. . . . What? . . . Oh, yes. I did too, even if we couldn't sit together. . . . What's that? Oh, thanks, May. I'll feel better in the morning. Next time I won't forget my glasses. But I'm positively *ashamed* to be so near-sighted—I really am! Well, good-bye."

There was an absent-minded laugh, the woman came into the hall, and the door closed.

"Dreadfully sorry to bother you, Mr. Wainwright," she continued. "Why, Mr. Wainwright, *don't* you look glum! Shouldn't get that way, you know." I imagined a playful forefinger shaken at the unfortunate Wainwright.

"Mrs. Balbirnie, will you come into the living room, please," we heard him request stiffly.

"Oh, yes, Mr. Wainwright, certainly." There was an excited pleasure in the woman's voice, a pleasure which, I fancied, was somewhat dissipated by the sight of us.

Nevertheless she came toward us in amiable surprise. We saw a fairly large woman, dressed in pronounced but unbecoming fashion, and wearing a tightfitting red hat that emphasized unfavorably the size and shape of her head and the prominence of her nose.

As she crossed the room, smiling at us with brightly rouged thin lips, she assumed a drawing room manner and affected to chat lightly with Wainwright, who followed her silently a step or two behind.

Kane, Moran, and I got up from our chairs. Mrs. Quincy leaned forward to speak. But Mrs. Balbirnie looked over her shoulder at Wainwright.

"Now I wonder what time it is," she announced. "As I say, that lecture . . ."

Wainwright flushed with annoyance, but as Mrs. Balbirnie still looked at him expectantly, he pushed back his cuff and glanced down at his wrist. His brief statement that his watch was not running did not, however, make an end to the question for Mrs. Balbirnie. This time Kane rose to the situation.

"It's exactly two minutes after ten, madam," he said.

"Oh, thank you so much. Would you believe it, I've been listening to a stupid lecture for almost two solid hours. Eight o'clock it began—now it's ten. Mercy me!" She raised her eyes in feigned exasperation. "It does seem to me that lecturers should—"

Mrs. Quincy drew herself together. "Mrs. Balbirnie," she began, "Mr. Kane has something to tell—"

But the name was enough. Mrs. Balbirnie glanced in wild surmise from the one to the other of us, and finally settled upon Moran.

"Oh, Mr. Kane," she broke in excitedly, "I've heard so much about you. Those mysterious bloodstains—what did you deduce? What is the end of the story?"

Moran, who had heard from Kane the events of the preceding day, coughed. "The end of that story, madam," he stated with dignity, "happens to be murder. Prendergast is dead."

The effect was electric. Mrs. Balbirnie's smile faded suddenly, and all natural color went from her face, leaving a rouge spot stranded on either cheekbone.

"Dead!" she chattered hoarsely. "He's dead!" Her staring eyes sought Mrs. Quincy's. Her mouth hung loosely. "For God's sake, Mrs. Quincy, what's happened?"

Kane explained to her quietly, and then, as she seemed unable to recover from her stupor, he motioned to Wainwright to take her to her room. When they had gone he closed the door.

"Are all the people in the house accounted for now?" he asked Mrs. Quincy, as he came back and sat down.

"Yes. They're all in now."

"Good. Then we won't be disturbed again. There are other things I want to find out from you."

Mrs. Quincy waited for Kane to continue. He had picked up a pencil from the table by his chair and was tapping his thumbnail gently, meditatively. A few seconds passed, and then, without warning, he turned on her.

"Mrs. Quincy, have you no idea who killed Prendergast?"

A shade of alarm crossed the woman's face at the sudden question, but fixing shrewd eyes on Kane, she answered steadily, "I have no idea."

"He had no enemies here in the house?"

"I knew of none."

"And outside this house?"

"I was not in the least acquainted with Mr. Prendergast's associates," she replied shortly.

"Then, as far as your knowledge goes," Kane persisted, "no one hated Prendergast sufficiently to kill him?"

Mrs. Quincy did not answer directly. Finally she said, "I can't conceive of anyone's hating a man such as he was. One could be contemptuous of him, certainly, with his queer ideas and his ridiculous fears. But as for hating him—he wasn't worth it."

Kane looked at her thoughtfully. "Contempt is fairly close to hatred," he said, "if the circumstances happen to be right. And hatred is the strongest inspiration for murder."

The woman was silent.

Kane went on. "Of course, there are other motives. Did Prendergast have money in his own name?"

"I suppose so."

"Don't you know?"

Mrs. Quincy cleared her throat. "I believe he did," she admitted.

"In the natural course of events, his mother would inherit, then."

"Mrs. Prendergast has money of her own," Mrs. Quincy interrupted coldly.

Kane seemed not to hear. "Do you happen to know whether Prendergast left a will?"

Mrs. Quincy's tone was distant. "You must understand that I have never concerned myself with my guests' personal affairs."

"I see. Well, I'll look that up for myself." Kane laid the pencil on the table and frowned down at it.

"Superficially," he mused, "there seems to be not even a shadow of reason for anyone's wanting Prendergast out of the way. First, we are to understand that he had no enemies. Second, we have yet to discover that anyone benefits unduly by his death. So—to start with—a motive for his murder is not only obscure, but apparently non-existent."

He shrugged his shoulders. "Anyhow, we'll let that go for the moment. Now, Mrs. Quincy," he began, turning again to the woman, "the medical examiner tells me that Prendergast was killed between eight-thirty and nine o'clock. Did you happen to see him between those times?"

Mrs. Quincy shook her head. "No, I didn't see him at all after dinner. But," she added slowly, "I remember hearing his voice upstairs—I think it was around half-past eight. I can't be sure."

"Where were you at that time?"

"In my own room, where I talked to you yesterday. That's across the hall, you know. I went there right after dinner, and stayed there until Mr. Lovejoy came."

"Do you happen to know who else was in the house at any time between eight-thirty and nine?"

Mrs. Quincy did not answer at once. Then she said, "I think I do. I know that Mrs. Prendergast was here until a little after a quarter of nine, because she stopped to ask me the time as she went out."

"Presumably her son was alive at a quarter of nine, then." Kane considered the end of his pencil thoughtfully. Mrs. Quincy made no answer.

"Mr. Vincent, the young man on the third floor," she continued, "was in. And Mr. Weed, of course."

Kane looked up quickly. "Mr. Weed? Oh, yes, I remember. He's the blind man, isn't he?"

"Yes. A friend came to see him."

"During the evening?"

"About eight-thirty."

"Is this friend someone you know?"

"Yes. He's been here before to see Mr. Weed. I don't happen to know his name."

Kane laid the pencil on the table and clapping his hands on either arm of the chair looked toward the ceiling.

"Then this, Mrs. Quincy, is what we are to understand," he said rapidly. "Mr. Vincent and Mr. Weed were in the house all evening, as far as you can say. Mr. Weed's friend came at eight-thirty. Mrs. Prendergast left a little after a quarter of nine. That means that your other guests—Dr. Spinelli, Mr. Wainwright, Mr. Lovejoy, and Mrs. Balbirnie were out. Right?"

"I am fairly sure that they were."

Out of the corner of my eye, I saw Moran move impatiently in his chair, and suspected that he was about to take a hand in the proceedings.

"Mrs. Quincy," he began abruptly, "it doesn't seem to me that your statements are consistent. You say you're fairly sure those four people were out of the house, and yet it wasn't a minute ago you said—and pretty positively too—that you never meddled in their personal affairs. What do you call their comings and goings, anyhow—a public concern?"

Mrs. Quincy turned to look at him in cold surprise, but answered without a trace of irritation. "I'm afraid you don't understand, Mr. Moran, perhaps because I haven't explained enough. I happened to be watching the door to-night for a reason of my own. You see," to Moran's obvious annoyance, she averted her face and addressed Kane, "there was a political torchlight parade on Boylston Street. Ellen and John, my two servants, asked for permission to go, and I said they might if they would stay only a few minutes. I intended to wait until they came back and then go over myself. A little before eight-thirty I put on my hat and coat. The bell rang, and as Ellen was out I answered it myself. It was Mr. Weed's friend. After I had let him in, I went back into my sitting room and sat down by the window, where I could watch the front door and see John and Ellen as soon as they came in sight. While I sat there no one entered or left the house, except Mrs. Prendergast, who went out, as I told you."

"How long did you sit there?"

"Let me see." Mrs. Quincy bent her head thoughtfully. "When Mrs. Prendergast asked me the time, it was eight . . ." She hesitated. "Eight forty-eight, exactly. I should say I waited at the window three or four minutes longer; then I decided it was too late to go to the parade, and so I took off my hat and coat."

"Mrs. Quincy," Moran called her attention forcibly to himself, "isn't there any other entrance to this house?"

"Yes. There's a kitchen entrance, of course, but that is always locked after six o'clock."

Kane hung a long arm over the back of his chair. "I suppose," he said, addressing her, "that since you haven't mentioned it, you didn't hear any noise from the upper floor, while you were in your room, which might have been the sound of a struggle."

"I heard no unusual sound."

"The house was quiet, then?"

"Yes, except while the piano was playing."

"What piano was that?"

"Mr. Weed's. He has an electric piano in his room. I heard him playing it to-night."

Kane pulled himself around in his chair, leaned forward, and studied the rug thoughtfully. "Well," he said at last, "you've told us a great deal, Mrs. Quincy. It's possible that you may be able to tell us more. However," he got to his feet, "that's all at present."

"You're leaving now?" There was a trace of alarm in Mrs. Quincy's voice.

"Not yet," Kane replied. "I expect to learn a great many interesting things before I leave."

CHAPTER 6

We waited in silence for a moment or so after Mrs. Quincy had left the room. Then Kane lit a cigarette and absent-mindedly flipped the match into a waste paper basket. Moran regarded his calm face impatiently.

"I don't see that that cuts much ice," he said.

"What?" Kane was hastily stirring about in the scrap basket.

"Her sitting by the window from eight-thirty till eight-fifty."

"Oh, that." Satisfied with his inspection, Kane leaned back and took a long drag from his cigarette. "Well"—he expelled a thin stream of smoke toward the ceiling—"I suppose it means that during that time no one passed through the front door except Mrs. Prendergast."

"But the murderer could have killed Prendergast and escaped before eight-thirty."

"Not according to Dr. Sloan, or Mrs. Prendergast either," Kane reminded him. "We can probably assume that her son was alive when she left the house."

Moran shifted his argument. "All right, then. But there's one more loophole. After eight-fifty, or eight-fifty-two to be exact, when Mrs. Quincy left the window, he could have entered, done the work, and cleared out."

"Perfectly true." Kane rubbed his chin slowly. "Unless Spinelli is right."

Moran seemed ready to advance another theory, when we heard light footsteps descending the stairs. There was a knock at the door, and in answer to Kane's "Come in," Lovejoy entered. His young, almost girlish face bore a look of apology. He stepped softly across the room and leaned down over Kane as if he had something confidential to say.

"I came to see if there was anything else you wanted to ask me. I'm tired, you understand." He passed his hand over his eyes. "This has been a very trying evening."

"Very," Kane agreed. "Yes, I do want to talk to you. Sit down."

Lovejoy sank into a chair and took on an apathetic attitude. He was of a very slight build, and his thinness made him look taller than he really was. For all of his assumption of delicacy, he seemed wiry enough. He moved with agility and a certain nervous intensity which was not concealed by the fact that all of his movements were very quiet. His expression was vague, but I noticed that his eyes were never still. As he sat there they darted restlessly from Kane to Moran and then to me, never pausing in their work of uneasy scrutiny.

"You don't mind if I smoke?" he asked suddenly.

Moran sniffed as Lovejoy pulled out a long Russian cigarette and lighted it.

The sergeant turned to me. "Have a cigar, Underwood?" He offered me one of a rank, five-cent variety which I declined as politely as I could. He struck a match on the seat of his trousers and glared at Lovejoy as he did so.

Kane paid no attention to him. "Suppose you tell us," he said to Lovejoy, "where you went this evening, what you did when you came home—in fact, the whole story."

Lovejoy glanced at Kane. "You want me to say what I was doing before I found poor Prendergast? It all seems so impossible! I find it hard to think back to my own doings."

Kane made no attempt to get him down to brass tacks, and Lovejoy talked on. "How could I have thought that I would return to such a scene! I was badly shaken. I shan't be myself for a long time." His mouth drooped pettishly. "I am really dazed," he went on. "What an ugly death!" He shivered a little, and a gray pallor crept over his face.

Kane finally brought him back to the question. "What time did you leave the house this evening?" he asked abruptly.

Lovejoy started a little. "Oh, yes," he said. "You must excuse me. I must have gone out a little after seven. No, it was practically half-past. I had to hurry through my dinner. I promised to join the parade on

Boylston Street. I was going to meet some friends, but I was too late. I didn't find them." His hands twisted nervously in his lap.

"You marched in the parade?"

"Yes." Lovejoy paused reflectively "I wish I had stayed quietly at home."

"Did you see your friends at all?"

"No. I couldn't find them." He toyed with his cigarette. "And it was only to please them that I said I would march. It rained so! I was soaked. I'm not really strong enough."

Again Moran cast a look of disgust at the fragile young man. "What time did you get back?" he asked impatiently.

Lovejoy was surprised at the interruption. "Why, you know," he said. "I came back about five minutes past nine. Mrs. Quincy must have told you that. I stopped to see her." He seemed to think the subject was exhausted.

Kane took charge of the interview again. "I haven't got it quite straight yet, Mr. Lovejoy," he said. "You stopped to see Mrs. Quincy about a leak in your room?"

"Yes. I thought you understood. You see, I knew the leak was there. The rain came in several days ago, but I'd forgotten to say anything to her. So when it rained to-night I thought I'd better speak of it."

"You asked her to go upstairs with you?"

"Yes."

"And when you got there?"

"We looked at the leak, naturally, and she said she would have it mended. Then we went to Prendergast's room."

"How did you happen to do that?"

"His room is below mine. There was a pool of water on the floor in my room, and we thought we had better look in Prendergast's room to see if it had gone through."

"You suggested that to Mrs. Quincy?"

"Why, yes. I think I did. The rain *had* come in there. Why, we could hear it dripping on the floor. We saw the leak at once." Lovejoy's eyes widened with horror. "We didn't see—the other for a second or two."

"What did you do then?"

Lovejoy took a quick breath. "I—I started to see what had happened. But I couldn't stand it. Blood makes me faint."

"Did you touch the body?"

"Oh, no! I couldn't have!" He shrank back in his chair. "Mrs. Quincy said he was dead. And then the others came. Dr. Spinelli had just come in. Mrs. Quincy called him." Again he passed his hand over his eyes. "It was a terrible shock to me."

Kane thought for a moment. "That's all, Mr. Lovejoy," he said.

Lovejoy seemed surprised and relieved. With a faint smile that included us all, he quietly left the room.

Kane offered no comment on Lovejoy's story. "Suppose we go upstairs and talk to Mrs. Prendergast," he suggested. "I'm afraid we can't help disturbing her to-night."

We went up to the second floor. Weed must have heard us mounting the stairs, for he opened his door and called to us.

"Mr. Kane," he said in a sorrowful voice, as we reached his side, "they've told me about poor Arthur." In spite of his tone, he was not moved as the others had been. I realized that his blindness had shielded him from the horror of Prendergast's room.

"Was that right, what I heard Dr. Spinelli telling you?" he went on slowly. "Did he die at ten minutes to nine?"

"So Dr. Spinelli says," Kane replied.

A look of bewilderment came over Weed's face. "Why—why," his expression was troubled. "The doctor is a dear friend of mine and such a good physician, too, but—" he faltered. and then went on, "but I really don't believe he could be right about that."

"What makes you think that, Mr. Weed?" Kane asked quietly.

"Well, now, it's this way," Weed answered. "Arthur couldn't have been killed at ten minutes to nine, if he was alive at five minutes of, now could he?"

"No."

Weed's air became triumphant. "I'll just tell you how I worked that out," he said. "It was just five minutes of nine—I'm perfectly sure of that—when I met that young Mr. Vincent in the hall, right outside Arthur's door. I thought to myself, now isn't that nice of him! He's been to see Arthur. You begin to see what I mean, don't you, Mr. Kane?"

"Not exactly," Kane admitted.

"Oh, Mr. Kane!" Weed admonished him. "If Mr. Vincent had just left Arthur at five minutes of nine, Arthur must have been all right then. Why, Mr. Vincent would have told me if anything was the matter, wouldn't he?"

"Of course!" Kane exclaimed heartily. "That was stupid of me. Thanks. I'm glad you told me. But I'm afraid we'll have to talk about that later. We must see Mrs. Prendergast."

Weed took the hint. "All right," he said amiably. "All right." He listened to our footsteps as we crossed the hall to her door.

Kane knocked. It was Dr. Spinelli's voice that told us to come in. As we entered he continued to talk soothingly to Mrs. Prendergast, who was lying on a touch, her handkerchief pressed to her eyes. She took it away long enough to see who was disturbing her. At the sight of us she gave a little cry and stretched out her plump hands in appeal to the doctor.

"Must you disturb this poor lady to-night?" he asked softly.

"I'm sorry," Kane answered gently enough. "But there are certain questions we must ask her."

Dr. Spinelli's disapproval was obvious, though unexpressed. He rose from his place beside Mrs. Prendergast, made a formal bow to us, and walked to the door, where he turned.

"As Mrs. Prendergast's physician," he said, "I must ask you not to excite her too much. She has a very sensitive nature."

As he made his exit Mrs. Prendergast began to weep again, and childlike tears coursed down her pink cheeks. She dabbed ineffectually at her eyes with her handkerchief and tried to quiet herself.

"I can't help it," she wailed finally. "I am trying, I really am." She turned her woebegone countenance to Kane. "What is it? What do you want?"

"We want to help you, Mrs. Prendergast," Kane said. "We want to find out how all this could have happened. So we have to talk to you."

For a second or two her frightened eyes bore a fleeting resemblance to Prendergast's. "But I don't know anything about it," she cried. "How could I?"

"Of course not," Kane soothed her. "But you can tell us when you last saw your son alive."

"Yes," she said, hesitating a little and catching her breath. "I was here with him this evening. Then I went out. My poor Arthur!" Her tears began to fall again.

"What time did you leave the house, Mrs. Prendergast?"

She seemed to take courage at Kane's kindly manner. "About a quarter of nine, I think. It's hard to remember now." Her words came in short bursts.

"You left him here?"

"Yes. In his room—in there." She shuddered as she pointed to a doorway on her left. "He was waiting to play chess." Her voice was still shaking, but for the moment she was distracted from her grief.

Moran pricked up his ears. "Somebody was going to come and play with him?"

Mrs. Prendergast's pale blue eyes drifted toward the new inquisitor. "Why, yes," she said. "Arthur was very much upset. Mr. Vincent was supposed to come at half-past eight, and he hadn't turned up at all. He himself had asked Arthur to play, too."

"Then," Kane shifted in his chair, "Mr. Vincent didn't come while you were here?"

"No-o." Mrs. Prendergast drew the word out. "Just before I went out Arthur decided he wasn't coming and went into his bedroom. He was disappointed."

"Except for his disappointment, did he seem unusually depressed or disturbed?" Kane was hurrying his questions, so that she would have no time to dwell on her sorrow.

"Oh, no. He was very cheerful at dinner. He was laughing and joking." The question had troubled her. Her face showed that she was lost in a maze of bewilderment. She looked like a woman incapable of understanding the ordinary world around her, least of all this abnormal tragedy that had been thrust into her life.

"Was Mr. Prendergast afraid of anyone? Did he have enemies?"

"I don't know. He never told me anything." She was aggrieved.

"You didn't see him after a quarter of nine?"

"No. I went for a little walk. Oh, if I only hadn't!" With a sudden yielding to emotion she sank back on the couch and sobbed without restraint.

Kane motioned to Moran and me. We left the room quietly. There was obviously no use in trying to question Mrs. Prendergast any further that night.

Dr. Spinelli was waiting for us outside the door.

"How is she?" he whispered, an expression of solemn concern on his dark face.

Kane reassured him, and motioning him to accompany us down the hall led the way to a window seat.

"I'd like to ask you a few questions," he said. "We may as well sit here."

The doctor pulled up a straight chair. The light, which came from a standing lamp, was behind him. "I am very eager to help you," he announced, concluding, with a slight shrug, "if only I could." He had a rich, flexible voice, and only the suggestion of a foreign accent.

"How long have you known the Prendergasts?" Kane began abruptly.

"Ah, I must think." He made a conscious pause. "It is five years now. Yes, five years. They were already here when I came to Mrs. Quincy's."

"You've known them well?"

"Yes. Mrs. Prendergast has more confidence in me than perhaps I deserve." He made a deprecatory gesture. "Also she is a patient of mine. I have been able to do a little something for her, for her health. She is very delicate."

"What did Prendergast do?"

"Work, you mean?" The doctor was mildly surprised. "He was far too nervous to have any occupation. It seems unkind to say so now, but he was even a little unbalanced. Very excitable, poor boy!"

"Mrs. Prendergast is comfortably off?"

"Oh, yes, I believe so."

"Her husband is dead?"

"Yes."

"You don't know, then, what kind of man he was?"

"Hardly. I think from what I have heard Mrs. Prendergast say that her husband was what you call a self-made man—perhaps a little rough but quick to make the money." The doctor smiled.

Kane had apparently satisfied his curiosity on that subject, for he shifted his inquiries. "Did young Mr. Prendergast get along with the other people here?"

"In general, yes." He made an explanatory motion of his hands. "You know how it is, living in a place like this. It is not always so amiable. And Arthur was peculiar. He had his little spats with the others, but nothing—" he drew the word out for emphasis—"more than that."

"He had no real enemies here, then."

The doctor made a shocked denial.

"How about friends?"

"He had more friends here, if you can call them friends,"—Spinelli shrugged his shoulders—"than elsewhere. In fact, as far as I know, he knew no one outside this house. He was not what you call a mixer."

Kane persisted. "How well did he get on with Vincent, for instance?"

The doctor hesitated. "Perhaps not so well as with some of the others," he replied cautiously.

"I see." Kane seemed to lose interest in the proceedings, and Moran took charge. The sergeant became red with importance as he drew a notebook from his pocket and jotted down the doctor's answers to his questions.

"Suppose you tell us what you did this evening." It amused me to see that Moran was consciously imitating Kane's methods.

The doctor turned to Moran with a tolerant air. "That will be very easy, Sergeant," he said. "I went out about eight, or a little after. I walked a little while, and then I went to the drugstore to have some prescriptions filled. I came home, as you know, at nine-ten."

"What time were you at the drugstore?" Moran's voice was very businesslike.

"I must have got there about twenty minutes to nine. I left there approximately at five minutes of the hour."

"Anybody see you there?"

Spinelli was beginning to dislike Moran's persistence. "The clerk knows me," he said. "He will verify what I say."

He gave Moran the address of a drugstore around the corner from Mrs. Quincy's. When the sergeant had written it down he shot a quick look at the doctor.

"Took you a long time to get home from there," he said, "didn't it?"

"I did not come straight home," Spinelli replied. "I walked along the Esplanade to get some fresh air before retiring."

Moran dropped the point. "When you came in, Mrs. Quincy called you, didn't she?"

"Yes. I was on my way upstairs when I heard her. Naturally I answered right away. You know what I found when I reached her side." The doctor's voice was smooth.

"You knew that Prendergast was dead as soon as you saw him?"

"Naturally."

"How much did you have to disturb the body?"

"Hardly at all. I knew he was dead. Obviously he had been killed. You see, Sergeant," he said pointedly, "we who read the newspapers know that the police do not like us to touch the body of a murdered man."

"How did you know he was murdered?"

"It was sufficiently evident, don't you think so?"

Moran was getting annoyed. "You said, didn't you, that he died at ten minutes of nine. Are you sure of that?"

"Beyond reasonable doubt. I can explain my decision to you in technical language if you . . ."

"Don't bother," Kane interrupted him. "Thank you very much, Doctor. Come on, Moran. That's enough for the present. I want to talk to Weed now."

CHAPTER 7

Kane crossed the hall to Weed's door. For a minute no one answered his knock; then we heard Weed's gentle voice. "What is it?" The door did not open.

"This is Kane, Mr. Weed. May we come in?"

"Oh." The answer was startled. "Why, I've just started to undress. I'll come downstairs and talk to you in a minute."

"All right," Kane agreed, and led the way to the living room.

"Well," Moran said, as he sank heavily into a chair, "that fellow Spinelli didn't tell us much of anything new." He smiled. "And, after all, it doesn't matter much," he concluded with brisk satisfaction.

"Why not?"

Moran looked at Kane slyly. "*You* know," he replied. "I guess you'll agree with me that Weed gave us enough to start on at any rate."

"Yes, I believe he did," Kane answered shortly.

"Well then—" But Moran was interrupted by a knock. All three of us turned toward the door. Weed was entering the room, his cane outstretched before him. He still wore the black skullcap, but it seemed to have been hastily donned, for several untidy white hairs were escaping from beneath it. He must have been familiar with the arrangement of the furniture in the room, for he walked without hesitation and made little or no use of his cane. As he approached he gave us a gentle smile. Halfway across the floor he spoke.

"Now, Mr. Kane," he droned, "I didn't realize you wanted me tonight, or I wouldn't have started to go to bed. Do you really want to talk to me again?" The end of the sentence was pitched in a higher key than the beginning, and he clung to the last word incredulously.

Kane rose to his feet. "Yes, Mr. Weed," he explained. "We must see everyone, you know. Now—"

"Certainly, certainly," the singsong voice interrupted. "May I ask who else is here? You, Mr. Kane, I know."

"My friend, Mr. Underwood."

"Oh, Mr. Underwood, I remember . . ." his voice trailed off.

"And Mr. Moran."

"Moran? How do you do, sir?" The blind man turned instinctively in our direction and held out his hand, but his eyes stared beyond us.

Kane made a quick gesture to Moran, who rose uncomfortably at the signal and gave the outstretched hand a clumsy shake.

"Glad to meet you," he shouted and sat down again abruptly.

Weed placed both hands upon the knob of his cane, and shook his head slowly. "What a horrible thing this has been," he began. "I couldn't believe it. Poor Arthur, he—"

Kane pulled up a chair. "Sit down, Mr. Weed," he said.

Weed eased himself into the chair, and sighed. "He came into my room so often, as I say."

Moran regarded him imperturbably. "Now, Mr. Weed, we've got to find out what we can from you. You were in the house when he was killed."

"And I know nothing but what I've told you." He was regretful, apologetic. "My room is next to his, too. Dr. Spinelli asked me—Mrs. Quincy asked me. They said—even the dear doctor said—I should have heard *something*. But I didn't. I know nothing at all," he repeated childishly. "I suppose I was too busy talking to my friend. And after he'd gone—even then I—"

"Who is this friend?" Moran interrupted him.

"My friend?" He looked wonderingly toward Moran. "His name is Hyde—Alvin Hyde. A fine man." His tone laid a token of universal esteem upon the name. "Interested in music

"What's his address?" Moran broke in, pulling out his notebook. "We gotta see him too."

"Let me see," Weed considered. "He lives on Newbury Street. Now what is that number?" He ruminated dismally. "Oh, yes. I remember now. It's 152. I remember it by fifty-two weeks in the year," he concluded with an air of triumph.

Moran wrote down the address and continued his questions. "What time did he come?"

Weed looked disappointed. "Now that, of course, I can't tell you exactly. But he was to come at eight-thirty, so I suppose . . ." He nodded his head in vague implication.

"And when did he leave?"

"Oh, he didn't stay very long this time. He just came to bring me a new record for my piano." His face brightened. "Some time you must let me play my piano for you. Of course, not now," he added understandingly, "but some other time, perhaps. It's a splendid instrument."

Kane covered up Moran's snort of impatience. "We'd like to hear it. Now, Mr. Weed, you haven't told us what time Mr. Hyde left."

Weed thought a moment. "Why, yes, I have," he said reprovingly. "I told you a little while ago when I saw Mr. Vincent. Alvin had just left then. I asked him what time it was before he went, and he told me. It was five minutes of nine. That's why I was so sure about meeting Mr. Vincent at that time. Alvin and I had had such a pleasant time. We'd talked, we'd played the new record—"

"Were you outside in the hall at any time during the evening?"

"Yes, I think I was. Once or twice before Alvin came."

"You met no one in the hall at those times?"

"I don't remember meeting anyone." The reply was plaintive.

"You didn't hear Prendergast's voice?"

"No-o."

"And after Mr. Hyde left, did you go out of your room?"

"No. I thought I'd go to bed. It was earlier than usual, but I'd taken a long walk in the afternoon—to Symphony Hall and back again, it was. It was too long—it tired me."

Kane brought him back to the point. "I don't quite understand how you happened to see Mr. Vincent."

Weed smiled. "I was just going to tell you," he rambled on, "that when Alvin left, I walked down the hall and part way downstairs with him. I *always* do that."

Moran tried to hurry him. "And you saw Mr. Vincent then?"

Weed's expression was patient. "I never *see* anyone, Mr. Moran," he reminded him. "But," he continued, "Mr. Vincent was there when

I came back, just outside Arthur's door. You know what I told you. I don't mean to contradict the dear doctor, but—"

Kane glanced at Weed quickly. "Mr. Vincent didn't say anything about Prendergast to you?"

"No." Weed's voice was placid. "I spoke to him, and he said, 'Hello,' just that, you know, and then I went into my room and closed my door. If I'd thought to ask him, of course—"

Moran threw a hard look at him. "How did you know it was Prendergast's door he was at?"

"Why, Mr. Moran—" Weed seemed at a temporary loss for words. "Why shouldn't I? I've lived here over a year, and," he concluded with dignity, "I know the house well."

No one said anything for a moment, and then Kane remarked that we had kept Weed long enough.

"Not at all," the latter replied courteously, "but I am a little tired, as I say, so if you've finished . . ."

Kane said that we had. Weed rose from his chair, and picking up his cane bade us a calm good-night. We watched him in silence as he threaded his way past the table and the chairs to the door. On the threshold he paused.

"On some less unhappy day," he reminded us, "you must come and listen to my piano." He stepped into the hall, and we heard him humming gently to himself as he mounted the stairs.

"Mrs. Prendergast, Spinelli, Weed," Kane murmured, when the blind man had gone. "Taken together they indicate . . . Let's go see the crux of the situation."

"What?" Moran did not understand him.

"I said," Kane translated, "let's go see Vincent."

CHAPTER 8

Vincent's room was dimly lighted by a student lamp. We found him sitting in a comfortable chair, smoking his pipe. As we entered he got swiftly to his feet. Somehow he must have given his pipe a knock, for it fell to the floor, leaving a bright trail of sparks along the rug. He stamped them out as he walked across the room to meet us.

"We want to talk to you for a few minutes, Mr. Vincent," Kane said easily.

"Sit down, won't you?" Vincent fell in with Kane's matter-of-fact manner. His voice was low and pleasant.

We made ourselves comfortable. "I see you smoke a pipe." Kane pointed to the forgotten object on the floor. "Guess I'll take to mine." He pulled out a rank corncob and filled it.

Vincent leaned over to pick up his briar. As he fumbled for it, I saw him look up at Kane quickly. For a second or two, his brows drawn together, he stared at the detective. Then he straightened up, threw himself back in his chair, and waited for Kane to speak. But after a little while the silence evidently became too much for him, for it was he who spoke first.

"You know," he said lightly, "you've come to the wrong place if you're looking for information. I don't know anything about the late lamented."

Kane nodded slowly. "Funny thing," he said with some malice, "nobody seems to. But I've decided people know more than they think they do." He paused. "You know, Mr. Vincent, you may be able to tell us something very interesting."

Vincent smiled his slow, attractive smile and made no reply. Instead he refilled his pipe and began to smoke steadily. As he sat within the circle of the lamplight, I had a good chance to look at him. In spite of the flippancy of his words, Prendergast's death must have had an effect upon him. His face was paler than it had been the day before, and a faint line had appeared between his eyebrows. His eyes were unnaturally bright.

"You were here all evening?" Kane began.

"Why, yes." Vincent gave a little tug at his mustache. "I didn't go out at all."

"You stayed here in your room?"

"Yes." He hesitated. "I came up here right after dinner. I was tired. You see,"—he leaned forward confidentially—"no matter what people say, we bond salesmen do have to work. Why, Mr. Kane, last night I had to go to a dance and stay up till all hours, and this afternoon I was forced into eighteen holes of golf." He gave a sly, sidewise glance at Kane, and went on deliberately. "And to-morrow I have to play squash. You know, every time I play squash, I sell a bond. People buy things when they get overheated." He seemed to be making an effort to amuse us, to exert the charm that must have brought many people to his side.

"Very nice for you," Kane murmured. "But speaking of games, Mrs. Prendergast tells me that you had planned to play chess with her son tonight."

Vincent put his pipe down on the table beside him. "Oh, well," he said carelessly, "it was hardly as definite as that. We thought we might play. Poor fellow!"

"Really?" Kane was entirely casual. "I thought the game was all arranged."

"N-no. As a matter of fact I didn't think much about it." Vincent's eyes were half-closed. He seemed to be contemplating the highly polished toe of his shoe. "I've got to admit," he went on somewhat apologetically, "that for a while I forgot all about it. I was tired, as I told you; so when I got up here after dinner I lay down on the couch and I fell asleep."

"What did you do when you woke up?"

"I didn't do anything," Vincent replied. "I didn't wake up till almost nine o'clock, and I'd meant to be at Prendergast's room at eight-thirty."

"Then you missed your game altogether?"

"Yes."

"And you didn't see Prendergast at all?"

Vincent shook his head. His loquacity had fallen before Kane's insistence on facts.

"That's too bad." Kane looked disappointed. 'Weed thought you could tell us . . . why!"—he seemed just to have remembered something—"why, Mr. Weed told us you had been with Prendergast just before nine o'clock!"

"Oh, no!" Vincent answered quickly, looking Kane full in the eye. "Weed's mistaken. I didn't see Prendergast at all after dinner." He turned away and picked up his pipe. He drew on it but it was out. He lighted it again.

"Then I must have misunderstood him. But I'm sure he said," Kane insisted, "that he'd talked to you in the hall, and that you were coming out of Prendergast's door. Of course, if you didn't leave your room all evening—"

"Wait a minute! Wait a minute!" Vincent hastily cut him short. "I didn't say quite that. You're misunderstanding me now." His smile was ready, and he went on with quick frankness. "This is the way it was. I slept till a little before nine, as I told you. When I woke up I looked at the clock. My God, I thought, I forgot about Prendergast. So I went downstairs." He paused.

"*That's* when I saw Weed. He was coming back from saying goodbye to a friend of his. We spoke. You can see why he thought I might have been with Prendergast. The poor old fellow, blind, and all that." Vincent gave a short laugh.

"Easy to understand," Kane agreed. "Then?"

"Weed went to his room," Vincent continued, "and I knocked on Prendergast's door. Nobody answered."

"You're sure you knocked loudly enough to be heard?"

"Positive."

"You didn't go in?"

"No."

"Did you hear any sounds in Prendergast's room?"

Vincent thought for a moment. "I really can't say I did. You see, when I didn't get an answer I went right back to my room."

Kane reflected for a minute or two. "By the way, how did you happen to be playing chess with Prendergast?" he asked. "Did he ask you to have a game?"

A queer look came over Vincent's face. "Perhaps," he said, "I don't remember exactly how it was."

"Were you and Prendergast great friends?"

"Oh, not exactly intimate, but . . ." He left the rest of the sentence to be understood.

"When he didn't answer your knock, I suppose it didn't occur to you that something might have happened to him?"

"Why should it have?"

"No reason at all," Kane replied smoothly. "Of course, you thought he had gone out."

He got up as if to terminate the interview, but for some reason Vincent was reluctant to have us go. "Funny business yours must be, Mr. Kane," he said, "always trying to find out things that other people don't want you to know. Unmasking the villain and all that. What do murderers look like, anyway? I've never seen one."

"Very much like you or me, Mr. Vincent," Kane replied absently.

Vincent seemed a little taken aback. The implied comparison between Kane's angular visage and his own regular features must have startled him. His lips twisted a little before he spoke again.

"Do you always catch them—murderers, I mean?" he asked.

"I try to," Kane answered. "We pick up small things, you know."

"Oh!" Vincent hesitated. "I wish you'd tell me—"

But Kane interrupted him. "Some other time, perhaps. I think we'd better be going along now." He moved toward the door. "Good-night, Mr. Vincent."

"Good-night." Vincent watched us intently as we left the room.

Once we were all out of earshot, Moran remarked to Kane, "Didn't want to tell us much, did he?"

Kane smiled. "You can hardly blame him, Moran. From his point of view the situation is a little difficult. Mrs. Quincy says everyone was out but Vincent, Mrs. Prendergast, and Weed. Mrs. Prendergast went out later. Weed was occupied with his friend, and that leaves . . . No," he smiled again, "you can hardly blame Vincent. And there's one thing I'm willing to take my oath on. When Weed said Prendergast must have been alive at five minutes of nine, because—you know the rest of the story—well, he was jumping at a conclusion. I'm sure that when Weed saw Vincent, Prendergast was dead."

As we stood talking McBeath came plodding slowly up the stairs. "Here's that cigarette case back again," he said, handing a small package to Kane. "Feller said he'd have the pictures for you in the morning." Without waiting for an answer he marched away.

Kane unwrapped the package. It seemed to give him an idea. "I think I'll try an experiment," he said. There was a speculative look in his eye. "An experiment to settle my own mind, to see whether we're dealing with stupidity or something else. If we can catch the man who killed Prendergast by using this we may as well do it. If we can't—" he shrugged his shoulders.

Catching sight of Mrs. Quincy's manservant at the other end of the hall, Kane called to him, "Come here, will you?"

The man obeyed, eyeing us suspiciously.

"This cigarette case is Mr. Vincent's," Kane announced. "Will you take it to him, please?"

"Yes, sir." The man took the case and walked over to Vincent's door. Kane drew Moran and me back so that we could not be seen.

At the servant's knock, Vincent opened the door and stood on the threshold.

"Your cigarette case, sir."

"What?" Vincent took it from his hand. For a minute, he looked at it in silence. Then he said, "My cigarette case? That's not mine. I never saw it before."

The servant excused himself, closed the door, and brought the case back to Kane. The latter, murmuring something about a mistake, took it and held it to the light.

"Two sets of fingerprints," he said. "Neither one like the first set." He laughed. "So much for Vincent."

"Well, by God," Moran exclaimed in disappointment, "I was sure he wasn't telling the truth. We both made the same mistake that time."

"You do me wrong," Kane answered good-humoredly. "I thought it would turn out that way. I only wanted to see if I was right. You see, this business has made our problem clearer and," he added, "a great deal more complicated."

CHAPTER 9

The next morning I met Kane and Moran at Mrs. Quincy's. When I got there, at about nine o'clock, I found them already at work. The table before which they sat was littered with newspapers whose scare-heads proclaimed the fact that Arthur Prendergast had been murdered. The crime had caught the imagination of the reporters. Prendergast's eccentricities, and those of the people who lived in the Quincy house, the story of the stains that were not blood, the brutality of the murder—everything combined to arouse public excitement. In each paper a section was devoted to wild speculation as to the motive for the crime, and it was widely announced that the police could offer no explanation of it, nor had they come upon any clues to the identity of the murderer. The accounts, much as they differed in presenting the facts of the case, agreed that it was one of the most shocking and spectacular Boston had ever known and that the Prendergast affair might, like the Borden murders in Fall River, remain forever unsolved.

Neither Kane nor Moran seemed very much interested in what the papers had to say. They were occupied instead with rough plans of the house. When I had finished my reading, Kane passed the drawings over to me.

"Just for the sake of thoroughness," he said, "take a look at these. That door there" (we were in the living room, and he motioned toward the rear of the house) "leads to the dining room. Off that there is a pantry; then the kitchen. Coming toward the street again, Mr. and Mrs. Quincy have their rooms. The stairs go up from the right-hand side of the hall and lead to a landing on the second floor outside Mrs. Balbirnie's rooms. Spinelli and Weed are in the front of the house, and the Prendergasts' rooms correspond to Mrs. Balbirnie's, on the other side. On the third floor are Vincent, Lovejoy, and Wainwright. The other rooms up there belong to the servants."

After I had examined the plans Kane folded them up and put them in his pocket. "Now, Moran," he said, "consult that valuable notebook of yours and tell us whom we have still to talk to."

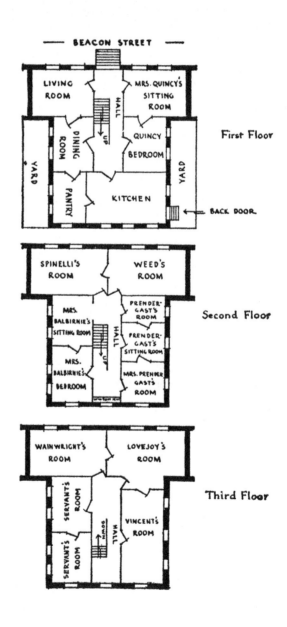

Moran grunted, but could not down his self-satisfaction as he pulled out his cherished record. He thumbed over the pages laboriously, licking his fingers to get the leaves apart. When he had found what he wanted, he took a deep breath.

"Mr. Wainwright, Mrs. Balbirnie, Mr. Quincy, Mr. Hyde, Ellen Hogan, John Hogan." He intoned the names as if he were reading a chant.

Kane reflected a moment, as though he were undecided. "We'll see them in a little while," he concluded. "At this moment I have other fish to fry. You stay here. I want to see Mrs. Prendergast."

As Kane left the room Moran looked after him irritably. "What's he got up his sleeve now?" he asked, as though I were to blame for the unforeseen interruption.

"Perhaps he'll tell us later," I suggested.

Moran glared at me. Fortunately our unpromising conversation was brought to a halt by the manservant, John Hogan, who appeared at the door.

"Mr. Hyde to see Sergeant Moran." The man's attitude was resentful. In his eyes we were rank intruders.

"Send him in," Moran ordered. He turned to me. "I sent him word to come here, and come quickly, too."

Hyde was in the room before Moran had finished his sentence. He was a thickset, almost stout individual, dressed in an alarming pepper-and-salt tweed.

"Sergeant Moran?" he asked, in a high-pitched voice.

Moran acknowledged the greeting and Hyde sat down, placing on his knee his spotless pearl gray felt hat which matched the gloves he was wearing. "I read in the newspapers . . ." he left his sentence unfinished, and went on, "and then I had word from you. Of course—"

Moran looked at him with distaste. Neither Hyde's clothes nor his way of speaking pleased the sergeant any more than they did me. He gave Hyde no opportunity for light conversation.

"You were here last night, weren't you?"

"Yes, certainly. I came to see poor old Weed. About eight-thirty." When it came to the point, Hyde was perfectly willing to answer Moran's questions directly.

"What time did you leave?"

Hyde hesitated. "A little before nine, it must have been. Yes, say five minutes of."

"You know Prendergast was killed while you were here?" Moran looked at him suspiciously.

"So I saw in the papers," came the calm reply. "Awful thing."

Moran went on with his examination. Point for point, Hyde confirmed the story the blind man had already told us. He had heard nothing. He and Weed had spent the time talking and playing the piano. Neither had had the slightest suspicion of what was going on.

As the two talked I decided that Hyde was intelligent even if unprepossessing. He must have been well past middle age, although his bushy hair was still black. His face was ruddy in color and his features gave an impression of heaviness, especially his nose, with its broad, flattened nostrils. He wore an unkempt black mustache and he had a trick of drawing his upper lip away from his teeth, which were badly discolored and filled with gold.

His quick, accurate replies made me revise the first estimate I had made of him. He was a good witness, no matter what he looked like.

The interview was soon over. As Hyde rose to go Moran stopped him.

"Wait a minute," he said. "Kane may want to see you later on. Can he always get you on Newbury Street?"

Hyde thought for a minute. "Perhaps I'd better give you my business address," he concluded, taking a card from his wallet. He scribbled something on it and handed it to Moran, who inserted it between the leaves of his notebook.

"All right, then," he said, in dismissal.

Hyde nodded amiably. "See you again, perhaps." We heard him speak to the servant who was in the hall, and then the front door closed behind him.

"That checks up with Weed, all right." Moran began to walk restlessly about the room. "Where the devil is Kane?" he grumbled. "Do we have to sit here all morning?"

The words were scarcely out of his mouth before Kane appeared.

"What have you been doing?" Moran asked him.

"Talking to Mrs. Prendergast, as I told you," Kane replied, "about that cigarette case. She is certain it wasn't Prendergast's and that it wasn't in his room in the early part of last evening."

"Then it must have belonged to the man who killed him." Moran was distracted from his ill humor.

"Apparently." Kane paused to light a cigarette. "I met Quincy in the hall as I came down, and told him to come here. By the way, have you heard from Hyde?"

"Sure, I heard from him," answered Moran. "He was here a minute ago." He gave Kane a resume of what Hyde had said.

"Agrees with Weed, doesn't he?" Kane commented.

"Yeah," Moran replied. "Same story. And what's more, it only took him about two minutes to say what that old rattlepate said in twenty."

Kane laughed. "Weed isn't so old, Moran. I'll bet you he isn't over fifty, in spite of his white hair and his skullcap."

"Well, anyhow," Moran retorted, "he's some talker."

"I'll agree to that, but here's Quincy now."

Our latest witness stood diffidently near the door. He was an insignificant-looking man, and since the flush of unaccustomed emotion had by now faded from his face, almost colorless. He was clean-shaven, and his hair, which had once been blond, had taken on a grayish pallor. He had the look of a man who has become a feeble second to his wife.

In answer to Moran's questions he said that he had not been at home for dinner the night before. Instead, he had gone early to the movies and had returned a little after nine o'clock to find the house in commotion. His wife had told him to telephone for Kane. Immediately after calling he had found us at the front door. No one, to his knowledge, had seen him before his return.

Neither Kane nor Moran pressed him for further information, and he was soon able to make a quiet disappearance.

The servants were brought in next. They could add little or nothing to our stock of information. They had left the house a little before eight, gone to the parade, and overstayed their time. The wife, Ellen, who served as maid of all work, was voluble enough, but her husband, the butler, was taciturn and disagreeable. They both verified Mrs. Quincy's statement that the back door was locked every night at six. The lock was an old-fashioned one, so that the door could not be opened from the inside, any more than it could from the outside, without a key The key itself John had had in his pocket.

The morning so far had been discouragingly fruitless. There was something depressing about the routine questions, and the answers which they had elicited had been far from helpful. The atmosphere of the living room was getting on my nerves, and I was glad enough when Kane suggested that we go upstairs to see Wainwright. The move would at least provide us with a change of scene.

We found him in his room on the third floor. It was a typical middle-aged bachelor's apartment, scrupulously neat. He evidently used it as a combination bedroom and sitting room, for a screen, behind which I could see a bureau and a four-poster, shut off a part of it. The walls were lined with bookcases. To the right there was a door, corresponding to the one downstairs between Weed's room and Spinelli's. which connected Wainwright's room with Lovejoy's.

Wainwright was sitting at his desk, putting in its various pigeon-holes the mail he had recently received. Like the rest of the room, the desk was unbelievably tidy. Its owner obviously lived by the ancient maxim, a place for everything and everything in its place.

He greeted us with a careful but reserved courtesy and invited us to sit down. When we had done so he seated himself. Now that I had a chance to look at him, I realized that he belonged to a type familiar enough in an old city—a type, I thought to myself, that might be called "the Descendants." Obviously he came of a good family, probably one that had been wealthy in its day. But his clothes and his room showed that he had inherited, instead of the wealth of his forebears, very moderate means. An imaginative person might see in his studied formality a vain attempt to hold on to a little of a past grandeur, a subconscious denial of a society that no longer paid attention to the things he stood for.

In a cold way he was fine-looking. He held himself very well and dressed with the quiet precision that was characteristic of his manner.

Kane studied him for a minute or two, and then began to speak.

"You understand, Mr. Wainwright," he said, "that we have to find out certain things from everyone living here."

Wainwright nodded slightly. "Yes. Quite."

"To begin with," Kane went on, "we'd like to know if you were here yesterday evening."

"In the early part of the evening, yes." He spoke almost as though he were reproving Kane for so general a question. "I had my dinner here as usual. After dinner I returned for a short time to my room. Just before half-past eight I went out."

"And where did you go?"

"To the library," came the meticulous answer.

"What time did you get there?"

"Not until nine o'clock."

Moran looked at him suspiciously. "Say," he interrupted, "the library's only ten minutes' walk from here."

Wainwright looked at him with well-bred insolence. "Quite so," he said. "Ordinarily, it only takes me ten minutes. Last night it rained, and I found refuge in a doorway until the storm was over."

Kane took over the interview again. "Did anyone see you in the library?" he asked.

Wainwright turned back to him. "Yes," he said, "the librarian. I talked to her for a short time while I was waiting for my books. At, I think, a little after nine o'clock."

"Did you know young Prendergast at all?" Kane shifted the subject abruptly.

"Slightly, of course. Not more. He did not appeal to me, as a person. He had hardly the manner one expects in people of one's own class." Wainwright's tone was matter-of-fact and his words were completely devoid of affectation. I realized that his was an innate snobbery, of which he was quite unconscious.

"He never talked to you very much, then? Never said he was afraid of anyone?"

"I wasn't in his confidence."

Kane rose and began to stroll aimlessly about the room. He peered at the few articles of decoration and then turned to the bookcases. After a few moments of silent deliberation he said to Wainwright, "You have some very unusual books here."

A sudden gleam of interest showed in Wainwright's face. "Yes," he answered, going to Kane's side. His stiffness of manner had relaxed a little. "I've been a long time collecting them, and even so the collection is not at all complete." His precise speech had an undertone of eagerness. "It is my hobby."

"History?" Kane asked, glancing at the titles of the old calf-bound volumes.

"Not all history," Wainwright corrected him. "I concern myself particularly with Spain and the Inquisition. It's an amazing literature." He took one of the books from its place on the shelf and turned its pages as though he knew their contents by heart. "Amazing," he repeated softly.

He began to read to himself, and for a few moments seemed to forget that we were there. Moran looked at him impatiently. "Why?" he asked abruptly.

Wainwright was startled out of his absorption. "Why?" he repeated coldly. "You mean, why is it amazing? Because, Mr. Moran, for hundreds of years the Holy Office was the most far-reaching, the most spectacular of human institutions. It dealt alike with princes and the riff-raff of the streets, queens and peasant women, priests and infidels. No man was so high that he was beyond its power; no man so low that it ignored him."

There was a growing intensity in Wainwright's voice. Having finished speaking he turned back to his book. Again he seemed to forget us, and when he looked up and began to talk it was not to arouse our interest but to satisfy his own obsession. He spoke of the doctrines of the early Christian fathers, of papal bulls, of auto-da-fé, and secret tribunals. His mind was packed with history and legend, peopled with the priests and kings of powerful and infamous memory. The pageantry of mediaeval courts and the bigotry of medieval religion were as real to him as the book he held in his hand. Even Moran, who obviously did not understand anything he was saying, stared at him as if fascinated. I could not believe that we were listening to the man we had come to see.

He must have talked for five minutes when, as suddenly as he had begun to speak, he stopped, and his attitude toward us changed. He looked at us resentfully, as though he regretted having taken us into his confidence, as though he had betrayed to strangers a part of his inner life. With an abrupt gesture he shut the book he had been holding and put it back in its place on the shelf.

When he turned to face us, he was again cold, precise, reserved. "Are there any more questions you wish to ask me?" he said pointedly.

Kane took the hint and turned to go. Wainwright conducted us to the door with much the same politeness that he would have accorded to uncongenial guests, and acknowledged Kane's abrupt leave-taking with a bow, ironic in its dignity.

"Odd fish," Kane commented. "Now for the last one. Mrs.—?" He looked at Moran.

"Balbirnie," the sergeant supplied. "Lives on the second floor opposite the Prendergasts."

We found Mrs. Balbirnie in her room, to which she had evidently just returned, for she was taking off her coat as she let us in. She greeted us with an excited stream of conversation, which continued without interruption as she bustled about, putting her things away. At the last moment before she settled down she remembered that she was still wearing her hat. She jerked at it absent-mindedly, and to my astonishment not only the hat moved but also the head of hair beneath it. I turned away, disconcerted, in time to catch Kane's smile and Moran's barely suppressed chuckle of amazement. At the same time I heard a hoarse, uncanny cry. I looked toward the corner from which it had come, and saw a cockatoo whose plumage glistened in the sun. He held his brilliant head on one side, and his wicked yellow eyes mocked his embarrassed mistress.

"Now be quiet, Jo-Jo," she admonished him. She turned back to us coquettishly. "He's such a bird! You don't know! And great company for me."

The cockatoo screamed at her again and then fell silent, his glittering eyes fixed upon us.

Kane began to question Mrs. Balbirnie patiently, covering the ground he had already been over with the others. It came out that she was very friendly with Mrs. Prendergast—"such a dear, sweet woman"—and had been in her confidence. No one could have foreseen this dreadful thing.

At this point Kane interrupted her to say, "If you were so friendly with his mother, I suppose you saw quite a lot of young Prendergast."

Mrs. Balbirnie pressed her lips together regretfully. "You *would* think so, wouldn't you, Clara and I being so much together? But I could not understand that boy—I say it frankly—I could not understand him. Many's the little cocoa party I had in the evenings, and I always asked him. But would he come! Never! I don't think he entered this room but once in all the time I've been here. I used to say to Clara, 'Can it be that Arthur has taken a dislike . . .'"

Once more Kane brought her back to the subject with careful tact. As she answered his questions her fear of the night before returned. Her face was both ridiculous and pathetic behind its blotched make-up. I noticed, however, that her terrors had not conquered her morbid curiosity. Unconsciously she slipped into her incoherent conversation a reference to the horror with which Prendergast's room had affected her.

"Then you stopped last night on your way upstairs," Kane asked, "and saw the body?"

"I wish I hadn't, Mr. Kane," she answered. "I don't know what made me do it. Mr. Wainwright told me not to, but I couldn't keep away from that—" She gasped. "I stood there, just outside the door. I almost fainted. If Mr. Wainwright hadn't been with me I would have. He helped me back to my room."

Evidently she could not bear to think any longer of the sight she had thrust upon herself and the reluctant Wainwright, for she jumped to another subject, and after that avoided as far as she could any reference to Prendergast and to his death.

When Moran asked her about her own movements she said she had been to a lecture—a travel talk at the Republican Club—with friends of hers. She had joined them shortly before eight.

"You were with your friends all evening?"

"What? Oh, yes. I came back here—why," she exclaimed in surprise, "you saw me when I came home with them! Don't you remember?"

Moran admitted that he did, and Mrs. Balbirnie plunged into further volubilities. At last Moran extricated himself from his chair.

"That's all," he said in a determined voice, breaking into her latest contribution.

"Well, now, Mr. Moran," she looked at him flirtatiously, "I do hope I've helped you. You know I . . ." Her strident voice followed us to the door, which Moran slammed behind him.

In the quiet of the hall we looked at each other helplessly. Finally Moran gave a sheepish grin. "Well, anyhow," he said, breaking into laughter, "it was worth a lot to see her take her hat off!"

Kane laughed with us, but absent-mindedly. His hands in his pockets, his head bent, he walked down the hall to the window seat. In a minute, however, he turned back to us, pulling out his watch.

"Twelve o'clock," he said: "Too early for lunch. We may as well fool away an hour or so. Let's go see Weed. I promised him faithfully we'd listen to his piano. He'll be disappointed if we don't."

Moran was about to expostulate, but Kane urged him. "Come on," he said. "You can't work all the time. You'll get to be a dull boy if you do."

"Damn nonsense," Moran muttered to himself as he followed Kane reluctantly. "Listen to that nickel piano . . ."

Kane ignored him, and at Weed's gentle "Come in," ushered us in to the blind man's room.

It was the first time I had seen Weed's apartment. It was large, and its two windows faced on the street. Its furnishing was commonplace, except that against the wall opposite the windows stood a large, upright piano.

Weed himself was sitting in an upholstered armchair, a shawl over his knees. On his lap lay the white cat. He stroked it gently, mechanically, as he turned toward us. For a moment the cat looked at us with wide, blue eyes; then, like a streak of lightning, it jumped down and took refuge under the bed.

"Now don't be so frightened, poor Sheba," Weed's voice was toneless. "Mr. Kane, isn't it, and the other gentlemen? Do make yourselves comfortable. Sit down, sit down."

As we obeyed him, Kane remarked, "Your cat seems to object to us, Mr. Weed. Doesn't care for visitors, does he?"

"She, Mr. Kane, not he!" His voice rose in slight horror and then fell back into tranquility. "I can see that you're not used to cats." He leaned over and clucked softly to the creature under the bed, but there was no response. "Well," he sighed, "Sheba is very, very high-strung. I suppose it comes from being so finely bred. Why, that cat, Mr. Kane, has bluer blood than royalty!" He chuckled, but in a moment proceeded to go even more deeply into Sheba's lineage.

Kane coughed discreetly. "You know you promised us something, Mr. Weed. And now we've come for it."

"Well, well." Weed was pleased, but uncertain. "Well, well. What was that? You know, we old fellows forget things. We're not like you young active men." If I was not mistaken, he was counterfeiting forgetfulness, so that he might have the pleasure of being urged.

"Why, you remember. Think what you said last night," Kane humored him.

"Of course, of course. Now I know." He slapped his knee softly, and his face lighted up with childish enjoyment. He laughed. "You want me to play my piano for you. Well, I certainly will."

Suddenly he was worried. He leaned forward in his chair and said in an anxious voice, "Do you think it would be all right? I haven't played it all morning. I haven't been able to touch it since last night when Alvin was here. And I've missed it so. But I didn't think it would be right." His sightless eyes appealed to us for confirmation. "You know, on account of poor Prendergast. But I wanted to." He breathed a deep sigh. "I wanted to."

"H'mm," Kane murmured sympathetically. Moran gave him an impatient look, but he let Weed ramble on.

"Alvin and I had such a good time with it last night. We played the new roll he brought me. He's very kind to me, always. Wasn't that nice of him? We both like music, you know, and after we'd talked a little while he put the record on and played it. To think I haven't been able to hear the piano since then! It's one of my few pleasures!"

"Wonder if I could manage to work it." Kane rose briskly and walked across the room. He looked at the roll in the piano, and from it to the boxes piled neatly on the top. "Mind if I make my own selection?" he asked.

"Oh, no, indeed!" Weed settled himself in his chair with as great anticipation as though the Metropolitan Opera Company had suddenly offered to perform for him.

"Now let's see." Kane was examining the instrument speculatively. "I'm not sure I know the combination to this after all. This little gadget down here—what—"

Weed leaned forward in nervous concern. "The roll, is it rewound, or isn't it?" he queried anxiously. "Because if it isn't—"

"It isn't."

"Then you must rewind it before you take it out. That little lever . . ." Weed went on to explain the mechanism, and soon Kane was able to set the roll in motion. "It should always be left rewound," Weed announced complainingly. "But that's the roll Alvin brought me. He put it on himself and turned it off, and I should certainly have thought—"

"Well, it's all right now." Kane had slipped the roll out from between the clips and was holding it in his hand. Presently he put it into its box which lay near by and took up another roll which he inserted in the piano.

"There she goes," he said triumphantly, as he pushed one of the levers and the roll began to turn. "Not many people have as fine a piano as this one," he remarked appreciatively.

"No-o." Weed beamed upon him. "I don't believe they have. I am very, very fortunate."

The music began. Moran, fidgeting with impatience, glanced at his watch. It was past his lunchtime, and he was hungry. He gave Kane a reproachful look but received no encouragement. His chief sat placidly rocking on the back legs of his chair listening to the music. I glanced at Weed. He was sitting motionless, his eyes closed in an attitude that might have been ecstasy, or—I laughed to myself—slumber. A satisfied smile played about his lips as the piece came to an end. The roll, still turning, flapped ineffectually against the bar which had held it. Kane stopped it, and with a grimace rewound the roll.

"That was fine," he said to Weed when he had turned off the current. "I certainly did enjoy it. Now, I'm afraid we must be going along. The roll's all fixed, ready to play again. All you have to do is to turn on the juice."

Weed thanked him profusely, and after we had listened to one of his long rambling speeches we were able to escape. Once in the hall, Moran prepared to give vent to his outraged feelings.

"Well, for the love of—" he began, but Kane silenced him.

"Shut up, Moran. He's not deaf. Wait till you get downstairs."

But when we reached the living room Kane gave Moran no opportunity for a further outburst. Instead he busied himself picking up his papers. Both Moran and I stood utterly ignored. When Kane had finished putting his affairs in order he glanced at both of us somberly, then walked over to the window and looked out into the street. After a moment or so he turned back to us. His thoughts must have amused him, for he was smiling.

"What's a feather, Moran?" he asked, a mocking light in his eye.

Moran revolved the question slowly. "What do you mean, a feather?"

"That's what I'm asking you," Kane retorted. "I'll be hanged if I know. What do I mean, a feather?"

He glanced at the bookcase. "After all, why not? The dictionary ought to say." He pulled out a heavy volume. "F-e-a," he murmured as he turned the pages. "Here it is. 'Feather: one of the epidermal appendages.' . . . H'mm . . . 'horny, pithy substance' . . . 'much like scales.' Not quite what I was looking for. Perhaps this little excerpt from Bacon will go better. 'With the feathers of these wings the muses made themselves crowns.' His eyes skimmed over the page until he stopped to read out, "'A sort of feather tossed about by whatever breeze happens to blow—a straw on the current of things!' By the Lord, and here's something, 'He hath plucked her doves and sparrows to feather his sharp arrows.' Very appropriate, that last line!" He spoke with enthusiasm.

Moran shifted uneasily, looked at Kane, and away again in sudden embarrassment.

"Never mind, Moran," Kane comforted him. "In spite of what I say or do, I'm not quite crazy. But I'm sorry you don't seem to appreciate the information I've been pouring into your ears." He clapped the dictionary shut, and, kneeling, put it back in the bookcase.

"By the way," he asked, as he stood up, "when Hyde was here this morning did you make any arrangements for me to see him?"

"I told him you might want to," Moran replied, glad enough to answer a reasonable question. "He left this card for you with his business address." He fished in his notebook.

"But you didn't make any definite appointment for me?"

"No. Why should I have?" He held the card toward Kane.

Kane took it from him without answering, read it, and gave a short laugh.

"'Alvin Hyde,'" he read aloud, "'Importer, 313 Summer Street, Boston.' And below the address, he's written 'P. P. C.'" He laughed again.

"'P. P. C.'" Moran repeated the letters after him. "What in God's name does that mean?"

Kane's laughter died. "Pour Prendre Congé," he said slowly. "In other words, 'to say good-bye.'"

"Good-bye!" Moran stared at him in utter bewilderment. "What does he mean—'good-bye'?"

"The usual thing, I guess."

"But," Moran looked at him stupidly, "is he going away? He didn't tell me."

"Yes, I should say he means to go away," Kane said slowly. He sighed. "Far away, probably from electric chairs, if you understand what I mean."

Moran scowled. "I don't get you."

"Then I'd better explain, hadn't I," Kane went on, "that Hyde killed Prendergast?"

CHAPTER 10

Twenty minutes later Kane was propelling me through the doors of Thompson's Spa. "Don't let a murderer get the best of your appetite, Underwood," he cautioned me, grinning down at my gloomy face, "whatever else he does to you. Here's an empty counter and an idle handmaiden. Sit down." He slapped a stool. Without a word I climbed up on it and he sat down beside me. "It's past eating-time and I know it. We'll have oyster stew, with flocks of oysters, and, let's see—for a climax—" He debated gravely, and then brought out with gusto, "Pumpkin pie."

I forced a smile. The mention of food brought me no pleasure. "That's just where you're wrong," Kane announced, when I explained this to him. "You know," he looked at me quizzically, "I'd lay a bet that nine out of ten really good murderers lose their appetites right after the shooting. And a hearty-eating gumshoe gets them on the hip every time. So forget your troubles."

He ordered for us both. When we were served I fished about in my stew with as good grace as I could muster. But Kane's startling words rang in my ears. Hyde was Prendergast's murderer! And Moran and I had talked to Hyde, had given him the scant attention we would have afforded a servant. He had been allowed to escape, to disappear from the face of the earth as far as we were concerned. I could not forgive my stupidity.

"Forget it!" Kane had said brusquely. "Stupidity doesn't enter into it. Neither you nor Moran had the information which would have convicted Hyde. Some of it I was getting from Mrs. Prendergast at the very time you were interviewing him. For instance, she told me that

Prendergast knew him, that her son had spoken of Hyde. The rest of it Weed told us afterwards. You don't understand now what I mean, but you will later. The murderer called on you at an auspicious moment—an incredibly auspicious moment, I might almost say," he added, his lips twisting ironically.

Moran had not come to lunch with us. Instead, burning with desire to make up for his mistake in letting Hyde go, he had stayed behind to trace our quarry. "By God, Kane, I'll find him before night," he had promised his chief. "There won't be a cop in the city who isn't looking for him. I'll have all the trains watched, and every city and town between here and San Francisco ready to arrest him."

Since we had left the Beacon Street house, Kane's spirits had risen, for no reason that I could fathom. I watched him curiously as he commenced on his pie. "Why so cheerful?" I asked at length. "This whole affair looks pretty black to me."

Kane looked up. "It is black," he agreed, "black as ink, most of it, but," he added softly, as he went back to his pie, "not quite all." He swallowed a large bite. "I've a fairly logical reason for being cheerful, Underwood. I think this case promises to be among the most interesting of my career."

"But we've lost out right at the beginning," I objected.

"And it's interesting," he continued, regardless of my remark, "because we're dealing with an enemy who possesses untold imagination. I suppose that's a curious way to describe a criminal, but I've reason to know that this one has that quality."

He laid down his fork. "Underwood," he went on, "you can combat most criminals with pretty dull weapons and come off victorious. But now and again one appears who threatens to overmatch you. Then you can draw your keenest blade and feel that the fight's a fair one." Kane was gazing beyond the stacks of dishes and the coffee percolator, a far-away look in his eyes. He smiled. "So that's why I'm cheerful. We'll have to do our best, or we're sunk."

He crumpled his paper napkin into a ball and deposited it on the counter. Turning to me, he said, "There's a day ahead of us that you won't soon forget. I've caught a scent that promises excitement. If it doesn't work out—well," he shrugged, "we'll start over again. But if it does—" He stopped abruptly. "Let's get on," he concluded, swinging himself off the stool.

"Where are we going now?" I asked in bewilderment.

"To buy some music."

I looked at him stupidly. He laughed, and pulling the check out of my limp hand walked over to the cashier's desk to pay our bill.

When we were out on the sidewalk, he started off rapidly. "The Variety Music Store is our first stop," he announced. "Number 765 Washington. That seems to be the place where Hyde bought the record he gave Weed. At least that's the name on the box."

We had walked not more than five or six minutes when Kane turned into a store whose show-windows carried the usual collection of sheet music, cheap ukuleles, and oversized harmonicas. The shop was small and there was only one clerk in attendance.

Without hesitating, Kane walked over to him. The man slipped a Victrola record into its envelope and looked up.

"Yes?" he queried.

"Do you carry records for electric player pianos?" Kane asked him.

The clerk nodded and took him over to another counter. "Any particular piece?"

"Yes," Kane replied. I could not hear what title he asked for.

The man started to poke about on the shelves. "I don't think—" he began, but left his sentence unfinished as he pulled out a long box and put it down before us. "There she is," he announced, and his hand crept toward a roll of wrapping paper.

But Kane had picked up the box and was examining it with care. "Yes, I guess that's it," he said doubtfully.

"Want it played?"

"If you don't mind." Kane sighed and rested his elbow on the counter.

The man broke the seal wearily, and taking the record out of the box inserted it in a near-by piano, but before he could turn the current on, Kane stopped him.

"Guess I haven't time to listen to it, after all," he said.

The man behind the counter removed the record and replaced it in its box.

"That's the one I want," Kane said. "Didn't know whether I'd find it here or not. Do you sell many?"

The clerk tore off a length of wrapping paper. "Sh'd say not. Those classical numbers rot on the shelves. We never carry more'n one or two of 'em."

"Then I'm in luck."

"Yeah." He broke off a piece of string, and holding one end of it between his teeth wound the other around the box. "S'matter of fact, I thought we were all out. Thought I'd sold the last one day before yesterday. 'Nother man asked for it. He was crazy about it too."

An expression of alarm crossed Kane's face. "Wait a minute," he ordered abruptly. "Maybe I don't want it after all." The astonished clerk halted in the act of tying the final bow knot.

"You see," Kane explained apologetically, "that man might have been my brother. And I was buying this record for him because he liked it so much. He wouldn't want *two*," he finished lamely.

The clerk was irritated. He looked Kane up and down. "Well," he seemed to say, "make up your mind."

"Did he look like me?" Kane pleaded, exasperatingly. I suppressed a desire to laugh.

"Not a bit," the man replied impatiently. "He was shorter—not so lanky."

Kane seemed slightly relieved. "Can you describe him a little more?" he asked.

The clerk started to unwrap the package, but thought better of it. "Well," he said. "I can't remember exactly, but he was kinda short, and seems to me he wore a black and white spotty suit." The description was vague, but I realized it fitted the man Moran and I had seen that morning. "And he had a mustache—a black mustache," he concluded.

Kane was delighted. "No," he shook his head violently, "my brother has no mustache. It couldn't possibly have been he. So go ahead." He waved an airy hand at the package. "I'll take it."

There was a threatening mutter behind us as we went out the door of the shop, but Kane was not affected. He was in high good humor, and as soon as we were out of earshot he laughed aloud.

"So far, so good," he announced, tucking the package under his arm. "Now,"—he seized me by the coat-sleeve—"let's cut across the Common. We'll take a peek at 152 Newbury Street."

I turned quickly to look at him. "You think—" I began excitedly.

Kane grinned. "No, I don't think our friend will be anywhere on the premises. Still it's a good idea to inspect the criminal habitat."

The house at 152 Newbury Street was shabby and unprepossessing from the outside. We mounted the steps and Kane glanced casually at the list of names near the mail boxes. Then he pushed the bell marked "Janitress."

He rang two or three times before there was any sound from within the house. Finally the door opened and a slatternly woman in a dirty house-dress confronted us.

"What do you want?" she asked hostilely.

"We're very sorry, madam, to disturb you from your work," Kane replied, "but we'd like to go to the room occupied by a Mr. Hyde. I believe he lives here."

"Ring his bell," she retorted.

"But no one answers."

"He ain't in, then." She began to close the door in our faces.

"Just a minute," Kane said peremptorily. "We want to see the room whether he's in or not."

"Nothing doing."

With a weary gesture Kane opened his coat and showed her his badge. Alarm succeeded hostility in the woman's face and she re-opened the door in haste.

"So he's crooked, is he?"

Kane stepped into the hall without answering her question. "If you'll tell us where his room is, we'll go up."

"It ain't up. It's right here." The woman started down the unlight-ed hallway. We followed her to a door not ten feet from the entrance. There she stopped and turned the knob. The door opened.

"Why, it ain't locked," she exclaimed in some surprise. "Most gen-erally it is." We went in the room.

It was dark and at first glance seemed to contain only the unat-tractive furniture of the usual lodging house. However, in a moment I noticed two objects which seemed out of place in that environment. They were empty boxes, about four feet long and three feet wide, made partly of wood and partly of wire netting. I thought they looked like small chicken coops.

In the rest of the room there were a brass bed, a table, a bureau, and one chair. To my surprise there was no indication of a hasty departure. The bed was made, the closet door was shut, and the bureau and table top were free from the debris of a hit-or-miss packing. Certainly the occupant of the room had collected his belongings with unhurried calm.

Hyde had left behind him no evidence of his tenancy, it seemed. But at this moment the landlady threw open the door of the closet.

"He forgot one of his suits," she said to Kane. I looked into the closet and saw, hanging by one of the hooks, a pepper-and-salt suit, of a loud pattern—the suit Hyde had worn that morning and the one that the clerk in the music store had described.

The janitress fingered it speculatively, but Kane, after one glance, turned away to examine the knob of the door and that of the closet.

"Fingerprints?" I asked.

"Not a one," he replied. "All the smooth surfaces have been wiped clean. But I'm not disappointed." He smiled. "I gave him credit in advance for that."

He crossed the room and turned his attention to the bureau drawers. They were empty, and he went over to the table and pulled out its single drawer.

Suddenly I heard him give a long, indrawn whistle. Then he spoke softly, between his teeth. "I'll—be—damned!"

I was at his side in two steps. He pointed downward. Lying within the drawer was a long, bulging white envelope. On the outside these words were neatly printed:

FOR THE POLICE
EXHIBIT A

I swung around excitedly. "What's in it?"

Kane's smile was twisted. "Can't you guess?" He ripped the envelope with his forefinger.

Within it was a bloodstained knife, with a blade five or six inches long.

CHAPTER 11

"Sit down, will you, please?" Kane's words were addressed to the woman and were more a reprimand than a request. While we had stood looking down at the knife she had edged nearer to see what it was we had found in the drawer. Now, as Kane confronted her, she backed away and settled herself uneasily on the side of the bed.

Kane slipped the envelope into his pocket. "I want to ask you some questions," he said. "You own this house?"

She shook her head.

"Lease it, I suppose," Kane supplied. "Well, that makes no difference. Are you the person who rents the rooms?"

"Sure." Her eyes slid vacantly from Kane to the floor.

"And collects the rents?"

"Uh-huh."

"Then you can tell me about Mr. Hyde."

The woman's eyes narrowed slyly. "No, I can't neither. Never seen him more'n three-four times. Ya can't get nothin' out o' me, see?" she finished triumphantly.

Kane was unperturbed. "When did he take this room?"

"Oh, long time ago."

"A year?"

"Longer'n that. Five years, I expect."

"Five years. H'mm." Kane fingered his lower lip thoughtfully. "Yet you've seen him only three or four times, you say."

"That's what I said." She shrugged her shoulders. After a moment Kane's steady glance made her uncomfortable. "That's right," she went on stubbornly. "I ain't seen him many more times'n that. He was a travelin' salesman, 'n away a lot."

"But the rent?"

"Oh, he always paid me ahead—three months it was, gener'ly. Cash, too—I used to find it in my mail box." Sudden regret clouded her face. "Will you be lockin' 'im up for long?"

"Can't say, yet." Kane answered. "However, I shouldn't hold the room for his return, if I were you. Another thing," he went on quickly, "didn't you ever see him coming in or going out?"

"Once or twice, maybe. But him bein' so near the front door, an' me bein' in my room in the basement, didn't happen that I ran into him much. Far's that goes," she volunteered, with a burst of heavy confidence, "I guess nobody in this house ever saw 'im to reco'nize."

"Thanks to the same reason, I suppose," Kane added, and then repeated slowly, "So nobody saw him much?"

"Hunh-huh. The other roomers wouldn't hardly know when he was in or out, 'ceptin' when those animals o' his begun to make a noise."

"Animals?"

"Sure. He kep' 'em here sometimes." Her expression was resentful. "An' they was the cause o' my losin' a good roomer. If I'd knowed then—"

"What was the trouble?"

"Oh, it was Mr. Guntz 'at complained. Lived up above then." She cocked a watery eye toward the ceiling. "Conducted on the street cars, he did, and paid reg'lar. But seems one o' Mr. Hyde's cats set up an awful racket. An' Mr. Guntz said nex' day 'at he wasn't payin' rent fer no cat music. So—I done the only thing I could."

"Which was?"

"I put a note under Mr. Hyde's door sayin' what Mr. Guntz said. Day or so after that they was ten dollars from Mr. Hyde in the mail box. So it seemed to me that if that cat meant *that* much to 'im —"

"How did you know the money came from Hyde?"

"Yellow envelope."

"No writing?"

"Hunh-huh. Never wrote." The woman snuffled. "Mr. Guntz, he went some'eres else. Always thought it was a pity, too. After that one time that cat never did yell so loud," she concluded reminiscently.

Kane nodded absently and walked across the room toward the wire boxes. "That explains these contraptions, I suppose," he remarked, kicking one of them with the toe of his shoe. "Cages for his pets."

"I expect."

Kane turned back to us. "Then he must have had more than one pet."

"Oh, yeah." The janitress indifferently plaited the folds of her skirt between her fingers. "They was a dog here once, I remember, but I don't think Mr. Hyde liked 'im much 'cause he didn't keep 'im long."

"What did he do with the animals when he went away on trips?"

"Can't say. Must a took 'em with 'im. The way it was, sometimes they was here, sometimes they wasn't. Hadn't been that Mr. Hyde paid so prompt, I wouldn'ta 'lowed it, not fer one second." She glared at us as if we had been two of the offending animals.

"Of course not," Kane agreed soberly, and bent down to pick up his hat which had fallen to the floor. "Well, Underwood, we'd better be on our way," he said, with a glance at me.

The woman watched us narrowly as we left the room and went out the front door.

As we walked back to Beacon Street I could control my excitement and my bewilderment no longer. The silence I had imposed upon myself was becoming irksome. I glanced doubtfully at Kane, but he gave no sign of appreciating my state of mind as he strode along, his eyes fixed on the sidewalk immediately before him. I cleared my throat.

"Kane—" I began. He looked at me sharply, and the expression on his face indicated that his thoughts had been far away.

"Yes?"

I hesitated and then plunged in. "You may think I've followed all this, but I haven't, and I don't mind saying so. There are lots of things that aren't clear to me. I don't understand, for instance, how you—"

But he cut short the rest of my sentence. "I know you don't," he said quietly, "but I promise that you will understand within a half-hour. As a matter of fact I intend to make the essentials of the case public property. By that," he continued, in reply to my look of inquiry, "I mean that I'm going to explain what we've found out to all those concerned. When we get back to the house I'll ask them all to come up to Weed's room. They've a right to know what has happened."

Moran was waiting for us at Mrs. Quincy's. Some of his buoyant confidence of the morning had disappeared.

"Nothing from Hyde?" Kane asked.

"Not a damn thing. But it's early yet," he added hopefully. "Anyhow, he can't get away from us entirely, not with the whole country looking for him."

Kane made no comment. In a businesslike manner he turned his attention to the meeting he proposed to hold in Weed's room. The blind man, a little perplexed by the nature of the gathering, lost himself in a sea of anxiety regarding the number of chairs necessary. He moved in aimless worry from one object of furniture to another, smoothing the bedspread or rearranging the articles on the table until the arrival of Wainwright and Vincent with additional chairs set his mind at ease.

Soon the rest of the guests began to come. A curious silence descended upon them as they entered the door. Each one gave Kane a quick, furtive glance, looked awkwardly for a chair, and sat down, seemingly glad that no more was required of him for the moment. Only Dr. Spinelli ventured to speak. Among the last to arrive, he looked in surprise at the assembled company.

"This is a matter of importance, then, is it?" he asked.

Kane turned to him slowly. "Yes," he said. "Sit down, please." The doctor obeyed. Still Kane did not speak. I realized that we were waiting for Mrs. Quincy, who had not yet come.

I fidgeted in my chair. The tension which hung over the whole group was preying on my nerves. I looked around quickly. Even Weed was affected by the unusual quiet. He seemed to be listening for some sound. Mrs. Balbirnie, seated at his side, rocked nervously at intervals, her gaze flitting from Kane to the door and back again. Vincent was biting the end of a match stick and then breaking it in his fingers, while Wainwright, next to him, held himself stiffly motionless, his eyes, for the most part, fixed on Kane. Lovejoy was rubbing the end of his cigarette holder with uncertain fingers, conscious that Moran was scowling at him from across the room.

We heard steps in the hall, and there was a movement of relief. Mrs. Quincy hurried in.

"I'm sorry—" she began, and then looked apprehensively around her. Kane moved away from the window.

"Mrs. Quincy," he said, "there's a chair by Mrs. Balbirnie. Will you sit there, please? I want to talk to you all for a few minutes. I haven't asked Mrs. Prendergast to come, for obvious reasons." He pulled a chair for himself into such a position that he faced us all, and sat down. Leaning forward, he rested his elbows on his knees. There was no indecision in his manner.

"You're all rather surprised, I imagine, and perhaps alarmed, to be called here in a body. But I've certain good reasons for wanting to talk to you." Kane hesitated, and then went on. "From what I know of you, I should say that you are all accustomed to fairly quiet lives. Certainly you are unaccustomed to murder. Arthur Prendergast's death has thrown you into a state very much like panic." He looked around, as if for corroboration, but there was no sound from any of the eight people who waited in tense anxiety for his next words.

"His murder presented a situation which you couldn't face. So you called on the police to help you. Doubtless by now you fear that it can't be explained, and that his murderer will never be discovered.

"But he has been discovered—that's why I've called you here this afternoon." There was a sudden movement in the room. "What I want to tell you is this—we know who killed Arthur Prendergast."

In the hush that followed, Kane drew a long breath. Then he went on.

"I'll tell you how we came to our conclusion. In the first place it was necessary to establish as nearly as possible the time when Prendergast was killed. That was a little difficult because Dr. Sloan, the medical examiner, was unwilling to state the exact time of death. All he would say was that Prendergast died between eight-thirty and nine o'clock. In the meantime Dr. Spinelli, who had also examined the body, said that he had died at ten minutes to nine." Kane did not look at the doctor as he spoke. "But on that point we couldn't take his statement as the truth, for Sloan is our authority, naturally, and his decision must be accepted. However, as it happens, Dr. Spinelli was very nearly right, according to the testimony of other witnesses." I glanced quickly at Spinelli but his face was expressionless. "Mrs.

Prendergast said that she saw her son at a quarter of nine, before she left the house. Mr. Vincent knocked on Prendergast's door at exactly five minutes of nine, and has said that he received no answer. Presumably, then, Prendergast was dead, and that means that we can logically set the time of death around ten minutes of nine."

Kane continued without a pause. "In the house at that time were Mrs. Quincy, Mr. Vincent, and Mr. Weed. They have said that they were in their own rooms. The rest of you," he looked around, "have testified that you were out. But during the evening a friend had come to see Mr. Weed. This man, whose name is Hyde, came at eight-thirty —Mrs. Quincy remembers that, as she was the one who went to the door when he rang. Mr. Weed corroborates the time, also. When Hyde left the house again, Mrs. Quincy did not see him, as she wasn't watching the front door, but Mr. Weed says that he left about five minutes of nine."

Kane leaned back in his chair. "Hyde was Prendergast's murderer," he said quietly.

There was a stunned silence, then Mrs. Balbirnie gasped. But no one paid any attention to her. All eyes were turned on Weed, whose face had become scarlet. He seemed to be choking for breath, and while he struggled to speak he held out his hands toward Kane in dumb protest. Finally the words came.

"That's not true," he cried. "It's not true. How could he? Why I— why I—"

Kane leaned over and put a hand on his shoulder. "Mr. Weed," he began, but he had to speak again and more loudly before the blind man's hands fell weakly into his lap and he ceased to cry out. "Let me finish, please." Weed bent his head and subsided.

Kane turned away from him. "Mr. Weed was trying to say that Hyde was with him all the time he was in the house." The blind man nodded his head eagerly. "And Mr. Hyde, who was interviewed this morning before we knew the evidence against him, said the same thing. But Mr. Weed happened to tell me something. He told me that Hyde had brought with him last night a new roll of music for his piano." As he spoke, Kane got up from his chair and walked across the room. The eight people watched him almost stealthily, but Kane seemed unaware of their scrutiny. Taking a box from the top of the piano, he turned to them again.

"I want to play that music roll for you," he said. They looked at him incredulously. Then Spinelli smiled and crossed one leg over the other. Weed was shaking his head sadly while Lovejoy rubbed the palm of one hand with the thumb of the other, his eyes never leaving Kane's face. Moran, after a gesture of impatience, looked disgustedly at the floor.

Kane had inserted the roll. He pulled a lever under the piano and walked back to his chair. Now the group's attention was transferred from Kane to the piano. As if it were a living thing, they watched the white roll unwind. Suddenly the first note, a low, soft minor, was struck and several times repeated. In these surroundings, in this terrified, bewildered company, the quality of the music was strangely disturbing. Now the notes fell more hurriedly, rising slowly to a crescendo. There was a menacing, prophetic undertone. I looked around me. Mrs. Balbirnie and Lovejoy shifted nervously. Mrs. Quincy was motionless in her chair, but her hands were tightly clenched on either arm. Wainwright's determined quiet, I knew, was not preserved without great effort, for his right foot was held in a strained, rigid position, and he cleared his throat softly at intervals.

The weird music had reached its height. The black and white keys of the piano rose and fell while the mad harmony crowded every impression but sound from my consciousness.

Then it softened—finally, it died. I saw Kane go over and remove the roll.

The unearthly silence that followed was soon broken. One by one, the listeners changed their positions, as if recovering from a trance. They remembered. Their eyes sought Kane again.

He was standing by the piano, the music roll in his hand. His voice sounded harsh and unnatural.

"The name of that particular piece of music," he said, "in case there are some of you who do not know it, is Saint-Saens' 'Danse Macabre.' It is a dance of death." Mrs. Balbirnie's eyes widened. Startled, the rest of the company waited for Kane's next words.

"A very appropriate choice, wasn't it?" He glanced at his watch. "It takes approximately eight minutes to play it from beginning to end.

Last night, while the 'Danse Macabre' was being played, Hyde stabbed Prendergast."

There was a faint cry from Weed. "It cannot be so! It cannot be so!" he repeated piteously. "For he was here with me."

Kane passed a hand over his forehead. "I'm sorry, Mr. Weed. You're mistaken." He looked speculatively toward the ceiling.

"Most of you have attended symphony concerts, I suppose," he continued. "At one time or another there must have been a person behind you who talked during one of the numbers. You probably turned round in your seat and made a polite remonstrance. Mr. Weed tells me that he is very fond of music. It would have been only courteous of Hyde, therefore, to refrain from conversation until the music was over." Kane's expression became harder. "Mr. Weed says that Hyde started the piano and turned it off. But in the six or seven minutes which elapsed between the beginning and the end of the music, it would have been possible for him to enter Prendergast's room, find him alone, and kill him.

"However, it so happens that we need not trade in possibilities," Kane went on quickly before Weed could voice a protest. "I have concrete evidence that Hyde was the murderer. For one thing, half an hour ago we found in his room the knife used to kill Prendergast. But," he shrugged his shoulders, "that was the end, not the beginning, of the trail." He stopped, and putting his hand in his pocket took out the tortoise-shell cigarette case. "Last night, I found this cigarette case on Prendergast's table. Mrs. Prendergast testified that it did not belong to Prendergast and that she had never seen it before although she had been in her son's room immediately before his death. It was reasonable, then, to suppose that the case belonged to the murderer. At any rate, I examined it carefully and I found several distinct fingerprints. I noticed that there was a small scar on the print of the thumb." Kane paused and slipped the case back into his pocket. He held out the music roll. "You can see that the ends of this roll are made of smooth metal. If you were near enough you could also see that on one end of it, which I have been careful not to touch, is the clear impression of a scarred thumb. I recognized it when I was looking at the roll this morning. It is identical with the print on the cigarette case. As you probably have learned, there are no two people in the world whose fingerprints are alike. Therefore, the same person who handled the music roll also handled the cigarette case."

He shot a glance at Weed. "Mr. Weed,"—the man raised his head—"it was you," Kane said, "who gave me the most damning piece of evidence against Hyde, for you told me that he alone had touched this roll."

No one spoke for what seemed at least a minute. Then Weed groaned and put his hand over his eyes. There was nothing defensive in his attitude now. He looked as though his last weapon had been stricken from him.

Kane put the music roll back into its box. He turned around. "That's all I've got to say to you," he announced.

Spinelli was the first to rise. He walked over to the door, opened it, and stood waiting for the rest to follow him. One by one they got up and went out into the hall. Some of them looked hesitantly at Kane as if they wanted to speak to him, but his manner was not encouraging, and after halting uncertainly they passed on.

As Mrs. Quincy was about to leave, Kane stopped her. "I'd like to see you downstairs for a moment," he said.

She nodded. Kane motioned to Moran and me to follow, and started out into the hall. At the door he paused and looked back into the room. Weed had not moved from his chair. Kane closed the door softly.

When we were seated in Mrs. Quincy's room, with the door shut behind us, Moran sighed deeply. "By God, Kane," he said admiringly, "that was a neat piece of work. Maybe I could have figured it out myself if I'd had more time, but I don't pretend to—"

"May I smoke?" Kane broke into Moran's sentence as if he had not heard it.

"Certainly," Mrs. Quincy replied.

Kane drew out a package of cigarettes. I wondered why he looked so dissatisfied, so perplexed. After lighting his cigarette he seemed to remember that Moran had been speaking.

He turned to him. "It was fairly easy, Moran—remarkably easy, in fact. All I had to do was to lay my hand on the cigarette case. The rest shaped itself," he paused, and then added, "a little too smoothly."

Moran grunted. "If I was you, I wouldn't fret my life away because a murderer's easy to catch." He looked around solemnly. "Say, what's the matter with you, anyhow?" he demanded.

For Kane was laughing, laughing as if he'd heard something too funny for words. I looked at him in startled surprise. His laughter stopped as suddenly as it had begun, and he asked seriously, "Do you think he is?"

Moran gave him a suspicious glance. "Well, of course," he said, apparently mollified by the earnestness of Kane's question, "we still got to locate him. It's a cinch he's skipped out of the city. But, great guns, man, what d'you want for a nickel? We've got his fingerprints—we've got his description. We'll notify the police all over this part of the country. Why, I remember exactly what he looks like."

Kane seemed very much interested. He leaned forward. "You do?"

"Why, sure. I never forget a face." Moran gave a snort of contempt. "Not his, anyhow," he added. "I could pick him out of a million."

Kane considered the statement. "How about a thousand?" he inquired.

"Easy. I'd spot him on sight."

"Suppose he were one of nine people. Could you?"

"I'll tell the world."

Kane blew a smoke ring toward the ceiling. "Well," he said finally, "I'm sorry, Moran. I wish I could believe you, but I can't. If you could pick Hyde out of even a small group of people our troubles would be over."

Moran's face grew red.

"The truth is," Kane went on slowly, "that neither you nor anyone else who has seen Hyde can recognize him now. Both you and Mrs. Quincy have been sitting in the same room with Prendergast's murderer for the last half-hour and didn't know it. Hyde is one of the people in this house."

CHAPTER 12

The expression on Moran's face changed from one of cool satisfaction to one of bewilderment. Kane's statement had swept the ground from beneath his feet.

"It surprises you then?" Kane queried, with a hint of mockery. "And you, Mrs. Quincy—you seem unprepared to hear that your house conceals a murderer." The woman's face was as white as chalk. She made an effort to appear natural.

"I am, indeed—unprepared, Mr. Kane. Unprepared to hear such a thing, and," her sharp eyes turned on him coldly, "if you'll excuse my frankness, unprepared to believe it." She set her lips in a straight line. "In the first place I see no reason why any of the people living here should have killed Mr. Prendergast."

"That I don't know," Kane admitted. "Not yet. That is still a missing link in my case. I do know, however, that one of your guests could tell us what his motive was, if he felt free to explain himself."

"Then this idea of yours is merely a personal opinion?"

Kane smiled a little sadly at her question. "I'll let you judge of that for yourself," he said. "At any rate you're entitled to hear what I have to say, since your interests are rather deeply concerned in this whole matter."

Mrs. Quincy nodded, but before she could speak Moran had taken the floor. He had a stubborn look on his face. "Excuse me, Kane, but what you just said about Hyde is a pretty sweeping statement. It don't go with me. Leastways, not yet." As Kane considered his fingernails without attempting a reply, Moran's voice grew louder. "How about that pretty story you just told us up in Weed's room! Eh? If that was a fairy tale, you certainly wasted considerable time for all of us."

Kane looked up calmly. "I admit a fondness for fairy tales, Moran, but I never make a point of telling them. What I told you happens to be true, word for word, as I saw it, and, incidentally, as the murderer wanted me to see it."

Moran impatiently flung aside the last phrase. "True! How could it be?" A new thought seemed to strike him. "Wait a minute, Kane," he said slyly. "You say the story you told us a while ago is true. All right. Now you say that the murderer is one of the people living in this house. Well, you've got those fingerprints, haven't you? Whyn't you go upstairs and check up on 'em—see who they belong to?" he finished triumphantly.

Kane was meditative. "That would seem to be the next thing to do, wouldn't it?" he mused. "However,"—his mouth curved into a smile—"I'm not going to do it. It's unnecessary."

"You mean to say you already know who they belong to?"

"I do."

This reversal left Moran nicely at sea. "Then you've got him!" he stuttered incredulously.

Kane's tone was decisive. "Yes, I've got him," he said, and then, before the other could speak, he added, "but I don't want him, for the simple reason, Moran, that he—the man to whom the fingerprints belong—has never set foot in this house, or laid eyes on Arthur Prendergast. I shouldn't waste my time in arresting him, if I were you."

Moran was not the only one to be taken aback by Kane's statement. Even Mrs. Quincy looked completely upset. I felt my bewilderment changing to indignation, and was glad when I heard Moran voicing the protest I too wanted to make.

"But Kane, you *said*," he pleaded, "you said that those fingerprints were the murderer's!"

"Not if I recall my words," Kane denied crisply, "and I think I do. What I said, Moran, was that the murderer had *left* the fingerprints. I did *not* say that they were his fingerprints." He shook his head and recrossed his long legs. "Now, I'll explain things to you, if you'll allow me the time and the opportunity."

There was no argument. Kane rubbed his forehead thoughtfully. "Guess I'd better start with this angle of the case," he began at last. "I want you to get things in the order that I got them. Now we know of three rooms that Hyde was in, that he spent some time in, either before or after he committed the murder. His own room on Newbury Street, Weed's room, and Prendergast's room. Presumably he spent more time in his own room than in either of the others. At any rate he changed his suit there and packed up his belongings. He was in Weed's room less than half an hour, talking to Weed, playing the piano. We don't know exactly how long he stayed in Prendergast's room, but he was certainly there long enough to kill him. Say five or six minutes.

"Now this is my point." Kane's forefinger tapped the arm of the chair. "An ordinary man, with no reason for concealing anything, can't be in a room even five minutes without leaving fingerprints all over the place. That is, unless he stands in the middle of the room with his hands in his pockets. He's bound to touch a table, part of a chair, the door handle, or a dozen different things.

"But there wasn't a single fingerprint in Hyde's own room—not even on the knife he carefully left for us. In Weed's room the only fingerprints on the piano were Weed's own. As a practical experiment I tried putting a roll in that piano without touching the piano itself. It can't be done. Yet Hyde played it and left no trace of his fingers on its surface. In Prendergast's room apparently he hadn't even touched the table or the knob of the door."

Kane looked up quizzically. "I suppose you wonder what I'm getting at," he remarked. "Naturally you're not surprised or even interested to hear that a murderer has been cautious enough to wear gloves or to erase his fingerprints. A clever murderer would do exactly that. I wasn't surprised at that, either. But what did surprise me—I may even say what shocked me—was the fact that although Hyde had left no prints on such casual objects as table tops, door knobs, and the like, he seemed to have lost all caution about wearing his gloves when he touched the two objects which might be supposed, even by the police, to lead straight to Prendergast's murderer. The cigarette case and the music roll both had clear thumb prints on them. And they were smooth surfaces too. Even a layman, I considered, ought to know that they would take beautiful fingerprints. Our murderer had been remarkably incautious—and, in view of other things, alarmingly inconsistent. A sixth sense tried to tell me that now if ever something was really rotten in that far-famed state of Denmark.

"Then I noticed another interesting fact. The cigarette case was a cheap one—you can buy them anywhere—and it was absolutely new. When I opened it I saw that the rubber band which holds the cigarettes in place wasn't stretched and that there were no little bits of tobacco in the corners. As far as I could see it hadn't ever had a cigarette in it. So I wondered why Hyde should have carried a case he never used. And above all I wondered why he should have bothered to take it out of his pocket and leave it in Prendergast's room, of all places. Particularly since he might have suspected that his fingerprints would be on it. Why should he have been so stupid as to leave an utterly damning piece of evidence against himself?"

Kane shoved his hands into his pockets and threw his head back. He had almost forgotten his audience. "But, damn it, I knew he wasn't stupid. More things than one had convinced me of that. And no matter how I tried to figure things, there could be only one solution. The fingerprints belonged to someone else.

"I was sure of it. But I had to prove it, naturally. And whose fingerprints could they be, if they weren't Hyde's? I dropped the cigarette case for the moment and tried thinking about the music roll which carried the same prints. I gathered from the information Weed gave me that no one had touched the roll since Hyde played it. That meant one thing to me. If those fingerprints belonged to someone else, they must have been on the roll *before* Hyde brought it to the house.

"I jumped to the most reasonable conclusion. It was easy to test out my theory."

Kane looked at me suddenly and smiled. "Underwood," he said, "when you accompanied me to the Variety Music Store this afternoon you probably thought I wanted to find out if someone answering Hyde's description had bought a record there. No, it was fairly obvious, from the name stamped on the roll, that he had. Of course, I had to make certain of it, but that wasn't my main purpose. What I wanted was the fingerprints of the clerk who sold the roll of music to Hyde. And I got them—very easily—on the ends of the roll he sold to me.

"They are the same—the scarred thumb—" Kane finished quietly, "as those on the roll Hyde put in Weed's piano."

Moran pulled at his lower lip, still frowning. "Yes," he said cautiously, "I begin to see. But wait a moment! How about the cigarette case?"

"That was the last link in the chain the murderer was making," Kane replied. "By themselves the fingerprints on the music roll served no purpose. It was necessary for Hyde to get the same fingerprints on another object which could be conveniently left in Prendergast's room. He bought a cheap cigarette case which he must have taken with him to the music store. It was easy to leave it on the counter, or drop it behind the counter in such a way as to give the clerk an opportunity of picking it up and handing it back to him. At any rate, he employed some such strategy, for the fingerprints on the case are undeniably the clerk's also."

Kane paused to light another cigarette. "You've got to understand the murderer's plan in full," he said after a moment, "before you can appreciate his ingenuity. This is the way he worked it out. He knew we would come upon the cigarette case in Prendergast's room and, finding out that it wasn't Prendergast's and hadn't been seen before the murder, would guess that it was the murderer's, and would assume therefore that the fingerprints on it were also the murderer's.

"Then we would hear of his—that is, Hyde's—visit to the house. Two witnesses would establish that—you, Mrs. Quincy, and Weed. He knew we would find out that while he was here Prendergast was killed. That, in itself, would bring some suspicion against Hyde.

"Finally, the fingerprints on the music roll would be discovered and identified with those on the cigarette case. Weed would be forced to incriminate him still further by admitting that Hyde alone had touched the roll. The deduction he laid out for the police to draw was simple and entirely reasonable. Hyde's fingerprints were on the music roll, therefore the fingerprints on the case were Hyde's, therefore Hyde was Prendergast's murderer."

Kane slowly tapped the ash off his cigarette. He laughed abruptly. "Oh, the trail was plainly blazed for us, no doubt of that. But he went even further—he took into account our possible stupidity. If we missed his signs by the roadside, then the discovery of the knife in his room at the lodging house could not fail to set us right. We would be sure Hyde was the criminal we sought."

Kane ceased speaking and took a few puffs from his cigarette. Moran began to fidget, and the expression on his face indicated that he was still laboring with a question which he was unable to solve. Presently he cleared his throat.

"That's a damn good piece of reasoning," he announced slowly, in the manner of one who dislikes to be thought too critical. "But—" his words became more uncertain—"but why should—that is, what's the sense of it all? I mean," he brought out at last, "where does all this scheming get the fellow? He's the murderer, isn't he, no matter what name he goes by, whether it's Hyde or—"

"Jekyll," Kane finished dryly. "Rather humorous of him to have chosen that particular alias. Yes, on the surface of things there wouldn't seem to be much in a name. However, Moran, your question leads up very nicely to the other thing I've got to say. I suppose the rest of you are wondering about that question, too." He turned to Mrs. Quincy. "Do you understand it?" he asked.

The woman looked surprised. "Why, no, Mr. Kane, I don't," she answered unemotionally. "If what you say is true, the murderer took very elaborate precautions."

Kane seemed satisfied with her reply. "Exactly," he agreed. "And I want to tell you why." His eyes narrowed. "Look here," he said, addressing Moran, "I want you to answer this question. Suppose, for the moment, that we didn't know that Hyde had killed Prendergast—suppose that such a man as Hyde had never entered the case. Where, then, would you search for Prendergast's murderer?"

Moran frowned and looked as if he did not quite understand what was expected of him. "Well, I dunno," he said at length, scratching his head. "I guess I'd corral the most likely people and see what they had to say for themselves."

"And whom would you classify as the 'most likely people'?"

"Oh," Moran's expression was vague, "people he knew. Men he worked with in business, say, or friends he'd been seen with."

"But, Moran, Prendergast had never worked in any business."

"Oh, yeah, I forgot that. Well, then, his friends or acquaintances would be the only ones who could have a motive."

"You know, don't you, that Prendergast had no friends, or even acquaintances, outside this house?" Kane suggested evenly. "Remember, Spinelli told us that."

Moran nodded. "That's right," he said. A gleam of sudden understanding came into his face. He stared at Kane. "By God," he muttered, "I think I get what you're driving at!"

Kane stubbed his cigarette out with an abrupt gesture. "Yes, I think you all do," he said, "without my telling you. In the supposititious case we've just been considering, the only people who could possibly be suspected of Prendergast's murder would be those who live in this house. But if a ready-made, practically self-confessed murderer—one Hyde, to be exact—were provided, then the situation changes. Not the slightest suspicion could attach to any member of this household. And if Hyde should disappear the police would be nicely buttonholed, and the less they made of the Prendergast affair, the better for their reputations."

Kane looked steadily at Mrs. Quincy. "I think you understand now," he said, "why the murderer devised such an elaborate scheme. Hyde was the mask assumed by someone in this house who wished to divert suspicion from himself. To throw us off the track, he provided himself with a false name and a disguise, which, I fancy, was very complete. He even provided himself with false fingerprints. The only vital mistake he made lay in neglecting to remove the name of the music store from the roll he brought Weed, for that enabled us to find out that the fingerprints did not belong to the murderer.

"Hyde has vanished from the face of the earth," he went on, "but not in quite the fashion his creator intended him to. It's true we have little to go on. His disguise has now, of course, been discarded forever. Nevertheless," he finished, "it's easier to pick a murderer from among nine people than from among nine million."

CHAPTER 13

As Kane concluded, Mrs. Quincy bit her underlip nervously. For the first time she seemed struck with the horror of the situation. "I couldn't bring myself to believe it," she began, in a voice which she tried hard to control. "I do believe you—now. But," she hesitated and then burst out, "must I live here knowing that one of these people is a murderer?"

Kane shrugged his shoulders. "Do as you wish, Mrs. Quincy. But, above all, you must let none of them know what I have told you. Whoever the murderer is, he must not be put on his guard. The account of the murder I gave them all should serve to put his mind at rest, and that's what I want. For our purposes it is better that he should think his plan has worked without a slip."

"But the difficulty of living in such a situation!" An overwhelming dread clouded Mrs. Quincy's words. "Of course, I must stay here. I can't leave my house to the mercy of the servants, and, if you'll pardon me, to the mercy of the police. How can I be sure that the murderer will ever be caught!"

"How can any of us be sure of that?" Kane replied calmly. "In any event, if you are uneasy I should advise that you go away for a while, regardless of what the servants and the police may do to the house in your absence." He brushed some cigarette ash from his trouser leg. "It depends, naturally, on what course is the more menacing to your peace of mind."

"Peace of mind!" She flung his words back at him derisively and gave a short laugh. "Do you imagine I can regain *that* by a course such as you suggest? Have you the slightest conception of what this

disaster has meant to me—to my future? My house has become noto-
rious—even my own good name—"

Kane interrupted her. "Your own good name is hardly in question,
Mrs. Quincy."

She disregarded his words. "I lie awake all night—even though I
take something to put me to sleep—thinking what my position will be
when this is over. Oh, no, Mr. Kane. A temporary absence from Boston, from this house, can hardly restore to me what I have lost by Mr.
Prendergast's murder."

Kane looked at her quietly and made no reply. After a moment she
continued more calmly. "What are you going to do? What can you do
to find out who the murderer is?"

"At the present moment," Kane answered, "there are two logical
things to be done. We can find out, for instance, which people were so
engaged on the night of the murder that they would not have had the
time or the opportunity to take on Hyde's disguise and kill Prendergast. That may or may not make the problem easier. The second thing
we can do is to find out from you and Mr. Weed, who saw Hyde on
that night, any additional details which might serve to identify him."

Mrs. Quincy made a slightly impatient movement. "I've told you
what I know, Mr. Kane. I saw him only for a minute at most. He had
come to the house once or twice before. I thought nothing of the
incident."

"But I want every detail of that minute," Kane insisted. "Understand, I'm not asking you to describe his appearance. That's unnecessary, first of all because I've had his description from several people,
and finally because I'm well enough versed in the arts of disguise to
know that a clever criminal can weigh all of two hundred pounds and
yet, under certain circumstances, give the impression of being frail
and undernourished. The shape of the nose, the size of the mouth, the
teeth, the eyebrows, the complexion, all of them can be unbelievably
changed. No, I don't want to know what Hyde looked like. But tell me
everything else you can. Start at the moment you heard the bell ring."

Mrs. Quincy frowned. "Well," she began a little helplessly, "as I
told you, I was waiting in my sitting room, ready to go out, when he
came."

"When you heard the door bell," Kane corrected her patiently.

"Yes. And I had to answer it because the servants were out. He was waiting in the vestibule."

"You could see him?"

Mrs. Quincy nodded. "The upper part of the door is glass, you know. He seemed impatient, too. When I didn't let him in right away, he said something. He acted very insistent."

"You kept him waiting, then?"

"The servants had left some kind of box right in front of the door," she explained. "A small packing box. I had to push it back—I thought I got it out of the way—before I let him in. He didn't even take his hat off. He seemed in a hurry. He said he had come to see Mr. Weed. Of course," Mrs. Quincy raised her eyebrows imperceptibly, "if Ellen had gone to the door she would have taken his name up to Mr. Weed. But as it was . . ." she was about to leave the sentence in mid-air when Kane interposed.

"As it was?" he repeated uncertainly.

"Well, I recognized the man as a friend of Mr. Weed's," she explained defensively. "Mr. Weed seldom leaves the house after dinner; so I was fairly sure he was in. And then—"

"You didn't want to go upstairs yourself," Kane finished. "That was natural. So you let him go up alone."

"Yes. I was in somewhat of a hurry. At any rate I stepped aside and held the door open. The man didn't say anything else to me."

"And that was all there was to it?"

'Yes." She hesitated. "Of course, I'd been stupid enough to leave that box in the way. I was provoked for a moment—not because he tripped against it, but because I thought he had cracked the glass in the door. He put out his hand, you see, to catch his balance, and knocked against the glass." For a moment the small worries of a housekeeper seemed to outweigh the tragedy we were discussing.

"I take it, however, that it wasn't broken—the glass, I mean," Kane suggested dryly.

"Luckily, no," she returned, unappreciative of his tone. "Actually, he didn't knock it hard enough for that, although for an instant I feared he had."

Kane stretched his legs and sighed. "Well, after that, I suppose you allowed him to continue on his way upstairs?"

She nodded.

"And you returned to your room?"

"Yes. And shut my door."

"There's one other thing, Mrs. Quincy. You say you had seen Hyde once or twice before last night. Do you know definitely any other times when he was here? Any times you can remember exactly and swear to?"

Mrs. Quincy shook her head. "No," she replied stiffly. "Naturally I didn't keep track of him."

"I see. Now," Kane looked at his watch, "I want to ask Weed a few questions; so we'll leave you." Moran and I rose from our chairs as he did. At the door he turned. "Let me know," he said, "if you decide to go away. And may I suggest again that our conversation remain secret?" As we left I had a last glimpse of Mrs. Quincy watching us with a steady, faintly hostile glance.

It was a saddened, anxious Weed who admitted us to his room without his usual word of greeting. He pulled at his skullcap with a frightened gesture and coughed apologetically. Finally he gave an uncertain laugh.

"It's so silly of me, but I feel almost responsible." He waited hopefully for some reply.

But Kane disregarded the opening. "I want you to tell me, Mr. Weed," he directed, "how your acquaintance with Hyde began."

"Oh, yes," Weed seized upon the straw. "That a chance meeting should have proved so unfortunate! It was chance, you know, Mr. Kane, pure chance. I used to go two or three afternoons a week to have tea at a nice little place around the corner from here. It was very refreshing after my walk. I still go there, in fact. However, I expect that now . . ." He sighed, and left his sentence unfinished. "Be that as it may," he continued heroically, "I was having tea there one day about a year ago when a man came over to my table. I think he said it was crowded—at any rate he sat down with me. As you may have guessed, it was . . ." he paused, perhaps to choose the right words, and finally came out with "that Hyde. He struck up a conversation with me about music, I remember. He was so fond of it—not that he really knew a great deal about the subject, but he was eager to hear what I had to say about it. So,"—his hands fell into his lap—"that was the way it was."

"And gradually you saw more of him?"

"Yes."

"And he began coming over here to see you?"

"Yes. There was the piano, of course. He enjoyed playing that. And then, he was a man who loved animals." Weed raised his head suddenly. "The strange thing, believe it or not, Mr. Kane, was that my Sheba was so fond of him. Why, Sheba," he spoke wonderingly, "why Sheba wouldn't let anyone but me touch her before Hyde came. She'd scratch anyone who tried to hold her, and never came to them. But she'd come to Hyde just as she comes to me and would sit right on his lap." He drew a long breath and his voice grew dismal again. "I cannot believe it, positively, I cannot. I've always thought," he went on tonelessly, uncertainly, "a man who loved animals—I ask you, yourself, Mr. Kane—could that man kill?"

Kane coughed gently. "Under the circumstances we won't generalize," he excused himself. He hurried to a new line of investigation.

"You couldn't tell us, could you, Mr. Weed, any definite date and hour, besides last night, when you were with Mr. Hyde?"

Weed bent his head. "Now let me think," he murmured, "now let me think. Was it last week Friday—no—it might have been—" He looked up helplessly. "You see I really can't remember." His hands dropped in his lap.

Kane shifted to a still more painful subject. "Did Prendergast meet Hyde through you?"

Again Weed sighed. "Yes, he did. Oh, I can see it now, Mr. Kane. I was responsible for this tragedy from the beginning. Arthur sometimes had tea with me too, and so they met. And I think Hyde sometimes dropped in on Arthur after he had visited with me." He bowed his head. "I cannot feel myself guiltless."

With this forlorn speech ringing in our ears we left. Outside, in the hall, Kane threw back his shoulders with an air of relief.

"I think we're through here," he said, "for the time being, at least. I'll meet you in half an hour for dinner, Underwood. Meanwhile Moran can be checking up on all the alibis." He turned to the sergeant. "Then meet us at my office. I want your report before I call it a day."

CHAPTER 14

"Well," Kane slipped into the swivel chair before his desk, "I don't mind saying I appreciate a change of scene, even such as this." We had finished dinner at about nine o'clock and had come directly to his office, where Moran was waiting for us. There was a matter-of-fact calmness about this room, high above the noise of the streets, that was a relief to us all. For the first time I felt a sense of detachment from the events of the day, and yet a keen interest in the facts we were about to discuss.

Kane turned the green lampshade downward and swept a bunch of papers to one side. As he pushed his fingers through his hair the reflected light shone on his long nose and the lines around his mouth.

Moran walked slowly to the desk, removing the cigar from his mouth. He laid a heavy hand on Kane's shoulder.

"Pretty far from anything, aren't we?" he said sympathetically. "You look stumped for once."

Kane pressed his lips together and glanced up. He smiled. "Stumped? No, that's the wrong guess. I'm just interested." Moran turned away, hunching his shoulders, and sat down in the shadows. His hat still on his head, he tilted back against the wall and sucked on his cigar butt.

Kane swung his chair around and crossed his legs. "You know," he announced, "it's just occurred to me how like a familiar game this particular case is. I mean the gambling one you used to find at all circuses and traveling side shows—they call it the shell game, I think. Ever play it?" he asked Moran.

The sergeant grunted an assent.

"It's this way," Kane explained for my benefit. "You have three walnut shells and a pea. You bet on the shell you think the pea is under. You know it must be under one of them. But try to pick the right one!"

He frowned. "Our particular game is about three times harder. We've got nine shells—by that I mean the nine people who could possibly be considered as Prendergast's murderer. It's not merely a figure of speech to call them shells, either. They're nothing more to us, at this moment. We've met them all, we've talked to them, we've heard something or other about each of them, but when all's said and done, what we actually *know* is just their surfaces. Add to that the uncomfortable knowledge that one of them is a murderer. You've got to accept the fact that under one of those nine shells, observation or hearsay to the contrary, is the character of one who kills. And that character, to retain the metaphor, is the pea of our game.

"Guessing won't get us very far. It seems to me it wouldn't be a bad idea to consider just what we know about this particular pea before we start saying where it's to be found. It might be a bit too large, or the wrong shape, to go under some of the shells. And that would eliminate a few of them and make the problem easier."

The front legs of Moran's chair hit the floor with a thump. Kane looked over the lamp at him and grinned.

"Moran," he said, "something in your expression intimates that peas come only in one shape. All right," his voice was rueful, "since you're so critical, I'll throw out the metaphor. But I still think it was good, up to the point you mention."

Moran fixed a distrustful glance on Kane, but the latter's mood had changed instantly, and he seemed occupied with more serious matters.

"There are certain things about the character of Prendergast's murderer that must be taken into account," he began thoughtfully. "First of all, we know that he was a person of great patience, of infinite regard for detail. He spent five years building up a dual life, a dual personality." With a frown, Kane interrupted himself. "That's a thing," he said, "that still puzzles me. If his reason for leading a dual existence was to kill Prendergast he need not have waited so long. More opportunities than one must have offered themselves. But still he delayed. Why didn't he strike almost at once?

"The fact that he didn't, might, with luck, have given us a lead. That's why I asked Weed to-day if he could tell us definitely any time except, of course, last night, when Hyde was with him. If Weed could have said, 'He was with me a week ago last Tuesday at five o'clock,' for instance, we might have found out where our various possible suspects were on Tuesday at five o'clock. Well, Weed couldn't help us, and neither could Mrs. Quincy. So we'll have to confine ourselves to the two appearances of Hyde's that we know about. But it's useful to remember that the mask known as Mr. Hyde has been in existence for five years. And that brings me back to the point—why did he wait so long?" He drew a deep breath. "As yet, we don't know."

With a gesture, Kane put the question aside and went on. "At any rate, if he knew how to wait, he also knew the exact moment to act. There's not a trace of faltering, of hesitation, in anything he's done. When his plans were laid he struck unerringly, never stopping to fear that they might miscarry. He killed his victim without haste, without trepidation, and then went about his business." He turned to Moran. "Think of his coming, at your summons, to Mrs. Quincy's house, to give you and Underwood a calm alibi for the very moment he had stabbed Prendergast, knowing that a second's miscalculation in the time of his appearance would mean his immediate arrest. And his handing you that calling card," Kane's mouth was set, "and then leaving the room as coolly as he might step out of an elevator. That was a neat piece of business."

"Why the devil should the man have taken such a risk?" Moran shot out impatiently.

"Possibly from a sense of the dramatic, Moran, if for no better reason."

Moran chewed viciously on his cigar.

"He had the audacity and the wit to call himself Hyde," Kane continued. "It's a perfectly good name. Why should we have thought about it twice? He could afford that little joke. And then he brought Weed the 'Danse Macabre,' and to the sound of the dance of death committed murder. He couldn't even make his disappearance without a flourish. P. P. C.! The commonplace initials of social usage. Something you might write on a card and leave for a lady who had had you to dinner!" His voice was appreciative.

"And he left us the knife he used to kill Prendergast and labeled it Exhibit A! Now you know he could have said the same thing in so many less striking ways. Well, I suppose you could call it a sense of comedy, if you wish. To me," he lifted his head, "it's more like a sense of tragedy."

There was a moment of silence. I heard the faraway rumble of the elevated and the rattle of a heavy wagon on the pavement below. The noises were like remote sounds heard through a fog.

Kane's hand fell heavily on the top of the desk. "That's the murderer we're dealing with," he said sharply, "and the qualities we've been talking about are, no doubt, his more striking characteristics, but don't forget that one of those people in Mrs. Quincy's house, one of those whose face, whose voice, whose manner alone we know possesses those same qualities. They're well hidden, I grant you, under the skin of appearance and personality, but they're there. Yes, they're there," he repeated, as if to convince himself, "but I wonder . . . which one it is."

Moran cleared his throat. "If you're going to go on that alone, it'll be a guessing game, seems to me."

"Yes, it would be," Kane agreed, "if we went on that alone. But we don't have to. We'll take the concrete facts first—the whereabouts of those nine people on the night of the murder. But while we're dealing with the facts—that is, whether any one of them had the time and opportunity to kill Prendergast—let's stop to consider in our own minds whether that person is capable of being the remarkable individual we know the murderer to be." He turned to Moran. "You checked up on all those alibis?"

His question brought Moran to attention. "You bet I did." He pulled a notebook out of his pocket. "And I got it all down in black and white."

"Good! But wait a minute before we start in on them." Kane reached for a pad of paper. "First of all I want to make a time schedule of Hyde's actions, as we know them, on the night of the murder. We've got to check those alibis against more things than the time of Prendergast's death." He picked up a pencil and began to scribble in a jerky fashion, occasionally pausing to consider what he had written.

Finally, he looked up, tore off the paper, and handed it to Moran.

When the sergeant had finished, I took it. It read:

8:30.   Hyde came to house. (Mrs. Quincy's and Weed's
             evidence).
8:30-8:45.   Hyde talked to Weed. (Weed's evidence.)
8:45.   Hyde probably started piano and went into Pren-
             dergast's room, for—
8:50.   Hyde killed Prendergast. (Evidence from various
             sources.)
8:53.   Hyde must have been in Weed's room to turn off
             piano, for roll plays only eight minutes.
8:53-8:55.   Hyde talked to Weed. (Weed's evidence.)
8:55.   Hyde, who was leaving, walked downstairs, accom-
             panied part way by Weed. (Weed's evidence.)

"There is something I didn't put down," Kane said, as I handed the
paper back to him, "and that's the time it must have taken the murderer to put on his disguise before coming to the house and to take
it off afterward. But we haven't any way of judging the length of time
involved in that. You see, we don't know in what place the changes
were effected, and that makes an enormous difference. Of course," he
added quickly, "it's the natural thing to believe that he changed in his
room on Newbury Street. But that may not have been the case. The
only time we are certain of his having been at Newbury Street is this
morning, after his interview with you. He must have been there then
because he left his suit in the closet and the knife in the drawer." He
picked up the paper. "Now, is this satisfactory to both of you?"

Moran and I agreed that it was.

"In that case," Kane suggested, "let's get on with your information,
Sergeant. We'll take each of the nine people in turn, and see where
he was between 8:30 and 8:55." Moran began to turn the pages of his
notebook. "How about Mrs. Quincy, first of all?"

Moran looked up blankly. "Mrs. Quincy? Why, Kane— I— Now,
look here, what's the point of that?" he expostulated. "I didn't check
her up, and I didn't check up on the other two people who said they
were in the house, either. We know what they were doing. Why, Mrs.
Quincy was right in her own room, and Vincent was sleeping, and

Weed— Well, my God!" he protested, in amazement, "I don't see what else I could have found out about *them!* No amount of pussyfootin' would of helped me there. They've told us what happened, and I couldn't—"

"All right, Sergeant, all right," Kane stemmed the tide of vehemence. "My idea was to make things shipshape, that's all. But I guess you're right," he decided. "You couldn't have discovered anything more than we already know. We'll let those three pass, and go on. What did you get on Quincy?"

Moran, somewhat mollified, turned over a couple of pages. "Nothing very definite. Wasn't home for dinner, he said. Ate a big meal at the Waldorf, which must have took him some time, then went to a movie up on Massachusetts Avenue. That was about seven. He got outa there a little before nine, then he had a —" Moran peered uncertainly at his handwriting, and finally came out with—"a Western."

"What?"

"It's a sandwich," the sergeant explained sheepishly. "Anyhow, he come on home after that. That's all I got on him. I couldn't get anything more exact." He looked at Kane expectantly. "Well, what do you make of him?"

"Always eating," Kane remarked, and waved his hand impatiently at the notebook. "Who's next?"

"Edward Lovejoy. You remember he said he marched in that torchlight parade. Well, I couldn't find out whether he did or not, but I know he planned to, because I asked him the names of the friends he was going to march with, and looked them up. They said they waited for him till half-past seven, on the corner of Boylston and Berkeley, but he didn't show up, so they went on. And that checks up with his story," Moran reflected, "because he was late and didn't leave the house till half-past seven. Didn't come back till five minutes past nine. That time's right. Mrs. Quincy says so. It was right after that they found the body."

"You couldn't find anyone who had seen him at the parade?" Kane asked.

"Not a soul. But it was a pretty big crowd, from what I hear, and he wouldn'ta been noticed."

Kane lighted a cigarette slowly and made no comment. After a moment Moran returned to his notes.

"Loring Wainwright," he pronounced distinctly, "says he went to the Public Library. I asked him, you remember, could he prove it, and he said yes, he talked to one of the librarians. So later on I asked him the name of the girl he was talking to, and after he got off a few snooty remarks he told me. I went right up there, but"—there was disappointment in the sergeant's voice—"he *was* there. She saw him a little after nine o'clock, before quarter-past, she thought. However," Moran spoke emphatically, "I'm not forgetting that he left the house a little bit before eight-thirty, and said he didn't get to the library till nine. I know one thing certain—I could get from Mrs. Quincy's up there in ten or twelve minutes at the outside."

"Yes, but you remember," Kane reminded him, "that Wainwright said he didn't go straight to the library. He stopped in a doorway to wait until the rain was over."

"Yeah, I know that," Moran agreed gloomily. "Anyhow, that's the dope on him." He licked his thumb and turned over to another page. "Here's Spinelli. He was a tough nut to crack, and nothing much come of it."

"Pretty well covered, is he?"

"Absolutely. Here it is. Spinelli went out a little after eight—doesn't know exactly when. He walked around and then he went to a drug store about twenty minutes of nine. Well, I moseyed over to see what the clerk in the drug store had to say. He told me a lot. The doctor had come in there just about the time he said—to have some prescriptions filled. As a matter of fact the clerk knew to the minute what time he come in, and what time he left. Something about leaving the prescriptions, it was. Seems Spinelli didn't want to wait for them if it was going to take too long. So he looks at the clock and says, 'It's eight forty-three now. Can you have 'em ready by five minutes of nine?' The clerk said he could, so Spinelli, he left 'em and went to the telephone booth in the back of the store to do some telephoning while he was waiting. When he come back—and it was exactly five minutes of nine then because the clerk looked to see—the prescriptions were ready. Spinelli took 'em and went right out. He got back to the house a little after that—about ten minutes past nine, I think. Prendergast was dead then, and he looked over the body, according to him." Moran sighed deeply. "So I guess we can cross the doc off our list," he said. "You can't get by that evidence, do you think?" he asked, tapping the page with his forefinger.

Kane examined with interest the growing ash on his cigarette. "It would seem like a clear case of innocence," he said, carelessly knocking the cigarette against the heel of his shoe.

"Seems so," Moran agreed morbidly. "Well, now," he looked at another page, "Mrs. Balbirnie is sittin' pretty too. She went to some lecture at the Republican Club—left Mrs. Quincy's at ten minutes to eight, she told me. Met two other ladies—friends of hers—at eight. I found out their names—May Murphy and Agnes somebody or other. Anyhow Agnes told me the same story Mrs. Balbirnie did. They heard the lecture, all right, and it musta been some lecture," the sergeant volunteered acridly, "from the amount of talk I've had about it. The man who did the lecturing was somebody by the name o' Holt, or—"

"Holmes, possibly," Kane suggested dryly. "He gives illustrated lectures, I believe."

"Yeah?" Moran queried politely. "Well, the lecture was out at half-past nine. The three of 'em went and had a soda, and come on home. We was there, don't you remember, when she got back to Mrs. Quincy's?"

"Yes, I remember." Kane dropped his cigarette and ground it hard into the floor with the toe of his shoe. "Did you find out anything further about Mrs. Prendergast?" he asked, looking up.

"Only the same old thing she told us in the beginning. She acted so scared I couldn't get much out of her. After all, she's had a pretty tough time, and I—"

"Don't get dismal, Moran," Kane directed curtly. "What did she say?"

Moran bent stiffly over his notes. "Stayed with son in own sitting room till 8:45," he read off. "Then son went into his room, and closed door. Few minutes after that, she went out."

"Why?"

"She said she wanted to take a short walk. It wasn't much before quarter-past nine when she got back. She went upstairs not noticing anything in particular, and when she got there . . ."

Moran's voice droned on, repeating the same old story. I found it hard to listen, and glancing at Kane I suspected that even his thoughts were elsewhere.

When Moran had finished, Kane said abruptly, "Well, so much for the alibis for Hyde's first appearance. There's another time when we know where Hyde was—the time when he talked to you, about nine-thirty this morning. I was with Mrs. Prendergast, but I've not been able to place anyone else definitely. When I asked the various people where they were, they gave exactly the answers I might have expected. They were in their rooms, or going about their business. No two of them were together. So there's no chance that we can catch Hyde on that."

He leaned back in his chair and began to rock slowly. "There's another thing we've got to consider," he said. "I mean the episode that first took us to the Quincy house. Underwood, you saw what happened to Prendergast's room, and I've already described it to Moran, but I want to remind you both of those pseudo-bloodstains. That incident doesn't stand by itself. It undoubtedly had something to do with Prendergast's murder."

"Sure," Moran interposed, "it was sort of a warning."

"That's the first thing that occurred to me," Kane answered.

Moran was still a little puzzled. "There's one thing," he said, "I don't see why—"

Kane got up, glancing at his watch as he did so. "Keep that for a few minutes, will you, Moran? It's ten o'clock, and I promised some of the boys on the newspapers I'd be downstairs to give them the latest dope for their morning editions. It won't take me long, I hope, so if you don't mind holding the fort till I get back—" He walked wearily toward the door and went out.

The sound of his footsteps had no sooner died away down the corridor than the telephone on his desk jangled sharply. Moran made no effort to rise from his chair, and so, after the second ring, I picked up the receiver.

"Inspector Kane is out," I said, and was about to replace it on the hook, when the person at the other end asked: "Is this Mr. Underwood?"

"Yes," I answered in some surprise.

"This is Mrs. Quincy speaking." Startled, I pressed the receiver closer to my ear.

"I understand. Is anything the matter?" I asked quickly.

"No, nothing. But," she went on hurriedly, "I wanted to tell Mr. Kane—I wanted to ask him to come over here soon, to-morrow morning if possible. There is something peculiar—I think I have found out—" the voice stopped suddenly. I wondered if I had missed the end of the sentence. Presently she resumed the conversation in a controlled manner which was more familiar to me. "It is merely this, Mr. Underwood," she said coldly. "I wish to talk to Mr. Kane to-morrow morning. Is that understood?"

"Certainly. I will tell him."

"Good-bye." The receiver at the other end was hung up abruptly.

"What was it?" Moran leaned forward eagerly as I replaced the telephone on the desk.

"I don't quite know," I replied, walking over to my chair. "I think Mrs. Quincy has discovered something. But she sounded so confused I couldn't make out. She wants to see Kane to-morrow."

"To-morrow!" Moran snorted. "If I know Kane he'll go to-night. God, I wish he'd hurry and come back."

"So do I."

But Kane did not return for what seemed hours to me, although my watch read 10:30 just before I heard his footsteps in the hall.

I commenced my story before he was well within the room, and before I had quite finished it he was reaching for his hat. Then he remembered the papers on his desk, and began to stuff them hastily into a drawer.

Moran and I stood near the door, impatient of the delay. In that second I heard the newsboys crying in the streets. To-morrow, I reflected, there might be more in their papers than the usual headline, "Police Frustrated in Prendergast Affair."

Again the telephone rang. Kane, ready to go, seized it roughly from the hook. It continued to buzz impotently for a moment. Then Kane spoke. "Yes?"

There was a loud metallic chatter.

Kane replaced the receiver very carefully. He looked like a man in a dream.

"We were going to see Mrs. Quincy, weren't we?" he said. "But Mrs. Quincy is dead."

CHAPTER 15

A minute later we were in my car, roaring through the silent streets. Kane had taken the wheel. He drove as if he were possessed. As we reached a corner he put the brakes on hard. The car skidded, rocked, but we made the turn. He pressed the accelerator. We shot past the Common and the Gardens. There was a traffic cop on the corner of Arlington. Kane ignored his signal and dashed by, threading a perilous way between the cars coming from the other direction. Whistles shrilled at us, but we were already blocks away.

The street lamps flashed by. Above them the sky hung black and threatening. The alternating light and shadow, the somber houses that wedged us in, the oppressive darkness overhead etched an indelible picture on my memory.

The brakes screamed and the car slid to the curb before the Quincy house. Kane was out, but Moran had reached the door before him. He pounded on it violently. Someone opened it; our haste suddenly arrested, we stood still in the hall.

Only one shaded light was burning. Half-hidden in the dimness, a group of people stood by the foot of the stairs. They were huddled together, as though our entry had startled them and they had sought each other for protection.

"Turn on the lights!" Kane's voice broke the silence.

The switch clicked and the dark hall leaped into brilliance. Their faces showed them clearly now—Vincent, Lovejoy, Spinelli, Mrs. Balbirnie, and the servants. A little apart from them, Wainwright stood stiffly by the banister. His face had the calmness of a mask.

Exposed by the naked, all-revealing light, they pressed still closer together, not away from us, but away from an intangible presence that ruled them. Once again in their comfortable, commonplace lives, they knew fear, and the knowledge stripped them of every other emotion. Terror was written on their gray faces.

Suddenly Mrs. Balbirnie burst away from the group. She stumbled toward Kane. "Who'll be the next one?" she shrilled. "Now she's been killed. You've got to let me go away. I can't stay here. We're all going to be murdered!" She clutched at his coat and stared up at him with wild eyes. "Let me go!" she whimpered.

Kane shook her off. "No one can leave the house," he said coldly. "I warn you all. Mr. Wainwright, where is—?"

Wainwright came forward. He alone showed no emotion. Without speaking, he indicated the door of Mrs. Quincy's bedroom.

Kane turned to the rest of them. "I'll want to see you all later," he said. "Go to your rooms now. Dr. Spinelli!"

The doctor faced him. "Where is Mr. Quincy?"

"In their—in his sitting room." His long, thin fingers stroked his lips. "Mr. Weed?"

"He went back to his room, after—"

"Mrs. Prendergast?"

"She is in her room."

As Spinelli went to join the others, already on the stairs, Kane stopped them. "Understand this clearly," he said, in a harsh, emphatic voice. "No one is to leave this house without my express permission."

They stared at him with dumb acquiescence.

Outside the door we heard the police car arriving. "Post your men, Moran," Kane ordered. "Sloan's been notified, hasn't he? You'll find us in Mrs. Quincy's room."

He did not go directly to her bedroom, however, but turned to the door of Quincy's sitting room. He opened it without knocking.

Quincy was sitting by the table, his body slumped in the chair, his head bowed in his hands. The circle of light from the lamp fell upon his thin gray hair. It seemed whiter than it had been in the morning.

He looked up as we came in. In his face were both sorrow and a shocked amazement. But one emotion dominated it. Like everyone else in that fateful house, he was afraid.

"You've heard—?" His pale eyes questioned us. He read the answer in Kane's face. "She's in there." He pointed to the door of the bedroom. His hand was shaking.

"Suppose you come with us, Mr. Quincy." Kane's cool voice seemed to steady the man, although he showed his reluctance as he rose. Before the closed door he hesitated a moment, then threw it wide open.

Kane stood quietly in the doorway, surveying the room. For the moment he ignored the recumbent figure that drew my eyes. He glanced first to his left, where stood a bureau and a couple of straight chairs. On one of the latter lay Mrs. Quincy's clothes neatly folded. In the wall to the left were two windows. They were up, but they were securely screened, and through the screens I could see that they were barred. Another wall was taken up by a heavy walnut bedstead. The pillows were arranged and the covers turned down. By the head of the bed, on the wall to our right, was a door that opened into the hall.

An unearthly quiet brooded over the room. No one moved or spoke. Not a sound came from the rest of the house. The old walls were thick. Nothing would disturb a sleeper here. But the builder might have spared his pains, for no noise, however loud, could awaken the woman who lay before our eyes.

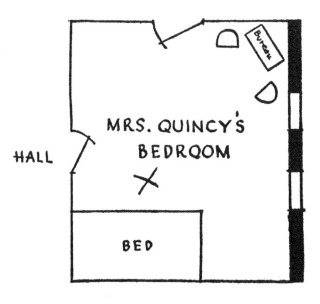

Quietness and order. The clothes so carefully arranged, the bed covers turned down, everything spoke of calm preparation and an easy mind. There had been no haste here, no struggle. But however peaceful the room had been, the silence was too deep to give comfort now. It was oppressive, horrible.

Suddenly a gust of wind blew against the shade. It flapped, and the noise was as startling as a pistol shot. But at least it broke the tension. As though he had been given a signal, Kane stepped into the room. Moran, who had joined us in the doorway, followed him. Both of them walked over to the bed, beside which the body of Mrs. Quincy, clothed in a dressing gown, was lying.

She was stretched out on the floor, one arm crumpled beneath her, the other extended as though she had attempted to catch herself. She had fallen forward, but her face was toward us, and I saw with horror that it was livid. But death must have come quietly to her. Her hair was neatly arranged for the night. The lines had faded from her forehead. Her brown eyes stared at us vacantly, their intentness vanished.

It was almost a shock to me to realize that there were no marks upon her body, no signs of a struggle of any sort. As far as I could see neither a knife nor a bullet had killed her. What, then, could have caused her death? If she had died by violence, how could her expression have remained so calm, so peaceful?

I glanced at Kane. He was standing motionless, looking down at the body, his keen eyes observing every detail of its attitude. He kept his thoughts to himself, however, until Moran aroused him.

"Kane!" he said, and then hesitated. "Say, she doesn't look as if somebody'd killed her. She must have had heart trouble."

He spoke doubtfully. Kane did not answer him at once. Instead he knelt down to make a closer examination. In a minute, he said, "I don't believe so, Moran. Look here. That didn't come from heart trouble."

He had pulled the dressing gown away from her shoulder. The sergeant bent down and looked where Kane pointed. There, on her arm, was a tiny round spot of red.

"But," Moran protested, "how could that have killed her?"

"I don't know," Kane replied, "but it must have. I wish I didn't think so."

Quincy, who had been standing behind us, put out a trembling hand toward Kane. A feverish red colored his pale cheeks. "But why—?" He bit his lip. "I—I can't understand. Why should anyone kill her?" A muscle in his cheek began to twitch. He put his hand to his face and tried to stop it.

"There's only one reason I can see, Mr. Quincy."

Kane's words came slowly. "Mrs. Quincy may have known enough to hang Prendergast's murderer. He may have killed her to save his own neck."

Quincy was badly shaken. "She told me she had noticed something. But she didn't know for certain—only something that seemed queer to her. Not anything important."

"Did she tell you what it was?"

"No. Why, she couldn't decide whether to tell you or not! She wasn't worried. She was going to bed."

"You knew she had telephoned me?"

"No." Quincy, half-hypnotized, stared at Kane.

"She did. She said she wanted to talk to us in the morning. I had decided it was better to see her at once. We were getting ready to come here when we heard she was dead. But all that doesn't matter. Her death proves to me that she could have given us the evidence to convict the man who killed Prendergast. Somehow he found out what she knew, and before she could talk he murdered her." Kane half-turned. "I wish to God," he went on, "that she'd told you what she found out."

He bent down over the body again and continued to examine it closely. As he did so he spoke to Quincy.

"I want to know everything that happened," he said. "Everything, that is, after dinner this evening."

Quincy looked at Kane uncomprehendingly. "But that's it," he said in a low voice, "that's what's so horrible." He faltered. "Nothing happened."

"Do you know where Mrs. Quincy was, or what she was doing?"

"Yes." He spoke with a little more assurance. "Yes. She was with me almost the whole time. In our sitting room."

"Then," Kane gave him a keen look, "from the time you left the dinner table till a short time ago you were both there?"

Quincy hesitated a little. "No," he replied uncertainly, "I didn't mean quite that. After we got up from dinner, we were busy for a while, both of us, seeing that everything in the house was all right."

"How long did that take you?"

"Three quarters of an hour, I suppose. It must have been half-past eight when we finished and sat down in there."

"Then what did you do?"

"We sat and talked. I read a book. That's all."

"When did Mrs. Quincy tell you that she had noticed something queer?"

"While we were talking. I asked her what it was, but she didn't tell me. She said she supposed it really wasn't anything."

Kane had been fumbling in the pocket of Mrs. Quincy's dressing gown. His expression changed a little as he drew out of it a small envelope. It was not sealed. He glanced at its contents; then turned to Quincy again.

"Your wife didn't break her glasses during the course of the evening, did she?"

Quincy was bewildered. "Why—no. Not that I know of."

Kane turned the contents of the envelope out into the palm of his hand. "Then I wonder where these came from," he said. He showed us some small fragments of glass. They were curved like pieces of a broken lens. He put them back into the envelope again and dropped it into his pocket.

He returned to the subject. "Neither of you left the room during the rest of the evening?"

"Yes. I did. I went to see that the house was locked up. We've been very careful about that."

"How long were you gone?"

"About ten minutes," Quincy answered thoughtfully. "It must have taken that long. I tried both doors, front and back, and all the windows on this floor."

Kane reflected for a moment. "What time was that?"

"Ten o'clock. I noticed the time when I first went through the hall."

"Then Mrs. Quincy must have telephoned me while you were away."

"I suppose so," Quincy replied. "But she didn't say anything to me about it. When I came back she was getting ready to go to bed. She always went to bed around half-past ten or a little before. I didn't go into the bedroom, but we talked through the door. It was open."

"You could see her then?"

"When she crossed the doorway. Not when she was in the other parts of the room."

"Was that door open too?" Kane pointed to the one that led to the hall.

"No. It was closed, but it wasn't locked."

Kane had finished his examination of the body. He stood up. "I take it, then," he said, "that anyone in the house could have got into this room from the hall. No one came through the sitting room, I suppose."

"No."

Kane looked at him sharply. "You're sure you didn't hear anyone in the room with her?"

Quincy shook his head helplessly. "No, I didn't hear anyone. I remember she said to me that she was very tired, that she was going right to bed, and not to disturb her. It wasn't a minute after that when I heard her fall. I couldn't imagine what had happened, unless she had fainted. I found her lying there. But she hadn't fainted. I knew that."

Quincy's face had begun to twitch again, but he went on talking. "I can't remember just what I did. They say I cried out. I don't know. I ran across the hall where they were playing bridge. They called the people down from upstairs. Then I went in there again, and they went with me, to see. . . . That's all."

He finished his story breathlessly and turned away from us to hide his emotion.

Kane asked him one more question. "What time did you hear her fall?"

"Just after half-past ten. I remember hearing the clock strike."

Quincy was exhausted. His face was so white that I thought he was going to collapse. When Kane told him that he could go he walked uncertainly away, his shoulders sagging and his head bent.

Kane went on with his examination of the room. As far as I could tell he found nothing until he bent over the small light blue rug, near which the body lay. He gave a sharp exclamation.

"Take a look at that, Moran," he said.

Moran leaned down, gazed at the rug, and then looked over at Kane. "Why," he said wonderingly, "that's blood."

I walked quickly over to where they were standing. At Moran's feet was a thin red streak about an inch long. Had the rug been a darker color we might never have noticed the stain on it.

"That's blood, all right," Kane was saying. "But I can't see how it got there. Can you?"

Moran's puzzled look cleared away. "Sure," he answered. "She must have fallen there first, and then thrown herself where she is now."

"Three feet?" Kane was not satisfied. "Granted that she could have moved her body that far, how does it happen that it's a streak, not a spot, of blood?"

Moran did not answer.

"Well, never mind that now," Kane said, glancing up. "Here's Sloan."

The medical examiner entered the room as Kane spoke. He nodded to Moran and me. "Well, Kane," he said, his cheerful voice in odd contrast to the business that concerned us all, "what's the matter now?" He glanced down at the body and gave a startled whistle. "So the lightning did strike twice, in the same house, anyway!"

"This is going to mean work for you," Kane answered shortly. "You've got to tell us what killed her."

Sloan took off his coat and knelt down to make his examination. In a minute or two he rose. "You must have seen for yourself," he said. "There's that incision on her shoulder, no other wound. If she didn't die a natural death . . ." he hesitated and looked at Kane.

"I know she didn't," Kane answered the unspoken question.

"Then she was poisoned through that scratch," Sloan concluded.

"Any idea what the poison was?"

Sloan shook his head. "Can't tell you that till I've performed the autopsy."

"And that means you can't tell me now what effect the poison had on her?"

"That's right." Sloan was already putting his coat on again.

Kane drew a determined breath. "Sloan, I've got to know those two things. Can you possibly do the whole business right away? Get the body down to the morgue and perform the autopsy to-night?"

"If it's absolutely necessary, yes."

"It is necessary."

"All right. I'll make the arrangements. Lord, I'm tired. Well, I'll phone you later." And Sloan took his departure.

Kane was deeply worried. He began to prowl restlessly about the room as though he hoped to find something that would relieve his uncertainty. His search was fruitless. Finally he turned back to Moran and me. "We can't do anything more here," he said. "We'll have to wait for Sloan's report. Lock up, Moran, and come along."

He led the way out of the room, but instead of taking the door that opened into the hall he went into Quincy's sitting room again. As before Quincy was sitting by the table. He looked up as we came in.

"There's one more thing I want to ask you, Mr. Quincy," Kane said, "and I want you to think about the answer very carefully. You told us that you heard your wife fall. Did you just hear that one sound, or did she fall and then throw herself into another position?"

Quincy was frightened by Kane's gravity, but there was no hesitation in his reply. "I only heard her fall," he said. "She didn't move after that."

CHAPTER 16

As we left Quincy's room I saw that Moran's satellite, McBeath, had been posted by the front door. Kane stopped to speak to him.

"You understand, don't you, McBeath, that until to-morrow no one is to come in or go out without my permission?"

"Yeah." McBeath turned his stolid countenance toward us. "They won't. You needn't worry. Say, some fellow told me to tell you they were all at Mrs. Balbirnie's waiting for you."

"All right." Kane led the way upstairs. The door of the room to which McBeath had directed us was open. As we came nearer we could hear voices, but the sound of our footsteps brought a sudden interruption to the conversation that had been going on. While we were still invisible in the dimness of the hall, we could see into the brightly lighted room. With the exception of Quincy and the servants, all the people who lived in the house had gathered there. They looked more normal, less frightened than they had at first, and yet they were still disturbed enough to find comfort for their overwrought feelings in one another's society. Mrs. Balbirnie had evidently been holding the center of the stage. Some of the others were gathered attentively around her. Apart from this group Weed sat in dreary silence, his hands folded in his lap. Behind his chair Wainwright was standing, gently shaking the perch to which Mrs. Balbirnie's cockatoo clung with indignant perseverance.

They turned instinctively as they heard us coming. There was something almost absurd about them as they stared at us, their talk suspended in mid-air. They were like a lot of children facing adult intruders. Only Wainwright was indifferent to our entrance. He glanced up with the rest, but soon turned away, and taking a cracker from a box on the table offered it to the cockatoo. The bird showed eager interest and advanced a scrawny neck toward the food, but Wainwright, smiling contemptuously, allowed the creature two pecks and moved the cracker out of reach.

Meanwhile the group around Mrs. Balbirnie eyed us with suspicious dislike. It was Spinelli who, for all his suavity, voiced their antagonism.

"Surely, Mr. Kane," he said softly, "you did not mean what you said—that no one was to leave this house. I beg you to consider what we are feeling. The ladies, they are frightened. They should be allowed to go away."

Kane eased his long limbs into a chair. "There are some things I can't help, Dr. Spinelli," he replied. "I won't keep you here any longer than necessary."

"Longer than necessary!" Lovejoy's voice was shrill. "When all our lives are in danger! You must know that's true, now. Last night, Prendergast—to-night . . ." He looked at Kane wildly. "We're afraid, I tell you, we're afraid!"

But Kane's face was as impassive as if he had not heard. "So you've all guessed," he said evenly, "that Mrs. Quincy didn't die a natural death. That's true enough. Furthermore, I can tell you this: she was poisoned by the person who killed Prendergast."

"Your Mr. Hyde?" Wainwright's voice was as smooth as oil, but his easy manner did not cloak the sneer. The resentful doubt of the whole company was expressed in those three words.

"Exactly."

"Then—" But a second outburst from Lovejoy prevented Wainwright from continuing. With a shrug he turned back to the bird, offering it, in place of the cracker, the lighted end of his cigarette. His chuckle and the cries of the cockatoo destroyed Mrs. Balbirnie's last vestige of self-control.

"I can't stay here, Mr. Kane. I can't." She was almost in tears. "I feel utterly defenseless." Her chin drooped in terror.

Kane was about to reply, but he was interrupted by a sudden movement from Weed. The blind man stood up. "And I," he said determinedly, "I must get back to my room. Sheba has not been fed. I am going now."

There was something laughable in the importance he attached to his cat, at this moment of all others. But Kane stopped him as he crossed the room.

"Just a minute, Mr. Weed. Where were you this evening?"

Weed turned to him with vague surprise. "Why, I was in my room, of course. Where else would I be?" He smiled tolerantly at Kane. A sudden idea seemed to strike him. "Oh, I see now." He nodded his head. "You want me to tell you what I can about poor Mrs. Quincy. What I heard and all that. It's too bad, but I can't help you. I didn't hear anything, and I didn't speak to anyone. I didn't leave my room at all."

"Then what did you do with yourself all that time?" Moran looked at him curiously.

"I didn't do anything, Mr. Moran." Weed was indulgent. "There is very little I can do. If you don't mind, I must go now. Poor Sheba!" No one stopped him this time.

Kane turned back to the others who were waiting in stricken silence. "I want you all to tell me briefly what you were doing this evening." He looked at Lovejoy, who answered the unspoken question.

"I played bridge, Mr. Kane," he said, with an effort at calmness. "That's all. Wainwright and Spinelli and Vincent and I made up a table. We played downstairs, in the living room."

Without comment Kane turned to Mrs. Prendergast. "And you?" he asked. Mrs. Prendergast replied that she had been in her room, as did Mrs. Balbirnie.

"All right." Kane came to an abrupt decision. "I want to talk to you, Mr. Lovejoy, now. I'll have to ask the rest of you to wait till later. I can't tell whether I'll need you or not till I get my bearings."

At Mrs. Balbirnie's suggestion Kane stayed in her sitting room while he had his conversation with Lovejoy. The others, Mrs. Balbirnie among them, left in a body. Apparently not one of them had the courage to go to his own room, or stay anywhere alone. Spinelli remarked as he left that they would wait for Kane in the living room.

Lovejoy, deserted by his allies in disaster, could not hide his uneasiness. For a moment or two he wandered around the room. When

Kane asked him to sit down he did so, but his hands continued their nervous, ineffectual movements.

"You know, Mr. Kane," he volunteered finally, keeping his eyes fixed on the floor, "I don't see what I can tell you. If it's Hyde you're after, I can't—"

"Why do you think it was Hyde who killed Mrs. Quincy?" Kane cut in sharply.

Lovejoy looked up in quick terror. "Why—why—you said so, didn't you?" he stammered.

Kane made a brusque movement. "My apologies, Mr. Lovejoy," he said. "I'd forgotten. Yes, it was Hyde. But," he glanced curiously at the man, "didn't you suspect that before I told you?"

Lovejoy nodded his head in relief. "To tell you the truth, Mr. Kane, I couldn't help thinking that from the very first."

"What do you mean, exactly, 'from the very first'?"

"When Quincy called us." Lovejoy drew a long breath. He was staring beyond Kane. "When we went in and saw her lying there on the floor. We'd all rushed in, you see—the four of us who were playing bridge and the others from upstairs." He closed his eyes for a moment. "Even then not one of us thought for a moment she'd died a natural death." Still he avoided meeting Kane's level glance.

"How did you know that? Did anyone say so?"

"No. No one said anything. Yes, they did, too— I don't remember what. We just stood there, stunned. But I could feel it." He made a vague gesture. "Afterwards—well, I found out they'd been thinking just what I had."

"Which was?" Kane prompted him.

"That Hyde had come back."

There was a faint uncertainty on Kane's face. "I don't see how he got into the house, Mr. Lovejoy. I know he did, of course, but hasn't Quincy been very careful about locking up?"

"I certainly thought so," Lovejoy answered nervously. "If I had ever dreamed—" He pulled out a large silk handkerchief and wiped his forehead. "Well, I wouldn't have been playing bridge, that's all."

Kane nodded. "You were having a game, weren't you? With Wainwright, Spinelli, and Vincent, I think you said."

"Yes." Lovejoy agreed wearily. "We got up a table. It was the first time we'd been able to think about anything but Prendergast. You'd told us about Hyde, you know, and it all seemed settled. I felt as if I could forget it all." He sighed, not without a touch of affectation.

"What time did you start to play?"

"Perhaps at half-past eight, perhaps a little later. I know it was shortly after the hour when Wainwright spoke to me about having a game. Then it took a little while to get the others."

"You played straight through till ten-thirty?"

"I guess that was about the time. We were in the middle of a hand when Quincy ran in and told us his wife was dead."

Kane showed his disappointment. "H'mm. I was hoping that if you had stopped at all some one of you might have left the table for a moment, and—" he motioned vaguely—"have seen or heard something which at the moment meant nothing perhaps, but now . . ."

Lovejoy was a little confused and showed it. "Oh! Wait a minute," he said. "I don't believe I understood your question. It wasn't that we stopped playing. But the dummy, you know." He looked expectantly at Kane, who seemed to comprehend. "You see," he went on, "whoever was dummy got up to fix the drinks, and so forth, in the next room. I don't know, but I suppose one of them might have—"

Kane interrupted him. "The living room, where you were playing, is, as I remember it, directly across the hall from Mrs. Quincy's part of the house. Also it opens into the dining room. Is that where you were mixing the drinks?"

"Yes. On a buffet in there."

"Mr. Lovejoy," Kane looked down between his knees at the floor, "was your game interrupted at any time during the evening?"

"Oh, no."

"I mean," Kane explained with some insistence, "were any of your hands ever held up because you had to wait for one of the players to return, say, from mixing a drink?"

The rubber sole of Lovejoy's shoe squeaked as he shifted his position. "I don't remember," he began, and then changed his reply. "Well, once, perhaps," he admitted. "The time Wainwright went upstairs to get his slippers. We had to wait a little after the cards were dealt, if that's what you mean."

"What time was that?"

"Let me see," Lovejoy murmured. "I remember thinking I would stop at the end of that rubber. I wanted to go to bed. I looked at my watch. It was quarter-past ten, exactly."

Out of the corner of my eye I saw Moran glance swiftly at Kane. I followed his look. Kane's expression betrayed nothing.

Lovejoy continued his explanation. "Wainwright had said that as soon as he was dummy he was going to get his slippers. I guess his feet hurt. Anyhow, he was limping a little. The very next hand, I made a bid and got it. Wainwright was my partner. So he went upstairs and came back in a couple of minutes."

"Wearing his slippers, I suppose," Kane murmured.

"Why, yes." Lovejoy seemed perplexed.

Kane was silent for a moment. Then he frowned. "You must be an almighty good bridge player, Mr. Lovejoy, if you can play through a hand in much less than a couple of minutes. You must have, if you had to wait for Wainwright to come back."

But Lovejoy was on surer ground now. "Not at all, Mr. Kane." He shrugged his shoulders. "It was hopeless from the start. You should have seen the hand Wainwright gave me. A singleton in my suit and one ace. Nothing else. I didn't even bother to play it out. He should never have given me a raise."

It was my turn to look sharply at Kane, but he was smiling as he replied, "Possibly Mr. Wainwright was more occupied with his feet than with the rules of bridge."

"It seemed that way to me," Lovejoy agreed morosely.

"Too bad you went down," Kane spoke with gravity. "However, even that may have its uses. It's an ill wind and so forth. It may be that Wainwright . . ." Lovejoy's obvious lack of comprehension made him hesitate. "Well," he lifted his eyebrows, "only time and Mr. Wainwright can tell us that."

After a moment's silence Lovejoy became restless. "Is that all you want of me?" he asked.

"Of you?" Kane seemed surprised at the question. "Oh, yes."

With little reluctance Lovejoy bade us good-night.

When he had gone Moran turned to Kane and me with heavy satisfaction. "Well," he announced, "I guess Lovejoy has started the ball rolling, all right, eh?"

"I believe he has," Kane said slowly. "But you know, Moran, it's dangerous to let a ball roll too fast." As he spoke he reached into his pocket and pulled out two or three old envelopes. "Never throw these things away," he admitted sheepishly. "My one economy." He took a pencil from another pocket, and his face was serious again. "Right at this moment we're all in a mood for theorizing. Before we go too far we'd better see how facts and theory go together. I propose to get the bare facts of Mrs. Quincy's death down in black and white. Then we can consider our theories." Without waiting for comments he bent over one of the envelopes.

When he had scribbled for a moment or two, he looked up and without a word, tossed the envelope to Moran. When Moran had finished reading it, it came to me, and I saw that Kane had written as follows:

8:30.	Mrs. Quincy and Quincy were in their sitting room.
10:00.	Quincy left to lock up the house.
10:00.	Mrs. Quincy telephoned and gave message to Underwood.
10:10.	Quincy returned to sitting room. Mrs. Quincy was in her bedroom, but he saw her and talked to her.
10:31.	Quincy heard her fall to the floor.

Below this list was another. It read:

1. The windows of Mrs. Quincy's bedroom were locked and barred.
2. Quincy's evidence would prove that murderer could not have entered Mrs. Quincy's bedroom by way of the sitting room from 10:10 to 10:31.
3. But door from her bedroom into hall was unlocked.
4. Quincy says he heard no disturbing sound from his wife's room until she fell.
5. There was a streak of blood on the floor three feet from Mrs. Quincy's body.
6. In the pocket of Mrs. Quincy's dressing gown were several small pieces of glass.

As I looked up from the paper I saw that Moran held another in his hand. He gave it to me.

"I want you to consider those particular facts," Kane explained, "in the light of the ones you've just read."

I looked at the envelope.

	Mrs. Prendergast, Mrs. Balbirnie, and Weed have said that they were in their respective rooms after dinner until they heard of Mrs. Quincy's death.
8:30.	Lovejoy, Wainwright, Spinelli, Vincent started to play bridge in the downstairs living room. It was possible for any one of them to have left the room unnoticed for a *short* time.
10:15.	Wainwright went upstairs.
10:17.	Wainright returned to table.
10:31.	Quincy discovered his wife's death.

When I had finished I handed the envelope back to Kane. He got up, and, walking over to the window, stared out into the silent street.

"Well," Moran said, thrusting his hands into his pockets, "now we've had the facts, how about those theories you were talking about?"

"I was just thinking about that," Kane replied slowly. "Considering, to be exact, a certain gentleman and a hand of bridge."

Moran nodded his understanding. Kane began to talk in a steady, almost monotonous voice.

"Suppose," he began, "we forget the decorations with which our murderer has provided us. Let's tuck the convenient Mr. Hyde, for instance, away in a bureau drawer. In fact,"—he passed his hand through his hair—"suppose we take this theoretical case and see how it sounds."

Kane left the window and came back into the center of the room, where Moran and I were sitting. He looked down with an enigmatic smile. "Now the theoretical case I've been thinking about," he went on, "goes like this. Two murders have been committed in a house. A man, Mr. A, has been killed—stabbed. A woman, Mrs. B, has been poisoned. We have reason to suspect a certain Mr. X. So far Mr. X hasn't provided us with an alibi for the first murder that is entirely conclusive. As far as the second murder is concerned, he has put himself in a very weak position. He spent the evening with three other men, but at a critical moment, 10:15 to be exact, he left them. He said he was going upstairs to put on his slippers. But he could have gone across the hall on his way, seen the woman whose evidence could hang him, and inflicted a slight injury on her, an injury so slight that she did not cry out. He could then return to his companions. Fifteen minutes later they are disturbed from their bridge game by the news that Mrs. B. is dead."

Moran looked up, his face heavily intent on what Kane was saying. "That's it," he said solemnly. "That's our case."

"That's our theory, you mean," Kane corrected him. "Now let's see how it works out."

CHAPTER 17

In the living room downstairs we found waiting for us the same group of people who had been in Mrs. Balbirnie's room. I could not keep myself from staring toward Wainwright who sat facing the door. His cold eyes swept with indifference from Kane to Moran. I suppose he also looked at me, but I dropped my eyes in time to avoid his glance. I was afraid he might be able to read my thoughts from the expression on my face.

As I sat down I saw that Weed had returned to the company. Evidently Sheba's society had not been entirely adequate to-night.

Mrs. Balbirnie hardly gave us time to settle ourselves before she turned persuasively to Kane. "Now Mr. Kane," she began, "you know you said you wouldn't keep us here any longer than necessary. Do you think it will be really necessary for me to be here after to-morrow?" She leaned forward, eager for his answer.

"That," Kane replied, "I can't say quite yet. Perhaps it won't be. On the other hand . . ." he left the rest of his sentence to be understood.

"But you don't mean, do you, that we can't go out at all?" Her voice had become anxious.

"Oh, no," Kane reassured her. "Understand, I'm by no means a jailer. After to-night, if anyone wants to go out for a short time, it's quite all right."

A cry of anguish interrupted him. Mrs. Balbirnie, distracted from her first preoccupation, was staring toward the door. "Don't let that thing in here!" she exclaimed hysterically. "I can't stay here, if you do! I can't bear it!"

Startled, Kane looked where she pointed. Weed's cat was crouched in the doorway, his bushy tail waving gently, his wide eyes staring at us with blank intensity.

No one seemed to know quite what to do. Kane, with a gesture of impatience, took a few steps toward the door. The cat, frightened by his approach, crouched lower, but did not retreat. He went still nearer, and the animal, out of its wits with excitement, jumped past him into the room.

As it did so, Mrs. Balbirnie screamed again and got up hastily from her chair. Weed, alarmed by the confusion, but apparently unconscious of its cause, repeated over and over again: "What is it? Someone tell me! What is it!" No one paid any attention to him.

Perhaps I felt an abrupt reaction from the strain I had been under. At any rate I was suddenly conscious of the absurdity of the situation. I could hardly keep myself from laughing out loud.

I glanced at Kane, but if the scene before our eyes was ridiculous to me, it was not so to him. He was not even smiling. Instead his face wore a look of strange interest. I heard him say sharply: "Mr. Wainwright! Call that cat! The rest of you, sit down!"

His tone was not to be disobeyed. Wainwright, startled at the command, flushed with irritation. He hesitated and then walked softly toward the animal, which was creeping away from him, its eyes on Mrs. Balbirnie. "Here, Sheba!" he called. "Come here!" But the animal gave no sign of hearing him.

Kane gave a short laugh. "That's that!" I heard him mutter to himself.

Meanwhile Weed had suddenly grasped the meaning of the commotion. He rose superbly from his chair, smiling with placid tolerance.

"If you had only told me that in the first place," he admonished them. "Sheba wouldn't let any of you catch her. Oh my, no! But she'll always come to me. Where is she?"

Vincent took his arm and gently propelled him in the direction of the cat, who eyed his approach impassively from her refuge on top of a tall bookcase. Weed held out his hand toward the animal, saying,

"Now, Sheba! Nice Sheba!" Uttering a purring cry, Sheba jumped for his shoulder, and was carried in triumph out of the room. As Weed left he turned to us, shaking his head in mild reproof.

"You frightened her very, very badly!"

Kane looked after him for a moment, checking a smile. Then he seemed to dismiss the incident from his mind. "As I was about to tell you all," he began abruptly, "when this—er—disturbance occurred, you may go to bed. With one exception—Mr. Wainwright. I must talk to you, sir," he concluded in answer to the other's frown.

One by one they drifted away. Only Mrs. Prendergast hesitated. With a sudden burst of decision she spoke to Kane.

"Are you going to want to talk to me at all?" she asked.

"Probably to-morrow, Mrs. Prendergast."

"Oh!" The exclamation was despairing. "Please, then, if you must talk to me, let it be to-night. I shan't be able to sleep, anyhow."

"Very well," Kane agreed. "I'll see you later." Half-satisfied, she left the room, and we were alone with Wainwright.

At the ladies' departure he had risen stiffly. Now he walked over and stood in front of Kane.

"I beg your pardon," he said with cool formality, "but I doubt if I can assist you at this moment."

Kane masked any annoyance he may have felt at the other's tone. "Perhaps you can't." He sighed. "We've just been talking over the case, Mr. Wainwright. Discussing Hyde and his ways and means, as a matter of fact."

"Indeed." Wainwright sat down and faced Kane calmly.

"As far as you are concerned," Kane went on, "there's very little I need to ask you. Really only one thing. Mr. Lovejoy tells me that you, Dr. Spinelli, Mr. Vincent, and he spent the evening playing bridge together. He heard nothing until Quincy cried out. He says you may have, however, since you left the rest of them about ten-fifteen. Is that right?"

"Quite." Wainwright made a curt acknowledgment of the fact. "I went upstairs to my room."

"Did you at that time see or hear anyone in the downstairs hall?"

"No."

"Well," Kane resigned himself, "that's all. I hoped you might have." He bent his head.

"You know," he continued, "this seems to me a peculiarly difficult and horrible business. I'm used to such things, of course, but it's rather terrible to think that both Prendergast and Mrs. Quincy were killed incold blood. We are as sure as we can be of anything that Hyde didn't commit the crimes on the impulse of the moment. He murdered them both because he had so decided beforehand. And Prendergast was young, and Mrs. Quincy was a woman."

Wainwright looked at him sardonically. "I'm afraid," he replied, "that I don't find myself moved by such notions. Mr. Hyde probably had reasons that seemed excellent to him."

"I must be getting sentimental, I guess," Kane admitted sheepishly. "By the way, how well do you know Mr. Lovejoy?"

"As one knows most people," Wainwright answered. "I see him occasionally. We play bridge together."

"Did it ever occur to you that he belonged to a type distinctly open to suggestion? I mean, that he might think he heard or saw something when he didn't?"

"Possibly."

"The reason I ask," Kane continued, "is that so much of our evidence comes from him. It's necessary to know how to value that evidence. Now let me take a small instance to illustrate what I mean." Kane looked thoughtfully at Wainwright. "Lovejoy and Mrs. Quincy found Prendergast. It happened this way. As you know, the rain had leaked through the roof into Lovejoy's room. He took Mrs. Quincy upstairs to show it to her, and they found a pool of water on the floor. Then it occurred to Lovejoy that it might have gone through into the room below his. That was Prendergast's. They went down, opened the door, and looked in. Prendergast was lying dead on the floor." Kane raised his eyebrow. "You saw the body, Mr. Wainwright, before it was removed. I believe you'll agree with me that it wasn't a pleasant sight."

Wainwright acknowledged the fact with an indifferent nod, and Kane went on. "I think I may say that such a sight would be, if anything, more unpleasant to Mr. Lovejoy than to you or me. Blood is particularly revolting to him. I imagine he made a swift retreat. Now," Kane leaned forward and tapped his finger on the palm of his other hand, "this is my point. While he was in that room Lovejoy couldn't have given much thought to anything except the fact that Prendergast had been murdered. Yet afterwards he was able to tell me without hesitation that the rain had come down through the ceiling into the murdered man's room." Kane paused and looked from Wainwright to Moran and me.

Wainwright frowned. "But," he objected, "there was a leak. I am not an imaginative man, and I heard it dripping."

Kane was a little put off. "I don't believe you get what I mean," he said. "Certainly there was a leak. I saw it myself. But the question is—would Lovejoy have noticed it, occupied as he was by that more ghastly sight?"

Wainwright looked at him with acid impatience. "I fail to understand, Mr. Kane," he said shortly, "how that question can be answered by anyone but Lovejoy himself."

Kane's good humor remained undisturbed. "You would be unwilling to say, then, that Mr. Lovejoy's evidence on small points could be trusted?"

"Not at all." Wainwright contradicted him. "As far as I know, he is an accurate observer."

"I see." Kane nodded his head once or twice; then turned swiftly on the other man. "There is one more interesting small point in Mr. Lovejoy's testimony. It concerns you, by the way. He says that at ten-fifteen you went upstairs to get your bedroom slippers. Furthermore, he says,"—Kane paused and looked down at the polished black oxfords on Wainwright's feet—"that when you rejoined them again you were wearing your slippers."

Wainwright's eyes had followed Kane's downward glance. Now he looked up and waited.

"Your opinion of Lovejoy's accuracy remains unchanged?" Kane queried, smiling.

The man's eyelids narrowed. "An interesting question," he replied. "But why not have Mr. Lovejoy psycho-analyzed?"

"Hardly necessary," Kane returned, "since what I want is your opinion."

"Well, then, let me repeat," Wainwright said distinctly. "Mr. Lovejoy is an accurate observer."

Kane chuckled. "Thank you," he said.

Across the hall the telephone rang. We heard McBeath answer it. Presently he appeared at the door.

"Dr. Sloan to talk to you." He stuck his head in and withdrew it like a jack in the box.

"Excuse me, will you?" Kane asked Wainwright.

"There is no more information I can give you?" Wainwright's tone was ironic. As Kane shook his head, he went on, "Then I'll go upstairs."

As he left, Kane went into Mrs. Quincy's room to answer the telephone. He returned in a few moments.

"Well," he said, in answer to Moran's look of inquiry, "that's conclusive, at any rate." In spite of his superficially nonchalant manner I knew he had just learned something of great importance.

"This is what Sloan says," Kane went on slowly. "Mrs. Quincy was killed by one of the most deadly of poisons—hydrocyanic acid. It was administered on the tip of a very small weapon stabbed into her arm. Her death was instantaneous, literally a matter of seconds."

"Well, that was just what you thought, wasn't it?"

Kane kicked at the rug with the toe of his shoe. "I don't believe you see what that means. It means," he continued, with precision, "that our theoretical case is smashed to pieces."

Moran stared at him uncomprehendingly. "But—but why?"

"For this reason. We knew that Mr. X.—we may as well call him Wainwright—had, at *ten-fifteen*,"— he emphasized the words—"a good chance to kill Mrs. Quincy. But if he had, she would have died at *ten-fifteen*. She did die a little after ten-thirty."

Moran nodded despondently. "I get it," he said. "Yes. That's right."

Kane began to speak again. "That was an obvious case, and after all you can't ignore the obvious. But it was too easy a way to catch the gentleman who called himself Hyde. He wouldn't make things so simple for us."

Moran slumped down in his chair. "Then we're up a blind alley. What are we going to do?"

"Quite a lot, Moran." Kane smiled at him. "A good many things have happened to-night. We haven't failed in everything. As far as I can judge, we have enough now to proceed directly against the murderer. If everything turns out as I think it will, that is. I'd almost take a chance and arrest him now, but not quite."

Moran was electrified. "You know who he is?" he cried out.

"I think we'll all know to-morrow," came the quiet reply.

CHAPTER 18

"To-morrow!" Moran echoed.

"For the present," Kane said, "we'll have to let to-morrow take care of itself. We still have to-night to consider. By the way, we haven't seen Mrs. Prendergast yet. I think I'll just send McBeath up to remind her."

He did so, and in a few moments McBeath returned with the delinquent lady. She entered the room apologetically. "I'm so sorry. I forgot. Arthur always said I couldn't remember more than one thing at a time. I started packing. I want to leave here just as soon as I can. Please excuse me." Her faded, childish face appealed to Kane.

He assured her that it did not matter. Somewhat relieved, she sat down and waited for his questions, but he was content to let Moran take charge of the interview with her. He seemed so occupied with his own thoughts that I doubt if he even heard her somewhat feeble answers to Moran's blunt questions. However, she had nothing to tell us. She had spent the evening in her sitting room. She had heard and seen nothing. Indeed, she was far more occupied with the state of her own nerves than with the new tragedy that had taken place.

"If I could only get away from this dreadful house!" she wailed. "I am never well, and now I feel like a very sick woman. I really don't think," she rambled on, "that anyone but Dr. Spinelli appreciates what I've been through. He's always so considerate. He was even considerate of Arthur, although Arthur was often rude to him. He had such unreasonable dislikes, poor boy."

With a complete want of logic she shifted to another subject. "Of course I know you can't help it, but just talking to you has upset me so. Well,"— she drooped with discouragement—"unless you have something else to ask me I will go back to my room."

She rose, but on the way to the door she continued her lamentations. "I must get away, I must get away," she murmured. "This depressing atmosphere is very bad for me. I need sunshine and fresh air. If I could just get out of doors even now. Just for a little while." She turned to Kane with artificial brightness. "Would it be possible," she appealed to him, "for me to go out? To take a little walk? I *might* get to sleep afterwards."

Kane seemed surprised at her request but offered no objections. "Why, of course, if you want to," he replied. "I'll tell the man at the door that I've given you permission to go."

She thanked him and bade us a grateful goodnight.

"Fine time to get some sunshine," Moran grumbled, but for some reason he looked after her with undisguised interest.

"Isn't it!" Kane murmured. "Well, it makes no difference to us."

He gave McBeath the necessary instructions and returned to the living room. As he came in I looked at my watch. It was a quarter-past twelve. I wondered if there was anything more for us to do to-night. I glanced at Kane and decided not to ask the question, for his expression was very thoughtful, and he had the air of waiting for something.

Moran was equally concerned with an idea of his own. His face wore a speculative look, and the results of his speculations seemed to startle him. After a moment or two he pulled his notebook out of his pocket and turned its pages rapidly until he found the place he wanted. He stared at his scribbled notes as if fascinated; then, on a blank piece of paper, he began to draw what appeared to be a plan.

A conspiracy of silence seemed to have taken possession not only of us but of the whole house. Most of its uneasy inhabitants must have gone to their beds.

As I looked out into the hall I could see McBeath nodding at his post. He was vigilant enough, however, to arouse himself at the sound of light footsteps on the stairs. Kane heard them too, and shifted a little.

But it was nothing more exciting than Mrs. Prendergast going for her walk. She spoke to McBeath timidly and he let her by. After a few seconds the front door closed behind her.

Moran was so engrossed in his thoughts that he did not hear it. He had apparently come to the end of his calculation, for he gave an eager glance at Kane.

"Look here," he said. "I've got an idea this time, and I'm going to show you I'm right. It isn't too late to find out, either. That place is open all night." He was already on his feet.

"What are you talking about, Moran?" Kane asked curiously.

"Never mind." The sergeant shook his head with decision. "I'm not going to tell you. I'm going to let you see for yourselves. Haven't I gone along with you lots of times when I didn't see any sense in it? It's my turn now."

"All right." Kane acknowledged the justice of his plea. "Come on, Underwood."

Moran led us out into the hall and bundled us into our coats. Then he was off, out the front door and down the street. We followed him to the corner, where he turned. In another thirty seconds he stopped and waited for us to catch up to him. When we had reached his side, he pointed to the lighted sign of a drug store.

"That's the place where Spinelli was last night when Prendergast was killed," he said. "Come on in with me through the side door."

He plunged ahead of us into the store. "Now just notice something," he said, as we entered behind him. "There's the telephone Spinelli used while he was waiting for his prescriptions." He pointed to a booth beside the door through which we had come in.

Without waiting to explain what he was getting at, he strode to the front of the shop, where a clerk was leaning wearily against a counter.

"That's the fellow I talked to," he whispered to us. The man evidently recognized Moran, for he looked at him curiously, and from him to Kane.

"Look here," Moran began, "you know what you told me this afternoon. Just say it over again. What time did Dr. Spinelli come in here yesterday?"

"I told you," the clerk expostulated. "It's the same now as it was the last time you asked me. Exactly eight forty-three."

"And what time did he leave?"

The man was annoyed. "Now listen," he said, "I told you that, too. He left here at five minutes to nine, because I had his stuff ready by then, and I saw him go out that door."

"The front door?"

"Yeah, the one he came in by."

"And during the twelve minutes he was waiting, he was in that booth back there, using the telephone?"

The clerk nodded.

"You couldn't see him, could you?"

"I can't see through a coupla counters and round a corner."

"Could you hear him?"

The man looked at him in disgust. "Say," he replied, "the reason we have that booth is that it's sound-proof."

"All right, then." Moran turned away satisfied. He looked at Kane, who nodded slowly.

In a good deal of bewilderment I followed the two of them back to the rear of the store. Standing in the doorway, Moran pointed in the direction from which we had come.

"Understand," he said, "when we go out this way we can't see that fellow and he can't see us."

Suddenly the point that Moran had been proving came to me. His next words confirmed my guess.

"Shoots his alibi to pieces, doesn't it? All he has to do is walk in there at eight forty-three, speak to the clerk, walk back as though he's going to telephone, and get out by the side door. He comes in again the same way. That's why he was so damned sure Prendergast died at ten minutes of nine. He'd fixed it so he was covered then, or thought he was. Isn't that so?" he appealed to Kane.

"Before we discuss it," the latter replied, "it's my turn to show you something." He glanced at his watch. "We have just time, I think, but we'll have to hurry."

He was off in the direction of Mrs. Quincy's, his long legs eating up the ground. It was hardly a minute before we reached the house.

McBeath let us in. "Is Mrs. Prendergast back yet?" Kane asked him.

"She come in just a second ago."

Kane turned abruptly and motioned us to follow him. There was a gentle smile on his face. He took us through the dining room and the pantry into the kitchen, which was pitch dark, except for the red glow of the coal stove.

"What—" Moran began, but Kane told him softly to be quiet.

"Well, then," Moran reduced himself to a whisper, "I'm going to turn on the lights. I can't see a thing."

Kane evidently caught his hand, for we remained in darkness. "You'll see something in a minute or two," I caught his faint reply. "Or I'm very much mistaken."

After that—silence. The kitchen clock ticked the seconds away. The fire hissed and shifted with a sudden clatter. Then there came another sound, slight, but not too slight. A creak. A key clicked in the lock and the bolt fell. I felt a draft of air. A door closed softly, the knob carefully released.

Kane's voice broke the silence. "Good-evening, Dr. Spinelli."

CHAPTER 19

The moment Kane spoke he flashed on the lights. In the sudden glare Spinelli shrank back against the wall, his hooded eyes darting from one to the other of us. His face was drawn and gray. For a minute no one spoke. Then, with an effort, Spinelli drew himself up, took a step toward us, and bowed slightly. "Good-evening," he said.

He reached into his pocket and pulled out his cigarette case. After offering it to each one of us in turn, he took a cigarette and lighted it. "I have been for a walk," he went on.

"So I see," Kane replied.

"Without your permission."

Kane refused the challenge.

"And now," Spinelli continued, "with your permission I will go up-stairs."

Without waiting for a reply he swung on his heel. Kane looked after him with something like admiration, but Moran was highly disturbed.

"Why didn't you stop him?" he exclaimed. "What's the sense of letting him get away with this?"

"I'm not letting him get away with anything," Kane replied, as he turned and went back to the living room.

Moran, following him, continued to protest. "Aren't you even going to find out what he went out for? God knows what he's been doing!"

"I think I share that bit of knowledge with the Almighty," Kane assured him.

Moran hardly listened to the answer. "We had him on the hip," he said despairingly. "We could have made him own up to everything, and you let him—"

Kane sat down and, lighting his pipe, proceeded to make himself comfortable. "Suppose we get this straight," he said, after a few puffs. "If I had stopped Spinelli you would have said to him, 'We know now that you murdered Prendergast and Mrs. Quincy,' or words to that effect. Wouldn't you?"

Moran nodded.

"And you would have advanced certain things to prove it," Kane continued. "But if he had asked you what you thought his motive was, what would you have said?"

Moran was nonplussed.

"Well,"—Kane pressed the tobacco into his pipe—"let me give you some help on that point. At the same time I can answer another question of yours, as to his reason for going out to-night. McBeath!" The weary officer lumbered to the door. "Go upstairs," Kane said to him, "and ask Mrs. Balbirnie to come down and talk to us. If she's already in bed, say you're sorry, but we have to see her."

"I've made a guess at something," he explained, as McBeath started up the stairs. "I want to see if I'm right. And I've a shrewd suspicion that Mrs. Balbirnie is the only person in the house who will tell me."

He had hardly stopped speaking when we heard McBeath on the way down again, with Mrs. Balbirnie in his wake. She was breathless with haste and surprise, but she began to talk at once.

"So lucky," she panted, "so lucky. I was just going to bed. I ought to have gone hours ago, but under the circumstances"—her face paled a little—"I suppose I'll have to expect to lose a little sleep."

"I'm afraid so," Kane replied. "I'm sorry to bother you again, but I have to ask you a few questions. Just sit down, won't you?" As she obeyed him, he turned away, as though he were a little uncertain how to begin.

"Mrs. Prendergast is a friend of yours, isn't she?" he said finally.

"Oh, yes, indeed. A very dear friend. Such a sweet woman. To have all this trouble!" Mrs. Balbirnie's answer was spasmodic.

"She confides in you, doesn't she?"

"Yes. And lately she says I've been such a comfort to her. You know I really think I have helped her. I do hope so." She sighed.

"How long," Kane asked casually, "has Dr. Spinelli been paying his court to her?"

Mrs. Balbirnie looked at him in pleased surprise. "Now, I didn't know you knew about that," she exclaimed. "She told me a week ago they were going to get married. Don't you let them think I told you." She shook a roguish finger at Kane. "I didn't, now, did I? I haven't said a word about it, but I could hardly keep it to myself. Are they going to tell everybody?"

"Not just yet, I think," Kane replied dryly.

"Well, I thought they weren't. Because only yesterday Clara told me again that it was a great secret, and that I mustn't say anything about it. The doctor thought it would be in bad taste so soon after Arthur's death."

"I can see his point," Kane agreed. "Well, that's all I wanted to ask, Mrs. Balbirnie. I needn't trouble you any longer." He whisked her, still talking, toward the door.

Before she left the room she insisted on asking a question that seemed to have a not unnatural importance for her. "Are we still not allowed to leave the house, Mr. Kane?"

"Go out as much as you want to," he replied. "I've given McBeath instructions to that effect. But no one can leave permanently, you understand." He avoided further argument by shutting the door behind her.

"That's one missing link," he said, as he returned to us. "Now here's another, which may interest you. I think I'm safe in saying that it also interests Spinelli."

But Moran was being hurried off his feet. "Wait a minute!" he cried out. "What do you mean—Mrs. Prendergast is going to marry Spinelli? How did you know?"

"I didn't know," Kane smiled at him. "I guessed, as I told you. And I guessed that she would have to tell somebody about it. Well, the person she would be most likely to tell was Mrs. Balbirnie." He paused. "But you don't seem very much concerned about the other thing I have to tell you."

"Yes, I am," Moran protested. "Go ahead."

The imp of the perverse seemed to have taken hold of Kane. "Not so fast as all that," he replied. "Let's just think back a little." He began to walk slowly up and down the room.

"When we first came here," he began again, "I felt quite sure, for no reason at all, mind you, that our friend the doctor knew something that he would prefer to keep from the rest of the world, for a while anyway. You see, by that time he had definite plans. There was one difficulty about them. He had to manage Mrs. Prendergast, and she was and is the weaker vessel." Kane was silent for a moment.

"Well," he resumed his story, "to go back to the place where we started. A week ago he offered the lady his heart and hand, and found that she was delighted to accept both, in spite of her son's opposition. It was natural enough to keep the secret for a few days. Then young Prendergast was killed. Now why, at that moment, didn't the doctor break his silence and take his rightful place as the poor lady's protector? It was at this point that I had to remind myself that Spinelli is a wise man, and one very unlikely to be swept off his feet by sentimental considerations. This morning I discovered his reason. It is a very good one.

"To put it briefly, I looked up Arthur Prendergast's will. He didn't leave one. But his father did. The elder Mr. Prendergast left his money in trust. A half of the income from the trust fund was to be paid to his wife, a half to his son. In the event of her remarriage, the entire amount went to Arthur. In other words, if she married again, she was disinherited. *But* in the event of Arthur's death, the estate came to her, without limitations."

Kane turned to face us. He was smiling but not with amusement. "You see," he commented softly, "why Spinelli thought the time of young Prendergast's death so unpropitious for the announcement of his engagement to the bereaved mother."

He broke off and turned his attention to lighting his pipe. When he looked up, he said abruptly: "We were talking about a possible motive, weren't we? And there was another question. Why did Spinelli go out to-night, and go so secretively? Do you remember who else found it necessary to get a little fresh air before retiring?"

Moran whistled between his teeth. "Mrs. Prendergast!"

"Precisely," Kane answered. "I'll bet you anything you like that the lady and the gentleman met, not exactly by chance."

"Takes us to find out things, doesn't it," Moran exclaimed in exultation. "You've got to give me the credit for the idea in the first place, even if you did get the facts that pin it on him."

"Pin what on him?" Kane inquired mildly.

Moran was too taken aback to reply.

"Two murders?" Kane continued. "Do the facts that we have collected prove that Spinelli is a murderer? I doubt it."

A deep flush crept over Moran's face. He tried to stammer a protest, but he could not find words in which to express himself.

"Look here," Kane began to speak very seriously. "You said just now that I had got the facts that proved your case against Spinelli. What are those facts? One, that Spinelli is going to marry Mrs. Prendergast. Two, that according to her husband's will she would be disinherited on her remarriage, unless her son were already dead. Three, that Spinelli has met her secretly, probably a number of times. Four, in order to do so he had a key to the back door made for himself. As far as I can see," Kane finished tranquilly, "those facts are self-explanatory, with one exception. The wording of the late Mr. Prendergast's will gives Spinelli a *possible* motive for murdering the son."

"Self-explanatory!" Moran echoed the adjective. "You've got to explain that to me."

"Very well." Kane settled himself in his chair. "This is the situation that existed before Prendergast's death. Dr. Spinelli wanted to marry Mrs. Prendergast. He probably knew about the will but thought it could be broken. He is not a sentimental type, and he was probably more moved by the material advantages she would bring with her than by the lady's charms. Her son opposed him. Both of the principals of the affair were living in a house which was also the abiding place of other people, people who were curious, who loved to gossip, who were always on the outlook for some bit of excitement to talk over. Spinelli was and is a sly fellow, with a natural taste for intrigue. Take those three things—Prendergast's opposition to Spinelli, the curiosity of the other people who live here, and Spinelli's love for shifts and strategies—and you have his reasons for obtaining a key to the back door, and for his secret meetings with Mrs. Prendergast, even *before* Prendergast's death.

"Imagine how much worse he found the situation afterwards! The will provided him with a motive, he realized, as soon as the news of his engagement to Mrs. Prendergast got out. He was in a fix. Now, more than ever, he wanted to avoid being seen with her, but she probably insisted on their meeting. And he couldn't throw her off altogether, for fear of what she might say. No," Kane concluded, "the facts we know about him show that he is cunning, dishonest, cowardly, not that he is a murderer."

Moran was adamant. "If you say so, all right," he answered, "*but* not one of the things you say gets around the fact that he gave us an alibi, and he hasn't got one." He brought his fist down hard on the arm of his chair.

"Are you sure he hasn't?"

The question made Moran flush angrily. "Didn't I take you to the drug store and show you?"

"You showed me that Spinelli could have been out of the store at the time when Prendergast was murdered," Kane replied calmly. "But I want you to remember that *Hyde* killed Prendergast. You've got to prove to me that Spinelli could have been Hyde." He turned on Moran. "Look here," he said, "suppose we consult that schedule of Hyde's actions on the night of Prendergast's death." He fished in his pocket. "Here it is. Read it off." He tossed the slip of paper into Moran's lap.

Moran read it slowly to himself.

"Now," Kane took up his argument when Moran had finished, "I want to call your attention to three items on that list: '8:30-8:45, Hyde talked to Weed; 8:53-8:55, Hyde talked to Weed; 8:55, Hyde, who was leaving, walked downstairs, accompanied part way by Weed.' According to Weed's evidence, Spinelli could not have been Hyde, for at 8:43 and at 8:55 Spinelli was seen in the drug store by the clerk on duty there."

"How about his saying exactly what time Prendergast was killed?"

"He made that statement," Kane replied patiently, "for a reason you've already given. He wanted to be sure that the police would settle on a time of death for which he had an alibi. Also, remember that, for his own purposes, he wanted Mrs. Prendergast covered. I'll hazard a guess that she had an appointment to meet him that evening, and that he knew she would have to be out of the house before ten minutes of nine in order to keep it."

Moran sat in abject silence for a few minutes. "All right," he said dully. "You've got me licked." He slumped down in his chair, the picture of discouragement.

Kane walked over to him and gave him a kindly slap on the shoulder. "Don't be downhearted, Moran," he said. "We've been up blind alleys before this, haven't we? But we always win out in the end."

Moran rose to the overture. "By God, you bet we do," he replied, swallowing hard. "Well, what's the next move?"

Kane made no answer. Instead he began to walk idly about the room. He pulled a match from his pocket and began chewing the end of it thoughtfully.

"I've been wondering," he said, "whether you like cats or not."

Moran scowled. "I can give you a straight answer to that, all right. I don't. Not one of 'em."

Kane took a last bite at the match stick and threw it into the grate. "I wasn't thinking of the ordinary cat, Moran. I was thinking of that animal of Weed's. It's a strange beast—has all the feline instincts, but they're so sharpened that to call it a mere cat isn't quite just."

Moran cleared his throat. "Guess Weed would agree with you there. My God! He treats it like it was sacred."

"It may be." But Kane was thinking of something beyond his words. "The cat seems to return his affection, at any rate. You haven't seen it trying to climb on anyone else's lap. That's a funny thing, too. People speak of one-man dogs, but I never heard a cat described that way. Now that creature of Weed's—"

Moran looked at his chief out of the corner of his eye. "Say, your memory's goin' back on you. Don't you remember hearin' how that creature fell for Hyde? That guy,"—his face brightened in appreciation of his joke—"musta had a way with cats that the rest of us can't get the hang of."

Kane laughed. "You're right. But in spite of that, I think it's a curious animal. You know, there's something peculiar about it. It may be my imagination, I suppose." He sighed. "But I'm sorry neither of you knows more than you do on the subject of cats. There's something—"

"Why don't you go to the Animal Rescue League and ask what it is?" Moran suggested with heavy sarcasm.

"That's not a bad idea at all," Kane answered serenely. "I might do that."

CHAPTER 20

We were all late in getting to the Quincy house the next morning. When I arrived there, about ten o'clock, I found that Kane and Moran had preceded me by only a few minutes. Kane was in the Quincy sitting room using the telephone as I came in the front door.

Apparently he had just got his call, for I heard him say, "Sloan? This is Kane. How thorough an autopsy did you hold last night? . . . Yes, Mrs. Quincy. . . I see. In other words, you merely answered the two specific questions I asked you. . . . Sloan, I must have a fuller report. Can you perform a second autopsy? And get in touch with me at the Quincy house sometime to-day? . . . All right." The telephone clicked faintly as Kane hung up the receiver.

He saw me standing in the hall. "Hello, Underwood," he said. "Come in here and bring Moran with you."

Moran, who had evidently been abandoned in the living room, joined us. I could not tell whether or not he had overheard Kane's telephone conversation or whether he shared my curiosity about it. However, Kane made no explanation of it, and Moran was busy thinking about a scheme of his own. He bit the end off a cigar and rotated it in his mouth.

"There's just one thing," he declared finally, "that I think we oughta do. We oughta go through this whole house—"

"A good idea," Kane interrupted, "but why don't you finish that cigar first?" He spoke quickly, as if there were other things on his mind, and I turned to see him abstractedly pacing the floor behind our chairs. "What I mean," he announced with sudden purpose, "is that I want to check up on something. You can stay here."

"We don't mind in the least," Moran retorted, as Kane's tall figure disappeared into the hall. "Anyhow, I don't. Just as soon sit right now as do anything else. I was pretty disappointed," he confided to me, "over that Spinelli business. Guess I'm just reacting to that, if you get what I mean." He looked up hopefully.

I nodded. "Kane doesn't act discouraged," I suggested.

"No, but you can't go by that. Now I'll tell you what I think we ought to do." He waved his cigar by way of emphasis. "We oughta search this house for the bottle, or the package, or whatever it was, that that poison came in. If we can find that—"

"It might lead us somewhere," I agreed.

Moran pressed his lips together with determination. "I'm goin' to put it up to Kane soon's he comes back."

But Kane did not come back immediately. By the time Moran's cigar was half gone I was growing restive. I got to my feet and walked around the room.

Then I heard a strange, scraping noise in the hall. It was repeated several times. I knew McBeath was out there, and wondered what he could be doing. Out of idle curiosity, and for lack of anything better to occupy my attention, I stepped over to the door. McBeath was sitting in his usual place, but he was staring with round-eyed absorption toward the door of the vestibule. I took another step forward in order to see what it was that so distracted him. Then I stood stock still with amazement at the sight before me.

Kane was down on all fours, a dust pan in one hand, a brush in the other. He was laboriously sweeping into the dust pan particles of dirt from the floor, and the expression on his face was at once so earnest and so pathetic that I was hard put to it not to laugh aloud. Presently he examined his sweepings, gave a deep sigh of relief, and struggled to his feet. It was then he saw me standing in the doorway.

He looked startled and a little sheepish as he stood there still clutching the dust pan.

"Well," he asked defiantly, "what of it?"

"For a man of your height," I objected, "it's not becoming. Furthermore, your tactics are rotten. You should sweep with the brush, not push with the pan."

Kane rubbed his nose with an embarrassed forefinger. "Perhaps that explains it," he admitted solemnly. "But you know this place is amazingly dusty. I wonder—" He paused. "Underwood, do you suppose you could round up one of those lazy domestics, the female one, if possible?"

"I'd do anything to prevent your becoming a household drudge," I replied, as I started down the hall toward the rear of the house. In the kitchen I unearthed Ellen, the maid, who followed me unwillingly to the front hall, where Kane was waiting. He looked more like himself now, having deposited the dust pan on a near-by table.

"I suppose," he began, addressing her, "that all this has been rather hard on you, hasn't it?"

"Oh, yes, sir," the maid agreed breathlessly, a little uncertain of his meaning.

"It's natural to let your ordinary duties slip," Kane went on, "at such a time. Now this hall, for instance,"—he looked around at the floor—"looks pretty dusty to me."

The woman eyed him uncomfortably. "I've meant to sweep it, sir," she said hurriedly. "I really have. But seems so I can't quite get to it, with all these awful things happening."

Kane's manner became suddenly insistent. "Ellen," he said, "I want you to tell me when you last swept this hall. It's important. Try to remember exactly."

The maid lowered her eyes and picked at the corner of her apron. "To tell you the truth, sir," she said at last, "it was the day that Mr. Prendergast—that he—" She hesitated.

"—died," Kane finished for her. "Yes,"—he drew a long breath—"yes, that would be it." He snapped his fingers. "Now, Ellen," he said, turning to her, "that's all. Don't worry about anything I've said, but try to get about in the ordinary way if only for . . ." He left his sentence unfinished, stuck his hands into his pockets, and walked away.

With a mumbled excuse the woman started back down the hall. I followed Kane into the room where Moran was still sitting, his cigar finished but his mood unchanged. He looked at us petulantly.

"Yes, Moran," Kane remarked without sitting down, "now we'll do what you want to do, if we can ease the members of the household out of their respective rooms. Looking for the remainder of that poison, or for the receptacle that held it, is undoubtedly a routine matter that shouldn't be neglected." He frowned. "It's my personal opinion that we'll draw a blank. However, let's to it."

"I'll wait for you here," I volunteered.

"Good idea. Come on, Moran."

The two of them left. I picked up a magazine and tried to interest myself in an article on child labor. When I had finished that, and two others, I heard them returning.

I got up and went out into the hall to meet them. Moran was standing at the foot of the stairs, leaning against the banister. He gave me a look of annoyance, turned his head, and began to chew his thumbnail silently. There was no need to ask my question. His attitude told me plainly enough that for him the search had been unsuccessful.

But Kane was smiling as he looked at me, and his smile was not that of one who tries to hide defeat. There was a briskness about him that I had come to recognize as the prelude to decisive action. He turned suddenly to the policeman sitting in the chair.

"McBeath," he remarked, "I've an idea that someone went out of the house this morning, before we came. Am I right?"

McBeath moved his head slowly to look at Kane. "Yeah, y'are." Alarm seized him. "But you said anybody could, didn't ya?"

"Quite." Kane paused, and then asked: "Who was it?"

"It was two. Mr. Lovejoy and a lady."

"Mrs. Prendergast?"

"No. That tall one."

"Mrs. Balbirnie?"

"Yeah."

"Did they go out together?"

"No, they didn't. First it was Mr. Lovejoy, and then—"

"All right, McBeath." Kane walked over to the vestibule door, jingling the keys in his pockets. He stood there with his back to us for a few minutes.

Moran slung his arm around the newel post. "What's up, Kane?" he asked curiously.

Without turning around, Kane made his reply. "Do you remember, Moran, what I told you last night?"

"Sure I do. You said by to-night we'd be able to lay our hands on the murderer. Well," the sergeant spoke acridly, "it's twelve noon, now."

"And," Kane lifted his head, "we've several more hours of daylight. So I see no occasion to doubt—anything." He turned and came back to us.

"You're pretty optimistic, seems to me," Moran volunteered.

Kane said nothing for a moment. Then he looked up. "Yes, I am," he replied.

"I s'pose you've got your reasons," the other hinted.

"Right again. But to tell you the truth, Moran, I'm not sure you'd think much of my reasons. However, want to hear them?"

"Sure."

"Well," Kane began slowly, "they concern a piece of evidence that we found in the room where Prendergast was killed." He paused and his face became grave. "I think you've been regarding that piece of evidence as a curiosity, as something that only confused the issue. As a matter of fact I wanted to disregard it myself. I couldn't explain it." He frowned. "I lay awake hours trying to figure out things without it. It couldn't be done. Again and again it came to my mind. It turned all logic upside down. 'A feather daunts the brave!' God! I'd reason to know it was daunting me, destroying every imaginable chain of circumstance I could conceive of." He drew a long breath. "Now, you see, I know what that feather signifies. And it straightens out a lot of things."

He stopped speaking and looked in the direction of the rear hallway. There was a sound of slow, approaching footsteps.

We waited in silence. Presently Quincy appeared. As he caught sight of us his expression of weariness changed almost imperceptibly to one of slight alarm. Without a word he continued toward the door of his sitting room.

But Kane stopped his progress. "Mr. Quincy!"

The man turned mechanically, as if he had expected to be called, and came over to us. "Yes, Mr. Kane?"

Kane spoke hurriedly. "It's very lucky you appeared just at this moment. As a matter of fact there's something you ought to be able to tell me better than anyone else in the house."

Quincy's eyes wavered uncertainly.

"I wonder," Kane went on, "whether you can tell me the names of the jewelers that your guests usually go to."

"Jewelers?" Quincy worried over the word, and finally said, "Well, I've heard someone speak of a place called Kingston's up toward the State House. And there's another on Temple Place, and, I think, one on Tremont across from the Common. I suppose there are some others, but I can't remember hearing—"

"That's enough," Kane said. Quincy hesitated a moment and then went into his room.

Moran moved impatiently away from the banister. "Will you kindly tell me why—" he began, when Kane interrupted him.

"You still recall what I told you last night?"

"Yes, I do," Moran replied with irritation.

"Well," Kane shrugged his shoulders, "only a jeweler can prove that I'm not a false prophet."

CHAPTER 21

Moran insisted on having some lunch before we started off on what he called our "wild goose chase." Kane laughed at the epithet, but consented to the lunch, so that it was almost an hour after leaving the house on Beacon Street that we set forth on our mysterious errand. We went directly to the jeweler that Quincy had first mentioned. There Kane asked for the man in charge of the repair department, and left us in front of a case full of earrings while he went to the rear of the store.

When he returned he snatched Moran from his admiring consideration of an elk-tooth watch fob and hurried us both out into the street again. He said nothing to us as we walked across the Common, but I suspected from his impatient haste that his first call had not been successful.

On the corner of West and Tremont he halted so suddenly that Moran and I went several steps beyond him. He stood there a moment, frowning. Then he came to an abrupt decision.

"Look here," he said quickly, "there's something else I must do. It's not our original errand, and it will take us down to Carver Street. You can come with me or wait here, as you like."

The idea of standing indefinitely on the curb appealed to neither of us, and we made this clear to Kane. Without a word he started down Tremont Street, and we kept as close at his heels as we could. After a few minutes' walk he stopped before a low doorway. As I looked at the sign above it I heard Moran snort with mingled surprise and indignation. My reaction to what I saw was sheer astonishment. Again I had failed to realize when Kane was not joking. The sign read "Animal Rescue League."

Kane made a curt gesture with his head. "Stay here," he said, and, opening the door, went in.

Five minutes later he emerged. Moran grinned. "Well," he asked impudently, "what can our sleuth have discovered here?"

Kane pulled his hat down hard on his head. "What he suspected, no more, no less," he retorted. "Let's move on, and faster, to the next stop." When he had set his long legs in motion, Moran and I became again the unwilling tail to the kite.

The next stop was another, and a somewhat larger, jewelry store. Moran and I were abandoned in front of the show cases, while Kane talked apart to one of the clerks. On his return to us this time he was unhurried. He bent over one of the cases.

"See that silver flask, Moran—the large one?" he asked, tapping his fingernail on the glass. "When you're a federal officer I'll make you a present of it. Don't forget to remind me."

Moran had become sour. He disregarded Kane's flippancy. "See here, what's all this about?" he asked crustily. "I don't mind runnin' up one street and down another, if there's any point to it. But—"

"There's no point to it any longer," Kane interrupted him. "That there was a point to it up to this moment, I can prove to you. Look here!" He pulled a small package wrapped in white paper out of his coat pocket and held it carefully in his hand.

Moran reached for it. "What is it?"

"Careful!" Kane warned him. "It's broken. I'll show you what it is almost immediately, but not," he looked around, "right here. Also, I'll tell you in detail why it means so much to me to have found it. It happens to represent one of the few slips ever made by that person who called himself Hyde." He put the package into his pocket. "Let's get out of here," he suggested, his hand on my arm.

"Where are we going?" Moran asked as soon as we were out on the sidewalk.

"Straight to the ultimate goal," Kane replied quietly. He stepped off the curb into the street and we crossed into the Common. I realized he was taking the shortest path to the Quincy house.

When we arrived there McBeath answered our ring. We entered the vestibule and Kane shut the door behind us. Then he turned to the policeman.

"McBeath, is anyone out at present?"

"No."

"Then listen to me," Kane spoke rapidly. "You are to let no one, no matter who it is, leave the house. You understand that, don't you? No one."

McBeath nodded silently.

"All right." Kane swung around on his heel. We followed him into the room we had occupied a few hours before.

After closing the door he tossed his hat into the corner. "Pull your chairs up here," he directed, choosing his seat by the table in the center of the room. "I want to lay some things out where you can see them."

We did as he suggested without delay. When we were seated he drew out of his pocket three packages, the one he had picked up at the jewelry store, and two others which were smaller and wrapped in brown paper.

He laid all three on the table before us and proceeded to unwrap the larger of the brown paper packages. When it was open we saw that it held four or bye shattered fragments of thin glass. Kane pushed it over toward me.

"Now." He reached for the second brown package and undid its wrappings. Pointing to the contents, he said, "There are some more smaller bits of the same glass. This morning I brushed them up from the floor of the hall."

Moran gave the package a cursory glance and looked back at Kane.

"You remember," the latter went on, "that I first thought the glass I found in Mrs. Quincy's pocket was from a pair of broken eyeglasses. The pieces are slightly curved, you see. But when I looked at them again, I realized that they were parts of a watch crystal. In this box,"— Kane tapped with his finger the third package, the one he had brought from the jeweler's—"is a watch with a smashed crystal. The pieces of glass I've shown you were broken from that crystal."

Moran frowned in bewilderment. "But what connection—" he began.

"The closest possible connection," Kane answered him. "Mrs. Quincy was killed because she knew too much about the murderer. The pieces of glass and the watch show us beyond a shadow of doubt exactly what she knew.

"I'll put it in as few words as possible," he continued. "Mrs. Quincy knew that the man whom, as Hyde, she had admitted to her house on the night of Prendergast's death had broken the crystal of his watch as he came in her front door. She had found, on the table in the downstairs hall, perhaps, or in one of the other common rooms, a watch with a broken crystal. She knew it belonged to one of the people in the house, to the one who had murdered Prendergast, but her knowledge stopped there. She intended to pass on the information to us in the hope that we could trace the watch to its owner, but before she could tell us, the owner discovered her intention and killed her."

For a moment we looked at Kane in utter silence, trying to understand what he had said. It was impossible.

"How do you know all that?" Moran objected impatiently. "How do you even know Hyde had a broken watch? And if he did, why do you think Mrs. Quincy knew it?"

"Now wait a minute, Moran," Kane directed. "You'll agree with me, won't you, that Mrs. Quincy had come upon certain information which she intended to give me this morning?"

"Yeah."

"And you'll also agree that it's rather strange for anyone to carry around shattered fragments of glass in her pocket. It's too uncomfortable. Therefore, you see my point in thinking that those pieces of glass had some bearing on the information which she was about to give us."

"Sure."

"All right." Kane seemed to be making an effort to speak with distinctness. "We've already said that those pieces of glass were from a watch crystal." He looked from the one to the other of us. "I picked up some of the pieces from the floor of the hall, near the vestibule door. Obviously, then, Mrs. Quincy found the larger pieces in the same place. If she had thought nothing of them, she would have thrown them away. But she didn't throw them away, because she suddenly connected them with Hyde.

"You remember that Mrs. Quincy, the last time we saw her alive, told us about letting Hyde into the house when he called to see Weed. As he passed her, he stumbled and caught his balance against the door of the vestibule. Do you recall her comment on that particular incident?" Kane paused, but as neither of us answered his question, he went on, "It was this. 'I thought he had cracked the glass in the door.' Well, as she found out immediately, he hadn't done that. So, when we saw her last, she was ready to dismiss the incident from her mind. But after we had left she chanced to make two discoveries. She found the glass on the floor and she saw a watch with a broken crystal, into which the pieces of glass she had picked up fitted perfectly. Then she realized that that watch had been broken the night of Prendergast's death, and furthermore that it belonged to the murderer."

"Kane," Moran interrupted, "why do you think she saw that watch?"

"Because I'm sure that nothing but the sight of the watch would have enabled her to fit two and two together. The pieces of glass alone would have meant little or nothing to her."

"Yeah," Moran admitted grudgingly, "but here's another point. You say that when she saw the watch it was downstairs in the hall, or some place like that. How do you figure that out?"

Kane sighed a little wearily. "That's simple," he said. "If Mrs. Quincy had seen it on anyone's person, or in anyone's room, she would have known who killed Prendergast, wouldn't she?"

Moran nodded.

"Well, she didn't know that," Kane concluded emphatically. "You've got to give her credit for a fair amount of nerves, after all. It's hardly likely that she would have talked over the telephone to Underwood, a half-hour before her death, as she did, if she had known who the murderer was. Don't you remember, she said she had something to tell me if I would come around *the next morning?* She didn't want to see me right away. She was going to bed. Perhaps she was tired. No, I don't think Mrs. Quincy would have been too tired,"—Kane's lips curled— "to see me that night if she had known the identity of the murderer. She didn't know, and that proves my point—the watch *must* have been in the hall, or in some common room, when she saw it. She thought it possible that it might turn out to be a clue against the murderer."

"By the way," Kane resumed after a pause, "it's my idea that the watch was about to be taken to the jeweler's at the moment Mrs. Quincy saw it. I'm sure the murderer thought nothing of it at that time. It was simply a broken watch, that's all, and it had to be fixed. So it came to be left out carelessly where anyone could see it.

"If it hadn't been left there," he went on, "Mrs. Quincy might be alive to-day. Without a doubt the murderer saw her looking at it, or heard conversation which showed him that she was about to pass on some vital information to us. And in our hands, he knew that information would lead straight to his discovery. So he took measures to silence her."

Moran was still unsatisfied. "And yet he went right ahead and took the watch to the jeweler's, just as he'd planned to in the beginning! Why didn't he get rid of it?"

"There was no need to get rid of it, if by that you mean destroying it. By having it fixed he could wipe out its value as evidence. If we had found it tomorrow the crystal would have been unbroken. As I see it, it was much more a matter of getting rid of Mrs. Quincy than of the watch. After her death he considered that the watch was in no way dangerous to him. You see, he didn't know that the clue hadn't died with her, that we would find the pieces of crystal in the pocket of her dressing gown.

"I guessed that Hyde might have felt that way about the watch," Kane concluded, "so I took a chance. And I hit it right." He laid his cigarette down in the ash tray. "The watch is worth looking at," he remarked, as he lifted the cover from the box and took out a fairly small gold wrist watch from which the strap had been removed.

In spite of the fact that the crystal was so badly smashed that only a few fragments of glass remained, I could see that it was a remarkably fine little watch of Swiss make. Kane turned it over. The back was heavily engraved, and near the stem was a small button.

After we had looked at it for a moment, Kane laid it face up on the table. "The hands got jammed, you see," he said, "the minute the crystal was broken. Eight thirty-two, to be exact."

He pulled the remaining pieces of crystal carefully away so that they no longer held the hands. "I wonder whether it'll still run," he murmured, and pressed the little button. Instantly a tiny gong within the watch sounded eight times, then there were two double rings, and finally two short rings. Moran stared amazedly. "I've heard of those," he said, "but I never did see one before."

Kane put the watch back into the box. "It's a neat little thing, isn't it?"

But there was one thing still unanswered, one vital piece of information needed to make the story complete. Moran was unable to wait any longer.

"Who's it belong to?"

Kane leaned over to extinguish the last sparks of his cigarette. "The jeweler told me," he said slowly, "that a young man had brought it in. The name was Lovejoy."

CHAPTER 22

"Lovejoy!" Moran echoed the name incredulously.

"Lovejoy," Kane repeated. "And that being so," he went on, "I propose to have a talk with him."

As we went out into the hall he turned to McBeath. "Do you know where Mr. Lovejoy is?"

"Sure I do." McBeath spoke with heavy satisfaction. "Five minutes ago I locked this door so no one could get out, see, an' I went all over the house. They're all in their rooms, every last one of 'em. I knew you'd be asking me something like that." He looked away, overcome with pride at his efficiency.

On the way upstairs Kane paused to give Moran a final injunction. "I want one thing understood," he said sternly. "No one is to interrupt my conversation with Mr. Lovejoy. Whatever you think, whatever you want to say, keep quiet. I'll do the talking."

Moran nodded a willing agreement. "This is your show," he said. "I won't bust in on it."

As we reached the third floor I saw that Lovejoy's door was open. I could not be sure, but I thought I saw Lovejoy standing near it, almost as though he had been listening as we came upstairs. He spoke to us easily enough, however.

"Sit down, won't you?" He pulled up chairs for us.

"Thanks." Kane glanced around the room as he sat down. Then he turned to me. "Sit over there, Underwood," he directed, pointing to a chair near the open door into the adjoining room. I went over to it, realizing as I did so that Kane had wanted Lovejoy, not me, in the chair I had been about to sink into. That chair faced the light.

373

However, when Lovejoy was once seated Kane seemed to become absent-minded. His whole manner puzzled me. He had reached the climax of his case, and yet he was content to chat idly with Lovejoy about the bridge game of the night before.

After a few moments he changed the subject. "You had dinner here last night, didn't you?" he asked.

"Why yes," Lovejoy replied. "Of course I did. I wish I hadn't, though. I simply couldn't eat a thing. The only reason I came down at all was for the sake of the others. We've all got to keep up, you know." He forced a brave smile.

"And after dinner?" Kane spoke carelessly.

"Oh, we stood around and talked a little. Before we played bridge, that was." Lovejoy was sitting with his knees crossed. As he spoke his right foot swung up and down.

"At that time," Kane paused to think, "you had in your possession a watch?"

Lovejoy's foot stopped moving. "I always carry one," he answered.

"The watch I'm speaking of was broken." Kane glanced out of the window. "Did you have a broken watch in your pocket at that time?"

"No." The reply was emphatic.

Kane smiled. "I'm glad to find that out," he said. "You know, I suspected that you didn't have it in your pocket then. In fact, you'd forgotten it, hadn't you, Mr. Lovejoy? You'd left it, box and all, shall we say, in the hall?"

Lovejoy did not answer and Kane went on. "I just thought you might have put it down on that convenient table in the hall. Surely you don't mind my thinking that?" His voice was soft.

Lovejoy gave a forced laugh. "Why should I? Of course, I *had* left it there. Just slipped my mind, as such things do," he concluded.

Kane nodded soberly. "You remembered it afterward, I suppose, and took it upstairs. But in the meantime Mrs. Quincy saw it—you know that, don't you?"

The mention of Mrs. Quincy's name alarmed Lovejoy. He hesitated and moistened his lips. "Well, yes, she did. I saw her looking at it, now I think of it," he hurried to say. "It reminded me that I'd left it there—that's the reason I remember seeing her standing by the table."

"Is that the last time you saw her, Mr. Lovejoy?"

"Yes, it was—no—I just can't remember. I'm so sick of it all." He put his hands wearily over his eyes.

"Curious thing, isn't it," Kane commented softly, "that Mrs. Quincy was killed because she looked at that watch?"

Lovejoy's hands fell from his face and fastened themselves slowly upon the arms of his chair. Before he could speak there was a sound from the hall.

"I just came up to talk to you, my dear boy." Weed, calm and benign, stood in the doorway. "Now am I interrupting you? Didn't I just hear Mr. Kane saying something? Don't let me bother you. I'll go right away again if you want to have a chat among yourselves." There was something almost inhuman in his detachment.

"Not at all, Mr. Weed! Not at all!" It was Kane who answered him. "Come in. I was talking to Mr. Lovejoy about a watch, that's all. Sit down and I'll show it to you."

As Weed made his slow entrance he continued to protest. "You're sure," he droned, "you're perfectly sure you want me? I wouldn't interfere for the world. Now just tell me, and I'll go right downstairs." But with very little urging he sat down, his hands, one above the other, pressing on the knob of his cane. If he had not been dressed in modern clothes he could have posed for some heathen idol, with his expressionless eyes and his bland, all-embracing smile.

"You were going to show me something?" He turned in the direction of Kane's voice. "You'll have to tell me about it instead, you know." His tone seemed to apologize for his infirmity.

"Just a watch, Mr. Weed," Kane answered cheerfully. He took it out of his pocket. "A very nice one, too. Nothing the matter with it except the crystal's broken. Listen!"

He pressed the little button and the watch again rang the hour.

At the unexpected sounds Weed lost his placidity. He looked up quickly, his face very pale.

"Anything the matter, Mr. Weed?"

"Oh, no! No!" Weed hastened to cover his momentary agitation, but his hands still posed on the knob of his cane shook a little.

"You seemed disturbed."

Kane's remark forced Weed to take a still lighter tone. "I'm sure I don't know why. We old fellows. . . ." He smiled.

But Kane ignored his explanation. "I thought you might know something about this watch," he went on. "It's a nice little one—gold, of Swiss make, too, Pathek Philippe, I think. The back is beautifully engraved. You know, I wondered if it wasn't yours."

Weed drew a deep breath of astonishment. "Why," he exclaimed, "I can't believe my ears! I really can't." He gave an amused chuckle. "I thought I recognized that ring. Of course, of course! It *is* mine! I should say so! And to think I didn't know the sound of my old watch!"

His expression changed from one of surprised amusement to one of sorrow. "Dear me!" he sighed. "What remorse that brings to me! And I used to be so fond of it, too. I was so fond of it that I gave it away to the man I thought was my dearest friend." He paused to give full force to his climax. "The man I gave it to was Alvin Hyde!"

Lovejoy stared at him as if fascinated. Then his eyes flickered toward Kane and back to Weed.

"Is that so?" Kane murmured.

Weed turned to him eagerly. "Now I wonder, Mr. Kane—" he began. "Of course, that watch means nothing to you, and I certainly don't want it left in Alvin's possession. Couldn't you just turn it over to me, now, as long as you know it really is mine?"

There was a touch of irony in Kane's reply. "Not just yet, I'm afraid. You see, it does just happen to mean something to me at this moment. Later on, I suppose, it will be treated as a part of Hyde's effects. I'm not quite sure how it will be disposed of legally. Perhaps in a couple of months or so you can get it, if by that time you care to put in a claim for it."

"I see. Well, later on, perhaps," Weed said resignedly.

No one spoke for a minute or two, and in the silence I heard McBeath's heavy tread on the stairs. "Telephone call for you!" he said to Kane.

Kane was irritated. "I don't want to be disturbed. Who is it?"

"Dr. Sloan," came the slow, indifferent reply.

"Sloan!" Kane repeated. "Yes. I must talk to him." He got up and motioned to Moran and me to precede him out of the room. Moran started to go. I hesitated because I saw that Kane was still standing by the table, fingering absent-mindedly a small ruler which lay there. He glanced in an undecided fashion from Lovejoy to Weed. I thought he was about to say something more.

However, I was mistaken. After a second he turned toward the door, still holding the ruler. He passed in front of Weed. At that moment he raised the ruler and, without touching him, brought it down within an inch of his face.

I was startled. And so was Weed. Instinctively, he raised his hand to protect himself.

"I beg your pardon." Kane laughed apologetically and went out the door.

Had he taken leave of his senses? For one short second I failed to understand what I had seen him do. Then, like a flash it came to me what else I had seen.

CHAPTER 23

Mechanically I followed Kane and Moran into the hall. Outside the door I looked back into the room. Lovejoy had left his chair and was raising the window.

"It's hot in here," I heard him say in a queer voice. Weed's head nodded slowly above his cane. "Is it?" he asked softly. I turned away.

Moran was saying something in a swift undertone to Kane. The latter shook his head. "No," he said hurriedly, "there's no need for you to stay here. He can't—"

Moran interrupted insistently. Again Kane shook his head. "There's no risk," I heard him say. "This is the third story of the house, remember." He took Moran by the arm. "I want you to come with me."

We followed him down the two flights of stairs, our heels making sharp, staccato noises on the steps. In the lower hall Kane paused long enough to say to McBeath, "Go up to the second floor. Don't let anyone get past you and come down here." Staring with surprise, McBeath got up from his chair. "Hurry!" Kane added. Then we followed him into the Quincy sitting room.

The telephone receiver was lying on the table. He picked it up quickly. "Kane speaking," he said. There was a pause. Moran and I leaned toward the telephone, hopeful of hearing what Sloan had to say. But we could not. Kane was listening intently. "Yes," he said, once or twice, rapidly. A few seconds later he asked, "It was enough to produce unconsciousness?" The reply was short. Then Kane said, "Yes, I thought it was possible. Thanks, Sloan. This closes this case." He hung up the receiver.

Like a bloodhound once more unleashed, Moran swung on his heel and started for the hall. Kane called to him angrily.

"Wait a minute! If you're going up to put the irons on him, you'd better know what you're accusing him of, hadn't you?"

Moran half-turned. "I know that well enough, don't worry. Once I've called him Hyde, I guess he'll confess!"

"Suppose he doesn't confess? How'll you prove he murdered Mrs. Quincy?"

Moran hesitated. Then his face clouded. He walked slowly back to Kane. "I'd forgotten," he admitted dully. "I don't know. He's got an alibi." He looked up eagerly. "But you know, don't you? You can prove he did, can't you?"

Kane frowned. "Yes, I can. I was about to suggest that we should all be able to prove it. Now listen to me carefully." His manner changed and he began to speak in a low, rapid voice.

"On the night of Mrs. Quincy's murder, Quincy testified that he heard her fall to the floor of her bedroom almost exactly at ten-thirty. At that time Spinelli, Wainwright, Lovejoy, and Vincent were seated at a bridge table in the room across the hall, while Mrs. Balbirnie, Mrs. Prendergast, and Weed were upstairs in their own rooms.

"There are two doors to Mrs. Quincy's bedroom. One," Kane point-ed to it, "connects with this room. That was open on the night of her death. Quincy was in this room, reading. Now the other door leads into the hall. It was not locked, according to Quincy. So you may say that it was possible—that is, physically possible—for the murderer to have entered her bedroom by the hall door.

"From the first, it struck me that that was a ridiculous idea. Quincy said that he heard no commotion in his wife's bedroom up to the time she fell to the floor, and after that he neither heard nor saw anyone escaping. It was absurd, on the face of it. If anyone had come into her room Quincy couldn't have failed to hear him, the door between the rooms being open as it was. Since he heard nothing except his wife's fall, the facts of the case are that no one *did* enter Mrs. Quincy's room."

"But, Kane!" Moran's bewildered thoughts failed to shape them-selves at once. Finally he said. "She was killed by poison in that scratch on her arm. And Sloan said her death would have been instantaneous." He looked up questioningly.

"Her death *was* instantaneous." Kane's tone was emphatic.

"But if no one came into her room right before she fell, how could—"

"I'll tell you," Kane interrupted. "Briefly, it was this way. Quincy found her lying on the floor and aroused the whole household. They all trouped in—every one of them—pale with fright, horror-struck by what they saw before them. You know, it doesn't take much imagination to picture their state of mind. As a group they're not very well acquainted with crime. Think, then, what Prendergast's death must have meant to them, the fact that his murderer was still at large, might reappear at any moment. They were a terrified, trembling lot as they looked down at the body—ready to accept anything. That is, all but Hyde. Of course he was one of the group. He wasn't so excited as the rest. You see,"—Kane drew a deep breath—"he knew that Mrs. Quincy wasn't dead."

Moran turned on him swiftly, a look of astonishment on his face. Kane hurried on.

"There was another reason," he said, "why Hyde wasn't excited. This was the climax of his plan, the moment of all others when he could least afford to lose his coolness. And,"—Kane shrugged his shoulders—"as we have reason to know, he did not lose it. Quite calmly, without the quivering of a single nerve, and in the presence of seven witnesses, not one of whom saw what he was doing, he finished his work. It was simple. He was standing very near the body, as were some of the others. He merely stuck a needle into her arm as she lay on the floor. That needle was hollow and contained enough hydrocyanic acid to kill her instantly. There was no sound, of course, and no movement to call the attention of the others to the fact that murder was being committed before their very eyes. Also, very little blood flows from a wound of that size. So you see there was almost nothing to indicate that Mrs. Quincy had been changed from a living to a dead woman during the time that the members of the household had been in her room."

Moran's eyes had narrowed incredulously. "Are you trying to tell us that when they all thought she was dead, she had only fainted?"

"Hardly. I imagine that it looked more like death than the most convincing fainting spell. Do you remember, Moran, that Mrs. Quincy once said to us, in reference to her uneasiness over Prendergast's murder: 'I lie awake all night, *even though I take something to put me to sleep*'? In other words, she was accustomed to taking a sleeping medicine every night. Hyde knew that. At any rate, Sloan, who performed a second autopsy at my request, has just told me that he found in Mrs. Quincy's body enough of a drug called chloral hydrate to have caused absolute unconsciousness or a trance-like state similar to death.

"There is nothing else to add," Kane went on, "except that Mrs. Quincy's ordinary sleeping medicine was a dilute solution of chloral hydrate. Hyde substituted for that a concentrated solution, so that her usual dose was powerful enough to produce a state closely resembling catalepsy."

"But why?"

"So that her death would seem to have taken place earlier than it did. So that he could protect himself."

"When could he have got at her medicine?"

"Any time before half-past eight, when he had a chance to get into Mrs. Quiney's room undetected."

"Huh!" Moran laid his hand flat on the table with a certain deliberate ease. "He sure planned things out. God, it gets me to think I never really suspected him till you told me about the watch. Now his alibi don't go for a damn! Even with three men to support it!"

I looked at Moran in perplexity. What did he mean by "three men"? Was it possible he thought . . .

But Kane put an end to my speculations. "No one's alibi counts," he said shortly. "However, at this moment that's neither here nor there." He moved abruptly and looked at us with keen eyes. "We've no time to lose. This is the end of the game. The trial of wits is finished. Now—" He did not end his sentence. "Moran, have you your revolver?"

Moran nodded and slapped his pocket.

"All right. We may not need it. However, we've practically told him that we know. He's had about five minutes to prepare himself." He drew a long breath. "Let's go." He swung toward the door.

Moran caught his sleeve. "We'd better send McBeath outside the house, in case—"

"Why?"

"Didn't you see him opening the window of his room?"

"Don't be a fool." Kane pulled himself away roughly and strode out the door. Moran went after him without another word. I hesitated, then followed them. We started up the stairs.

Mechanically, I put one foot above the other. My mind was in a daze. It was a matter of seconds. Did Kane know what he was doing? What Moran had said—"opening the window of his room" . . . But that meant Lovejoy! It *couldn't* be!

The second landing. McBeath, standing there, was told to follow us.

It couldn't be Lovejoy. He wasn't the type. Moran was a fool to think that. Suddenly, in a flash of understanding, I realized that it wasn't so much that Moran was a fool. It was just that he hadn't seen what I had seen as we left Lovejoy's room. Kane knew!

We had reached the third floor. There was no light in the hall, and no noise, except our footsteps, from anywhere Kane led the way swiftly to Lovejoy's door. We went in.

For a moment, because the light was dim, I thought the room was empty. Then I made out the figure of Lovejoy standing by the window, looking toward us. I saw Moran reach into his pocket.

But where was Weed? The chair in which he had been sitting was empty. He was nowhere in the room.

Suddenly Kane's voice rang out harshly, imperatively. "Who closed that door?" He was pointing toward the door leading into the adjoining room. Without waiting for an answer he walked over and wrenched at the handle.

"It's locked!" I heard him mutter. He turned and ran past us into the hall. "Come along!" His tone was not to be disobeyed. Even Moran came immediately.

Kane threw open the door of the next room, Wainwright's room, I remembered. The door swung back and hit the wall. Within, it was almost dark. As I strained my eyes to see, something like a fleeting shadow moved and slipped from the bed to the floor. But it was not that which struck me cold with terror. There was something lying on the bed!

Kane felt with his hand along the wall. "I'm going to turn on the lights," he said. There was a click, and an overhead lamp shone down on the bed. A man was sprawled across it. It was Wainwright.

"He's dead!" Kane walked across the room, bent over, and looked at one of the man's wrists. He turned it over and pointed. I saw a scratch and a small spot of blood. I remembered the incision on Mrs. Quincy's shoulder. "The poisoned needle," Kane said briefly, and let the wrist drop.

Moran's eyes were starting from his head. "Then he's been murdered too!"

"My God!" I said hoarsely. "Weed! Where is he?"

Moran leaned forward. "Wait, Kane," he cried., "There's something in his hand!" Seizing it by the wrist, he pushed back the clenched fingers and pulled out a folded scrap of paper. He unfolded it hurriedly. I could see some rough letters printed on it. Moran drew in his breath.

"Kane!" His voice was harsh. "It's Hyde's writing! Only this time it says 'Exhibit Z.'"

Kane was staring at the floor. "The last show," he said.

Moran swung around to look at him. "What are you standing there like that for?" he cried despairingly. "We've waited too long already. Now Wainwright's dead. We've got to get his murderer!"

Kane did not move. "Look in his other hand," he said. "That will tell you all you need to know."

After a moment we understood. Between the thumb and forefinger of Wainwright's right hand was a needle about an inch and a half long.

Kane pointed to the bed, then turned away. "That was Hyde," he said. "He heard us talking to Lovejoy. He knew it was the end."

I do not remember how much longer we stayed there, or what else was said. But the last glimpse I had of that room of death was one I shall never forget. We had all gone out into the hall. I had turned to close the, door, and as I did so something came from beneath the bed on which the dead man was lying. It was the white cat. Springing from the floor, it settled itself softly upon the body of the man who had called himself Hyde, and began to purr.

CHAPTER 24

"A strange case, wasn't it?" Kane stared dully at the green blotter on his office desk. "One of those volcanic eruptions of the dark side of human nature. Hardly credible even when you understand the facts." He ceased speaking abruptly.

"But, there seems to be no reason for those facts," I began slowly. "Moreover, I don't see why Weed pretended to be blind, if he—" Kane's look of surprise stopped me in the middle of my sentence.

"You don't see why Weed pretended to be blind!" he repeated, and then laughed. "The answer to that is simple enough. He didn't *pretend* to be blind. He is!"

"But when you waved that ruler at him—" I protested in amazement.

"He jumped back. Yes, he did." Kane was serious again. "Underwood, I did that to show you the truth. I knew you suspected Weed. And when we were in Lovejoy's room, things were looking pretty black for him. If he wasn't blind, if he'd been shamming, then you were right to suspect him. But I knew you were wrong."

"But how—"

"Hold on, now," Kane admonished me. "Remember this. A man who shams deafness won't jump if you come up behind him and make a noise—a noise loud enough to startle him. He reasons this way: 'I am supposed to be deaf. Therefore I don't hear this noise. Therefore I won't jump.' But a really deaf man would. He'd feel the vibration and know something had happened. It's the same way with a blind man. Weed wouldn't have jumped if he'd been shamming. But he felt the current of air, and he heard the thing. Of course he recoiled. That's all there is to that," Kane concluded. He fell silent, frowning. I knew that he had dismissed Weed from his thoughts.

I waited for a few moments, and then, since he did not speak, asked him the other question that weighed on my mind. "Why should Wainwright have done it, Kane? I can't understand it."

Kane turned to face me. "There was one immediate reason," he said. "Prendergast was on the point of exposing him. It was in the boy's power to ruin Wainwright's life. Do you remember the first time we saw Prendergast?"

I nodded. I could never forget that afternoon, the man opening the door of his room in quivering terror, saying, "You can see for yourself. It's everywhere. Blood!"

"Then you know how desperate Prendergast was. And in his despair he found a courage he had never risen to before. 'I won't stand for it any longer. I know who—I'll—I'll—'" Kane paused for a minute and then continued. "Prendergast had found out that the man he'd known as Hyde was Wainwright. And what was more important, Wainwright heard him say those words, and knew that Prendergast had pierced his disguise and was at last brave enough to threaten him." He took a cigarette from his pocket and lighted it.

"Still I don't understand," I said. "How could Prendergast threaten Wainwright with anything? And why had Wainwright masqueraded as Hyde?"

Kane took a long drag on his cigarette and put it down to smolder in the ash tray. "One answer will fit both those questions, Underwood," he replied. "This is part of it." He opened the bottom drawer of his desk and took from it a white feather. Without comment he laid it on the blotting pad before him. As I looked at it with startled surprise, he went on. "Then there was Hyde's excessive fondness for animals. And something we saw last night—Wainwright playing with the bird. All those things are important."

Moran stared impatiently. "I don't know what you're talking about," he said. "I wish you'd come down to brass tacks. I want to know why you didn't arrest Wainwright last night, when we suspected him. You said then that he wasn't guilty."

"That's not quite fair, Moran. I said, if I remember correctly, that Sloan's report had shot our *theoretical case* against Wainwright all to pieces. We were going on the theory that Wainwright injected the poison in Mrs. Quincy's arm at ten-fifteen, when he left the bridge table. And that couldn't have been true, for Sloan told us that hydrocyanic acid causes *instantaneous death*. Mrs. Quincy didn't fall until ten-thirty. Wainwright was then playing bridge, and had been for the last fifteen minutes." He shook his head. "As far as the facts we then knew went, it was physically impossible for him to have killed Mrs. Quincy."

"And yet, in spite of the impossibility," I objected, "you still thought he had. I don't see how you could have gone on thinking that."

Kane smiled. "Underwood," he said, "I'm not one of those crack detectives who know who the criminal is the moment a murder is committed. I ought to confess that with shame, I suppose. There was a certain length of time when there was hardly anyone I *didn't* suspect. Until we figured out that it was Hyde who had killed Prendergast, until we knew the kind of criminal Hyde must be to have made such plans and executed them as he did, I had an eye on every one of them. But when I had that knowledge, it seemed to me that Wainwright alone was cool enough, strong enough, and resourceful enough to be the man we sought. At first I suspected him on those grounds.

"Then, with Mrs. Quincy's death and Lovejoy's testimony about the bridge game, my suspicions grew. But I was going too fast. Sloan's report of the instantaneous effect of the poison was one of the reins that pulled me down to a slower pace. But there was still another. My best witness, the only living thing, that could tell me who Hyde was had just gone back on me. That was Sheba."

"Sheba!"

Kane nodded. "It's not so ridiculous as you think, Moran. The cat, you remember, was afraid of everyone but Weed and one other person. Weed had told us that she would come to Hyde, just as she came to him. Well, think for a moment of that scene in the living room."

"Yeah."

"I thought I saw an opportunity of identifying Wainwright with Hyde. I told him to call the cat. And he did. He called quite loudly, too. But the cat didn't come to him."

Kane looked over at Moran. "It was you who suggested, as a joke, that I go to the Animal Rescue League. I found out there that what I suspected was true. Sheba is a pure-bred white Persian. Incidentally, she has two blue eyes. Usually, I've discovered, they have one pink eye and one blue. If they have that curious combination, they can hear. But if both eyes are blue, and if the cat is absolutely purebred, it is stone deaf. So," Kane concluded, "the explanation is simple enough. The cat wasn't looking at Wainwright when he called, hadn't had time to smell him out, and couldn't hear him."

"I'll be damned!"

Kane frowned. "Foolish as it may seem, the failure of the cat to respond to Wainwright that night stumped me quite badly. Coupled with what Sloan had to say, it might have convinced me that I was on the wrong track. That is, it might have, if, five minutes before Sloan's telephone message, I had not been talking to Wainwright. In that conversation I got the certain knowledge that Wainwright was Hyde, that he had killed Prendergast. Curiously enough, the information came from Wainwright's own lips."

Moran was bewildered. "What do you mean?" he asked truculently. "I was there when you talked to Wainwright. So was Underwood."

"Then you were both asleep," Kane returned shortly, "for in that interview Wainwright convicted himself of Prendergast's murder. This was the way it was."

Kane tapped his finger slowly on the desk. "The night Prendergast was killed, you remember, it had rained. When we left my hotel, at nine o'clock, Underwood, the storm was over, but as you said, half an hour before it had been pouring. Now when we got to Prendergast's room the rain was dripping through the ceiling. Under the circumstances, it was horrible—that tap, tap, tap, like drops of blood falling on the floor. No one who heard it could forget it. Certainly not a man who had just committed murder, and who, in the silent moment that followed his crime, had to listen to that hideous sound. Wainwright did not forget. Instead, he forgot something else, or never knew it—that the dripping had stopped before he made his public appearance in the house.

"I drew him on with some rigmarole about Lovejoy's reference to the leak. Wainwright said, 'But there was a leak. I heard it dripping.'

"That's why I just told you that Wainwright had convicted himself, for in those words he said in effect that he had been in Prendergast's room at the time he was supposed to have been on his way to the library."

Kane seemed to have grown less tired and to have regained the first enthusiasm of the chase. "You see," he said, "all along we've had the pieces of the puzzle given to us. It only remained to fit them in correctly. The watch, for example.

"By the way," he went on, "I talked to young Lovejoy to-night after Wainwright's death, and found out that the way I'd figured things out was correct. The afternoon after Prendergast's murder, Wainwright, thinking nothing about the matter, asked Lovejoy to leave the watch at a jeweler's for him. Lovejoy agreed to and took the watch from him. He had intended to take it to the jeweler's that same afternoon. But his plans changed. He didn't go out, and he left the watch on the table in the downstairs hall. That's where Mrs. Quincy saw it. The next morning Lovejoy took it to the jeweler's. And that's the whole story as far as Lovejoy is concerned."

"It was a funny mix-up," Moran commented. "Didn't it put you off to find that it was Lovejoy who had left it there?"

"I can't say it did," Kane replied. "You see, I knew from the very beginning of things that Wainwright wore a wrist watch and that it had been recently broken. Do you remember the night Prendergast was murdered? When we were talking to Wainwright, and he let Mrs. Balbirnie in?"

"Yes."

"She asked him what time it was, and he looked down instinctively at his wrist. Then he said that his watch wasn't running. At the time that little fact meant nothing. But I remembered it later, when a smashed watch crystal entered our scheme of things. And I knew that if Wainwright's watch hadn't been running that night, it was because the watch had been broken. Can you imagine Wainwright letting his watch run down? I can't, and if you'll think for a moment of his meticulousness, of his precision, of the careful order of his room, the neatness of his desk, you'll agree with me. He was incapable of even the smallest shiftlessness. And that being so, I knew it was Wainwright's watch I had found at the jeweler's no matter who had left it there."

Kane leaned back in his chair. "There was another small piece of evidence against Wainwright, by the way. Have neither of you wondered why he left the bridge table?"

"Well, yes, I have," Moran answered abruptly. "If he didn't kill Mrs. Quincy then, I don't see there was much point to it. And you can't tell me he went upstairs to get his slippers."

"As a matter of fact, Moran, he did. And he came down wearing them. I looked up those slippers of his while we were searching the house for the poison. The toe of the right slipper was particularly interesting. There was a little hole cut in it between the sole and the leather." Kane paused for a moment and then went on. "Mrs. Quincy was stabbed in the arm, as you know, in the presence of seven witnesses. Under those circumstances, which he had planned for in advance, Wainwright couldn't run the risk of *bending over* the body as it lay on the floor. So he stuck the poisoned needle in the toe of his slipper. That would account for his walking stiffly, or limping a little, as Lovejoy put it, when he came downstairs. It also accounts for the smear of blood we found on the rug, three feet away from the body. As Wainwright walked away, his device betrayed him."

There was a silence after Kane's last words. He got up and walked over to the window. I heard him sigh, and turned to look at him.

He made a vague gesture with his hand. "It's black as pitch out there now," he said dully. "But in the visible world there is nothing to compare to the darkness, the secrecy of the world that some men carry within themselves. Wainwright was that way." Kane walked quietly back to his seat at the desk.

"I'm not a judge of men," he began slowly, "and don't pretend to be, but sometimes I vaguely see the reasons for the things they do. Wainwright was never a weak man. Under other circumstances he might have been a strong man. But he had a desire for power he could never reconcile with his own position, could never satisfy in the world he lived in. It turned his strength into perverted channels, made him, in the end, a criminal.

"Obviously he was a survival. He allied himself with a society that had gone by. He clung to formality, to the manners and ways of speaking of another generation. If you look into his family history you will find that he came of fine stock. His ancestors, a hundred years back, were men of wealth and power. For three generations they belonged to the leisured class, just as Wainwright did, except that by the time he came along the family fortune and prestige had dwindled. He had just enough to get along on, and nothing to support the position he considered that he should have had. Every day he must have suffered under the spectacle of his own insignificance. And he was proud. The energy that he inherited with his name was bottled up.

"A few minutes ago, Underwood, you asked me why Wainwright masqueraded as Hyde. Think of him as he must have been five years ago, in the fifties, thoroughly embittered and disappointed. He had made no mark in the world, nor was he likely to. His legitimate ambitions had been thwarted. But he had others that were not legitimate. He took to a double life to give vent to those instincts for evil which, if he had shown them in his own person, would have made him an outcast from any society, would have lost him completely his place among his own kind. As Hyde he could safely indulge his vices. And he did. If we could follow Hyde's career in detail it would probably make an ugly showing. We know this much about it: the janitress at Newbury Street said that he often brought animals there and kept them in his room. One of the cats cried until people in the house complained. She didn't know what he did with them when he went away. They disappeared. Everybody was willing enough to believe in Hyde's fondness for animals. Fondness! I should hardly call it that, myself. But remember that phase of his career. Then think of his passionate absorption in the history of the Inquisition, a chronicle as dark and bloody as any I can think of."

Kane rubbed his hand over his eyes. "A moment ago," he said, "I reminded you of the time when we saw Wainwright playing with Mrs. Balbirnie's bird. He offered it a cracker first, then the burning end of his cigarette. When the bird cried out with pain, he laughed. That's the situation in a nutshell. Wainwright was what is known as a sadist, and in order to indulge in his abnormal pleasures he played the part of Hyde.

"You asked me a second question, Underwood—what hold Prendergast had over Wainwright. To answer it I have to remind you that Prendergast was in every way Wainwright's opposite, and yet he possessed opportunities that would have made Wainwright what he wanted to be. He was young and well-to-do. Yet if Wainwright envied him his opportunities, he had nothing but scorn for Prendergast as a person. Do you remember the way Wainwright summed him up? That 'he had hardly the manner one expects in people of one's own class.' Wainwright disliked him—that was natural enough. But it was stronger than that. From the beginning Wainwright resented the boy's very existence.

"That resentment might never have led Wainwright to murder, had Prendergast not been uncontrolled, weak, and hysterical—the ideal type for Wainwright's purposes. The older man tortured him, as earlier in his career he had tortured animals."

Kane looked over at Moran. "I asked you once what you meant by a feather. You thought I was fooling, but I wasn't. In the back of my mind I knew all along what that feather meant. 'A feather daunts the brave!' That has two meanings. A feather daunted me for a while. And a feather daunted Prendergast.

"You've heard of the intense fears that are called phobias. Some people are thrown into hysteria by the sight of certain animals. Freud has shown the prevalence of phobias of horses, dogs, cats, and birds. Prendergast was afflicted with such a fear. You remember he wouldn't go into Mrs. Balbirnie's room—certainly on account of her bird. Moreover, he couldn't endure the sight of a feather. I knew there was such a thing as a feather phobia, but at first I didn't connect Prendergast's feather with that psychological phenomenon. I should have.

"When we first saw Prendergast he gave us the clue, but we were too blind to see it. He said, 'People do awful things to me.' He wasn't suffering from hallucinations, as Mrs. Quincy thought. Wainwright was doing awful things to him. The boy was terrified, not so much by the stains on the floor of his room, as by that dancing white feather that Wainwright had put there. He had such a horror of the object that he wouldn't even speak of it. I know now, too, why we found a feather near Prendergast's body. That night was Wainwright's last opportunity to indulge in his ghastly sport.

"Now you can see what hold Prendergast had over Wainwright. Somehow or other he had discovered Hyde's real identity. The moment Prendergast said, in Wainwright's presence, 'I know who . . .'—Wainwright knew that the end of the game had come. At any moment Prendergast might expose him. Unless he were willing to see his world crashing about his ears, he had to silence Prendergast. There was only one way to do it."

Kane paused, and for a few moments we sat in silence. Then he began to speak again.

"Remember that to him, Prendergast was despicable. Remember that in the course of tormenting the boy, Wainwright had come to hate him. Remember that by killing him brutally, Wainwright merely carried out the ultimate sadistic impulse."

COACHWHIP PUBLICATIONS
COACHWHIPBOOKS.COM

COACHWHIP PUBLICATIONS
COACHWHIPBOOKS.COM

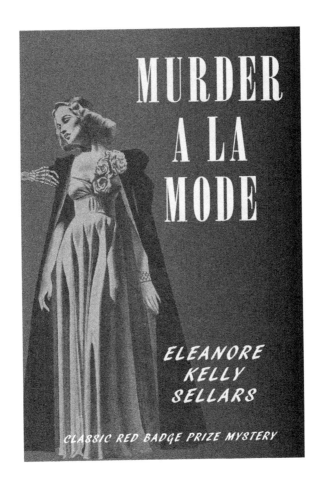

MURDER
A LA
MODE

ELEANORE
KELLY
SELLARS

CLASSIC RED BADGE PRIZE MYSTERY

COACHWHIP PUBLICATIONS
COACHWHIPBOOKS.COM

THE GOLF CLUB MURDER | OWEN FOX JEROME

COACHWHIP PUBLICATIONS
COACHWHIPBOOKS.COM

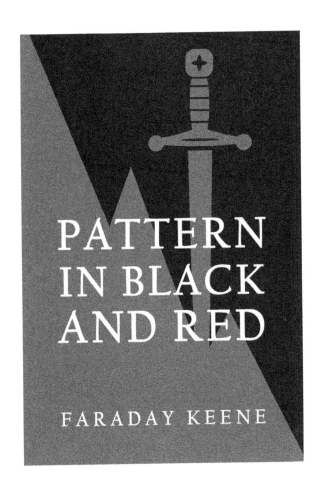

PATTERN
IN BLACK
AND RED

FARADAY KEENE

COACHWHIP PUBLICATIONS
COACHWHIPBOOKS.COM

MURDER
IN BERMUDA

WILLOUGHBY SHARP

COACHWHIP PUBLICATIONS
COACHWHIPBOOKS.COM

ANITA BOUTELL

DEATH BRINGS
A STORKE

CRADLED
IN FEAR

COACHWHIP PUBLICATIONS

COACHWHIPBOOKS.COM

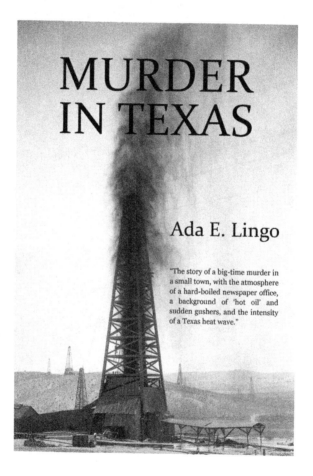

MURDER
IN TEXAS

Ada E. Lingo

"The story of a big-time murder in a small town, with the atmosphere of a hard-boiled newspaper office, a background of 'hot oil' and sudden gushers, and the intensity of a Texas heat wave."

COACHWHIP PUBLICATIONS
COACHWHIPBOOKS.COM

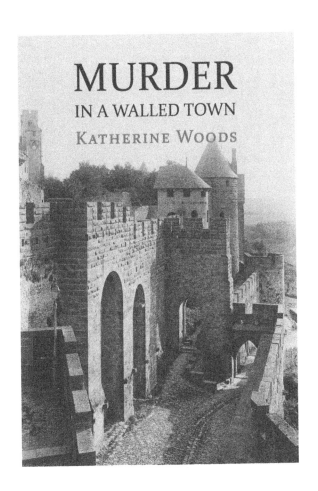

MURDER

IN A WALLED TOWN

KATHERINE WOODS

CPSIA information can be obtained
at www.ICGtesting.com
Printed in the USA
BVOW09s1736180318
510796BV00001B/145/P